BEAUTIFUL CARNAGE

By

Caroline Peckham & Susanne Valenti

Sloan

FOUR YEARS AGO

It was a cold day. The type that drilled into your bones and licked and bit at exposed flesh. Port Diavoli was a place of sin where even the wind would gut you if it got the chance.

I clipped my seatbelt into place as I dropped into the back of the shiny Bentley and Uncle Sergio patted my knee. He patted it a little higher every year. I'd just turned sixteen. Where was the line for old Uncle Serg with his dyed black hair and greasy moustache? Was this the year he'd try his luck?

I carried mace – wasn't allowed a gun – and my fingers got twitchy for it every time I had to spend time with him.

"Sensible, Sloan. You've got your mamma's brain."

I peeled his hand off of me when he didn't remove it, planting it back in his lap with an overly sweet smile. He didn't put his own seatbelt on. Most of my family never did, like they thought their name alone was a sure-fire shield from death. But like he said, I had Mamma's brain. Not that that had saved her in the end.

She'd hung herself from Inverno Bridge high up in the eastern forest eight years ago, leaving nothing behind but tainted memories. Had she ever really been happy? Had the smiles she'd given me been painted on with lies? I guess I'd never have my answers. And thinking about it only made my heart hurt.

I whipped out my iPhone, tapping on Pinterest. My bodyguard, Royce, glanced around from the passenger seat in the front and shot Sergio a look as powerful as a gunshot. My uncle missed it, but Royce gave me a nod to say he had my back and my lips twisted into a smile. He was the only guard I liked. Tall, as hairy as a beast and as big as one too. Royce could shoot a tin can off a wall a hundred feet away. He'd shown me that once then I'd begged him to let me try it. But he'd said what he always said when I asked to do something reckless. "A tuo padre non piacerebbe, Miss Calabresi."

Translation? *Your father wouldn't like it, Miss Calabresi.*

Not to sugar coat it, my father was a mob boss. And not just any mob boss, he owned the whole city and everyone in it. Including me. My name was tattooed between a ring of barbed wire across his entire chest. How was that for messed up? I loved Papa, but holy shit, he was controlling.

I was on my way to a gala to schmooze a bunch of new business owners into signing over a percentage of their company to him. He did it all under the guise of flashy lights, expensive wine and enough food to bust your gut. But what it really was, was a threat. Papa was the king of the city and with our rivals looking to cut us down at every opportunity, he wanted to have something on everyone to keep them from screwing us over in favour of the Romero family.

It was all pretty boring to me, but Papa dragged me along to every event, showing off his shiny princess. I was expected to smile and look pretty. Apparently he hadn't heard of the twenty first century. And I couldn't say I'd stepped a foot into it either outside of Netflix shows. The cruel truth was, men ruled my world whether I liked it or not. I was trapped in an invisible cage, my wings thoroughly clipped. I was home schooled, my friends were chosen for me, as were my books and daily activities. But Papa's downfall was his old fashioned ways, like the way he'd forgotten about restricting my access to Netflix. Pinterest was the only social media I was allowed though. He hadn't let Instagram or Snapchat slip through the net.

The one thing I knew for sure? I was going to escape this life soon enough. Papa was sending me to study in Italy. I had just two more weeks to kill then I'd be free. Sure, he was sending Royce and the rest of the team with me to hound my every move, but I'd be far, far away from America and Papa. How much control could he really exercise over me then?

I tugged at the bottom of my silver dress to cover my knees more thoroughly, feeling Sergio's gaze dripping over me. He wasn't flesh and blood. He'd married into the family and I pitied my aunt for his company. Not that she was much fun either. She had a Botox addiction and her only hobby was counting calories.

"Road's closed," our driver murmured, glancing over at Royce for direction.

His lips were tight and his posture rigid. I swear he was made of stone sometimes. The only place he bent was at the hip.

"Go around," he decided, pointing to the diversion sign.

The driver veered down a dark road where the tall buildings seemed to close in on either side of us and dark alleys sat between them. Lights flashed behind us as the other car full of bodyguards signalled to us. Papa was always overprotective with me. Did I really need to travel with eight people just to go to his stupid gala?

Royce's phone buzzed and he answered it with a heavy sigh. The predictable snap of Eddie's voice sounded down the line as he shouted angrily in Italian. I rarely used the language unless Papa insisted. I personally saw it as another way to control me. We lived in America so I spoke goddamn English thank you very much.

"What do you want me to do, huh?" Royce hissed, silencing him. "There isn't another way around. We're almost through the-"

A huge crash sounded and everything lurched, my gut tumbled. My whole world flipped – no the car goddamn flipped!

I screamed, my phone falling from my hand and hitting the roof before whacking me in the face as we spun over once more. Sergio's foot slammed into my gut as he was tossed around like a rag doll. Another limb smashed into my mouth and I tasted blood. Adrenaline ran wildly through my veins and all I could hear was the deafening shriek and crunch of metal against concrete.

We finally came to a stop and I hung upside down, panting as I gazed into Sergio's lifeless eyes below. Blood dripped from my nose onto his face and I screamed once more.

"Quiet!" Royce commanded and I forced myself to obey.

The rat-tat-tat of several gunshots cut the air apart and I fell entirely still.

"It's the Romeros," Royce breathed and fear latched onto my heart with ice cold fingers. My favourite bodyguard in the whole world tried to force his way to me from the front seat as smoke seeped under my nose and made my heart tumble into oblivion. He couldn't fit. The roof was badly bent and the gap wasn't wide enough for his huge shoulders.

I'm going to die. I'm going to fucking die.

I reached for the seatbelt, pressing the button again and again, but it didn't come free. Panic licked its way up my spine as I yanked at it.

"I can't get out," I stammered, my voice trembling violently as I locked eyes with Royce.

My gaze slipped to the broken windscreen, the person-sized hole, the blood, the empty driver's seat.

"Don't panic," Royce said too calmly like there wasn't a thing in the world to panic about. He leaned through the front seats and I could tell his other arm was broken as he winced every time he tried to get near, clutching it to his chest.

A boot crunched on glass on the other side of the vehicle and we both fell still. Royce twisted around, drawing his gun but a deafening bang made my whole world stop as a bullet hit him squarely in the chest. He jerked and fell still and it took everything I had not to scream again.

"Check everyone's dead, Rocco," a cold voice reached my ears and the boots thumped away slowly. "Finish off anyone who's still twitching."

I reached forward as far as I could, my fingers flailing for Royce's gun. It was still in his grip and I could reach it, I was almost sure.

I swallowed a whimper of fear as footsteps sounded close again. The scent of smoke was growing unbearable and a thick plume was coiling its way through the car.

I battled the urge to cough as my fingers grazed the gun and I desperately wrangled it into my grasp.

I was dead. I knew it. But I'd go out fighting. I'd take out a few of the bastards who'd done this. I'd never shot a gun in my life, but *hell*, I'd figure it out. I just needed a few seconds.

My seatbelt unclipped itself and I fell from the seat with a gasp of horror, landing with a muffled thud onto Sergio's body.

Someone yanked on the door handle with brute strength but the twisted metal stopped it from opening all the way.

I scramble around and lifted the gun, my fingers shaking violently as I gripped the trigger.

I fell back on my ass the second the guy wrenched the door open. A breath lodged in my lungs as I held the gun up, my hands trembling like crazy, my tongue wet with blood.

My life didn't flash before my eyes, I didn't see a bright light at the end of a tunnel. All I could think of was one word. *Wasted*.

I'd wasted my life. I'd never really lived during my short sixteen years in this world.

I waited to see his face to pull the trigger. I'd make these final seconds count. I'd let him look me in the eyes. Show him who killed him. Sloan Calabresi. A girl who could have been someone if only she'd stopped listening to what everyone else told her to do.

He dropped to a crouch with his gun raised and our eyes locked. My finger twitched against the trigger and so did his. At least one of us should have been dead but we just remained frozen, staring at each other like it meant something. But my mind wouldn't work to tell me what.

His eyes were two inky pools flecked with silver, the stubble lining his jaw was as jet black as the hair sweeping over his head. His features were harsh, ruthless, stunning. His mouth was set in a hard line and my death awaited me in the depths of his eyes. The worst thing of all was that I knew who he was. Rocco Romero. Oldest son of Martello Romero, king of the underworld and bringer of terror.

He was me in reverse. A prince to an empire. The only difference was, women didn't inherit. He was his vicious father in the making. A man who slaughtered our people on the streets, who left a trail of fear in his wake. His family were the reason Port Diavoli had been nicknamed Sinners Bay. But I was not going to be afraid in my final seconds on Earth. I'd take out one of my mortal enemies instead.

"Il sole sorgerà domani," I hissed my family's motto at him, squeezing hard and pulling the trigger. *The sun will rise again.*

Click.

Rocco didn't even flinch, he smirked. And it was the coldest, most deadly smile I'd ever seen. "Safety catch, principessa. Didn't

Giuseppe Calabresi teach his little girl how to protect herself?" he mocked, then snatched the gun from me as horror bled through my soul.

I refused to give in, reaching for anything I could use as a weapon. My fingers grazed my phone and I slammed it against his temple with a gasp of exertion.

His hand locked around my throat in an instant and he pushed me down to lay on Sergio's lifeless body. I clawed at his arm, terror wrapping around my heart as he reared above me. His body flattened mine with a weight of sheer muscle and panic swept through my blood. I was small, nothing compared to this animal of a man. And with no weapon, no nothing, he did to me what men had done to me my entire life. Crushed me beneath him.

I kept my eyes on his, never looking away, determined that he would see no fear in me no matter what my thrashing heart thought of that. I recalled Mamma's final words to me all those years ago, the only hint she'd been going to take her own life. *Death is the truest freedom in the world, mio caro.*

"Sleep," Rocco whispered as blackness curtained my vision and set off warning bells in my head.

I despised how beautiful my killer was and spat a curse at him on the final scrap of air in my lungs. Then the devil sent me deep into the darkest sleep I'd ever known. And it was surely death.

Sloan

FOUR YEARS LATER

I stood on the porch of the stately manor house where I'd grown up on the outskirts of the city. The sheer white walls stretched up above me, the pillars either side of me seeming more ostentatious than I'd ever realised. Snowflakes cascaded onto the lawn, silently circling and dancing through the air. The wind carried the sound of gulls down at the west dock on the bay and the cry of fishermen bringing in their morning catches. That wasn't the only thing they'd have onboard. The men down there made most of their money smuggling goods for my family.

My little white Pomeranian, Coco, was tucked under my arm as I stood there, hesitating. The driver placed my bags down outside the door and I dismissed him. I'd managed four years in Italy without a porter and I didn't want to fall back into old habits. I might have had a whole crew sent with me to cater to my every need, but I'd wanted the real world experience. And as they were under my command and a thousand miles away from my father, I'd managed to get a bit more freedom than I'd hoped for.

Now, I was home for the first time in four years. I hadn't looked back when I'd left this place. Hadn't wanted to look back. I was a prisoner here and returning felt like putting the shackles back on. I'd sobbed into my friends' arms just yesterday while we drank wine and watched the sun set on the balcony of my apartment. It broke my heart to leave them. But I'd known deep down my papa would tighten the leash eventually. I had what he wanted. A shiny classical degree. Another gold badge to place on my lapel.

I was still hesitating outside the door, putting off the inevitable. I loved my papa because he was flesh and blood, but I couldn't say I'd missed him. I was afraid to walk back into his life and let him wrap me in chains once more.

Coco licked my arm, wriggling in an effort to get down. At least he wasn't afraid to be here. But he hadn't met my father yet. I'd picked up the little pup in an animal shelter after I'd volunteered there with one of my friends. He'd been a constant companion since and I was glad at least to have been able to bring one friend home with me.

I straightened my spine, lifted my chin and held onto what my friend Marina had told me before I'd left Italy. *You are who you choose to be.*

So I choose this: I am not a prisoner.

I slotted my key in the lock, pushing the door wide and finding two bodyguards flanking the doorway. I said hello but they said nothing and I sighed, missing Royce. I'd insisted he go home even though he'd driven the other car right up to my family's property to ensure I got here. The guy hadn't slept in twenty four hours and Papa had ten men at the gates. I wasn't exactly in danger once I was in the Calabresi fortress. With the open heart surgery he'd had after the Romero attack, I was determined he rest as much as possible these days. It was a miracle he'd stayed in his job at all. But I knew deep down, he felt guilty for what had happened that day. By staying, he was trying to make it up to me.

I placed Coco down and he scampered up the stairs, disappearing along the balcony. *Just don't pee in papa's office you little beast.*

"Papa?" I called into the echoing quiet as a servant hurried out to grab the rest of my bags. "I can do it," I told the man but he just smiled and jogged upstairs with my two carry-ons. I sighed. I wasn't going to be able to do a thing for myself here. But there was one thing I was determined to hold on to. In Italy I'd grown a passion for cooking. I could make my own pasta from scratch, my own sauces and seasonings. But the thing I'd fallen in love with the most, was baking. Little pastries, cakes, sweet breads and sugary treats. It was a passion I never would have found a love for if I hadn't been given the freedom to discover it.

"Papa?" I tried again, walking through the huge hallway across the dark wood floors and into the lounge. Two men sat by the fire with a bottle of port between them on the coffee table. My heart started beating harder at the sight of them. One was my father and the other was Nicoli Vitoli; the nine year old boy Papa had adopted when I was just four. Nicoli had answered all of my father's prayers; he was the boy he'd always wanted. We used to be so close, causing mischief in the house, winding up the guards, spending our summers building camps in the woods and swimming in the lake.

As he'd gotten older, I'd seen less of him. Papa had taken him under his wing, teaching him the 'ways of the family', spending more time with him than I ever got. It had made me resent him plenty of times, but I'd long since forgotten the days where I'd looked upon Nicoli with any envy in my heart. These days, I just wanted to keep out of the family as much as possible. I didn't want to inherit, I wanted to be set free.

Papa stood, spreading his arms with a welcoming smile on his face. He'd put on weight since I'd last seen him and his full head of hair was entirely grey. The smell of smoke wafted from two cigars sitting in a dish on the table and I wrinkled my nose. Nicoli rose to his feet too, turning to look at me and my breath snagged in my lungs.

The boy I'd spent my childhood with had hardened into a man. There was no mischievous smile or dare in his eyes like all those times we'd played games together in this very house.

Nicoli had put on pounds of muscle and his boyish features had toughened to a steely jaw and iron eyes. I could have sworn his hair was darker than before, swept back stylishly and enhancing the cut of his cheekbones.

He had been well and truly moulded into my father's prodigy. A man able to do what I wasn't allowed to and inherit the Calabresi empire.

His mouth hooked up at one corner as he took in my outfit. The leggings and sweater I wore were overly casual, perfect for a plane journey and completely normal for someone my age to wear. But Papa's brows knitted together and I swear a tut passed his lips.

"Come hug your old papa," my father asked and I hurried forward to embrace him, the familiar smell of mint and tobacco washing over me. He placed two kisses on my cheeks then turned me around in his arms to face Nicoli.

"You remember Nicoli?" Papa asked.

"Of course," I said, fighting an eyeroll. *How could I forget the guy you adopted and groomed to be your heir?*

"It's good to see you again, Sloan. How was Italy?" Nicoli asked and Papa prodded me toward him.

"Amazing. I'd live there if I could," I said lightly, trying to ignore the way Nicoli's eyes scraped over every inch of me. Or the way my heart reacted to that, pounding wildly in my chest. Handsome didn't even begin to describe what he was. The skinny boy who'd wrapped me in his arms the day my mother had died had transformed entirely; he'd been my knight in shining armour in the worst moment of my life, and now he had the features to match.

"Nonsense," Papa tsked. "Then you would miss the great life I've organised for you here."

"What life?" I asked a little sharply.

"Perhaps Nicoli can explain," Papa said, his tone soft but somehow setting me on edge.

I looked to Nicoli and my heart cracked and splintered as he dropped down onto one knee and produced a ring in a velvet box. The rock was so big it caught the light and half blinded me.

Panic seized me as I stared at my fate. Because the worst had happened. Papa had sold me. This wasn't a request. It was a demand. A life sentence.

No.

Hell no.

"Marry me, Sloan Calabresi. I'll make you happier than you can imagine," Nicoli promised and something in his gaze said maybe he really could offer me that. But I didn't want to be chained to a man I didn't choose for myself. I'd known Mamma's marriage was arranged with Papa and it certainly wasn't a happy one. I'd hoped that fate wouldn't ever be forced on me, that I'd be left to my own devices. But now I realised how foolish a dream that had been.

"Papa, please, can we talk?" I begged of him, my voice choked as the world seemed to tilt and fall.

Just moments ago I was swearing never to be a prisoner again, now a ring that looked like a collar was staring me right in the eye.

Nicoli glanced at Papa with a hint of confusion and a manic laugh escaped me. Because he didn't know. He thought this was already arranged. He thought I *knew*. But of course Papa had never told me. He never cared what I thought about anything.

"Of course, amore mio," Papa crooned, but it was all an act. "As soon as you've given Nicoli his answer. It's not right to keep a gentleman on his knees."

"But Papa-" I started and his arm clamped around my wrist. Too tight.

He'd never struck me, but I'd seen him hit Mamma once. His grip was bruising and the threat in his eyes was clear. But my one advantage was that he would try to save face with Nicoli, so I tugged away from him and he had to let me go.

I stormed from the room, heading upstairs to my old bedroom, flinging the stark white door open and entering the princess pink room which didn't feel like mine at all. Coco came running down the hall into the room and dove onto my bed, looking to me with his tail wagging.

I pulled my cellphone from my purse, bringing up Royce's number as my heart thumped unevenly in my chest. He was the only person in America who I trusted, but what would I say? Now that we were back home, my father was his boss, not me. But he felt like more than just some employee to me. He was the guy who played card games with me while he was guarding me, who had taught me to shoot hoops at basketball, who had wiped my snotty nose as a kid. He'd been more of a father to me than my papa ever had. And he'd come if I called. I was sure of it.

Papa marched through the door and Coco started yapping furiously in an attempt to warn him off. He kicked the door shut and my blood turned to ice.

"Give it to me," he demanded, striding forward with his hand outheld for my phone. But this wasn't just a phone, it was my life, my connection to the outside world. Giving it up meant losing contact with my friends in Italy, the people who'd been there for me through the years, who'd laughed with me and spent hours in my company.

I turned away but Papa caught my arm and wrestled it from my grip.

"Wait a second-" My words died as he popped the SIM card out. "No!" I yelled, clawing at him to get it. Panic coiled through me and I fought harder, desperate for him not to take this from me.

He held me back with one hand and crushed it in his other palm with a vicious crack. "No more of this, Sloan. What has gotten into you?"

He dropped the two pieces of the SIM on the carpet before pocketing the phone. Those two pieces mirrored my heart.

"You dare to leave Nicoli on the floor of my home, offering you the world?" He grabbed me by the shoulders and Coco snarled furiously, jumping off the bed and gnawing on his trouser leg in a desperate bid to save me.

Royce had been training me in self defence in secret for the past four years, but I wouldn't dare lay a hand on my father. Even if I could break his hold on me physically, I couldn't do anything about the hold he had on me mentally.

"I won't marry him," I hissed and Papa's eyes turned to a deadly dark shade. He clutched me tighter, his fingers bruising my arms as he shook me. "Without Nicoli, this family has no future. I've been preparing him to follow in my footsteps for fourteen years! You know I need a man I can trust to inherit my title when I die. Your husband can't just be anyone, it has to be the right man. It has to be *him*."

"But-"

"But nothing!" he snapped. "Without this marriage to secure heirs for our family, the Romeros will take over the city. Is that what you want? Those filthy fucks who left you half dead in that car to take everything from us?"

Horror swam through my veins and I shook my head frantically as the memory of that day seeped over me. Of Rocco Romero pinning me down, his rough hands tightening around my neck.

I'd woken in hospital wondering why I was alive. It still haunted me to this day. He was my nightmare. My one true fear. And I hadn't ever overcome it.

"No Papa," I said, realising tears were streaming down my cheeks.

"Then you will be grateful for the life Nicoli is offering you. He is a fine man and will treat you with respect. You will want for nothing, what more can a father give his daughter than that?"

A choice.

I stared at him mutely, unable to believe the chains had tightened around me so quickly. And they were more unbreakable than ever before.

I could see my life stretching out before me. Becoming the wife of the man my father had built in his image. Bearing him children. Being expected to cage those children in this life too. And the cycle would never end. The Calabresi women would be eternally bound, eternally caged.

My breathing grew rapid and Papa caught my chin, forcing me to look up at him. "I need you, Sloan. You're a good girl. Now be what the family needs you to be. We all have a role to play, this is yours."

Coco stopped tugging on his leg, the fight going out of him the same time it did me. Papa released me and I sank down onto the edge of the bed while my little pup jumped into my lap and licked my hands.

"The wedding is in a month. It's already organised. You need do nothing but look pretty on the day." Papa closed the door and it felt like his fist was tightening around my heart.

It was already organised. I was just a pawn on a chessboard being pushed into place.

I stared down at the broken SIM card, wondering if I'd ever be able to contact my friends again. I still didn't have social media and if I ever got another phone, I wouldn't be allowed it. Coco nuzzled into me as my tears dripped onto his silken white fur.

I hated that I could feel myself giving in. Because there was no war to fight. Papa had already occupied my world and forced me to surrender.

I thought of running away but where would I go? How would I get out of a city full of Calabresis and Romeros?

A gentle knock came at the door and I scrubbed the tears away from under my eyes.

"Come in," I called, expecting a servant with tea, but finding Nicoli stepping into my room, his broad shoulders nearly as wide as the door.

He took in my miserable appearance with a frown. "That wasn't quite the way I wanted things to go."

"Sorry for wounding your pride," I said hollowly. "But I didn't expect to be sold like chattel the moment I arrived home."

Nicoli sighed, stepping closer and Coco growled low in his throat.

"I would never buy you," he said earnestly. "But I'm not a fool. I'm aware this is a transaction of sorts. Your father wants me to take his place one day and frankly, Sloan, you are better off in my company than whoever else your father might push you toward."

My throat thickened as I stared at him. "So you're not getting anything out of this?" I asked dryly. *Apart from an empire that should have been mine.*

"I didn't say that. I have admired you for my entire life. You're beautiful, passionate, and your heart is so big you could fit the whole world inside it with room to spare."

I frowned, taken aback by the sweetness of his words.

He stepped closer, glancing at the door, knowing he shouldn't really be alone with me. Father would die before he let any man lay a hand on his daughter. But I'd defied that rule in Italy already and a part of me wanted to defy it again now.

"We both know this world," Nicoli said gently. "We've shared it together. Don't you think we could make this work?"

I looked up at him as he halted before me, so close I could smell his subtle cologne and the general scent of power rolling from him in waves. But beneath it all, I detected the outdoorsy smell of that boy I used to know. The one I'd played with and adored.

He took my hand, guiding me to my feet and my heart stuttered as I stared into his familiar eyes. I didn't want to look anywhere else than there, trying to capture that piece of him I knew so well. But I couldn't hold onto it for long.

"You're not the boy I once knew," I breathed and his brows knitted together.

He dipped his head, threading his fingers between mine and awakening a reckless part of me. We were going against my father. He brazenly touched me with the door wide open and it felt so intoxicating that I wanted to give myself to that feeling entirely.

"I'm still here," he promised, his head lowering and his gaze burned with desire as his metallic eyes fixed on my mouth.

A kiss with him would feel like a sin. But we were in Sinners Bay after all…

I tip-toed up, hoping for the kind of spark which could make this better, a hint of passion in our future. This man before me was going to be my husband, there wasn't any way out of it and I'd loved him once as a boy, so maybe I could do so as a man.

Our lips brushed and the thrill of his boldness spurred me on, my mouth parting for his tongue. He suppressed a groan, his arm looping around me and dragging me against his firm chest. His heart thumped furiously against my flesh and some part of me started to hope there really was a chance for us.

Coco yapped angrily and I finally pulled away, feeling hot all over.

"I can't imagine a more fitting bride for me, Sloan," Nicoli said in a gravelly tone. "We are made for each other and I vow to keep you safe. Always."

I frowned as he moved away across the room. I didn't want to be safe. Safe was another word for confined.

He placed the ring box down on my nightstand before heading back to the door.

"I'm staying for dinner," he said. "If you'd like to get reacquainted tonight, I'll be waiting for you. Either way, we will be married by the end of the month, Sloan. So let's try and make it work."

My mind whirled as I sank down onto my bed, staring after him with an ache in my soul. Nicoli may not have chosen me, but it was clear he wanted me. And maybe the universe would be kind. Maybe he would be enough. But the reckless girl he'd awoken in me was still wide awake. And I wasn't sure yet if he was ever going to be enough for her.

Rocco

Forgive me, Father, for I am about to sin.

The church confessional was cramped and dark, the scent of polished wood and incense wrapping around me until my head was full of it.

I rolled my shoulders back, trying to alleviate the ache in them from a night hidden in the tiny space. I watched the congregation file into the huge church through the small, cross-shaped holes carved into the door of my hiding place.

The Calabresis were loud and brash, their arrogance shining through beneath their designer clothes and overly quaffed hair. The women crowed at each other, complimenting bright dresses and layers of makeup while internally sneering and trying to score points with exclusive purses and one-of-a-kind shoes. The men spoke in voices that boomed off of the vaulted ceiling as they puffed their chests up like peacocks in their expensive suits.

I didn't spot any weapons. No one came to church armed. Not even me – Mamma never would have forgiven us if my brothers and I had come into a holy place bearing arms.

My gaze slid to the altar where a pristine white table cloth hid my brother, Enzo, from view. He was no doubt twitching with energy, desperate to make our move. But we couldn't yet. Not until our other brother, Frankie, did his part.

The groom strolled up the aisle, muscles straining against a black suit as his dark gaze swept over the gathered mobsters like they were his to command. Nicoli Vitoli. Soon to be heir to all of this. All he had to do was get a ring on Sloan Calabresi's finger and his position as next in line would be confirmed.

I'd take him out too if I could. But not before we hit her father, Giuseppe. *If you want to cut down your enemies, then it makes sense to chop off their head first.*

And he wouldn't appear until the bride did. Because what proud father would miss the opportunity to walk their little girl down the aisle, binding her to his adopted son and solidifying their power in one fell swoop?

My hands curled into fists, my heart beating solidly in my chest as I watched. And waited.

The timing had to be just right.

Father Mariellos stepped up before the altar and those onlookers who had still been lingering in the aisles swapping stories of bullshit and bloodlust quickly moved to take their seats.

A choir readied themselves to sing, their pristine white robes and innocent expressions making me wonder if they really didn't know they were standing in a room filled with killers and cutthroats. Or maybe they just didn't want to know. Perhaps they left the judgement down to the almighty.

The first long note was struck on the organ and the congregation stood as all eyes turned to the doors at the back of the enormous church.

The mahogany doors were drawn wide and a beat passed before Giuseppe Calabresi himself stepped into view, his considerable bulk squeezed into a suit which must have been custom made just for him. He held out an arm and from the other side of the doorway, a girl stepped forward dressed head to toe in white.

The wedding dress pooled out around her, the train dragging along the floor in a waterfall of delicately embroidered lace.

A full length veil covered her features so it was impossible for me to see if Sloan Calabresi had changed much in the years that had passed since I'd spared her life. Since I'd let a pair of wide, brown eyes filled with fear talk me out of violence. There weren't many things that had managed that in my life. I was always ready with my fists, a blade or a gun if the situation allowed it. And yet that day, in that moment, something in the gaze of a terrified girl made me stay my hand.

I'd convinced myself that it was because she was young, innocent and no threat to me. But the truth was, I could have struck a heavy blow against her father by taking her life alongside her uncle's. I could have. And maybe I should have. But I hadn't. And even after all these years, I wasn't entirely sure why not.

Nicoli kept his gaze firmly fixed on the back of the room, not turning his head to see his bride's approach.

An eternity passed as Giuseppe and Sloan walked up the aisle. Every face in the room was locked on them and I could have sworn the slowness of the bride's pace was reluctance, not nerves.

I dismissed that thought as soon as it came. Sloan Calabresi was just a pawn in her father's games. His only child and the key to securing his family's claim on this city. He was marrying her off to bring Nicoli into the fold officially. The girl wasn't even going to be taking his name. From this day on, Nicoli would be a Calabresi too. The boy Giuseppe had plucked from nowhere and moulded into a monster in his own image, finally being elevated into the position he'd been groomed for.

If any of the congregation here took exception to this arrangement, they clearly weren't voicing it. Nicoli might have sprung from nothing, but he'd proved his worth to the man who had taken him in. Paying for his bride in blood and death a thousand times over. I had him to thank for my cousin Mario's death alongside many others. And I had his life marked as mine just as soon as I'd taken down Giuseppe.

My heart beat harder as the priest began his sermon. Tension was building in my muscles, violence coiling in my heart. This was what I lived for. The release of unleashing the beast which dwelled within me. The war my family waged against the men who filled this room with the stench of superiority and entitlement. I'd give my entire being in the pursuit of their demise. It was what I was born for, bred for. I'd bathe in their blood and dance on their graves before this creature in me would ever be satisfied.

I glanced at my watch, wondering how long it would take for Frankie to do his part. I couldn't move until he did, but the idiota was taking his sweet time with our distraction. Knowing him, he'd be waiting for the part where the priest asked if anyone here had any objections. He always did have a flare for the dramatic.

I snagged my phone from my pocket and shot a text to the group chat.

Rocco:

Stop stalling and get moving.

Frankie:

Keep your panties on, I've had a wiring issue.

Enzo:

My ass is numb and my muscles are twitching. If you don't hurry up, I'm gonna burst out of here, bodyguards or not.

Rocco:

Calm down stronzo, Frankie's about to stop fucking around. Aren't you?

Frankie:

Thirty seconds, hold on to your asses…

I pocketed my phone, a dark smile pulling at my lips as expectation burned through my limbs.

I began counting down the seconds just as Giuseppe reached out and drew Sloan's veil off of her face. He blocked my view of her, kissing her cheeks and releasing a hearty laugh as he took her hand and passed it into Nicoli's.

Giuseppe stepped back, moving away to take a seat on a pew at the front of the congregation. My gaze slid from him, landing on his daughter.

Four years had changed Sloan Calabresi beyond recognition. The terrified girl I'd spared in that car had grown into a woman whose dark features and wide eyes had a breath catching in the back of my throat.

Full lips painted red turned down ever so slightly at the corners like she wasn't satisfied with her lot in life and those same big, brown eyes were filled with secrets I wished to tease from her mouth.

I pursed my lips, anger trickling through me as I looked upon the face of the girl who had caused me so many problems.

One moment of weakness where I'd chosen to spare her life had haunted me daily ever since. Our father had been furious. He'd accused me of being incompetent. Failing. And he didn't even know that I'd done it on purpose. That was a secret I'd take to the grave. He merely thought I'd failed to finish her properly. If he knew I'd chosen to let her live, I'd have paid for it in blood.

Still, the shame of that failure had followed me like a shadow and the name Sloan Calabresi had become a weapon my brothers used to taunt me time and again. If ever I had the chance to rob Giuseppe of his child once more, I wouldn't hesitate. Her death would come at my hands, and my name would be wiped of the shame of that failure.

As my heated gaze burned into the side of Sloan's perfect features, she turned her head. Her gaze fell on the confessional and I stilled. She couldn't see me hidden in the shadows, but for a moment it was like she had sensed the heat of my hatred pouring over her and turned to face it. Her chin raised defiantly, her jaw set with determination like she was marching into battle, not about to marry the man of her dreams. If mindless pawns even had dreams...

BOOM!

The sound of the explosion tore through the church, echoing off of the vaulted ceiling and drawing terrified screams from the congregation. Everyone was on their feet in moments and adrenaline spilled through me as I held myself back through sheer force of will.

Just a few more seconds...

The bodyguards ran straight for the doors at the far end of the church led by Royce Belmonte, heading out front to see what the hell had happened and to defend the family they were paid to protect.

The wedding cars would be flaming towards the heavens right about now and Frankie should be well on his way to the back of the church with our getaway vehicle.

I bit the inside of my cheek as Nicoli failed to follow them, standing protectively by his bride-to-be instead and blocking my route to Giuseppe.

Looks like I'll be spilling his blood after all.

The moment the bodyguards pulled the doors open and rushed outside, I sprang into action. My boot collided with the confessional door so hard that the whole thing flew off of its hinges.

People were screaming, some of them looking our way as Enzo burst from beneath the altar, up-ending it and sending the huge, golden cross crashing to the floor by my feet.

Nicoli turned to face me, his gaze ramming into mine and a roar ripping from his lips as he dove at me.

A wide smile captured my mouth and I raced to meet him, jumping from the raised dais as I collided with him.

Nicoli cursed as my weight sent us crashing to the ground and I threw punches into his jaw with all the force of my muscles behind them.

Blood flew but he gave as good as he got, his knuckles hammering into my sides, battering my ribs and sending pain splintering through me at the impact.

I swung my fist back again just as a foot slammed into my side, knocking me off of him.

I rolled away, scrambling up and glaring at Sloan goddamn Calabresi as Nicoli leapt to his feet between us. Her fucking stiletto had made me bleed and my white T-shirt was stained with the evidence of her attack.

Enzo had grabbed the large bronze pitcher which had fallen from the altar and was swinging it at Giuseppe's head again and again as he fought to keep his arms up between them to defend himself. A howl of rage escaped my brother as he fought to batter the life from our sworn enemy.

Cries of panic rang out as the women and children in the congregation all tried to run for the exit while the bodyguards and mobsters fought their way closer to us.

The echoing bang of a gunshot rang out and Enzo fell back, a torrent of curses pouring from his lips as I spotted Carlo Fabrini, Giuseppe's right hand man, battling to line up a second shot through the chaos.

A snarl of rage left my lips as my brother crawled back towards me, blood pouring from his bicep as he clutched the wound.

Giuseppe scrambled back too, moving out of reach and sending rage shuddering through me.

Nicoli charged straight for me again, his eyes wild and their family's motto spilling from his lips. "Il sole sorgerà domani!"

I rolled away, getting to my hands and knees, my fingers brushing something cold and hard.

I spared a moment of my attention for the thing I'd touched and a manic laugh spilled from me as I snatched it into my hands.

I swung the heavy, golden cross with all of my strength and the metal end of it hit Nicoli in the side as he leapt straight for me.

Blood flew, my muscles strained and Nicoli fell back with a cry of rage and pain.

I followed him, swinging the cross again and again, blood speckling my arms as my muscles burned with the pressure of wielding the heavy thing and I battered his huge frame with it.

On the fourth strike, I caught his temple and Nicoli collapsed. For a moment, the only thing I could hear was the silence that followed his fall.

I gave myself a second of triumph, looking down at him before my head snapped up and took in the room again. Giuseppe had disappeared into the crowd, the throng of bodyguards and mobsters were making it past the panicking congregation and Carlo was aiming his gun my way. Our momentary advantage was up and we'd fucking failed.

I leapt aside as Carlo fired, turning away from him and the rest of the Calabresis as I ran for the back of the church.

Enzo had made it to the stained glass window and his fingers fumbled the catch as blood poured freely down his arm.

I sprinted straight for him, swinging the cross as I went and throwing it at the window with all my might.

The sound of glass shattering filled the air and Enzo ducked aside as it rained down all around him.

I reached him, cupping my hands to help him up and he fell through the window to safety on the other side.

His curses called back to me as he fell on his injured shoulder and a growl of rage left me, knowing these assholes had hurt my kin.

I gripped the frame just as the third bullet hit the stone window ledge beside me, my heart pounding a frantic beat that begged for me to escape this mess before I paid for this failure with my own life.

I hauled myself up, but before I could pull myself outside, something heavy collided with the back of my head.

I spun around, teeth bared and fists clenched just as Sloan Calabresi hefted the bronze pitcher in her arms again.

Her white dress was stained with Nicoli's blood, her brown eyes wild with rage. Those same eyes that had watched me fail before.

A snarl of hatred tore from my throat as I glared at her and her family charged towards us, crying out for her to move aside.

She swung the pitcher at me again but I reached out and caught it, absorbing the strength of her blow before yanking the thing right out of her hands and tossing it aside.

I could just hear my brothers and father now, taunting me over failing because of this girl yet again.

I should kill her.

My fingers flexed and I lunged for her. But as I caught her wrists in my grasp, those brown eyes widened in fear and a better idea occurred to me.

"Your papa's gonna have to rearrange the wedding, Principessa," I taunted, yanking her towards me and lifting her into my arms.

Sloan screamed as I threw her towards the window, her arms flailing as she fought to catch herself before she fell, her fingers snatching hold of my wrist.

I laughed cruelly, prising them from my flesh and shoving her hard so that she fell outside with a cry of panic.

I leapt up a moment later, Carlo's gun ringing out again as I dove out of the church, rolling across the glass and concrete outside with a hiss of pain.

Frankie was blasting the horn at the far end of the street and Enzo was staring at me with wild eyes from the back seat of the black BMW as he gripped his bleeding shoulder.

Sloan was on her feet, her veil whipping off of her head as she ran as fast as she could, desperately trying to get away from me.

A savage smile pulled at my lips as I charged after her, quickly gaining on her as she fought against the swathes of material that made up her wedding dress.

I collided with her, catching her around the waist as she screamed bloody murder and I threw her over my shoulder.

"What the fuck are you doing?" Frankie yelled, his window down and eyes wide as I raced for the car.

"Pop the trunk!" I commanded, ignoring his question as the sounds of pursuit came from behind me.

There wasn't any more gunfire though. Not while I held their precious Sloan.

Enzo started laughing like this was the funniest fucking thing in the world and I ran even faster as the trunk sprang open.

Sloan was screaming, cursing, scratching and even biting me in an attempt to make me release her. But that wasn't gonna happen.

We may not have succeeded in killing her father, but I'd just come up with the best plan B in the history of the world. Because if we had his precious daughter then we held his empire in our hands. We could bend him over a barrel and make him dance to whatever goddamn tune we wanted.

"Let me go you fucking psycho!" Sloan screamed as I hoisted her back over my shoulder and threw her straight into the trunk.

Her lips parted, eyes wide and full of panic for half a second before I slammed the trunk door and blocked her out.

I leapt into the passenger seat and Frankie hit the gas as the car tore away from the crowd of screaming gangsters who were racing after us.

I watched them until we turned a corner and then threw my head back against the headrest with a bark of laughter.

"What the fuck was that about?" Frankie demanded as Sloan's screams filled the car.

"I've decided to branch out into hostage taking," I said with a victorious smile. "And I think I'm gonna be really damn good at it."

Nicoli

A hand crashed into my cheek and blinding pain splintered through my skull as I blinked my eyes open.

"Svegliati! Wake up, Nicoli!" Giuseppe's voice came at me in a harsh snarl as he slapped me again.

I growled a curse, rolling onto my hands and knees as blood poured from the side of my head where that Romero bastard had struck me with the fucking cross from the altar.

"That piece of shit is kidnapping your bride!" Giuseppe snarled and somehow that one small piece of information slipped through the agony and confusion of my battered skull and lit a fire of rage burning in my soul.

"Where?" I demanded, getting to my feet and ripping my jacket off, throwing it to the ground.

"He took her out of the window!" Giuseppe cried and I was running before he could get another word out.

The broken window at the back of the church let in the howling winter air, the cold biting at the wound which gaped open on the side of my head.

Blood poured along my cheek and dripped all over my once pristine white shirt and I snarled in rage at the scum who had ruined one of the first things I'd ever truly been able to call my own. This wedding should have bound me to the Calabresi name in every way possible. The sons Sloan and I would have were the future of this city and I refused to accept the idea that someone was trying to steal that fate from me.

I dove out of the window, landing on the frozen ground outside and rolling across broken glass which cut and bit at my flesh, adding to the wounds the Romero scum had given me.

I was on my feet a moment later, my gaze zeroing in on the black BMW at the far side of the wide green where Rocco fucking Romero was forcing my bride into the trunk.

Her screams pierced the air and tore at my heart and I bellowed my rage as I ran for her.

I'm coming, Sloan. I will rip the world in two to save you!

More members of the Calabresi fold were racing across the grass already, shouting curses as they tried to get to her. But my pace outmatched them all because none of them could match my rage. She was my destiny and I'd die before I let her slip through my fingers.

"Romero!" I bellowed, a challenge and a demand. "Stand and face me like a man!"

My feet pounded across the hard earth as I tore up the distance between us, but that filthy-blooded asshole was already leaping into the car and the engine growled hungrily as it was thrown into gear.

"No!" I cried. "Will you run from this fight like the cowards you are!?"

A high pitched *yip yip yip* came from somewhere beside me and I glanced down, spotting Sloan's little white dog, Coco, running at my side, his rage meeting mine as those fucking assholes stole her away from us.

The car sped off down the street and Carlo fired his gun once behind me.

"Don't shoot at her!" I roared, challenging him to defy me without once looking back.

My gaze was fixed on that fucking car. My life lay in there. My bride. My inheritance. The one true claim I was to have on this empire I'd given my life to.

I was a boy plucked from nothing and groomed to fill the shoes of the greatest mobster this city had ever seen. Giuseppe Calabresi had taken me into his home as a kid and I'd repaid that debt every single day of my life since then. I worked tirelessly to be the best I could be. For him. The closest thing to a father I'd ever known. And he'd entrusted me with the responsibility of taking care of his most prised possession. Once I married Sloan, I would be a Calabresi in every single sense of the word. She was my reward for every foul and dangerous thing I'd done for him. He'd chosen me. Given her to *me*.

She was *mine*.

And I'd chase these assholes to the ends of the earth to return her to her rightful place at my side.

"Sloan!" I bellowed, charging down the street as fast as I could in my dress shoes.

My head spun dizzily, blood dripping into my eyes. I swiped it away with a white sleeve which was quickly stained red as I refused to slow, ignoring the protests of my battered body.

Coco still ran at my side, barking his love for the girl in that car.

One of the Romero assholes leaned out of their window and started firing on me.

I didn't slow, my arms pumping, legs pounding as I ran on. Only a bullet would stop me and even then it would have to hit me square between the eyes.

But as they accelerated further, the distance between me and my destiny only grew.

"Come back!" I demanded, my voice tearing as I roared my fury to the heavens.

The BMW took a corner at speed, bullets hitting the concrete around me and gouging up lumps of grit to pelt my legs. I only ran faster but as they sped beyond a building, my heart sank and a ringing started up in my ears.

I raced on with Coco at my side while the rest of the Calabresis fell too far behind to even hear anymore.

But it didn't matter. If I caught the Romero brothers, I'd tear them apart with my bare hands. Their lives were marked, their deaths belonged to me.

No one stole from Nicoli Vitoli. I was going to be the heir to the Calabresi name. Everyone in this city feared me. And the Romeros would soon find out exactly why that was.

I raced around the corner, my heart falling as I failed to spot the BMW anywhere.

"Cowards!" I screamed at the sky, still running despite the fact that they were gone.

I couldn't give up. I wouldn't. Sloan was counting on me.

To have and to hold.

To honour and protect.

She was mine.

And I'd get her back, no matter the cost.

I ran down street after street, taking turns on instinct but never catching sight of the BMW again.

My heart was pounding so hard that the only sound I could hear was my own pulse in my ears.

My footsteps faltered.

My will shattered.

She was gone.

I doubled over, hands on my knees as I gasped for breath in a desperate bid to recover from my run.

Coco fell panting at my feet, his eyes frantic with concern as he swung his head back and forth like she might somehow spring from the shadows.

"We'll get her back," I promised him and he looked up at me almost as if he'd understood.

A car horn started honking and I looked up at the man who dared to try and make me move out of the road for him.

I strode straight towards his white pickup, my dark gaze pinned on the asshole behind the wheel.

His eyes widened with panic as he took in the full force of my rage.

I roared in challenge, swinging both of my arms above my head and slamming my fists down on the hood of his truck.

The hood crumpled beneath the force of my attack, two huge dents forming beneath my arms.

"Nicoli!" Giuseppe's demanding voice sounded behind me and I spun away from the man I'd been moments from ripping apart as I spotted my boss looking out at me from the rear window of a large, black Bently. "Get in," he snapped and I fell to heel instantly.

I scooped Coco into my arms and wrenched the car door open before falling into the seat opposite my boss.

"She's gone," I stated hollowly as if he couldn't tell.

"Then you're just going to have to get her back, aren't you?" he snarled, the venom in his voice making it seem like he was somehow holding me to blame for this disaster.

"Yes, boss," I agreed, hanging my head in shame as Coco growled beside me.

"Clean that fucking head wound," Giuseppe added irritably as the driver took off. "You're bleeding all over the upholstery."

I tugged the buttons of my shirt open and yanked it off of me, balling it up so that I could stem the blood which still poured down my face.

We pulled up outside Doc Dariello's and I followed Giuseppe as he got out.

Coco leapt from the car behind me, staying close to my heels and I glanced at the little dog in surprise, united with him in our desire to return Sloan to her rightful place at my side.

We headed straight through to the back room of the clinic and I took a seat on the paper-covered bed as Giuseppe pointed me towards it.

"I should be out there tracking her down," I protested, though I didn't make any move to go against him without his permission on the subject.

"Yes, you should be," Giuseppe growled. "But if you collapse and bleed out in the street, you'll be no good to anyone."

My heart twitched at that declaration. The fact that we were here made me think he must care about me. Even just a little. More than just for what I could do for him.

Though I'd been welcomed into the Calabresi household when I was a boy, earning a place in Giuseppe's heart had always felt out of reach. He'd sharpened me into a tool. Honed me into a man not to be trifled with, but there was little place amongst that for anything so simple as love. He just wasn't the kind for declarations and shows of emotion, but at times like this, I wondered if I'd done enough to secure my place at his side or not.

The doctor walked in, eying my wounds without making comment.

I dropped the shirt from my head and sat still as he set to work cleaning it.

"I have every one of my men scouring the city for leads," Giuseppe said darkly. "They'll find her. But I want you hunting too. You do anything and *everything* it takes to get her back. You hear me?"

"Yes, boss," I agreed. I'd tear this city apart until I found her. No one stole what was mine and got away with it.

"Good. And once you've got her, you kill those fucking Romeros. You do it slow and you make sure the pieces are left for the cops. I want everyone in the city to know precisely what happens to a man who crosses Giuseppe Calabresi."

"I'll tear them limb from limb," I snarled, violence calling to me like an old friend.

The doctor started stitching and I gritted my teeth against the pain.

"You will," Giuseppe agreed fiercely. "Because if you don't do this, you're no heir of mine. So I don't want you to eat, sleep or even take a shit between now and when you find my daughter. This is all you live for now. And if you can't get the job done, I might as well cut your throat myself."

"Understood," I growled.

I didn't need the threat of his rage to urge me into action though. The moment the doctor was done stitching my head back together, I'd be back out on the streets. I'd rip open every door, search every alley and kill every fucking Romero I discovered hiding in the gutters until I found her.

I wouldn't stop. I wouldn't rest.

Sloan Calabresi was *mine*. And I'd die before I gave up on her.

Sloan

Oh my god. I've been kidnapped - fucking kidnapped!

I must have been in the trunk for hours and I hadn't stopped screaming. I thumped and kicked the walls, the seat, bashing at everything I could find until my arms and legs were bruised as hell.

Panic crashed through me in the dark as I tried to think of a way out. Anything I could do at all, but I was trapped, the walls seeming to press in on me and the air seeming too thin to inhale.

When we started bouncing along a dirt track, fear stole my breath and sent images flashing through my brain of what might be about to happen.

They've taken me to the woods. They're gonna drag me out of the trunk, kill me and bury me in the ground or dump me in a lake.

It was the middle of winter so the ground would be frozen solid. But they could drill a hole in the ice of a lake…drop me through it dead or alive. Either way I wasn't coming back.

Stop it Sloan! Find a way out before that happens!

I was jostled around, hitting my head, disorientated as I tried to brace myself against the roof. I'd hunted every single inch of the trunk and even torn up the carpet in hopes of finding a tyre iron or something I could use as a weapon, but there was nothing there. Nothing but what I had on me. Just a huge damn dress and-

With a jolt, I kicked off my shoes and snatched one firmly in my grasp. It wasn't much against a gun, but maybe all I needed was a chance to run, to scream, for someone to hear me. Someone who could help.

The car rolled to a halt, sending another flash of terror through my body.

I tried to recall everything Royce had taught me about self-defence, steadying my breathing as best I could and focusing on the task. But nothing could relax me about being at the mercy of Rocco Romero again. I was terrified to face him. I could almost feel his hands around my throat and a tremor ran through me. For the sake of the sixteen year old girl who'd almost died once because of that monster, I was going to fight him with everything I had. I wouldn't go down easy. But there were three of them and no doubt they were armed too.

Shit shit shit.

Heavy footsteps drew my way and my throat closed up as I clutched the high heel in my hand, ready to launch myself out the second I was free.

A beat of silence passed and the wind howled beyond the car like a wailing ghoul.

The trunk popped. My heart juddered. I leapt up with all my might, screaming in defiance.

I slammed into a hard body and smashed the heel of my shoe against his head again and again.

Huge hands caught my wrists and as the trunk shut behind me, my captor slammed me up against the car, prising the shoe from my hand.

"*Fuck*," he snarled as blood poured down his brow.

Rocco Romero was as terrifying as the first day I'd met him. His hardened gaze peeled me apart as he clamped my hands together in one of his then dragged me back upright. My bare feet sunk into snow but I couldn't feel the cold as adrenaline swept through my veins. I tugged desperately at my wrists as he turned me around and I found his two brothers standing further up the drive, watching us.

Frankie Romero, the younger one with floppy black hair, looked on the verge of laughing while the other one with his piercing eyes and dark top knot was nursing a gunshot wound to his arm, staring at me like *I'd* shot him. That one was Enzo, I guessed. His brutal reputation preceded him, but of all the Romeros, none scared me in the way that Rocco did.

A huge manor house sat up on the hill in a nest of trees, covered in snow. The wooden walls reached high up toward the sky, casting an imposing shadow across the ground. The windows reflected the white of the snow and the hills surrounding this entire valley. I didn't know where we were, but I committed it all to memory. We had to have travelled north into the mountains, but the fact that they were letting me see this place at all could only mean one thing: they were going to kill me.

Rocco shoved me along, but I dug my heels in, wriggling and fighting in a furious bid to get free. I used every move Royce had ever taught me, but Rocco was well trained and had at least three times the amount of muscle I had, if not more.

"Enough," Rocco commanded, but hell did I listen. I swung around and bit into the arm of his leather jacket as deeply as I could. Rocco flipped me off of the ground, tossing me over his shoulder and locking his arms around my legs with a huff of frustration. My wedding dress flipped over my head and I screamed in fury as I fought to escape the folds of netting to land a punch on his back.

He carried me along until the sound of a door opening reached me then I was dumped onto a hardwood floor. I shoved the skirt of my wedding dress down so I could see, my hair tumbling around my shoulders in a mess. Rocco kicked the door shut and darkness fell. I shuddered as I found myself at the heart of the three men in a vast entrance hall, moving close to form a triangle around me.

"What are we gonna do with her?" Frankie looked to Rocco for direction.

"We could cut off little pieces one by one," Enzo said with excitement in his eyes.

"No," I gasped.

"Go get that bullet out your arm for a start, fratello," Rocco ordered. He was the eldest of the three so I guessed he was in charge.

Enzo sighed and walked away, clutching his arm which was tied with a tourniquet. I scrambled forward into the space he vacated, launching myself to my feet and trying to bolt. Rocco's arms closed around my waist and he yanked me back against him, sliding his hand up to grip my throat.

I froze, terror gripping my heart as his hand squeezed threateningly.

"We'll put her in the cellar," he decided and a murmur of fear escaped me.

Frankie nodded, looking slightly out of his depth as he hurried off to open a black door beneath the huge staircase at the centre of the hall. Rocco guided me forward and a sheer will to survive flooded me. I elbowed and kicked and screamed, praying there was a neighbour nearby who might hear.

Rocco's hand slammed over my mouth and a tear escaped my eye. His mouth dropped to my ear, his rough stubble biting into my cheek. "No one can hear you, you're miles away from anywhere but you're really giving me a fucking headache. So shut the hell up."

I nodded, reaching my hand back as Royce had taught me once, gently feeling if he had a gun holstered on his hip that I could get to. My fingers grazed his belt and Rocco chuckled in my ear.

"Are you looking for a gun or for my cock, principessa? Because neither will do you any good right now."

I couldn't answer beneath his hand, but I could bite. And I did. As hard as I freaking could.

Rocco growled in my ear as I tasted blood, dropping his hand as he shoved me through the cellar door. Frankie was still looking wide-eyed and I turned to him for help, praying he might have a bout of conscience.

"Please!" I begged of him. "Please don't let him do this."

Frankie rubbed the back of his neck, glancing at Rocco. He didn't answer, but maybe for a second it looked like he cared.

"Please!" I screamed at him as Rocco manhandled me down the staircase.

At the bottom, he shoved me to my knees and the cold stone bit into my skin. I gasped as I braced myself on the floor and my dark hair fell around me in a curtain. This was it. He was going to finish me now, in some dank cellar with no dignity. Then he'd put me somewhere no one would ever find me, my body left to rot.

The sound of the door slamming and a lock clicking made all of the air leave my lungs in a wave. I turned to look behind me and a ragged breath ripped free of my chest.

He was gone.

I sagged forward, bracing myself on the ground and letting a few tears fall as relief and fear mashed together inside me.

I'm not dead yet. Which means they want me for something.
Either that, or Rocco is just fetching tools to do the job.

I gagged on the bile building in my throat then shakily got to my feet. It was almost as cold as the wintry air outside down here and it was entirely dark. I hunted for a wall, running my hand along it in a desperate search for a light switch. The rough stone rubbed against my palm as I hunted and hunted.

My fingers finally met a switch and I flicked it on, illuminating a large wine cellar full of racks of bottles and rows of huge barrels. I hurried forward, reaching for one of the bottles, but the door sounded before I grabbed it and I placed my back to the rack instead, my fingers locking around the neck of one of the bottles in preparation.

A bucket was tossed into the cellar, bouncing down the steps with a series of metallic clangs. Rocco's shadow fell over the room, looking huge as he blocked the light at the top of the stairs. "You can piss and shit in there. You eat what we give you and you never set a fucking foot on these stairs. If you try to escape, I'll kill you." The door slammed and my heart lurched in time with it.

I released my grip on the bottle, eyeing the bucket with disgust.

What do they want from me?

I shivered in the freezing air, wrapping my arms around myself, wondering how long they were going to keep me down here. I'd get hypothermia within a day. And I'd die of humiliation if I used that bucket.

I collected my fears and stuffed them as deep down inside of me as I could.

What would Royce tell me to do?

With a slow breath, I started moving through the room methodically, hunting for anything that might be of use to me. I could use a wine bottle as a weapon, but I'd only get one shot at it. And if they carried guns on them, I might not get close enough…

I moved around the walls, looking for a door, a vent, a window at the top, but I found nothing, my hope failing by the second.

Think, Sloan, think.

I soon gave up my search, sitting down with two wine bottles hidden beneath the folds of my dress and another beside me in easy reaching distance. I couldn't believe that mere hours ago I'd sat in my bedroom getting ready for my wedding day, thinking marrying Nicoli was the worst fate I could face.

This was far worse than that. I'd been placed straight into the hands of three devils, one of whom had tried to kill me before. Would he finish the job this time? The bucket told me I was safe for a while longer. But maybe they were going to torture me first. Maybe they thought I had information on my father. But Papa never told me anything and even if he had, I'd never give it up to the likes of the Romeros.

Dark thoughts flickered through my mind and I made the quiet but resolute decision to try and escape. Whatever it took, no matter the cost. I would get out of here. I just needed a plan, something to give me a chance to run. Then I'd find my way to the nearest neighbour. I'd run as fast as I could and never stop until I found someone, *anyone*. But the beautiful dreams of the outside world were crushed away by the reality of the cellar staring back at me.

I still had one advantage. They hadn't tied me up. So the next time that door opened, I needed to be ready to run.

Rocco

I strode away from the cellar door, my feet thumping across the hardwood floorboards in the hallway as I headed to the living room.

I pushed the door wide and found Frankie building a fire in the hearth while Enzo sat cursing beneath his breath over the bullet wound on his arm.

The room was at the east end of the house and had been built with the height of two floors. Enormous floor length windows sat at the farthest end of the room, filling the entire wall there and looking out over the mountains and forest beyond.

There was a wooden balcony above us and a small, curving staircase led up to it and into the master bedroom where I slept when we stayed here.

The room was full of comfortable furniture and soft rugs in pale colours to contrast the dark wood of the room itself. Papa said this was Mamma's favourite place in the whole world, but since she'd been killed when we were children, he didn't like coming up here often. It had become something of a retreat for me and my brothers, somewhere we'd come to think of as our own. And though I'd never said as much out loud, being here made me feel closer to Mamma.

I was the only one of us who truly remembered her. I'd been six when she was killed. The Calabresis had broken into one of our houses in the city while Papa was away on business. Our brother, Angelo, had come down with a fever and she'd sent me, Enzo and Frankie to stay with our Nonna so that we didn't catch it too. That was the only reason the three of us were still alive.

The Calabresis had come to our home that night and burned the house to the ground with the two of them inside it. I'd lost my Mamma and my closest brother in one night. And our Papa had never been the same again. Angelo had been four when he died. Enzo was two and Frankie just a baby. Neither of them remembered it, but they'd certainly felt the hole left in our home by the people who were torn from it.

We'd been brought up by various nannies after that and moulded into cold men by the rage and loss our father had been left with the day they'd died.

It was why we fought so hard to tear this city away from the clutches of the Calabresis. And why I'd never stop fighting until Giuseppe Calabresi lay dead at my feet.

Before doing anything else, I pulled my phone from my pocket and set some music playing over the speakers which ran through the house, cranking the volume up to be sure our new house guest would hear it.

Rupert Holmes sang Escape (The Pina Colada Song) and I smiled to myself as I shrugged out of my leather jacket, letting it fall to the floor and closed my eyes, tipping my head back to the ceiling as I danced. I sang the lyrics at the top of my lungs as I pulled off my bloodstained white T-shirt and my brothers rolled their eyes at me while trying their damn hardest not to join in.

Sloan had gifted me a ring of perfect bloody teeth marks on my index finger and I painted two bloody lines across my cheeks like I was a warrior headed into battle.

"This is the start of something great," I called over the music. "Can't you feel it, fratelli?"

"I can feel my arm still pissing blood all over the couch," Enzo growled, pouting like a little bitch.

I sighed dramatically, lowering the volume of the music and Frankie took pity on me, belting out the chorus before I could switch it off entirely. I joined in with a wide grin and by the last line Enzo was singing too. We might have been a bunch of crazy motherfuckers, but we just so happened to be the best people I knew.

When the song ended, I killed the music and moved across the wide open space, dropping down to one knee before the cupboards which had been built into the wood panelled wall to the side of the room.

I grabbed the first aid kit out and tossed it down on the couch beside Enzo as I approached him.

"Is there still a bullet in there or did it go through?" I asked, grabbing a wooden chair which stood beside the small table in the corner.

"It went through. I'm going to have a fucking scar right through my ink though," he grumbled, pulling away the ruined shirt he'd been using to stem the flow of blood to give me a look at the damage.

Sure enough, the bullet had punched a hole straight through one of the tattoos on his bicep, the howling wolf that sat there was now missing an ear and half of an eye.

"Now your wolf has a battle scar too," I joked, flipping open the first aid kit and grabbing the bottle of antiseptic.

"Fucking Calabresis," Enzo growled, shifting in his seat so that I could cover the wound with the strong smelling liquid.

"Well we're paying them back for it by taking the little principessa," I growled darkly.

"Can you imagine Giuseppe's face right about now?" Frankie asked enthusiastically behind me. "I bet it's all red and angry like a big fucking beetroot bastardo."

I snorted a laugh as I caught Enzo's elbow and turned his arm to look at the exit wound. If he thought the wolf was fucked up with its missing ear, he was gonna shit a brick when he saw the big ass mess the bullet had made of the skull on the back of his arm. The fucking thing was nothing more than a bottom jaw now.

"It looks like someone's been fighting in a zombie apocalypse back here," I joked as I smothered the wound in antiseptic.

"Per amore di Cristo!" *For the love of Christ!* Enzo cursed, twisting his arm to try and get a look at it then hissing in pain as he tugged on the wound. "What have they done to Isabella?"

"Isabella has lost the top half of her head. But her smile is just as beautiful as always," I teased. Enzo had names for all of his tattoos and sometimes I got the impression they were his best friends in all the world.

"Mother fucker," Enzo growled. "I'm going to carve Carlo Fabrini a few new holes of his own in retaliation for this one day!"

"Keep your mind on that while I'm sewing you up," I replied, taking the needle and thread from the kit next.

"Fuck that, I'm going to opt for oblivion if you're going to be poking me with a needle," Enzo said, rising to his feet and stalking across the room to the liquor cabinet. He grabbed a bottle of thirty year old scotch and unscrewed the cap before tossing it on the floor.

"We don't have a maid up here," Frankie scolded him irritably. "So pick that shit up."

"Fuck off," Enzo replied before putting his lips around the mouth of the bottle and drinking from the neck until more than half the contents were gone.

He slammed the bottle down on the table and walked back to me with a slight stagger in his step.

"Give me five minutes before you start poking me, fratello," he slurred, laying back on the couch and offering me his arm like I was his fucking nurse.

"You want me to kick you in the balls so you have some other pain to focus on while I work?" I asked.

"Vai a farti fottere," he muttered. *Go fuck yourself.*

"That's gratitude for you," I deadpanned before pushing the needle into his skin.

Enzo proceeded to call me every name under the sun in both English and Italian and I smirked to myself as I kept stitching.

Frankie tossed some big logs onto the fire as it started blazing and the warmth of it began to chase the freezing cold of winter from the room at last. It must have been fucking freezing down in the cellar and the thought of that brought a cruel smile to my lips.

"So are we going to talk about the elephant in the room?" Frankie asked, pouring himself a measure of bourbon and taking a seat in the armchair beside us. "Or more accurately, the bride in the cellar?"

I snorted a laugh and Enzo winced as I stuck him a little too hard with the needle.

"I'm sure we can do rather a lot with her," I said, my gaze staying on Enzo's wound. "Namely luring her father out somewhere that he'd be vulnerable so that we can finish what we were supposed to do today."

"You think he loves her enough to put himself at risk for her?" Frankie asked doubtfully.

"What father wouldn't trade their life for their child's?" I asked.

"Ours wouldn't," Enzo put in, his voice a little slurred.

"Alright," I conceded, though I wasn't entirely sure that that was true. Papa may have liked us to fight our own battles and never balked at the idea of putting us in danger, but if we'd been taken hostage I was pretty sure we'd find out just how much he loved us. "What father wouldn't put himself at risk for his *daughter?*"

"I dunno," Frankie said, leaning back in his chair and shaking his head. "He might give a shit about her, but trade his life for hers? Nah, I can't see it. Giuseppe Calabresi doesn't have it in him to be that self-sacrificing. No one could have done the things he's done and walk around town with a big ass smile on their face if they had that much of a conscience. My guess is, we hurt his pride more than his heart when we stole his little Sloan."

I growled my agreement to that point and finished up stitching Enzo's arm before I added anything further.

"Well, even if he won't trade himself, I'm sure we can make plenty of demands on things he *will* agree to."

Frankie nodded at that, a smile dancing around his lips. "We must be embarrassing the fuck out of him."

"We should go down to the girl and cut off a finger," Enzo said with a snigger. "Then post it to him so he knows we're serious."

"Fuck, Enzo, we're not doing that!" Frankie blurted in disgust.

"Yeah," I agreed, clapping my idiota brother around the ear. "We can't go around cutting off fingers like a bunch of savages. At least not until we have to-"

"Why the fuck would we have to?" Frankie demanded, his lip curling back.

"To send them a message!" Enzo pressed.

Frankie looked to me for help and I rolled my eyes as I pushed myself to my feet. "We aren't sending a fucking finger message," I said flatly, no room for negotiation.

Enzo sighed like I'd just told him he couldn't have a puppy and Frankie shot him a look which said *what the fuck is wrong with you??*

I wrapped Enzo's arm in a soft, white bandage and he patted me on the cheek affectionately just before his eyes fell closed as I finished up. I was pretty sure he'd still be right there on that couch come morning if everything went the way it usually did. Aside from the girl I'd stolen who was hanging out in the basement of course.

"Sometimes, I worry that he was born without that part of the brain that makes you empathise with other people," Frankie said, taking a long drink from his bourbon as he watched our brother through narrowed eyes.

"Don't worry about Enzo," I teased. "He only needs a firm hand to keep him in line."

"Easy for you to say," Frankie muttered. "He listens to you. I'm the one he always torments."

"And yet you still haven't seen him cut off any fingers and send them out in the mail, have you? Just forget about the stupid shit he says. Until I see him chopping fingers, I'm not going to worry myself over it. He's no Guido."

Frankie cringed as I mentioned our creepy ass, psychotic cousin and I smirked as I walked across the room to claim a drink too. Frankie blew out a breath that said he wasn't wholly convinced about Enzo, but he wasn't gonna push it any further either.

"Fine. So what *are* we going to do with our little house guest?" Frankie asked, his gaze trailing after me as I drained a glass of bourbon.

I took my sweet time drinking. Because I actually didn't have an answer for that. Stealing Sloan Calabresi from her own wedding had seemed like a brilliant fucking plan when I'd done it. And I had to admit that the idea of Giuseppe and Nicoli racing all over Sinners Bay in a desperate bid to find her had me feeling all kinds of happy. But the reality we were now in was that we had a girl locked in the basement who would need watching constantly, not to mention some level of care to keep her alive.

I sighed, placing my glass down and the look in Frankie's eye said he knew I'd just let myself get carried away back at the church. I hadn't wanted to lose face. Didn't want it to be another failure. So now I had to make good on this plan.

"For now, we have the Calabresis shitting themselves and crying themselves to sleep over their missing principessa," I said. "So I say we let them squirm for a few days until Papa gets back from his trip. Let him make the call on where to go from there."

Frankie's face broke into a smile at that suggestion. He always had been a papa's boy. He much preferred it when his instructions came from the man in charge and though that kinda riled me up sometimes, in this instance I had to agree with him. Because taking Sloan hostage had been the easy part. Figuring out what was best to do with her now was a little trickier.

I glanced down at my blood stained clothes and decided on a shower as my next port of call.

"Can you fix us something to eat?" I asked Frankie as I headed for the door. Being the getaway driver had plenty of perks, including the fact that he was the only one of us who wasn't bleeding all over the hardwood floors.

"Sure. I'll put together some sandwiches," he offered, following me out of the room before heading to the kitchen. Sandwiches were about the best any of us could do food wise and the closest town was too damn far away to order take out. I'd probably go pick up a bunch of food we could reheat tomorrow though or we'd be in for days of sandwiches and junk food.

I took the curving staircase in the hallway up to the second floor, walking along the wood panelled balcony to the master bedroom at the far end of the walkway. I crossed through it to the huge en-suite, stripped out of my ruined pants and stepped straight into the hot flood of water in the shower.

Dirt and blood swirled down the drain as I tipped my head back and enjoyed the peace of the shower.

A slow smile spread across my face as I stood there.

Sloan Calabresi had brought shame on my name when I'd failed to kill her all those years ago. But now, finally and somewhat unexpectedly, I was going to wipe that memory from everyone's minds.

I was making it right, evening the score. And this time, I'd be doing whatever it took to keep my reputation spotless.

Sloan

I opened every damn wine bottle in the cellar, pouring them all over the floor instead of smashing them. I wasn't going to draw the Romeros to me until my plan was ready. First, I had to make this place inhospitable so they couldn't leave me down here even if they wanted to. It was a gamble, but my life was worth the risk even if the consequences of this terrified me.

What if they punish me?

What if they decide I'm not worth the trouble and put a bullet between my eyes?

I couldn't let myself dwell on those possibilities. I had to try something, I couldn't just lie down and accept this, because that option would surely lead to my death.

I'd found a corkscrew on one of the racks and it had taken me nearly an hour to drain every bottle. Then I started on the barrels, opening the valves and letting them pour out like a river of blood, washing over my feet as it spilled everywhere.

When the job was done, I grabbed the two bottles I'd saved and tucked the corkscrew down the front of my dress.

I took a moment to will away the fear burning through me and though it didn't work completely, it gave me enough strength to keep going.

Just do it, Sloan. Be brave.

With all my might, I threw a bottle at the wall and a huge crash sounded as glass shattered everywhere. Then I screamed for help like I was in pain, flicked the light switch off and ducked under the gap beneath the stairs. There was no banister on the wooden steps so I'd be able to climb up past whichever bastard came to find me. It was reckless, crazy and my heart was pounding out of control as I finally put my plan into action. But I had to try. I couldn't give up.

The door wrenched open and a rectangular patch of light illuminated the steps. "What the fuck is going on down here?"

It was Enzo's booming voice and he jogged down the stairs in a wife beater, the muscular, tattoo-covered bicep of his right arm bound with a bandage. "Merda santa!" he cursed as he switched the light on.

With a surge of adrenaline, I hauled myself up onto the steps, wielding the wine bottle and swinging it at the back of his head. A hollow donk sounded as it connected and Enzo crashed forward into the pool of wine face first. The bottle slipped from my fingers but I couldn't waste the time trying to retrieve it. I fled up the stairs, trailing wine behind me which had soaked into the hem of my dress. My feet were bare, giving me a silent ascent and as I reached the hall, hope shone through me like rays of sunshine.

I ran to the door, unlocking the latches with fumbling fingers then yanking it open and spilling outside.

Glorious fresh air rolled into my lungs. I darted forward with no plan but to run for my life and search for help. I made it to the first step of the porch when strong arms closed around me from behind and my gut lurched in horror.

I screamed to the dying sun which hung low in the sky, praying my voice would reach someone, *anyone*. The noise echoed back from the mountains and was cut off as Rocco slammed the door, whirling me around and throwing my back against it. "You wanna die out there in the snow, principessa? Because that's what'll happen if you go running out into the wilderness. Either that or the wolves will get you."

I spat in his face and he laughed, rubbing it into his cheek. "Thanks for the free facial."

"Psycho!" I snarled and he laughed harder.

I struggled to break his hold on me, but it was no use. He dragged me back across the hall toward the cellar then paused at the top of the stairs, tugging me against his hip.

"Fuck!" he roared as he spotted Enzo lying in an inch of wine at the bottom. He was struggling to get up, seeming drunk and disappointment flared inside me that he wasn't dead.

I scratched and clawed at Rocco's hand and he caught my chin in a tight grip, making me fall still in fear.

"Enough," he commanded, his angular face looking sharp and unforgiving as he frowned at me. "You can't win." He turned and I spotted Frankie striding towards the cellar, throwing a dark scowl at me which I felt right down to my bones. If there had been any hesitation in him before about keeping me here, it had vanished at the sight of his brother at the bottom of the cellar stairs. He hurried down to help Enzo and I feared what was about to happen to me in penance for this.

Rocco's eyes slid down to the wine dripping from my dress and he growled low in his throat. "What am I going to do with you, hm?" He didn't wait for an answer before hauling me toward the staircase and dragging me up them. I stumbled, nearly falling but his grip was too tight to let my knees touch the ground.

He swung me around on the landing, pulling me along and I dug my bare feet in to the floorboards to try and stop him, but I kept slipping in the wine which trickled from my dress. My eyes fell on a door up ahead and I glimpsed a bedroom beyond it. Fear like nothing I'd ever known took hold of me and I started screaming again, battling against his hold, but he just kept tugging me along. I used every trick Royce had taught me, but none of it overpowered sheer strength. I was powerless to stop him and terrified of him bringing me into that room.

I'd rather die than that.

At the last second, he turned sharply into a bathroom and kicked the door shut. My relief at not going to the bedroom was short-lived as he shoved me forward, letting go of my hand. The wine made a red stain on the white bath mat beneath me as I curled my toes up in the fluffy material.

He took out a switch blade, flicking it open with a loud snap. Adrenaline bled into my veins. I hooked the corkscrew out of the front of my dress, wielding it at him with a shaking hand even though I knew it was stupid, useless. But it made me feel less out of control.

Rocco smiled darkly then lunged at me, snatching the corkscrew from my grasp before turning me sharply and sliding his knife down the back of my dress. The icy blade kissed my skin and with one sharp cut from top to bottom, he sliced the material open then yanked it down to reveal my white bridal underwear beneath. I gasped as his hand closed around my arm so I couldn't escape. His breath rolled over my bare shoulder and a shudder rushed along my spine in response.

I tried to cover myself up as he lifted me out of the remains of the dress around my legs. I stumbled back against him then shoved him away, trying to cover my breasts with one arm whilst holding him off with the other.

"Shower. Now." He pointed with the knife. "And if you get any ideas about using any bathroom products against me, you'll regret it."

I nodded, hating that I had to comply, but at least he wasn't cutting off the remainder of my clothes. And I had to hope that meant he wouldn't force himself on me either. If he did, Royce had taught me a few tricks that might give me a chance to run. But in this house, it didn't seem like I'd get anywhere far without a Romero hunting me down.

I slid the shower door open with trembling fingers then glanced back at him to find him watching me without any hint of him leaving.

"Can't you wait outside?" I asked with as much strength as I could muster.

"No," he said simply. "Start the shower in the next two seconds, or you don't get one."

I clenched my jaw, glaring at him for a beat longer before stepping into the shower and turning the hot water on. It burned against my frozen skin and I had to ease into the stream to adjust to it. But when I did, it was a godsend. It felt crazy to appreciate anything right then, but just a couple of hours in that freezing cellar had driven ice into my bones and I was finally about to thaw out.

I sighed, placing my hand against the wall as I let the water run down my back and soak into my hair. I didn't know what would come next, but I hoped the ruined cellar meant I wouldn't be going back down there. Being out of there wasn't even close to freedom, but it was something.

"Out. Now," Rocco commanded and I shut off the water, a prickle of fear running over my skin at this beast watching me.

I'd only had one man's eyes on my naked flesh before. A boyfriend in Italy who could have besmirched my name if anyone ever found out about him. I'd risked it for freedom. I didn't want to covet my virginity like some precious flower, I wanted to make my own choices when it came to my body. Choices I knew I'd be unlikely to get again when I came home to America.

Ironically, I was now left with even less choices than I'd had just yesterday. My whole life I'd felt like a prisoner and now I knew what it was really like to be bound and chained. Had I tempted fate with all my thoughts of being a captive?

Rocco tossed a fluffy white towel at me and I wrapped myself up in it as my wet hair hung around my shoulders.

"Dry off. Don't do anything stupid." Rocco walked out the door and I cursed his name. If he was happy to leave me in here, he could have done so before I had a damn shower.

The door clicked shut and a key sounded in the lock.

I immediately hurried to the window. It was frosted and small, but maybe I could wriggle through. I didn't know what lay beyond it though. We were on the second floor.

I jumped up onto the toilet seat, my fingers trembling as I twisted the catch and pushed it wide. I stuck my head out as an icy wind crashed over me, my stomach swooping at the sight of the drop below. But there was a ledge beneath the window and the roof of the porch was just beyond that. I could make it.

Footsteps pounded along the hall and I dragged the window closed, hopping off the toilet with panic in my heart as I grabbed another towel to start drying my hair. My pulse pounded wildly as Rocco stepped back into the room, his eyes sweeping over me, assessing. Something about him was so penetrating, like he could see beneath my skin and peel apart my darkest secrets.

He tossed a large black T-shirt at my feet along with a pair of white boxer briefs. I eyed them with my nose wrinkling, looking up again to find him smirking.

"Unless you want to stay in that damp underwear – which is entirely transparent when wet by the way – I suggest you put these on."

My mouth fell open and I gaped at him in horror. "You looked," I accused.

"It was hard to miss your pointy nipples, one of them nearly took my eye out." He grinned like a wolf and I scowled at him.

"Leave me to change," I demanded, hugging my towel tighter to my chest. *I do not have pointy nipples.*

"No one tells a Romero what to do. Least of all a Calabresi. So I'm going to stand right here."

"Like a pervert," I muttered and his eyes flashed with hate.

"As if I'd lust after the daughter of my mortal enemy. You repulse me."

His words were as sharp as knives, but I hoped they were true because I didn't want this man or any of his brothers laying a finger on me.

I turned around, pulling my towel up and over my shoulders to give me cover then slid my lacy panties off. When I'd put them on this morning, I'd imagined laying beneath the weight of Nicoli's muscular body, giving myself to him as his wife. The thought had been kind of terrifying. I'd barely had any time to get used to the idea of him being my husband and I'd been more than a little nervous about what he'd expect on our wedding night. And though I'd resigned myself to that fate, I'd never wanted to have those kinds of choices made for me. But I'd take a marriage bed over this any day.

Stupid Sloan, you wished away a miserable life for an even worse one.

The bra was more difficult to shimmy out of and I swear Rocco laughed at me under his breath as I tried to keep my body hidden from him. It was stupid as he'd already seen through my underwear, but I hadn't chosen that. I didn't want his eyes scouring my flesh. He didn't deserve to look at me.

I tossed the bra aside with a small flutter of accomplishment before wrapping the towel back around myself and turning to find Rocco had the T-shirt in his grip. "You're taking your sweet fucking time, principessa. This isn't a spa retreat."

"Oh I must have wandered into the wrong mansion, I thought this was a five star hotel. I'll just be leaving then."

His brows lifted ever-so-slightly and his mouth twitched at the corner. A beat of tense silence passed. I made a mental note that my kidnapper had a sense of humour and wondered if I could use that to my advantage.

He came at me so fast I didn't manage to stumble back two paces before his arms were around me. He ripped the towel off of me and I screamed half a second before he dumped the T-shirt over my head, leaving my arms trapped beneath it. He bent down, lifting one of my ankles and I forced my arms through the T-shirt then clung on to the sink for balance. My eyes fell on a brass toothbrush holder. It didn't look like it could do much damage, but I'd sure as hell give it a try. As Rocco forced my foot into a hole in the briefs, I smashed it over his head with a yell of defiance.

He growled in anger, dropping my foot and lifting the other one, forcing it through the hole without reacting further to what I'd done. He stood up fast, yanking the briefs over my ass and pushing the T-shirt up to my hips. They were too big even though the elastic waist held them in place, but *god* whose were they?

Rocco's burning fingers lingered on my outer thighs as he leaned into my face with a sneer. "You fight me again and you won't get clothes."

A sharp lump formed in my throat and I nodded as I tried to swallow it back.

He grabbed my wrist then tugged me out of the room. Fear skittered through me as he led me downstairs and a breath of relief passed my lips as he pulled me away from the cellar door. He guided me through to a huge kitchen with a marble-top island at the heart of it.

Enzo sat on a stool, holding a bag of frozen peas to the back of his head, his eyes narrowed on me. "Frankie's cleaning the cellar," he told me with a twisted smile. "Won't be long and you can go back down there. Maybe this time we'll lock the door and throw away the key. The rats will have a feast."

My blood ran cold and I took an instinctive step back, immediately regretting it as I knocked into Rocco's hard chest. He pushed me toward the seat beside Enzo. I didn't want to sit anywhere near him, but Rocco gave me no choice as he lifted me up and dumped me on it.

"If she moves, shoot her," he commanded Enzo and his brother grinned.

"Gladly."

A sandwich sat in the centre of the island and despite myself, my stomach growled for it. I hadn't eaten anything today and I must have burned through countless calories on adrenaline alone.

I looked away from it, fixing my gaze on the window instead. A mountain stood in the distance and I scoured every inch of it as I search for a house, a line of smoke, any indicator that someone lived there. If I got the chance to run again, I needed to know which direction to take.

Enzo placed the peas down then took a huge hunting knife from his hip, admiring it casually like he wasn't threatening me. But it was clear he was.

Rocco made coffee and the scent of it reached me as he filled his mug from the machine.

I endured a full ten minutes of watching Rocco nurse half the cup of coffee before pouring the rest of it down the sink. I was so thirsty I could have swallowed a gallon of water in one go.

Frankie finally appeared with a mop and bucket, frowning as he strolled into the room and his eyes fell on me. "All finished. You just cost our father a lot of money in wine."

"She'll pay for it when he arrives," Enzo said excitedly and a shiver clutched my spine.

I had to get out of here before he showed up. Martello Romero's name amongst our family was a curse. And I did not want to come face to face with the man who'd produced these three ruthless boys.

"You should eat," Frankie said, moving to the island and pushing the sandwich towards me. The scary glint in his eyes was absent now and I hoped that meant he'd gotten over what I'd done to his brother.

My gaze fell to the sandwich. It looked like cheese salad but it didn't matter what it was, I was desperate for it.

Frankie nodded in encouragement and I pulled the plate towards me, picking up one of the triangles. I lifted it to my mouth but before my teeth closed around it, Rocco slapped it out of my hand. I blinked in surprise then flinched as the plate and the rest of the sandwich followed it onto the floor with another swipe of his palm. "If the principessa is hungry, she can eat like the chained dog she is." He marched away across the room, reaching into a cupboard and taking something out. I couldn't see what he was doing, but a foul scent reached my nose and a second later he slammed a metal bowl of dog food under my nose.

I inhaled in horror, looking up to find him smirking like it was the funniest thing he'd ever seen.

"You pig," I hissed, pushing the bowl away, but he shoved it firmly back at me.

"Time to go back into your cage, pup." He snared my arm, holding the dog bowl in the other hand and I screamed as he forced me back to the cellar door out in the hall.

"No!" I yelled, trying to twist my wrist out of his grip, but it only caused me pain as his hand didn't yield. He pulled me down the stairs so fast I almost fell and when I reached the bottom, I was terrified of what I found there.

A wine rack had been pushed back against one wall, the floor still glistening with the residue of the wine around it. Attached to it was a chain and a padlock.

I shook my head in a panic, knowing as soon as I was tied up, I was never going to get out of here.

I swung toward Rocco, jamming the heel of my palm against his jaw hard enough to throw his head back as adrenaline crashed through my veins.

He snarled, catching my other wrist and forcing me along. I kicked his shin then went for his balls, but he was too fast, swinging me around and shoving me to my knees in front of the rack. He dropped the dog food and the bowl clanged on the ground as he fell on me.

I fought furiously, but he used his knees to pin me down while binding my wrists together then chaining them to the rack. I reared forward and sank my teeth into his shoulder, but he just laughed like he enjoyed it.

"Bastard!" I spat as the padlock clicked into place and he stood up with a satisfied look. He kicked the bowl of dog food toward me, reaching up to his shoulder then bringing his fingers away wet with blood.

"What did I say about fighting back?" he asked in a deadly tone.

I curled my legs to my chest, desperation filling me as I thought about him leaving me down here naked and chained. I clenched my jaw, refusing to give him an answer.

"Come on," he purred. "I know that mouth does more than bite. Did you enjoy the taste of my blood, little vampire?"

I kept my lips sealed, refusing to rise to his bait.

He leaned down into my face with a smirk, a crazy glint in his gaze. "Answer me and I won't punish you."

My throat closed up from the dare in his expression. I didn't want to invoke the wrath of this ox of a man. But he didn't say I had to answer nicely.

"You taste delicious, give me a knife so I can try some more." I stared him dead in the eyes, refusing to flinch.

His face twisted into a grin that was half maniac, half clown. "Looks like you've got a lot of spirit for me to break." He headed toward the stairs, jogging up them and flicking the light off. A chill ran through me at being alone in the dark. "Eat up, principessa, or you'll have to share with the rats."

Rocco

I groaned as I woke, the stiffness in my body reminding me of just how many times I'd been hit by Nicoli Vitoli's hammer fists in our fight yesterday. Not to mention the wounds his bride had given me too.

I rolled out of bed, a shiver running along my bare chest at the kiss of cold air which hung in the room. I snatched a pair of sweatpants from the chair beside my bed and drew them on as I glanced at the clock. It was half nine so I guessed Enzo wouldn't be up, but Frankie might be.

I never closed the curtains over my window and one look out of it showed a thick frost and a new thin layer of snow coating the ground. Everything sparkled and glimmered with the power of winter and I released a slow breath as I looked out over that view, letting the peace of our surroundings wash over me. I always felt calmer when we stayed here, away from the rush of the city and the pressure of the family business.

I quickly brushed my teeth in the en-suite and headed out onto the balcony which adjoined this room before taking the twisting staircase down to the bottom floor of the living area.

The fire had died down but a few embers lingered in the grate and I stirred them with a poker before adding some kindling and some new logs to them to get the blaze going again and warm this place up. We had the central heating running but nothing could really banish the cold in this house like a good fire once winter had set in.

I yawned as I padded out into the hallway, heading for the kitchen and wishing I'd grabbed a shirt before coming down.

I pushed my way into the kitchen and found Frankie buttering a slice of toast which I instantly snatched from his grasp.

"Stronzo," he swore as I bit into his breakfast with a wide grin. "That wasn't even for me," he added.

"Aww were you gonna bring me breakfast in bed, bella?" I teased.

"No, idiota, we have a house guest now and thanks to you she hasn't eaten in over a day."

"I gave her dinner," I joked, wondering how long that dog food would go uneaten if I didn't give her any other options.

"Well now you can stop being such a jackass and give her something real to eat. Unless you want her starving to death and us losing our leverage against her father?" Frankie gave me a judgemental look and I rolled my eyes at him.

"Fine. Let's feed the principessa," I agreed with a sigh like the idea of it bothered me. Though in all honesty he had a point.

I made myself some coffee while Frankie put some more toast on for her and I looked out over the drive as a few more flakes of snow tumbled lazily from the sky.

"Here," Frankie said and I turned to find him holding a plate with two slices of toast on it and a plastic sports bottle filled with water.

"Why am I the one going down there?" I asked.

"Because you're the idiota who snatched her," he replied flatly. "And you know what Papa always said about bringing strays home. If you wanna keep it, you gotta feed it. And clean up after it. So you should probably check her bucket too."

I rolled my eyes and took the food and water from him before heading out into the hall.

I unlocked the cellar and pulled the door wide, a rush of cold air washing over me even before I'd gone down there.

I flicked on the lights and headed down the stairs at a casual pace, my feet thumping heavily on the wooden steps and the cold wrapping around me, making goosebumps rise along my arms.

I stilled at the foot of the stairs as I spotted her huddled in the corner beside the wine rack I'd chained her to, her arms wrapped around her legs as shivers wracked her body. Her wide eyes fell on me and her jaw locked tight as she forced herself to raise her chin in defiance.

It was fucking freezing down here. Like, take your balls and dip them in dry ice 'til you hear them pop *cold.*

Fuck.

I moved towards our little prisoner at a casual pace and she fought to control the chattering of her teeth. Her lips were blue and she looked on the verge of hypothermia. The cellar had clearly been a terrible fucking idea. Not that I'd be admitting that to her.

"Good morning, principessa," I said casually like we'd just bumped into each other at brunch in some swanky restaurant in town.

The hatred in her eyes hardened, but she didn't deign to respond. Or maybe she couldn't stop her teeth from chattering long enough to do it.

"I brought breakfast," I said, waving the plate of toast at her. "Assuming you're not still too full after your dinner?"

Her scowl deepened and I glanced at the untouched dog food on the floor.

"F-fuck you," she hissed, fighting hard against the chatter. In all honesty I was fairly impressed she'd made it through the night. It was as freezing as the fucking Antarctic down here.

"Thanks for the offer, bella, but I'd sooner cut my dick off than stick it in a Calabresi. So are you gonna eat or what?" I took a piece of toast from the plate and held it out in front of her where she knelt on the floor before me.

"I c-can feed myself," she growled.

I smiled like the honest to god asshole I was and lifted the piece of toast out of her reach as she tried to take it from me.

"No, no," I said. "You're my little doggy. And I'm gonna feed you like a good little doggy."

I pushed the slice of toast close to her full lips again and the scowl she gave me was so full of venom that I couldn't help but laugh.

"Eat it my way or go hungry again," I said, taking a step back.

"Wait!" she bit out, her gaze on the food and her pride burning away to nothing in the face of her hunger.

I smirked cruelly at her as I offered the toast again. "Open your mouth then, sweetheart."

Sloan glared at me for a moment longer before letting her mouth fall open.

I stepped closer, looking down at her on her knees in my t-shirt with those full lips parted hungrily and my dick twitched with the kinds of ideas I really didn't want it to be getting about a Calabresi. But *fuck* she looked hot like that. My fingers tingled with the ache to grip her hair and drive the full length of me into her mouth.

I banished the thoughts with a grunt of irritation and pushed the toast between her lips instead. She took a savage bite which had me feeling glad it hadn't been my dick after all and I stood over her as I continued to feed her the rest.

When she'd eaten the final mouthful, I reached out and swiped my thumb across those full lips, brushing crumbs from them and savouring the way they felt against my skin. Fuck, this girl was going to be trouble if I let myself keep thinking about her like that.

"See you at lunch time," I said, placing the water bottle down beside her and turning away.

"No! P-please!" she called after me and a twisted satisfaction poured through me at the desperate tone to her voice.

"What?" I asked, looking back at her with about as much interest as I might take in reading my horoscope.

"You c-can't leave m-me down h-here. I'm g-going to f-f-freeze." She gave me those big eyes again and some deceitful little prick deep down inside me squirmed uncomfortably at the desperation in her gaze. I kicked him back down hard enough to silence him permanently, my gaze trailing over her cold, dank surroundings like I couldn't really see what the problem was.

"Well try not to," I said casually. "If you die before we're ready, you won't be much use for blackmailing daddy now, will you?"

Her lips parted in horror as I turned and jogged back up the stairs, flipping the lights off again and plunging her into darkness.

A soft whimper of fear reached me just before I pulled the door shut on her and that sympathetic asshole I thought I'd just killed raised his battered head again.

For fuck's sake.

I headed back into the living room and found Frankie and Enzo both sat eating their breakfast before the fire.

"What's up, fratello?" Frankie asked as I stalked into the room and moved to stand before the fireplace to warm myself. The cold of the cellar clung to me like the touch of frozen fingers and I'd only been down there ten minutes.

"Our prisoner is going to die if we leave her down in that fucking cellar," I said darkly. "I wouldn't be surprised if she's got hypothermia already."

"Shit," Frankie replied, placing his coffee down on the table.

"Good," Enzo cut in. "She's a fucking liability anyway. I say we let her die then toss her in the woods for the wolves to eat…after we cut off a finger for her papa of course."

"Quit it with that finger shit," I snapped. "But if we don't make an alternative plan for her soon they might all freeze off anyway."

"Well she'll have to come up into the house then," Frankie said like that was just so fucking simple.

"We can't possibly keep her secured in the house, every room has windows with old shitty catches securing them. She'd escape as soon as we went to sleep," I said, rubbing a palm down my face in frustration.

"So we sleep in shifts and watch her," Frankie suggested.

"You know I'm no good at staying up late," Enzo interrupted. "What if I fall asleep and she runs off?"

I sighed irritably. "Then we'll have to chain her to the bed."

"Which bed?" Enzo asked. "Everything in this house is antique, she'd be able to break it without much trouble and if we're in another room then we might not hear her."

"So what do you suggest then?" I asked, growing tired of this back and forth.

"She'll have to sleep in a bed with one of us," he replied with a dirty as fuck smile.

"You turning into a rapist now, Enzo?" I growled and he blanched like I'd struck him.

"Fuck off. I'm not offering to have her in with me. I'm not the one who snatched her up like the prize pig at the fair and stole her back here. You made your bed so you can lie in it." He grinned tauntingly as he pushed his chin length hair away from his face. He usually tied it in a top knot, but I was guessing that was pretty hard with a bullet hole through your bicep.

"I can't have her in my bed," I protested weakly though the set of Frankie's jaw told me he wasn't going to volunteer either.

"Why the fuck not, stronzo?" Enzo demanded.

"Because if she sleeps in my bed every night, she'll end up falling in love with me," I joked. "And that'll be awkward as fuck when I have to kill her."

Frankie snorted a laugh. "You wish. That girl would sooner carve her own eyes out than stare lovingly into yours."

"Please. I could make her fall in love with me in the blink of an eye if I wanted to. Haven't you ever heard of Stockholm Syndrome?" I folded my arms across my chest and stared them down with my bullshit.

Enzo barked a laugh. "I think he can do it," he said, smirking at Frankie with the game. "Girls always buy into his asshole persona and his pretty face."

"I do have a pretty face," I agreed.

"Pretty doesn't have stubble in my book," Frankie said, rolling his eyes. "Besides, I'm the one with dimples so if anyone's the pretty brother then it's me."

"And it's not an asshole persona," I added. "I'm just a dick."

"Noted. Girls still seem to like that though for some reason," Enzo said with a shrug.

"Not enough to make up for the fact that he kidnapped her!" Frankie said in exasperation.

"Wanna bet?" Enzo asked and I snorted a laugh.

"Fine. A thousand dollars says he can't do it," Frankie said, holding out a hand.

"A thousand says she's parting her legs for him before we cut her pretty head off," Enzo disagreed, slapping his palm into Frankie's and shaking on it.

"I thought the bet was that she'd fall in love with me, not fuck me?" I asked, raising an eyebrow at them. "A thousand says she says the three little words and means them."

"You think you can make Sloan Calabresi fall in love with you?" Frankie scoffed.

"Yeah. And I'm not even gonna have to work hard at it." I grinned cockily as my brothers laughed.

"It's a bet then," Enzo said, raising his coffee at me and draining the whole cup.

"Right. Then let's get this house fit for a principessa, she's gonna need a hot bath if we want her keeping her fingers and toes and someone's gonna have to go into town and pick up some chains and shit to keep her contained," I said.

"I'm still recovering," Enzo said with an innocent shrug.

"Fine. I'll go to town," Frankie agreed. "I'll pick up some pre-cooked meals from the diner while I'm there."

"Looks like I'm bathing a Calabresi then," I said and I smirked to myself at that idea. First I'd tossed her in a freezing cold cellar and almost let her die, now she'd see me as the saviour who brought her back from the brink of death with a hot bath and a warm bed.

Sloan Calabresi would be in love with me before the end of the week.

Sloan

The ice in my bones was burning. This wasn't freezing to death, it was dying in a pit of flames that gnawed at me from the inside out.

My throat was hoarse and my wrists rubbed raw from how hard I'd fought against the chains. I thought I'd have longer than this, more time to plan. But maybe this was all they'd wanted. Perhaps they had cameras in every corner, capturing my death at all angles.

How much longer can I last in this cold?

Another day at the most.

I eyed the water Rocco had brought me with a heavy realisation pouring over me. No, they didn't want me dead. The water was proof of that. But then they must have been idiots, because what use was I to them frozen into a lump of ice in their basement?

Maybe the dog food was proof they had no idea how to look after a living thing. Where was the dog? I certainly hadn't seen one. I thought of my little pup, Coco, wondering if he was being looked after okay. My father was useless with animals, so who would take care of him if I didn't come home? He needed affection. He needed *me*. And he was the only creature I'd ever known who I could say that about.

The cold was starting to do strange things to me. That and the sleepless night made my thoughts hazy, my breathing shallow. Every time the scent of dog food wafted under my nose, bile rose in my throat but nothing came up.

I hadn't done enough with my life. I wasn't old enough to die. I hadn't scratched the surface of all I wanted to do.

All I could hear was the chattering of my teeth and the clinking of chains as I shivered in the dark. I started to lose track of my thoughts, grasping them for a second before losing the thread of them again. A haze was descending and the darkness left me disorientated. I settled on saying my name over and over again, the one solid thing I had to hold onto. The one, unchangeable thing in all my life.

I will live.

I am Sloan Calabresi.

And I will *live.*

Over the noise my teeth were making, I missed the footsteps on the stairs, but I heard them as they drew close. I willed my eyes to open, but they felt sealed shut as strong hands took hold of me. The chains came free and I was pulled against a warm chest which made me groan with need. I curled into their arms and hunted for bare flesh to rest my icy fingers against.

"Fuck," he hissed as I wrapped my hands around his neck.

My eyelids unglued themselves and I gazed up at the devil himself. *He has hellfire to spare so I'll happily take it from him.*

He carried me from the cellar and even now my mind drifted to running, though I knew there wasn't a hope in the world of me even escaping Rocco's arms right then. And my body was in such desperate need of heat that I didn't have any intention of leaving them.

He took me through doors and long halls until we arrived in a steamy room. Heat seeped over my skin but it was like there was a barrier of ice shielding me from it.

My gaze slid over the huge bathroom where a large, claw-foot bath sat at the centre of it. Steam plumed up from hot rocks on the other side of it where glass doors led into a steam room.

Rocco held me over the bath and I suddenly clutched onto him with all my might as he tried to lower me into. "N-no," I forced out.

He paused, frowning at me and waiting for me to elaborate.

I knew a little about hypothermia from the stories Royce had told me about his ex-army days. He'd been posted at a base in Russia for three years and a few of his fellow soldiers had succumbed to it after a storm had left them stranded out in the wilderness. It could set in within less than an hour and it was stupidly dangerous to heat up quickly once it had. I couldn't be sure whether I was that far gone or not, but I wasn't going to take the risk.

"T-towels," I said, pointing to them. "C-can't heat up t-too fast."

Rocco placed me down on a wooden bench built into the wall beside the steam room, gathering up towels and moving toward me. The worst of the chill had started to ease, but I was a long way from being warm.

I tried to lift my shaking hands to help but soon gave up, letting Rocco wrap me in towel after towel. Then he sat down and pulled me into his lap. My cheek touched his and I pushed eagerly against it, not giving a shit in that moment what he thought of me. It might have looked affectionate to anyone watching, but I was taking what I damn well needed from this bastard. I wasn't going to escape this place in a body bag, I'd do it on my own two legs. Which meant I had to get better as soon as I could.

He continued to say nothing and I was fine with that as my heart rate finally found a normal beat and feeling returned to my toes. It took over an hour, maybe longer, but I kept shutting my eyes and time would drift by so I couldn't be sure how long I stayed wrapped in his arms. The shivers started to come in wracks instead of a constant vibration and my teeth eventually stopped chattering.

Time continued to tick by, but Rocco simply sat there until my body came back to life then I pointed to the bath when my skin felt warm enough to face it and he pulled the towels off of me.

He carried me over, lowering me into it and the heat enveloped me like an embrace. I sighed as I sank deeper, all the way down to just below my nose. I watched Rocco as he moved to the end of the bath, leaning his hands on the edge and staring at me.

"Better?" he asked his first word in all this time and I nodded. "Good. We can't have the principessa dying on us now, can we?"

I lifted my chin so my mouth was freed from the water. "If you mean to keep me alive then you've done a terrible job so far."

"Well I'll expect a bad review on TripAdvisor." He smirked and I scowled.

A knock came at the door and Frankie stepped in a second later.

"You know you defeat the point of knocking if you walk in anyway?" Rocco said dryly.

"Yeah, yeah," Frankie said, his eyes falling on me. He frowned, glancing at Rocco. "Is she okay?" he asked like I wasn't capable of answering that question.

"I'm fine," I said. "Apart from the kidnap and the hypothermia, oh and the fact that I've barely eaten in over twenty four hours."

"You can't please some people," Rocco said with another cruel smile.

I set my gaze on Frankie, ignoring his brother. He was clearly the kinder of the two, even though I sensed something deadly beneath his smile. "Any chance of some food?"

"Sure," Frankie said and hope shone through me. "You can get dressed too. I brought you some clothes."

Rocco snatched the bag from his hand and peered into it, muttering something under his breath.

"There's more upstairs," Frankie told his brother and I sat upright, my brows lifting.

"Is that where I'll be staying?" *Oh please Lord if you ever loved me let me stay upstairs away from that freezing cellar.*

"Yeah," Rocco said, shooting me a look that said I wasn't going to be happy about that fact for long. "In my room. With me."

"No," I said immediately, almost choking on the word in horror. "No way."

"You don't get a choice," Rocco snarled.

I looked to Frankie, my heart pounding desperately in my chest. "Can't I stay with you?" God, was I really asking that? Anyone was better than Rocco though, even the bloodthirsty Enzo.

"You're with me or you're back in the cellar," Rocco growled and the threat in his voice was clear. He would put me back there and no matter how much I despised the idea of having to spend the night in his company, it had to be better than going down there again.

I wondered what I had to negotiate with here, but it wasn't a whole lot. "I want more freedom," I blurted. "A shower every day and human food." It was embarrassing that I had to bargain for things that were my right to have anyway.

Frankie smiled. "Done."

"You don't get to answer," Rocco snapped at him, glaring at me and silence rang out.

"Well…I suppose Sloan will just hate your guts forever," Frankie said with a shrug and Rocco seemed to get even angrier at that.

"Get out of the bath," Rocco commanded. "Get dressed. You can have your daily shower but only so my bed doesn't smell like dog piss." He strode from the room, slamming the door and Frankie frowned.

"Do you need any help?" he asked.

I shook my head and he slipped out of the door, leaving me alone. My limbs felt like lead as I climbed out of the water, peeling off the soaking T-shirt and men's underwear, tossing them across the room without care before drying myself on a soft towel.

I moved to the bag Frankie had brought and found a thick white pair of winter pyjamas inside. I pulled them on, followed by the fluffy pair of socks in the bottom of the bag then started towel drying my hair.

My mood had brightened by the time I was dry. Because if I was out of that cellar, I would get a chance to observe the brothers, figure out their habits, their weaknesses. And when I found a chink in their armour, I was going to strike for my freedom.

***

I glanced at the window across the living room. Night had fallen and snow was fluttering down beyond the pane, coming to rest on the sill.

I'd been in here all day while the brothers watched Netflix and ate takeout food from the diner Frankie had been to earlier. They didn't offer me any. Despite my current company, my eyes kept fluttering closed. My body felt weak and as much as I didn't want to sleep in front of these assholes, I knew I needed to rest soon. Though how I was going to share a bed with Rocco Romero and get any sleep at all was yet to be seen.

Frankie passed out on the couch around eleven and by midnight my head was lolling. Rocco suddenly beckoned me toward him across the room, curling a finger at me. I almost didn't go to him, but then I saw the pizza sitting on a plate in his hand. I wet my mouth, practically drooling as he smiled at me like he was enjoying having something to control me with.

"Come with me upstairs and you can have this. Fight, and it goes in the trash. Your call."

I got to my feet and moved toward him, too hungry to complain and he took my arm with a look of satisfaction, leading me to the staircase that led to the balcony above.

"Have fun." Enzo smirked.

I glanced at Rocco's left hand holding the plate, wondering if this asshole had a wife, but I hadn't heard of any Romero weddings recently.

"What are you looking at?" he growled as we arrived up on the balcony.

"I was just wondering if there's a beat down housewife hiding around here somewhere like a frightened mouse. It seems like you like women chained."

"I like *Calabresis* chained and begging at my feet. But women tend to beg me to tie them up."

I tsked, but the light in his gaze didn't fade.

"You probably have only one sweet memory of a man to hold onto, don't you principessa? I bet your Nicoli kept you nice and virginal for his pea-sized cock."

I glowered at him. I wasn't going to correct him. He had no right to any of my secrets, especially not my deepest one. "Which man are you referring to then?"

"Me," he said, grinning like he knew it was true. Which it definitely wasn't. "I bet you've dreamed about me night after night, pressing you down beneath me in that car."

"While you tried to strangle me?" I scoffed in disgust as he guided me along a hall past a series of doors.

"Some women like that."

Acid rose in my blood and slid into every corner of my body. "You tried to kill me. The only dreams I've ever had about you involve me pulling that trigger."

"That's a strange thing to touch yourself over," he mused, that permanent smirk still stamped to his face.

"I do not-"

He cut over me, "No need to be ashamed, principessa. I have that effect on women."

"The only effect you have on me is making my skin crawl."

"Crawl with desire," he taunted and I rolled my eyes.

Asshole.

Rocco released a dark laugh as we arrived outside a room and he pushed me inside, still keeping those heavenly pizza slices from me.

He kicked the door shut behind us and my heart stalled as I was suddenly in a bedroom alone with him. A soft white rug was spread at the base of the double bed. A large window was framed by heavy red curtains with a balcony beyond it and antique furniture sat around the edges of the room. A door at the far end of the space gave a glimpse of an en-suite bathroom which meant Rocco wouldn't need to leave me alone at any point in the night.

A large picture of a deer hung at the head of the bed in a woodland scene, its expression wary as if a hunter with a gun sat out of shot. *I know the feeling.*

My gaze fell to the thick blanket folded on the end of the bed and my gut lurched as I spotted a pair of handcuffs there.

A click sounded as Rocco locked the door then moved past me, placing the plate down on the bed and taking up the cuffs.

I backed away, fear licking up my spine as I retreated against the door.

"If you behave, you can eat without the cuffs on."

I suddenly didn't feel so hungry but I knew I needed my energy if I ever got a chance to run from this place again.

I moved forward cautiously, his penetrating eyes following me as I swiped up the plate and headed over to a table across the room to eat the pizza in relative peace. I turned my back on him, dropping into the plush armchair there and swallowing a slice down in a few bites.

When I looked back at Rocco, he was pulling his shirt off and my gaze snagged on the cut muscles of his torso, firming and flexing. My eyes dragged across an old bullet wound scar on his right shoulder and the tattoos sprawling across his chest. Two pistols crossed at the centre of his sternum, the artwork spreading out around them in a network of wilting roses. Amongst the flowers were the names Enzo, Frankie and Angelo. I frowned, unsure who that last one was. I didn't know any Romeros by that name.

Rocco reached for his belt buckle, his gaze slamming into mine as he dropped his shirt and despite myself, a line of heat channelled into my cheeks.

I looked away and finished my pizza, my knee bouncing anxiously as I thought about being in that bed with him. I didn't trust him one bit. What if he touched me against my will? Forced himself on me?

My throat was thick and for a second I thought the pizza might make a reappearance.

A shadow fell over me and I glanced up at Rocco in nothing but his boxers, his eyes gleaming as he held the handcuffs in his hands.

"I don't need to be tied up. I won't run." *Lies*. As soon as I felt strong enough to try and escape again, I would.

He ignored me, grabbing my hand and yanking me to my feet. He pulled me toward the bed and I pushed back into him in alarm, his huge body penning me in.

"Wait – just wait a second!" I cried, but he didn't listen. He knocked me onto the bed, lashing a cuff around my right wrist and locking the other one to the bedpost. I tugged immediately, but it was tight as hell, biting into my skin.

He leaned right over me, so close I couldn't breathe, the scent of pine and freshly brewed coffee snaring my senses. It wasn't the worst scent in the world, but because it belonged to him, it was now my least favourite.

He crawled over me, dropping into the space beside me and yanking the covers out from beneath me. He tossed half of them in my vague direction before rolling over, placing his back to me and dropping his iPhone onto the nightstand then switching the light off.

My breathing was heavy, filling my ears alongside the sound of him shuffling around to get comfortable.

My heart hammered a wild tune as I tugged at the cuffs and they clinked loudly.

"Quiet or I'll tie your other hand too," he muttered and my jaw clenched.

I lay down fully and the blood soon drained from my arm as it hung at the awkward angle over my shoulder. As the minutes ticked by and Rocco's breathing became softer, I started to relax. He clearly wasn't planning on forcing himself on me and I was more than happy for him to remain disgusted with me and my heritage for that reason alone.

A notification lit up Rocco's phone screen and I eyed it hopefully across the bed. I didn't have a huge amount of chain to work with on the cuffs, but I was flexible and if Rocco was a deep sleeper…maybe I could get my hands on it.

I remained quiet for at least an hour before I made my first move. I rolled slowly towards him as far as my cuffed arm would allow, dreaming of sending a message to my father. Giving him a clue of where I was. There couldn't be too many places like this, surely he could narrow it down?

The idea drove me on and I carefully pushed myself up onto my knees, reaching over Rocco's head and making sure I kept my body from touching his. My fingers grazed the nightstand, but I couldn't get any further and nearly bumped Rocco as I reached as far as I could. My heart juddered and I took a slow breath, staying still to make sure he didn't wake.

I cursed internally as I stared at the phone, wondering if I could use my foot to scoop it closer.

I brought my arm back over him, bracing myself on my pillow then slowly raising my leg and swinging my hips around to reach for the cellphone. My toes grazed it and excitement filled me as I drew it right to the edge of the nightstand. I pulled my leg back, reaching over his head again with my hand and grabbing hold of it.

A huge palm locked around my wrist and I lost my grip on the phone with a gasp. It tumbled onto the sheets beside him and all of my hope crashed away with it.

"Passcode, principessa. It's like the safety catch on that gun all over again." He snorted, shoving my hand away before tucking the phone right into his boxers. "Feel free to try and get it, but don't be tempted to give me a hand job while you're in there. I think my cock would fall off if a Calabresi touched it."

"Asshole," I hissed as I fell back onto my pillows with a breath of frustration. "I wouldn't touch it if it was the doorbell to heaven and Satan was running up behind me."

I swear a laugh escaped him and I rolled my eyes, turning over so I didn't have to face him and shuffling as close to the edge of the bed as I could manage.

I closed my eyes, tired as hell but not sure how I'd be able to drift off. It was going to be another difficult night, but I had to admit I was happy not to be in that cellar anymore.

Rocco

I rolled onto my back as I woke, yawning as I stretched my arms above my head and worked out the kinks in my spine.

My arm brushed against a warm body as I laid it down beside me again and I turned to look at Sloan in surprise. She'd rolled towards me in her sleep, laying on her back with her dark hair spilling over her forehead and her long eyelashes kissing her cheeks.

The light of dawn illuminated the pale colouring of her skin and the natural pinkness of her full lips.

When she wasn't talking, she really was something to look at. If she hadn't been a Calabresi, I was fairly sure I'd have been planning to do more than just toy with her emotions. But it wasn't possible for me to forget who or what she was. This wasn't going to be some Romeo and Juliet story, two lovers from warring families trying to build a great romance against the odds. They both died in the end anyway. Silly fuckers.

I got out of bed and crossed to the window to look out at the new frost, taking a deep breath as the utter peace of this spot filled me, calming all the rage in my soul and leaving me with a void in its place. Everything felt so damn still up here, like no matter what we did or where we went, this little slice of wilderness would never change. I was looking at the same view my mother had loved so much twenty years ago. The same view that had been here long before this house or even the Romeros had even existed. And nothing made me feel better than reminding myself of my own irrelevance. My time on this planet would come and go and the world would keep on spinning, the snow would thaw and fall again. And again. Forever didn't care about what I loved or what I hated. It hardly had time for me at all.

I turned away from the view with a wrench in my heart as it slowly began to fill with all the mundane pressures that filled my life.

My eyes fell on the girl in my bed, her right hand above her head and twisted at an awkward angle where the handcuffs secured it in place.

I moved closer to her, pursing my lips as I looked upon the spawn of my enemy.

I reached out and shook her shoulder lightly, seeing if she might wake, but her only response was a slight tightening of her brow and a pout of those lips which kept drawing my gaze.

I sighed. She probably hadn't slept down in that cellar and no doubt her body needed time to recover from almost freezing to death too.

I had to head back to Sinners Bay today. Nicoli and Giuseppe needed to receive a little message from the Romeros and I planned on delivering it in person. Minus the finger that Enzo was still determined should accompany it.

I took a step back, meaning to head for the shower just as Sloan shifted in her sleep, tugging fruitlessly at her chained arm before relaxing back into sleep again as she gave up.

I eyed the awkward position of her arm and headed across the room to fetch the handcuff key. I carefully unlocked the cuff attached to the bed and locked it again on a lower piece of the headboard before pushing a pillow beneath her arm to support it.

My gaze caught on the sparkling diamond engagement ring on her finger and a smile tugged at my lips as I reached out to relieve her of it. No doubt Nicoli would like it back when I spoke to him.

Her skin was cold to touch and I hooked the duvet up around her without thinking about it. I pursed my lips as I realised what I'd done, but I wasn't quite enough of an asshole to yank them back off of her again. At least not while she was asleep and had no idea about it anyway.

I turned away from my irritatingly tempting prisoner and headed into the en-suite for a shower, stepping out of my boxers as I set the waterfall flow running.

I left the door open so that I could keep my eyes on her as I washed, half laughing to myself as I wondered what she'd think if she woke up now and found me butt naked and staring at her. At least I wasn't jerking off. That would definitely scare the fuck out of her.

I kept my shower brief and dressed in a perfectly tailored Italian suit which cost more than some of my cars. I buttoned the charcoal grey waistcoat over my white shirt and left the jacket off, straightening my tie in the mirror beside the bed. Our Papa always said that when you faced your enemies head on, they should see that you're the superior man in every way. From the look in your eye to the set of your jaw and the cut of your suit. Every movement, every word and every look should be carefully selected to show them exactly who they were dealing with. And if I was going to walk into the Calabresi stronghold armed with nothing but my balls and a threat, then I was damn sure they were going to see exactly who the fuck I was on first glance.

My black hair curled enough to fall into my eyes when it wasn't styled but I swept it back, fixing it in place with product and making myself look harsher in the process as the sleek style accentuated the hard lines of my face.

I took one more look at Sloan, focusing on her heavy breathing for a moment to reassure myself that she was still fast asleep before I stepped out of the room. I strode along the corridor to the next door and knocked once before pushing it open.

"Whosit?" Enzo mumbled, snatching a revolver from his nightstand and vaguely aiming it my way. The bullets still lay next to an untouched glass of water beside his bed so I wasn't overly concerned about him shooting me.

"Get up. You've gotta watch Sloan while I go deliver a message to her family."

"Get Frankie," Enzo complained, pulling a pillow over his head and tossing the revolver back towards his nightstand. It hit the wood, bounced off and fell to the grey rug beside him.

I growled at him as I flicked the lights on and stalked across the room to rip his duvet off.

"Get up," I snapped again, more forcefully this time so he'd know I was willing to kick his ass if that was what it took to make him.

"For fuck's sake." Enzo got out of bed and grabbed a pair of sweatpants before stalking past me and into my bedroom. "Did you at least fuck her yet so that I can win my money?"

"Shut the fuck up," I snapped as I followed him to the doorway and he slumped onto the couch at the foot of my bed. "If she hears you saying that shit, the only one winning will be Frankie."

Enzo sighed dramatically. "Okay. I'm here now so why don't you get going? And maybe you should pick up some baby monitors while you're out, so that the next time you do this I won't have to get out of bed to watch over her?"

I opened my mouth to argue with him about that, but it actually wasn't a terrible idea so I agreed instead. "Fine. Just make sure you keep a close fucking eye on her while I'm gone." I tossed him the handcuff key and turned to leave.

"Last chance to bring a finger with you!" Enzo called cheerily and I rolled my eyes as I walked away.

It was a three hour drive back to Sinners Bay, plenty of time for me to think up exactly what I wanted to say to Giuseppe Calabresi when I saw him. So by the time I pulled up outside The Hall of Dreams, the Calabresi run Casino that they used as a front for their illegal activities, I was more than ready to get out and deliver my message.

An eager little valet with a pencil thin moustache leapt forward, reaching out for the keys to my Ferrari, but I didn't relinquish them.

"Someone might wanna run on in to your boss and tell him Rocco Romero is here to talk about his little girl," I said, leaning back against the hood of my car and crossing my ankles. "I'll give him five minutes to grant me an audience or my brothers will start cutting off her fingers."

The valet stared at me like I was a complete fucking psycho, and if he was smart he'd probably realise that that was exactly what I was.

His lips parted, his gaze dropped to my car key as I span it around my finger then he turned and scurried inside like someone had lit a fire up his ass.

I checked the time on my Rolex, then folded my arms as I set myself up for a wait.

One stronzo had the great idea to pull his car up behind mine and start honking the horn. But as I casually rolled my shirt sleeves back and approached his car with a look in my eye that promised him a quick death, his balls promptly shot right up inside him and he sped away instead.

"Mr Romero?" a voice came from behind me and I turned to see Royce fucking Belmonte glaring at me as if he'd like nothing better than to snap my neck with his bare hands. I didn't know how that fucker had survived a shot to the chest, but he shouldn't have. He'd been there the night Giuseppe had my mother and brother killed. He could have been the one to light the fucking fire for all I knew. And for that I'd take his life one day. The only reason he still drew breath now was because he'd been too hard to get to while he was in Italy with Sloan while she studied. But now he was back, I had him marked.

Not that I could do a damn thing about it at that particular moment. I was unarmed and walking into the viper's pit.

I smirked at him tauntingly as I strode towards him and if looks could kill I would have gone up in flames like Satan's ass-fucked bride right then and there. As it was, my smile only grew and his hatred only deepened.

One day soon I'll give you the fight you want with me, stronzo. And we'll see which one of us is bathing in the other's blood by the end of it.

"How's Sloan?" Royce demanded, his eyes glimmering with enough emotion to show just how much he cared about her. Which suited me even better. Every time I hurt her, I now knew I'd be hurting him too and this stronzo deserved a lifetime of suffering for what he'd stolen from my family.

"Surprisingly willing for a virgin," I taunted. "She doesn't even seem to blame us for what we're doing to her either. She just keeps asking where her bodyguards were when she needed them."

Royce lunged forward a step and I grinned as he forced himself to stop again.

"I swear on everything I am that if you've hurt one hair on her head, I'll-"

"Can you quit wasting my time, monkey? I'm here to talk to the organ grinder. And if my brothers get bored of waiting to hear from me, they'll start coming up with ways to entertain themselves with your principessa."

"This way," Royce growled and I was flanked by eight more bastardos, each of them armed to the teeth, though none of them had drawn a weapon. Yet.

They led me through the lavish casino where gamblers were losing their money and convincing themselves to place just one more bet before we headed into a brightly lit room through a door in the back.

"Spread your legs," Royce growled, moving forward to search me.

"Aren't you gonna buy me dinner first, bella? I don't usually give it up on a first date," I mocked.

Royce didn't laugh surprisingly enough and he was none too gentle as he frisked me either. The only things he found on me were a roll of hundred dollar bills, my car key and my cellphone because that was all I had.

"If my brothers don't get a text from me every five minutes to let them know it's all going to plan, then they'll have to start taking pieces from your principessa," I warned. "So you might wanna give me back my phone."

Royce's upper lip curled back as he shoved my cellphone into my hand and I smiled brightly like we were old buddies and he'd just done me a solid.

I couldn't say he liked that much but fuck it, it seemed like that only made me want to do it more.

The goons led me on into another corridor before finally opening the doors to a huge lounge where Giuseppe and his closest men all stood waiting for me, arms folded, eyes narrowed and a wish for violence dancing in the air.

"What is this insult?" Guiseppe growled, looking me over like he'd been expecting someone else. "Why have I got you when I should be speaking to the man in charge?"

"Papa had an appointment at the optometrists," I said innocently. "He's concerned that he might need reading glasses. You know how pressing these things can be."

Nicoli suddenly lunged forward, pointing a finger at me and near spitting with rage. "If you disrespect the leader of my family again, I'll cut you in two," he threatened.

I raised an eyebrow at him before looking away as if he hadn't spoken at all. He wouldn't touch me. Wouldn't fucking dare. Not while I held their precious Sloan.

"I do believe we have come into possession of something that belongs to you," I said slowly, my words for Giuseppe as I ignored every other person in the room.

"What do you want for her?" he asked, cutting to the chase. Man after my own heart.

"For now, we're gonna start off with you backing out of Romero Territory. And you're gonna keep your noses out of Romero business too. So that means we don't wanna see any of your people dogging our streets or lurking in our bars. We want some hassle free, lucrative time to focus on our businesses without Calabresi interference."

"That's it?" Giuseppe growled.

"For now," I reiterated, giving him a taunting smile. "When you prove you can follow simple instructions, we'll be back with a few more."

"When I have my wife back in my arms, I'm going to hunt you down and gut you like a pig," Nicoli snarled.

"Wrong," I replied, turning my gaze on him as my smile widened. "She's not your wife. You never said *I do*." I pulled her engagement ring from my little finger and tossed it at him. "And she said you can have that back. Seeing as you already failed at the whole *to honour and protect* part of your vows before you'd even spoken them."

Nicoli looked about ready to leap on me, but at a flick of Giuseppe's hand he controlled himself.

"How do I know she's even still alive?" Giuseppe growled.

"I can send you daily photos," I said easily, already aware he'd demand that. "Just pop your number in my cell and you'll get the first one tonight. So long as you keep up your end of our arrangement, she'll be just fine."

I painted a cross over my heart innocently as I held my cellphone out towards him.

He snatched it from my grasp, cursing in Italian as he keyed in his number.

"We won't pull away from Romero Territory until we receive that confirmation," Giuseppe warned.

"Then I'd better get back to my sweet Sloan and get you that photo."

I offered the room at large one, final shit-eating grin then turned and strode out.

The Calabresis parted for me like the tide, letting me stroll right out of their stronghold as if I owned the fucking place.

And fuck it. That might just have been the best feeling in the entire world.

Sloan

I woke from a dream that guided me along little Italian streets and past familiar faces to a dark reality which cut into my soul. I sat upright sharply and the cuff knocked against the wood as I reached the end of my tether.

A pillow sat where my hand had been and I frowned as I realised Rocco must have moved the cuff further down the headboard. *Probably so he could save himself the bother of amputating my hand when it died from lack of blood.*

My gaze swung to the empty space beside me with a flood of relief. It was short-lived as the need to pee grabbed onto me and I stared longingly toward the en-suite on the other side of the room. I was torn between stubbornly wetting the bed and calling out for help. But I didn't like the idea of Rocco finding me here in a puddle of shame.

"Hello!" I called, hoping the kinder-faced one, Frankie, might appear. Footsteps pounded toward the door and I set my jaw as I prepared for the worst. Rocco.

The door swung open and Enzo stepped into the room, his muscular frame almost filling the doorway. My throat thickened as he rubbed the back of his head as if in memory of me hitting him there with a wine bottle.

"Good morning, little shrew. Or should I say afternoon as you've slept half the day away?"

I pressed my lips together, my heart thrashing as he sauntered his way toward me.

"Quiet today," he mused. "Has Rocco finally broken your spirit? Or is your throat just sore after a night of happily sucking his cock?"

"As if I'd ever touch that creep," I spat.

"Ah, she speaks." He smirked, his dark eyes making me squirm. I noted the hunting knife strapped to his hip and my breathing quickened.

"I need the bathroom," I said, lifting my chin high, determined to hold his gaze.

Enzo was as beautiful as his brother, but in a rougher way. His hair was wild, his eyes raw and full of cruel thoughts that he didn't try to hide. He was infamous for being unpredictable and the crimes his name was attached to made my skin crawl.

Enzo reached into his pocket, taking out a key without a word. He moved forward, unlocking the handcuffs and I immediately pulled my arm free. He was leaning over me, close enough for his hip to press against my leg – and the hilt of his knife. My fingers itched for it and I shifted my arm so my hand grazed the strap.

In a flash of movement, I went for it, my hand locking around the hilt and a surge of adrenaline rushing into my veins.

Enzo snatched my wrist as I drew the huge knife free and he smiled manically. "What now, little shrew? Will you kill me?" He lifted the knife, in full control of it as his fingers clutched mine so hard that I winced. He held the tip of the blade to his own throat and my eyes widened.

A dare filled his gaze and I shoved the hilt with a growl of fury. He jerked backwards with a wild laugh, taking the blade with him. "You really would do it, wouldn't you? I like your spark. But be careful, sparks cause fires."

"Why would I be careful? Maybe if I'm lucky, this whole place will burn," I hissed and his brows arched.

He gestured to the bathroom with the knife and his cold eyes followed me as I slid off the bed and headed into it. The second I closed the door, it flew open again and I stumbled back as Enzo rested his shoulder against the doorway.

"You'll go with the door open or not at all." He turned his back on me, but remained standing there and I didn't know whether to be relieved that he wasn't going to watch me or furious that he was giving me almost no privacy.

I pulled my pyjama bottoms down in defeat and dropped onto the toilet, tugging my top over my thighs in case he decided to look.

I shut my eyes in concentration, cursing his name as heat rushed up my spine and made it impossible to pee.

"Just move away from the door!" I snapped in frustration.

Enzo chuckled, but walked away all the same and a breath of relief escaped me.

I finally peed and moved to wash my hands. I blinked as I realised my engagement ring was missing. No doubt Rocco had peeled it off my finger either to taunt me or to send to my father. But little did he know, it actually felt good to be rid of it. Wearing that ring meant my promise to marry Nicoli was still intact, but without it I felt like one of my chains had been broken.

Enzo reappeared with a pile of clothes in his grip. "Get dressed." He tossed a pair of jeans, underwear and a white tank top at my feet and headed away again.

I soon had them on and stepped back into the bedroom, finding Enzo waiting by the door with the handcuffs in his grip. "Wrists together," he commanded and I clenched my teeth.

"Is that really necessary?"

"Unless you want to lose a few fingers, it is." He gave me a demonic grin and my heart lurched in warning. I held my wrists out and he locked the cuffs in place, keeping hold of them and pulling me out of the room.

He guided me downstairs and the scent of something burning filled my nose. As we stepped into the kitchen, Frankie appeared striding across the room and planting a fiery pan of something that looked like tar into the sink. He turned the tap on with a curse and smoke and steam coiled into the air.

"Please tell me that's not lunch," I said and Frankie whipped around, looking dishevelled.

"It *was*," he said in frustration, cursing under his breath in Italian.

Enzo dragged me to the island and planted me down on a stool. He strode toward the refrigerator, taking out a tub of butter then moving over to a loaf of bread on the counter. "We'll just have sandwiches again," he grumbled, taking out his hunting knife and proceeding to butter a slice with it. *What the hell?*

Frankie fetched a spoon and started scraping the remains of what was left in the pan into the trash.

"Ridiculous," I muttered.

"What's that?" Enzo snarled, turning his razor sharp gaze on me.

I glared at the butter on his hunting knife and pointed. "*That* is ridiculous." I looked to the burnt pan Frankie was holding. "And *that* is pathetic. Did no one ever teach you how to cook?"

"We usually have maids for that, but we can't exactly bring one here while you're in the house," Frankie said with a dark frown.

Enzo took some questionable-looking brown thing out of the refrigerator and I grimaced.

"Let me cook," I insisted. "I'm good at it."

Enzo tsked. "No chance."

"Why not?" Frankie shot back and my brows arched hopefully. "She can't do anything to us, we've got guns." He lifted his shirt to expose the pistol there pressed to his cut abs and I was sharply reminded that Frankie might have had a face like an angel, but his soul was encased in sin.

Enzo gazed at his wholly unappetising sandwich for a long moment before shrugging his uninjured arm. "Fine. But if she runs, it's on you when I put a bullet in her."

Fear wrapped around my heart as I looked between them. Frankie didn't object and I knew they meant it.

Enzo approached, unlocking my cuffs and I slipped off of my seat, tentatively moving around him and heading to the refrigerator. It was well-stocked and a jar of fusilli on the side gave me an idea for a meal. I took out the ingredients I needed, glad to have something to focus on other than my current situation as I started preparing the food.

Enzo and Frankie took seats at the island, watching me silently. I soon forgot they were watching, falling into the familiarity of cooking and taking some comfort in the thing I loved doing most in the world.

The snowy scene beyond the window reminded me I wasn't anywhere near Italy anymore, but for a second I captured the feeling of the freedom I'd had there. Cooking what I wanted, when I wanted. Living in my home, never having to answer to anyone. *What I'd give to have that back.*

"Where's Rocco?" I inquired, half expecting him to jump into the room like a jack-in-the-box at any moment.

"Out," Enzo replied and it was clear I wasn't going to get any more information than that.

I made a simple but tasty dish of fusilli with spinach and ricotta, placing down three bowls on the island and handing the men a fork each. I dropped down beside them, my stomach rumbling, but I waited for them to try it first.

Enzo ate one mouthful then scoffed the whole lot down within about thirty seconds. Frankie ate his slowly, devouring every piece like it was his first and smiling in between bites.

"Oh Dio, questo è buono," *Oh god, this is good,* Frankie groaned in delight and I couldn't fight a grin of pride as I tucked into my own meal.

I tried to savour my bites like Frankie had, but I was soon scraping the last piece of pasta out of the bottom of the bowl and placing it on my tongue.

"I wonder if she cleans as well as she cooks," Enzo said to Frankie with a taunting grin.

I didn't really care if they made me wash up, that would only give me more chance of getting my hands on one of the sharp knives I'd used to chop the spinach. *If I could just slip one up my sleeve, maybe I could use it tonight against my vicious sleeping partner.*

"What the fuck is going on?" Rocco's voice crashed over me and I lurched around in alarm as he strode into the kitchen looking like the definition of power. His shirt clung to his muscles, his sleeves rolled up to reveal his bronzed forearms. His hair was styled, but a lock had fallen loose, caressing his forehead and speaking of the wild man who could so easily burst out of that business attire.

"We're just making use of our house guest," Enzo said with a shrug. "She might as well cook and clean for us while she's here."

"And give her a chance to stash a weapon or put cyanide in your meal?" Rocco scoffed.

"I'm fresh out of cyanide," I said coolly and his eyes whipped back to me, full of hate.

"Enough of this," he hissed, marching toward me and I nearly fell off of my stool in my haste to escape him.

He caught me around the waist, launching me up and over his shoulder and locking his arms around my legs.

"Hey!" I yelled, throwing my fists into his back. "Put me down!"

He carried me through to the living room and up the stairs as easily as if I weighed nothing. My stomach lurched as he kicked the door open to his bedroom and tossed me on the floor. He kicked the door shut and I flinched as he locked it, pocketing the key. He stepped over me and my heart ricocheted off the walls of my chest, but he kept walking, heading to a closet across the room where I spied some women's clothes Frankie must have put there for me. He took a little leather bag from a shelf, unzipping it and producing two lipsticks.

I leapt back to my feet, hurrying to the door and pressing myself against it. "What are you doing?" I asked, trying to force my voice not to shake.

"Are you a rose red kinda girl, or cotton candy pink?" he asked, ignoring my question.

"What?"

"You're too much of a virgin for the red," he muttered to himself and my upper lip peeled back.

He walked up beside me, facing the mirror hanging on the wall next to the door. He pulled the lid off of the pink lipstick and I stared at him in shock as he started putting it on himself.

What the hell is happening right now??

He took his sweet time, painting it on just right then turned to me with a sadistic smile on those cotton candy lips.

Oh holy shit! I tried to run but he lunged, throwing me back against the door and stamping his mouth to mine.

My senses were drowned by my heart-jack-hammering, the divine scent of him, the deadly taste of him. *How dare he fucking touch me?!*

He pulled back, smacking his lips together to make a kissing noise, smirking at me. I slapped him as hard as I could then grabbed his shoulders, throwing my knee up to catch him in the balls. He jerked backwards before I could land the shot then caught my wrist with a malicious glint in his endless eyes. He dragged me forward, flipping me into the air and my legs kicked and wheeled as I tried to fight.

"No!" I screamed, my voice echoing around the whole house.

He launched me onto the bed and I bounced on the mattress, scrambling to my knees. He followed me onto the bed, snatching the strap of my tank top and ripping it with a sharp pull. It hung loose, almost exposing my breast and a true fear found me. He snatched hold of my hair, knotting it up between his fingers and ruffling it over my head.

"Please don't!" I gasped.

I fought back with a keen desperation, landing a solid punch to his chest, but he didn't even blink. I could see a monster behind his eyes and knew I couldn't win. I had to run.

I wriggled away and crawled backwards, leaping to my feet on the bed. He lunged forward to catch my ankle, uprooting me once more. I threw a sharp kick at his face as I fell and he goddamn laughed when my heel connected with his chin. I was off the bed in a second, sprinting toward the window.

His hands latched around my waist and he tossed me back to the bed with sheer force. I bounced off the edge and crashed to the floor, pain flaring up my spine. He marched after me and my pulse thumped wildly in my ears. I scrambled backwards and made it to the bathroom, kicking the door closed.

It bounced off his shiny Italian loafer as he wedged it in the doorframe and I pushed myself up in a panic, diving into the shower unit and slamming the glass door closed between us.

He stood looking at me with a smile hooking up his lips then folded his arms. "Now what, principessa? Are you going to wash yourself down the drain?"

I glanced around me for any sign of a weapon, but all I could see were my options fading. I put my middle finger up and pressed it to the glass in a last act of defiance, baring my teeth at him as some wild part of me took over.

His eyes skidded down my neck and over my breasts, giving me just long enough for an idea to spark in my mind. I swiped the shower head from the holder above me, flipping on the hot water and shoving the door open.

He dodged the scalding water with a snarl, grabbing the hose and yanking hard enough to make me stumble into him. Then he wrapped it around my shoulders as the water continued pouring. It crashed over my feet and I yelped, but he lifted me in the same moment, reaching into the shower and switching the dial.

I gasped as he held the shower head above me and an ice-cold torrent drenched me right through.

"Asshole!" I tried to kick him and when that didn't work, I bit deep into his arm until I tasted blood.

"I think you enjoy biting me." He laughed like *he* was the one who enjoyed it then untethered me from the hose and tossed the shower head into the unit, turning off the water. He carried me soaking wet into the other room and dumped me unceremoniously onto the bed.

I stared at him, panting and shaking as blood seeped through his shirt where I'd bitten him. Triumph filled me at marking his impenetrable exterior. I'd hurt him. Even if he wouldn't admit it. Even if he laughed through the pain. It didn't make my victory any less real.

Rocco reached into his jeans pocket, taking out his phone and snapping a picture of me.

"This could have been a lot easier," he mused. "But I rather enjoyed that." He walked out of the room, throwing the door shut and the lock clicked a second later.

I screamed my rage after him as I realised he was going to send that to my father. If he'd just told me what he wanted, I wouldn't have fought him with all my might. I wouldn't have panicked at the thought of him pinning me down and forcing himself on me.

It suddenly hit me that I was alone and untied and I quickly ran to the window, but it was locked with a key. With a curse, I headed to the bathroom, finding the same problem.

I huffed in frustration, striding back to the bedroom and searching every drawer and cupboard for something I could use to escape.

When I came up short, I unscrewed the bulb in the lamp on my nightstand, then I pulled Rocco's pillowcase off and put it inside. I dropped it to the floor and used the base of the lamp to crush it into a fine powder of glass, imagining it was Rocco's face as I pulverised it. Then I sprinkled that glass all under the sheets where he slept and placed the cover back on the pillow filled with the remnants of the bulb.

A sweet satisfaction filled me and though I knew he'd probably punish me for it, I didn't care. I wanted him to bleed for me.

Besides, if I didn't do something, it meant I was giving up. And there was no force on earth which could make me do that.

Nicoli

I sat in Giuseppe's study, my fingernails digging into my biceps as I forced myself to remain still with my arms folded as we waited for the proof of life from Rocco Romero.

My teeth were grinding so hard that I was surprised they hadn't ground right down to dust yet.

My body was a strange mixture of utter exhaustion and coiled energy just waiting for an outlet.

I'd barely slept since Sloan had been stolen from me. Since that creature came and took what was mine while I stood helpless as a lamb. The shame of that moment would haunt me for all eternity.

I kept going over that morning in the church, turning over all the details in my mind again and again as I tried to figure out what I'd missed. How hadn't we noticed two Romero rats sneaking right into the church? There had been people going in and out of there all morning, setting up decorations and laying flowers. I just couldn't understand how they'd gotten in unnoticed. But I'd interrogated every parishioner, church warden, priest and bell ringer who even so much as blinked in the direction of that church in the week leading up to our wedding and it seemed like not one of them had seen a thing. Which either meant we had Romero spies in our midst or we were surrounded by idiots.

I'd wanted to take that side of my investigation further, but even Giuseppe Calabresi wouldn't sign off on torturing a priest and the members of his congregation. But I wouldn't forget this. There was something missing from the equation and though I didn't understand what just yet, I'd get to the bottom of it and find out who needed to pay the price.

Giuseppe and Carlo sat talking business at his desk, discussing which places the Romeros might use to hide Sloan and what they might be doing with her. Royce stood glaring out of the window, seeming as tense as me as we waited.

At the muttered suggestion from Carlo that the Romeros could be abusing her body, I shoved out of my chair and stalked to the window too.

Sloan's little white dog, Coco, leapt up as well, trotting at my heels as if he thought I was on my way to retrieve her right now. But I was as useless as the chair I'd just vacated. I had no idea where she was or what they were doing to her. I should have been getting to know my wife better right now. We should have been enjoying each other's company and sharing our marriage bed. Instead I was here, like a wind-up toy with a missing part, unable to function without it and filled with all the promise of the purpose I'd been meant to fulfil.

A ping sounded from Giuseppe's cellphone on the desk behind me and I snapped around, striding across the room in four long paces just as he snatched it into his grasp and opened the message.

"Figlio di puttana!" *Son of a bitch!* Giuseppe growled, glaring at the cellphone before thrusting it my way. "See what they're doing to your poor bride? My precious daughter?"

I snatched the phone from him roughly, flipping it around so that I could see the photo for myself and Royce pushed close to look too.

Sloan lay sprawled on a bed, wearing a white tank top which was ripped at the shoulder and turning transparent from the water drenching her. Pink lipstick was smeared across her mouth, making her look like some kind of beat up whore.

But that wasn't even the worst of it. The thing that had my heart pounding was the look of utter terror in her wide eyes. The way her hand was raised as if to ward off the man wielding this camera. She was fear embodied, desperate, alone, in need of rescuing more than anyone I'd ever known. She needed me. And yet I was utterly useless.

"There's nothing in this picture to help us narrow down her location," Carlo said analytically as he leaned over my shoulder to get a look for himself. "She's sprawled on a bed. It could be anywhere. The only implication it gives us is that they may be defiling her."

An actual growl spilled from my throat, echoed by the little dog at my ankles as the desire to beat Carlo's head in with the cellphone currently locked in my fist overwhelmed me. My vision narrowed to two pinpricks of light and all I could see at the end of them were death and blood and vengeance.

"Control yourself, figlio," Giuseppe said firmly and only that word on his lips saved Carlo's life. Figlio. *Son.* For years Giuseppe had been the only real parental figure I'd known. He'd taken me in when I was nine, raised me up from the foster system and brought me into the fold. I'd had nannies and tutors and all kinds of practical care, but the love and respect of this man was the only thing I craved. To know he'd selected me as a husband for his daughter had been the brightest moment of my life. But to actually hear him refer to me as a son was the truest sense of love I'd ever felt from him.

"So what do we do now, boss?" Carlo asked, dropping back into his seat like the whole world didn't hinge on the way we handled this.

Royce started pacing, holding his tongue through pure force of will.

"We pull out of Romero Territory," Giuseppe growled, the cost of that decision clearly weighing heavily on him. "We can't risk them hurting my little girl. All the time we're sure she's alive and relatively unharmed we will need to be seen to be doing what is asked of us."

"Yes, boss," Carlo agreed. "I'll put the word out."

"I'll go and check in with some of our informants," Royce announced, clearly needing to do something. "If anyone has heard even a whisper about the Romeros' current whereabouts, I'll find them."

Giuseppe nodded his agreement and Royce strode from the room without another word.

"What about me?" I growled because we both knew there was no way in hell I'd be hanging back while the Romeros sucked this city dry and held us over a barrel.

Giuseppe turned his dark eyes on me, a hand raking down his face as he considered how best to use me. I was a tool at his disposal. The fiercest, meanest object in his grasp and I would destroy anything he aimed me at.

"Find out where they're keeping her," he said in a low voice. "Do anything you have to to get the locations of every property they own, then start searching them. This city is only so big and the Romeros won't be leaving it for the sake of one hostage. Not when they just tightened their grip on their power here. Besides, that pezzo di merda, *piece of shit,* Rocco Romero, sent that photo within three and a half hours of leaving us at the casino. I'm willing to bet that means he either made us wait just because he could or that it took him that long to get back to her. Either way, that means she's within a certain radius of the casino. There are only so many destinations he could reach in such a short space of time. So find it. Find her. And kill every man, woman, child and goddamn cat hiding in that prison before bringing your bride back home."

"Yes, boss," I agreed with a dark smile.

I turned and strode from the room as Giuseppe and Carlo began to discuss what else they might do and how far they were willing to follow Rocco's rules. But I had my instructions. I didn't need to waste any more time on talking. It was time for action.

I headed straight downstairs and out of the house with Coco racing along at my heels. I frowned at the little dog as he continued to hound me. It wasn't like I'd taken to feeding him treats or anything. The only possible reason I could come up with for him following me was that he knew I was hunting for Sloan. And I could respect his dedication even if he did seem to be as clueless as me on where to begin our hunt in earnest. But that was all about to change.

I headed straight for the garage to the side of the sprawling estate and unlocked it using the keypad attached to the wall outside.

I walked in, passing by the family cars and heading for the rack of tools at the back of the room.

I snatched a wrench, hammer and nail gun from the rack and stalked towards my Harley Davidson at the far end of the garage. I flipped open the saddle bag which hung beside the rear wheel and tossed the tools in before moving across the room to claim the key from the lock box on the wall.

I headed back to the bike and paused as I spotted Coco perched inside the open saddle bag.

"No, boy," I said firmly, moving closer to lift him out of the bag. "This is too dangerous for little dogs."

As my hand slid beneath him to hoist him out of the bag, he snarled at me, twisting suddenly and sinking his teeth into my finger.

I cursed as I snatched my hand back, glaring at the dog as he lowered himself further into the bag, giving me an expression that said he was coming no matter what I thought about it.

I rolled my eyes and flipped the top of the bag down over him as I gave in. I buckled it closed, leaving it loose enough for him to stick his nose out of a small gap at the top then swung my leg over the motorcycle. I took the helmet from the handlebars and placed it on my head, drawing the visor down to hide my face.

The beast growled beneath me as I started up the engine and I tugged on the throttle as I directed it out of the garage and down the drive. The guard at the gates recognised me and opened them as I approached and I was soon speeding down the streets towards downtown Sinners Bay with my destination in mind.

Calabresis were no fools and we knew our enemies well. The Romeros had men all over the city who did various jobs for them and Lucio ValPenza, their accountant, was one of the best known amongst us. Not that it had ever made sense for us to go after some pen pusher before now, but I was willing to bet that asshole had the answer to some of the questions I needed to ask.

I soon drew up outside his office and cut the engine, flipping open the saddle bag and hooking the hammer through the loop in my belt. If I needed any of the others tools then that would require a new location to work anyway. Coco shifted aside obligingly and I left the bag open for him to hop out.

It was late but that didn't matter; the accountant always worked through the evening for the Romeros. We had his routine pegged.

I headed straight up to the glass door and walked inside.

I wasn't even surprised to find Sloan's dog at my heels again, his tiny strides as determined as mine.

I headed to the left as we made it inside and pushed open the door to the stairwell, climbing the five floors to his office and avoiding most of the CCTV cameras on my way. Not that I was too worried about being caught on them. The Calabresis had the local police in their pockets and even if some footage of me showed up in an investigation, it would get lost long before any court date came up.

I strode straight down the carpeted corridor to his office and threw the door open as I reached it.

Lucio looked up in shock as the door bounced off of the wall and I pulled my helmet from my head so that he could see exactly who had come calling.

"Oh sweet baby Jesus," he gasped, scrambling to his feet and backing away toward the windows which spanned the wall behind him.

"Not quite," I replied as I advanced on him.

He waited until I moved to the left of his huge desk then darted right like he thought he might be able to outrun me.

I released a merciless laugh as I hefted the helmet in my hand and threw it at the back of his head.

He hit the floor like a sack of shit and I was on him before he could do any more than roll over.

I threw my fists into his face, one, two, three times as he cried out for mercy.

"I want a list of every single property Martello Romero and his sons own!" I demanded as blood flew and something cracked beneath my knuckles.

"They'll k-kill me!" he gasped.

"*I'll* kill you," I promised. "But if you give me what I want then at least you'll have a chance to run before they find out what you did."

Lucio whimpered beneath me and Coco leapt forward to bite his leg.

"Ahh!" Lucio wailed, kicking and flailing like he was being attacked by a Rottweiler instead of a Pomeranian.

"Off, Coco," I commanded and to my surprise, the little fucker listened. He backed up, growling at the man beneath me as I yanked the hammer out of my belt.

"Last chance to give me what I want," I warned, raising the weapon with intent.

Lucio whimpered in fear, lifting a trembling hand to point at a set of drawers beside his desk. "The deeds to everything I know about are in there."

I got off of him and moved to claim the information I needed.

Lucio started crawling for the door, dripping blood all over the carpet as he went, but I ignored him.

I ripped the drawer open and searched through the files until I found the one I needed. I flipped it open and found a thick folio of documentation on various properties all over the Romero-run part of the city and beyond.

The first one was an apartment on the west side and I smirked to myself as I snapped the file shut and stalked towards the door.

I snatched my helmet from the floor as I went and whistled for Coco to follow me.

I'm coming for you, Romero. And I'll have your head swinging from my fist before the night is up.

Rocco

I sat eating my breakfast in the kitchen while Sloan nursed a bowl of porridge beside me, her hand cuffed to the heavy stool she sat on. She was pouting. And I was smirking about it like an asshole. Which I was, so that was fine.

Her nasty little trick with the lightbulb had backfired on her rather spectacularly when I'd spotted the glass lining my bed. I'd made her clean the whole lot with her bare hands before she'd had to change the sheets and hoover the mattress. All in all, I'd been pretty damn pleased with the way it had worked out, not least the cuts which marred her fingertips from the broken glass she'd meant for me.

Frankie's cellphone started ringing and he hooked it out of his pocket, raising an eyebrow at me.

"It's Papa," he said a moment before he answered.

Sloan stilled beside me, peeking up and clearly attempting to eavesdrop on their conversation.

"Ciao, Papa," Frankie said, standing up a little straighter as if our father might hear the slouch in his voice. Which he damn well might. "Oh, okay…are you sure you want to drive all the way up here, though?"

I raised an eyebrow at that. We'd been waiting for him to fly back into the country so that he could decide how he wanted to deal with our hostage situation, but Papa hardly ever came up here. It was our little safe haven. I didn't want to relinquish control of it to him if he came. Hell, he might even want to take the master bedroom from me. Though as I thought about that, I doubted it. He didn't sleep in any of the rooms my mother used to sleep in. In fact, he'd sold most of the properties he'd owned when she'd been alive after her death, the memories of her in them too present for him to bear their company. I was pretty sure the only reason he'd kept this house at all was because she'd loved it so much and selling it would have felt like a betrayal to her memory.

"Okay," Frankie said. "We'll see you in a minute."

He hung up and I frowned at him. "What do you mean 'in a minute?'" I asked.

"He's almost here, just called ahead so that I could have coffee waiting for him," Frankie explained.

"Fuck," I muttered, getting to my feet and unlocking Sloan's cuff.

"What's going on?" she breathed in alarm, sensing the tension spilling through the room.

"You're about to meet the head of our family," I said. "So put your best smile on, bella, because he doesn't appreciate a frowny face."

I snapped the open cuff around her other wrist, keeping hold of the chain that linked them and tugging her along after me as I headed out of the room.

"Enzo!" I barked, striding straight into the living room where my brother was sprawled on the couch in his boxers.

"What's got you twitching?" he asked me, casting his gaze over Sloan. "Are we cutting off a finger after all?"

Sloan flinched, jerking back a step like she expected him to come at her with a meat cleaver right then and there.

"Stop with the finger shit," I snapped. "Papa's coming. Like, right now. We need to clean this place up!"

"Merda." Enzo growled, getting up instantly and tossing empty beer bottles into the fire basket.

This was why Papa had really called ahead. He hated mess and he knew we let our standards slip when he wasn't checking up on us. So long as we had the place looking respectable by the time he showed, he pretended not to know about it. And I'd rather run about like a whipped little kid cleaning up than hear all about the state of the place for the duration of his stay.

"You, *sit,*" I commanded, shoving Sloan so that her ass hit an armchair beside the fire.

She curled her legs up as she stayed where I'd put her and I helped Enzo toss the chip packets from last night in with the beer bottles.

Enzo headed out of the room with the trash and I straightened the cushions on the couch before throwing some more logs on the fire.

The sound of a car approaching along the drive came from the front of the house and I grabbed Sloan's elbow and yanked her out of the chair again.

"Come on," I snapped as I dragged her after me up the stairs.

"What are we doing?" she asked but I ignored her, pulling her into my room and releasing her as I kicked the door closed behind us.

I dropped my sweatpants and tossed them in the laundry basket before grabbing a clean pair of jeans from the closet and tugging on a red T-shirt followed by a thick, grey sweater.

"Your Papa doesn't like sweatpants?" Sloan teased as she watched me.

"My Papa doesn't like stupid observations so I suggest you keep your mouth shut in front of him," I snapped.

She pouted at that and my gaze fell on her lips.

"Get on your knees," I commanded, striding away from her so that I could style my hair in the en-suite.

"Why?" she asked, fear creeping back into her voice.

I ignored her question as I worked on smoothing my curls back, but I glanced in the mirror to see that she'd done as I'd said anyway. A smirk tugged at the corner of my mouth as I washed my hands then stalked back over to her.

"Do you know why I like it when you're on your knees?" I questioned her as I stopped before her with her face right in line with my crotch.

"Because you're an asshole?" she guessed, looking up at me beneath long lashes.

"No, principessa. It's because it reminds you who you belong to now. You're mine and that means you have to look up at me from your position down there."

"So you're just getting off on having a Calabresi at your mercy?" she spat.

"No, bella. If you want to get me off you'll need to open your mouth a little wider."

"*Pig,*" she growled.

"You don't know the half of it," I mocked. "But I do know you're thinking about it, aren't you? That virginal little mind of yours is wondering what it would feel like to suck on my cock."

"Shut up!"

"Well you know what to do when you're sick of tormenting yourself with imagining it," I said, thriving on her rage and feeling my dick twitch at this talk of her full lips wrapped around it. "Just beg me for the real deal."

"I hate you," she growled.

"Yeah. But you still wanna fuck me."

I reached out and grabbed the chain in the centre of her handcuffs just as I heard the front door open downstairs.

My brothers were greeting our Papa enthusiastically and I tugged Sloan after me to join them.

We made it into the living room just as Papa and my brothers entered too and I gave Sloan's handcuffs a hard yank, forcing her to her knees again beside me.

She yelped in pain as her knees hit the rug in front of the fire and Papa closed in on us with a look on his face like he'd smelt something bad.

He was as tall as me, as broad too and years of brawling had scarred his striking face, painting a line through his left eyebrow which was now pale and white with age. *Romeros fight their own battles.* His black hair was streaked with grey around the temples and he wore an expensive as shit designer suit as always.

"So, this is the Calabresi principessa, is it?" he mused, inspecting her like she was a horse at a market.

"It is," I agreed, keeping my voice level. Because fuck it, I wasn't going to start regretting this choice to steal her even if she turned out to be a fucking liability. I swore I'd wipe the shame of sparing her life all those years ago from my name and I was determined to make this insanity pay off.

My Papa was a cold man with cruel eyes and a crueller heart. He had little time for love or affection, though we knew he felt both for us because of the fierce way he pushed and protected us in equal measures. I had faded memories of him chasing me and our dead brother, Angelo, around the park with a football and of him dancing with our mother in the kitchen, but either I'd dreamed them up or the man who had featured in them had been murdered alongside her. This creature left in his place was harsh and cold, distant and unforgiving. But he'd also taught us how to be strong in every way, made us proficient in dishing out pain as well as receiving it and forged us into creatures of war. And the battle we fought was against the family of the girl who currently knelt before us.

"Get rid of her so the men can talk," he said, looking away from Sloan dismissively and I drew her back to her feet without a word.

Sloan didn't even protest as I led her out into the hallway but she dug in her heels as she realised where I was about to put her. There was only one room in this house that was truly secure and if my father wanted her locked away then this was where he meant.

"But-" she began, her eyes widening with fear as she snared my wrist in her grasp. Her gaze caught mine like she was searching for some twinge of sympathy in me, but she'd be a long time looking if she ever expected to find that.

"What's the matter, principessa? Did you think that just because we don't want you to die just yet that we actually care about your wellbeing?" I taunted.

Her jaw tightened, her eyes blazing with the desire to hurt me and fuck it if that didn't just make me want to break her more.

I grabbed her by the arms and whirled her around until her back was driven against the door to the cellar before I pressed my body flush with hers to hold her there.

I smirked at her as she cursed me and reached out to turn the key in the lock beside her.

"What's wrong with you?" she hissed as the door swung open and I stood back to let her descend.

"If you want a full list we might be here a while and I've got a meeting with my family to attend. Suffice to say that I'm a special brand of fucked up, created in the depths of your darkest nightmares and dirtiest fantasies. But if you think you've seen the worst of me, then you really have no idea. So I suggest you be a good little hostage and start playing by the rules. Because the sooner you fall in line, the better it will be for you. And I promise that when I'm nice to you, it'll hurt in all the right ways."

Sloan stared at me like she didn't even know what to make of this fucked up creature before her, but if she thought I was a mystery she might be able to solve then she was going to find herself severely disappointed.

I reached out and flicked on the light in the cellar for her and she slowly turned and headed down the first few steps.

I leaned against the doorframe and waited for her to descend, a smug sense of satisfaction filling me as I watched this enemy of mine bowing to my commands.

"Good girl," I mocked as she made it to the cold floor at the base of the stairs.

I reached over my shoulder and caught the material of my sweater in my grip before dragging it over my head. It was thick and warm and would stop her from freezing quite so much while she was stuck down here again. I tossed it to her and she caught it with a frown that said my kindness only confused her further.

Lap it up, baby. You'll be all mine before you even realise what's happened to you.

I closed the door on her, locking it and tucking the key into my pocket as I strode back to the living room in my T-shirt, wondering if Papa would question my sudden outfit change.

"I say we kill her," Papa said firmly, the moment I re-entered the room.

"What?" I asked, feeling like a little kid being chastised for doing the wrong thing. "But you haven't even heard my plan yet-"

"Don't try and fool me with your bullshit, Rocco, I know you didn't have a plan when you took her. You fucked up and you just tried to save face with the insanity. But it's gone on long enough. Giuseppe Calabresi killed my child. I say we kill his in kind."

"Wait," Frankie said, stepping between Papa and the door like he might just march out there and murder Sloan right now.

My jaw ticked with fury. He didn't even want to hear me out and worse than that; he'd seen straight through me as always. He hadn't even been in the country when I'd taken it upon myself to snatch Sloan from her wedding, but he knew me so well he'd already figured out what had happened without even having to look me in the eye and ask.

"I have an idea," I ground out, determined to make him at least listen before he overruled me.

"It's a good one," Enzo piped up, having my back as always.

"Fine," Papa said wearily, folding his arms as he moved to stand before the fire. "Then spit it out."

"I've already got the Calabresis backing out of Romero territory," I began but he waved a hand to silence me.

"Don't bore me with the details you've already given me, tell me what this plan of yours is," he snapped.

"I say we use her to draw Giuseppe out somehow. Find a way to manipulate him into a situation we can take advantage of. We can use her to orchestrate his assassination," I insisted, keeping it short and to the point. Papa would want to make any definitive plans himself anyway.

He sucked his bottom lip between his teeth as he considered that, his gaze flitting from me to my brothers.

"And the two of you agree with him on this?" he asked.

"Yes," they both confirmed instantly and I suppressed a smile at that. The three of us may have disagreed constantly in private, but in front of our father we always stood united. It was the one tactic we could employ against him that got his attention.

As expected, his gaze flashed with pride at the three of us showing solidarity and he nodded curtly.

"Fine. I'll work on a plan to use this to finish her father. Do what you want with her until then and once he's dead we'll have her head too."

The tension in my posture fell slack as I got my way and I allowed him to see my smile.

Papa only rolled his eyes at me like I was some tiresome child. "Well in that case, I may as well get back to the city. I'll be in touch with further instructions shortly," he promised.

I raised my eyebrows at his sudden decision to leave again, but I wasn't sure why I was surprised. He hated to linger in this house and the sweeping glance he gave the room we stood in only made the point more strongly. He damn near shuddered before turning and striding for the door.

We followed him into the hall and he pulled the front door wide, pausing as snowflakes swirled in around us on a freezing breeze.

"Make sure you don't fuck this up, Rocco. It's your head on the block if she escapes," he warned.

The door slammed between us before I could reply and I was left in the wake of my father, feeling somehow like that little boy who'd just been told his mother was dead.

Sloan

I sat at the top of the cellar stairs with Rocco's jumper swamping me. I couldn't put my hands through the sleeves with them cuffed together but in a way, that was better. My fingers drank in the warmth of his lingering body heat and I tried to ignore the freshly cut pine smell that always seemed to hang around him.

His actions had contradicted his nasty words. Giving me this sweater was screwing with my mind. But maybe that had been his intention. I didn't imagine I could unravel the inner workings of a psychopath like Rocco Romero anyway.

It was warmer by the door and I refused to spend more time down in that icy pit. I tried not to consider the possibility that Rocco's father would take charge now. That he'd insist I was kept down here, or worse…if he decided to kill his enemy's daughter.

The hatred between him and my father was like rot, gnawing deeper and deeper into the bone until it infected every part of them. I didn't even know why they hated each other so deeply. Our families had been in a feud for a hundred years over territory in Sinners Bay, but with them it was personal. And that was why I needed to escape this place as soon as possible. Because every day that passed meant I was drawing closer to the day the Romeros would kill me. There wasn't a chance on earth they were going to let me return to my family. I knew it in the depths of my soul.

The door opened and I shot to my feet, looking up at Rocco as he stood barring my way out.

His shoulders were pressed back, his head cocked to one side. Enzo muscled in beside him followed by Frankie looking between their heads. I took an involuntary step backwards onto the lower stair as they leered at me like a three headed hellhound.

"What now?" Frankie murmured.

"We put her to good use?" Enzo suggested hopefully.

"Hmm, the kitchen floors need scrubbing," Rocco said with a wicked grin.

"Do they?" Frankie frowned and Rocco threw his elbow back into his ribs.

I glowered at all three of them, refusing to react to their display of power. I didn't care if they made me clean the entire house from top to bottom. That would just give me more opportunities to find a way out.

Rocco moved onto the stairs, a shadow falling over his face as he blocked the light of the bulb above. "Yeah, Cinderella had to earn her way to the ball. But in your case, you can earn your way back into my bed tonight. If you fuck up, you can stay down here again."

He snatched a handful of the sweater and tugged me out of the cellar, the two brothers parting for us and sniggering as Rocco led me away.

"Cinderella didn't earn her way to the ball," I tutted. "Her fairy godmother showed up to help her."

"Well maybe Frankie will sprout wings and Enzo will turn into a turnip for you."

"Pumpkin," I corrected, shaking my head. "If you want to threaten me with a fairytale, at least get the story right."

Rocco gave me spine-melting look, leaning in close to my ear. "Fine, how's this for a story? Three hungry wolves made a principessa clean their floors. Every time she fucked up, they took a bite. By the end of the day, the principessa was nowhere to be seen but the wolves all looked a little fatter. The end." He shoved me to the floor in the kitchen and I huffed in rage as I found myself on my knees beneath him once again.

He tugged the sweater over my head, tossing it onto the counter and I immediately shivered. The house never felt truly warm, the vaulted ceilings too high and the rooms too large to keep the heat contained. He knelt down, taking the key from his pocket and unlocking the cuffs from my wrists. Then he set about filling a mop bucket with soapy water then tossed a scrubbing brush in front of me before dumping the bucket down and sploshing it over my knees. "Get cleaning or I might take my first bite."

"Bet you can't bite as hard as me," I muttered, glancing behind me to see he'd paused beside the door, his fingers pressed to the place on his shoulder where I'd sunk my teeth into him.

A purely animal look entered his gaze and there was something so deeply carnal about it, I found myself looking away again. I cursed my body for the heat tingling right through to my core and the way a breath snagged in my lungs. He was too dark of a fantasy to dare indulging in and I forced my mind away from him in an instant.

"Don't tempt me into a competition I'll easily win, bella," he said before heading out the door.

I sighed as I picked up the scrubbing brush and dunked it in the water. It wasn't like I could refuse to do this and at the very least, it gave me something to occupy my time. Spending the day gazing at a wall wasn't exactly much better so in a way, this was an improvement. The only issue was that it was also degrading as hell. Sloan Calabresi cleaning the Romeros floors. Humiliating.

My father will have your balls for this if I don't get them first, Rocco.

I thought of Nicoli and wondered if he missed me at all. He was no doubt hunting me down on my father's orders, but would he have done it for me alone? He'd always been my saviour as a kid, but would he still be that for me now?

I sighed, directing my frustration into every stroke of the scrubbing brush. Nicoli might have been coming for me, but I wasn't going to wait here and hope for his arrival like a bird in a cage. I'd keep rattling the bars, checking every corner for a way out. *And who knows, maybe I'll save myself.*

After an hour, the kitchen floor was clean and I was directed into the hallway to start scrubbing there. I could hear the brothers talking in the living room, apparently not giving a damn about watching me. I supposed if the scrubbing noise stopped, they'd notice.

I settled into cursing them with every stroke of the brush, coming up with as many colourful names for them as I could to stop me from going insane.

My hands were already sore from cleaning the broken bulb from Rocco's bed this morning, but now blisters and bruises were added to the mix. I was working my rage out on the floor but it was only growing. The longer I cleaned, the angrier I became.

My blood mixed with the soapy water as I dunked the brush once more and hissed between my teeth as it stung my wounds. I cursed my luck as Rocco appeared the very same moment a blister burst on my palm and I winced.

His jaw was locked tight and his eyes narrowed to slits. "You're done for the day," he growled, striding forward and plucking me up from the floor.

I pushed away from him, marking his shirt with my soapy hands and leaving a patch of blood there too. He glanced at it with a scowl then dragged me into the bathroom across the hall.

"Clothes!" Rocco barked out at his brothers and someone's footsteps sounded in response.

"Shower," he commanded me, pointing at the unit. "Make sure you're clean enough to cook for us."

I glared at him in fury. "So princess is off the menu then?" I asked coldly.

"Why would I want to eat a dirty Calabresi princess?" he asked with a sneer.

"Why would I want to cook for a greasy Romero who has no class? Calabresi men would never treat a woman the way you do." I spat at his feet and a dangerous shadow slipped into his eyes.

"I know how to treat a woman, bella, but all I see before me is a rat."

My lower lip quivered with rage and my heart beat painfully hard in my chest. I wanted to scratch and tear at his face, destroy the beauty and unveil the evil beneath. He deserved to be ugly, his face marred and twisted just like his soul.

"Get out," I hissed and he stepped back without complaint.

Frankie appeared behind him and Rocco took the bag of clothes from him, tossing it at me. The door slammed shut and I stood there, shaking with rage. I turned to the shower, about to turn it on when I noticed the window was open a crack.

My world halted as I stared at it. It was a tiny thing at the very top of a frosted pane of glass. One of the brothers had probably taken a dump in here earlier today and I thanked the lord for that particular shit because it was about to save my neck.

I turned the shower on then stripped out of my sodden leggings and pulled on the black onesie Frankie had supplied. It was lined and the thick pair of socks they'd given me would have been perfect if I'd had shoes. But I'd have to go without. Instead, I carefully tore the plastic bag in half and tied the two pieces around my feet to make the soles as waterproof as possible. Then I climbed onto the toilet seat and pushed the window as wide as it would go. It was seriously small but I was petite and come hell or high water, I was getting through that gap.

I hauled myself up, sticking my arms and head out before bracing myself against the wall outside.

A foot of snow and miles of forest spread out before me, but I didn't care. There had to be someone out here who could help me. I'd just keep running until I found them.

Adrenaline pounded in time with my pulse, making my muscles twitch with the urge to flee. I squeezed my way through, wriggling hard to get my hips out and bruising my sides along the way. I twisted to cling to the top of the window frame, praising the world for my Pilates classes as I slid my legs out and dropped into the snow.

For a full second I froze, drinking in the icy air and endless space around me. *Holy hell, I'm free!*

I charged across the snow covered yard and into the trees, needing to put as much distance between me and the Romero brothers as possible. I ran and ran, my lungs burning as the cold air dived into them and made my heart pound even harder.

Even sprinting flat out couldn't chase away the cold. It bit at my hands and slid beneath my clothes like grasping fingers. Still, I raced on, never slowing, wondering how long I had before someone checked the bathroom. The thought of Rocco's shocked face brought a smile to my lips and a small laugh bubbled from my throat as I tore through the trees.

When I escaped, I was going to bring the full force of the Calabresi household down on their heads. They were going to rue the day they ever stole me from that church.

A noise reached me that made my heart clench with terror. I hoped on all the stars in the heavens that I was imagining it but as it drew closer, a sick kind of dread made me certain it was real.

Footsteps crashed through the snow, moving far faster than my legs could manage.

I powered on, running as fast as I possibly could as panic rushed through me.

As the light of the house was left far behind, I was plunged into almost total darkness. The trees were grouping tighter together, forcing me to slow and raise my hands so I didn't crash into them. The snow had barely made it beneath the thick canopy of the pines here and I praised my luck, leaving no more footprints as I fled into the dark, begging the shadows to swallow me away and hide me from my pursuer.

A man howled not far behind me and I recognised Rocco, my skin crawling as I realised he was taunting me. Playing wolf.

I charged on, my lungs labouring and my limbs aching as I kept hunting for a prick of light ahead. A house, a farm, a car. Anything. Any*one* who could help.

The trees thinned up ahead and the snow caked the ground beyond them. An idea struck me and I ran out into it, racing for another line of thick woodland ahead. When I darted onto the drier ground beneath their branches, I turned sharply back, racing across the tracks I'd just left, hoping I hadn't just made a terrible mistake.

I could hear him crashing through the trees ahead and dove back into the cover of the pines before he appeared.

I darted behind a huge trunk, pressing my back to it and holding my breath as I waited, my eyes burning from the icy air. It was too dark for him to see the tracks well enough to know I'd crossed back over them. At least, I hoped it was.

His footsteps pounded right beyond the tree I hid behind and my heart soared as he continued off across the snowy path I'd laid.

I waited for a full minute before I moved again, heading away from the direction he'd taken and breaking into a run. I glanced over my shoulder as a victorious smile pulled up my lips and my heart rose like the sun in my chest.

I collided with something hard and too warm to be a tree and a scream ripped from my throat. Strong arms closed around me then threw me back against the solid trunk of a pine. I could barely see him in the dark, but I knew it was Rocco from his scent, his imposing height, his terrifying aura. He crushed me back against the bark and I fought hard not to yelp as a hard knot dug into my spine.

"I've hunted people in the dark before and they all ended up in ditches, principessa." His heated breath washed over me and his hips ground into my stomach as he tried to draw a whimper from my lips. I ground my teeth, refusing to let a noise escape me apart from the frantic pace of my breaths.

He shifted his weight against me and I inhaled as I felt the solid length of him digging into me. The sick bastard was turned on by this. My hands were crushed between us and were altogether far too close to that monstrous appendage than I liked.

"I thought you weren't attracted to Calabresi girls," I taunted, heat invading my body as I tried not focus on the immense size of him. I prayed he had too much pride to act on his urges, because there wasn't a thing I could do right then to escape.

Rocco growled at my words, moving back enough to relieve me of his hard-on and I tried to duck under his arm. He caught me by the hair, yanking me back into his body and turning me toward the house. "I'd sooner fuck a hole in the ground. It'd be far more satisfying than your god-fearing pussy anyway."

"Just make sure you don't traumatise a family of rabbits while you're at it," I said dryly and he laughed. Like actually freaking laughed. I didn't want to like the sound but it was gravelly and rough, like a wave crashing against a rocky beach. The worst thing of all, was the thrill of that chase had left me light-headed. And I hated to admit how much some twisted part of me had enjoyed it.

His hands closed around me; not tightly like before, but the threat was still there. My heart sank deeper and deeper into my gut as the house came into view through the trees.

I was a prisoner of war. But this solider had fight left in her yet.

Rocco

Sloan sighed in her sleep as she rolled over onto her back and her side brushed against mine.

I tore my eyes from the view beyond the open window where I'd been watching the sun rise over the mountains and looked at her instead.

I cupped my hand behind my head and shifted to get a little more comfortable as I assessed my new pet.

In all the hours I'd spent training for fights or learning about strategies to employ against your enemy, I'd never once pictured a foe who looked like her.

Sloan sighed again, wriggling closer, no doubt subliminally chasing down some more heat from my body.

I stayed still as she rolled onto her side, her arm twisting awkwardly over her head where it was cuffed as she laid her head on my chest and pressed the full length of her soft body against the length of mine.

I hung in that moment with a frown pulling at my brow, wondering what strange twist of fate had delivered us both here. We'd been born to hate each other, destined to ache for the other's demise and take pleasure in their pain. But what if we hadn't been born a Romero and a Calabresi? What strange opportunities might fate have dealt us then?

Sloan shifted against me, a soft moan escaping her full lips which had my dick twitching to attention. She was either dreaming about food or sex and I was struck with the desire to find out which.

She shifted again, her cuff clattering against the wood as her hips shifted against me and I cleared my throat loudly.

She gasped as she woke and I watched her in amusement as she took a moment to figure out where she was and what was going on. Not to mention whose chest she was currently half on top of.

"When you're done dry humping me, we should probably get up," I deadpanned, breaking through any lingering remnants of sleep she was clinging to and laughing as she jerked away from me in horror.

"Are you sure you're a virgin, principessa? Because the noises you were making in your sleep sounded a hell of a lot like you knew what you were doing."

"I'm not the one who keeps claiming I'm a virgin," she growled as she moved to the edge of the bed on her back, trying to create some distance between us even though there was none to be had.

"Is that so?" I asked, genuinely surprised as I shifted suddenly, moving on top of her and catching her free hand in my grasp so that I could hold it above her head with the other.

I looked down at her pinned beneath me like that and I had to admit it was a pretty spectacular view. Even the hatred in her gaze was a turn on. I wanted to stoke the flames of that rage in her until it burned her alive and the only release she could get from it would come in the form of her body bowing to mine. Her gaze dipped to my bare chest as I pinned her there and I could have sworn she was thinking about it too.

"Did Nicoli take a ride on his bride before the wedding night?" I tutted at her like she was a bad girl and she squirmed beneath me in discomfort which only really served to grind her body against mine.

"Get off," she snapped, defiance flaring in her gaze. I leaned down to speak into her ear, my stubble grazing her jaw.

"La ragazza disubbidiente," I growled. *Naughty girl.* "It wasn't him, was it? What would Papa Calabresi think of his little girl getting hot and heavy with someone beneath the sheets before her wedding day?"

My only answer was a scowl and a pout of those goddamn lips. That girl's mouth was becoming my own personal brand of temptation. Every time a smart comment spilled from them I wanted to push her to her knees and feel her wrap them around the hard length of me.

I eyed her raven locks for a moment, imagining them knotted in my fist as her body fell prey to mine and felt myself growing hard at the mere idea of it.

Besides, as much as I claimed not to want to fuck a Calabresi, I had to admit that I wouldn't hate to know I'd bent Giuseppe's little girl to my desires and made her scream my name. Hell, I could even tape it and send it to him as a Christmas present.

"Well I'll be sure to inform Nicoli of his bride's wandering attention the next time I see him," I promised her before shoving off of the bed and heading into the en-suite.

I pushed my boxers off as I set the shower running and smirked to myself as I heard her gasp in surprise behind me.

"You don't have to look if I'm making you blush, principessa," I said as I stepped under the water and turned back to face her.

She'd pushed herself to sit up in the bed and was glaring at me with narrowed eyes, working pretty damn hard at looking unimpressed. She fought to keep her gaze on my face as the water spilled over my body.

"You're not making me blush, you're making me gag," she hissed, still not looking away from me.

"I can really make you gag if that's what you want?" I offered and her gaze instantly fell to my dick before she turned away sharply, yanking on her cuff as she refused to look at me.

"I'll vomit on my own time, over here, thanks," she growled and I laughed.

I made quick work of washing and quickly dried off, dressing in a pair of boxers and black sweatpants and leaving my hair damp and curling.

I opened the closet and pulled out some underwear, a pair of jeans and a green tank top for her, tossing them onto the bed so that she could get changed before I unlocked her handcuff.

She instantly drew her wrist closer to her body and rubbed at it where the skin had grown raw and red.

"Are you just going to stand there and watch me get changed?" she demanded.

"Are you going to make a show of it for me?" I countered.

She didn't so much as twitch a smile and I smirked at her as I turned my back obligingly.

"I'll give you to the count of ten," I said. "Then I'm turning back around. One, two, three…"

The sound of the zipper being drawn down on her onesie was quickly followed by material falling on the mattress and her shuffling into the new clothes.

"-ten." I turned back to face her just as she drew her shirt down over her bra and I reached out to tug the hem down for her.

She didn't recoil like I'd expected, just looked up at me with those big eyes like I was a puzzle she was trying to solve. I smirked as I turned her around and pointed her towards the en-suite. "You can pee with the door open and brush your teeth."

Sloan huffed and I was struck with the desire to spank her for it as she strode away to do as I'd said. There was no window in the en-suite and from now on, that would be the only bathroom she was allowed to use.

I reached for the handcuffs, unlocking them from the bed as I waited for her to finish up and moving to the doorway just as she stepped back into the bedroom.

I reached for her hand, snapping one manacle closed around her right wrist and the other around my left.

"As you can't be trusted, you'll be spending your days locked to one of us from now on," I informed her.

"And I thought this was already hell," she complained and I chuckled, pocketing the handcuff keys.

"Oh no, principessa, you've barely even begun to scratch the surface of the darkness inside me."

We headed downstairs to the kitchen and I couldn't help but smirk to myself every time she brushed her shoulder against my arm or her fingers nudged mine. She reacted like my skin burned her, trying to jerk away only to find that she pulled my arm with her when she tried.

We headed into the kitchen and found Enzo sitting on the counter by the sink, halfway through a slice of toast.

"Good morning, love birds," he teased, eyeing the handcuffs which linked us with an amused expression. "Did you sleep well?"

"Aside from the girl who was all over me while I tried to sleep, I can't complain," I replied and Sloan scowled.

"You wish, asshole," she spat at me.

You have no idea, baby.

I took the handcuff keys from my pocket and tossed them down on the kitchen island as we headed towards the coffee machine and Sloan waited as I poured myself a cup.

I added cream and held it out to her, watching her eyes widen in surprise at the gesture. She reached for the coffee, her fingers brushing mine just before I drew it away from her again and drank it myself.

Her lips parted, her eyes blazing with rage as I smirked into my coffee, fighting down a laugh so hard that I choked on it as I swallowed.

I bet the Calabresi Principessa never had to deal with anyone who didn't fall all over themselves for her before.

Her lips parted like she wanted to chew me out, but before she could get a word out, the kitchen door opened again.

"I got everything you asked for from town last night," Frankie said to Sloan as he came into the room. "Are you going to make us something good?"

I frowned in confusion as Sloan gave him a smile that looked damn near genuine.

"Thank you," she said, hurrying towards the fridge and tugging me along behind her.

I followed her out of curiosity as she drew it open and raised my eyebrows at the mounds of food inside.

"What's all this?" I asked.

"If you're going to make me cook for you then you might as well let me do it properly," Sloan said defensively like she thought I might take all the food and dump it in the trash just because it pleased her. Which actually wasn't the worst idea, aside from the fact that we'd all go hungry too…

I shrugged like I didn't give a shit and she started pulling out ingredients right away.

She tugged me around the kitchen and even shoved things into my arms as she went, clearly in her element and I indulged her to see where this would go.

She piled up eggs, milk, butter, yeast, vanilla, flour, cinnamon and finally grabbed a big bag of sugar before hooking a huge mixing bowl out of a cupboard and stepping towards it with intent.

I jerked her to a halt using the cuffs and she frowned at me in confusion.

"I don't like sweet things," I said, eyeing the bag of sugar with distaste.

Her lips curved into the ghost of a smile. "Well you haven't tried my baking yet. I'm sure I can convince you to enjoy something sweet."

"Come on, Rocco," Enzo begged. "Maybe you'll enjoy her sweet things when she gives you a taste."

"Yeah, let her make her buns," Frankie piped up. "I bet you'll love her buns!"

I snorted a laugh as Sloan fought a blush at my brothers' terrible innuendos.

"Fine," I gave in, moving to stand before the worktop as Sloan started putting the ingredients together.

She struggled a bit with my hand locked to hers, little huffs of irritation spilling from her lips each time she was forced to tug on my arm. And as I'd locked myself to her right hand, that was more often than not.

I didn't exactly make it easier for her either, letting my arm hang like a dead weight from the cuff as she worked.

As she started pouring the flour out into the scales, I suddenly tugged my wrist back. The bag fell from her hands, landing with a solid thump in front of her and sending a cloud of flour up to coat the front of her clothes.

She gasped in surprise then dove her left hand into the bag of flour and threw a handful of it straight into my face.

Frankie and Enzo burst into laughter behind us but I kept my gaze fixed on Sloan, scowling as I swiped my arm over my face to get rid of the worst of it.

"Is that how you want to play, bella?" I asked her in a dangerous growl.

I expected her to shrink back down or shake her head. I didn't expect her to grab another handful of flour and throw it at my chest. My heart beat faster at the game and the wild glint in her brown eyes.

I growled at her as I reached out and caught the edge of the packet, tossing half of it over her head in one go.

She tried to run but I jerked her back towards me using the cuffs and a cloud of flour engulfed her as she squealed again.

A deep laugh escaped me as I spun her in my arms and she was forced to face me.

"Oh fuck this!" Frankie exclaimed and the two of them hurried out of the room before our food fight descended any further.

"Do you surrender?" I teased, gripping Sloan's hip and pushing her back so her ass hit the counter.

"Never." Her left hand whipped up between us and she slammed an egg straight against my bare chest, cracking it and spilling the yolk all over me.

My lips parted in surprise as she laughed, the sound of it pure and genuine and catching me completely off guard. The second egg was crushed against the side of my head and I felt it sliding right down to the roots of my hair.

"You asked for it now," I warned her and she shrieked as she tried to escape me again.

I grabbed the box of eggs, snatching two into my grip before breaking them on the top her head, pinning her back against the worktop as she tried to escape.

I laughed in victory as she wriggled against me, trying to break away. The friction between our bodies only made my smile grow and it didn't seem like she was trying all that hard to shove me off either.

She lurched to the side, dragging me against her more firmly as she grabbed the pint of milk.

"Don't you da-"

Stone cold milk spilled straight over the top of my head in a torrent. It ran over my shoulders, down my back and chest, mixing with the egg and flour to form a paste against my skin. I shook my hair to clear it of the milk and lunged at her, driving her back against the worktop as I dumped the whole bag of flour over her head.

A huge cloud of it rose up all around us, covering me as much as her and we started coughing and laughing all at once.

Sloan's free hand landed on my bicep and she held me just tightly enough to discourage any further attacks without actually restraining me.

The cloud slowly dispersed around us and I found myself holding her close as my heart beat to an unusual rhythm.

"I think that was a draw," she murmured, her eyes bright.

I snorted a laugh. "I think you might have won that one, bella," I disagreed as I dripped milk all over the kitchen tiles. "And I have to say, I don't think much of your baking skills either."

She rolled her eyes at me but it was almost playful. "Well you haven't actually tasted it, so…"

I leaned forward quickly and ran my tongue straight up the length of her neck. Her grip on my arm tightened, but she didn't try to push me away and I had to fight the urge to linger with my mouth on her flesh. A mixture of flour, milk and raw egg coated my tongue and I pulled a face as I leaned back just enough to meet her eye.

"It's fucking awful," I informed her seriously.

"It'll taste better when it's cooked," she replied lightly. "So why don't you just stick your head in the oven…"

I barked a laugh and reached out to push her eggy hair back over her shoulders. "I think I'd prefer a shower, wouldn't you?"

"I dunno, I kinda like your new look," she countered and my smile widened.

"Well as much as I'm enjoying being covered in this shit, I don't think it will go so well with the upholstery in the living room." I turned away from her and moved to the kitchen island to find the handcuff keys, but they weren't where I'd left them.

I shoved some things about, dragged Sloan to the coffee machine and frowned around at the huge kitchen in confusion.

"Did you see where I left-"

"Lost something, fratello?" Enzo asked casually as he pushed the door open.

I frowned, striding forward with my hand outstretched.

"Give me the keys," I demanded and he widened his eyes innocently.

"Didn't you hear? They fell down the toilet."

"That had better be some kind of joke," I growled.

He grinned tauntingly and I knew in my gut that he wasn't bluffing. He was trying to win this fucking bet. And he thought locking us together would make it happen.

I snarled at him and lurched forward with my fist clenched, but he darted away with a laugh and I stumbled as I almost yanked Sloan off of her feet trying to catch him.

"Does that mean we're stuck like this?" she asked me, not even trying to disguise her horror at the idea.

I clenched my jaw, the amusement I'd felt just moments ago fleeing like it had never existed at all.

"Yeah, principessa. It looks like we are."

Sloan

The moment of madness where Rocco and I had laughed together was thoroughly gone. His smile had been replaced with a cold, hard fury. He dragged me into the living room after his brother, Enzo, his muscles tensing as he moved.

"Tell me where it is!" he roared and Frankie sniggered, looking to Enzo who was stretched out on the couch.

"I told you, fratello. I flushed it," Enzo said with a shrug.

Rocco bulldozed toward him and I stumbled after him as he snatched Enzo's collar in his fist. "This isn't funny."

Enzo grinned broadly, looking to me. "You'll just have to get used to each other, I guess."

Rocco shoved him away and I was forced to hurry after him as he stalked out of the room, crossing the hall to the front door. He unbolted a bunch of locks then pulled it wide and freezing air washed over me.

"Where are we going?" I demanded as he dragged me out onto the porch.

He didn't answer me, jogging down the steps, his shoulders rigid. My bare feet stung as they sank into the snow and I cursed as I had to half run to keep up with his furious pace.

I spotted a wood shed on the border of the forest and was soon hauled inside it. Rocco flicked the light on and my stomach churned as I took in the rows of tools hanging around the place. There was a red Cadillac gathering dust and a large work bench beside it. He snatched a wood-chopping axe off of the wall and my heart lurched into my throat.

"Wait, you're not actually going to try and cut through this are you?"

He continued to ignore me, forcing me over to the workbench and standing on the opposite side of it to me. He slammed his arm down on it so mine was dragged down too.

"Are you crazy!?" I yelled, my pulse thundering in my ears as he lifted the axe high with his free hand.

"Hold still," he growled, his brows pinching in concentration.

Fear splintered through my chest. "Stop!" I screamed as he slashed the axe through the air.

I jerked my hand away in terror and the axe slammed into the wood half a centimetre from Rocco's little finger. I'd yanked his arm forward when I'd moved and the look he gave me for it was a death sentence. Fear slithered into my chest and took root in my soul.

He left the axe in the wood, practically snarling as he ripped his arm backwards so I was dragged onto the workbench. He flipped me over so I lay beneath him on my back and a tremor racked through my bones.

"Idiota!" he spat and I winced as he wrenched the axe from the wood beside me. My hair tumbled everywhere as I struggled to get up, my breathing ragged. He pressed his hand to my shoulder to keep me down and I lifted my hand to shield myself from his fury. The low light of the bulb glinted off of the sharpened edge of the axe and for a second I didn't know what he'd do.

He stared down at me, the milky mixture covering his head and shoulders doing nothing to take away from the terrifying look in his eyes. I had no idea how we'd shared such a carefree moment just minutes ago; I couldn't imagine this man ever cracking another smile. Not unless it was at the sight of my butchered body beneath that blade.

He tossed the axe down and the clatter it made as it hit the floor made me flinch. He scooped me off of the workbench, crushing me into his chest as he headed out of the shed and kicked the door closed with an echoing bang.

Rocco was a livewire, his temper as potent as my father's. I hated the idea of leaning into him, but I knew one tactic that usually worked to ease Papa's rages. I didn't want to try it with this mad man but if it worked, it might save me from whatever punishment he had in mind for me almost causing the loss of his finger.

I reached up with my unchained hand, cupping his jaw and raking my nails up into his hair. He glanced down at me, his brow creasing in confusion, but I continued because confusion was better than anger.

"I'm sorry," I breathed. "I was afraid."

He grunted, his eyes lifting and I could have sworn a bit of tension left his body.

Keep going.

"Do you even know how frightening you are sometimes? I'm half your size, Rocco."

His jaw ticked, but he remained silent as he marched up the porch steps and muscled his way into the house. He didn't stop, stomping straight through the living room and up the stairs toward his bedroom. My breathing increased as I wondered what the hell he was thinking.

The second he shut the door, he dropped me onto my feet and I waited for an explanation.

He reached into his pocket, flipping out his switch blade and my throat constricted. "What are you going to do?"

"Shower. I'm not staying like this and neither are you. One of my useless brothers will drive to town and fetch us some bolt cutters."

He dragged me toward the bathroom and I caught the edge of the doorframe, refusing to go in there.

He turned to me, his muscular chest drawing my attention for half a second as my nails bit into the wood. His eyes softened and he reached forward to brush his fingers across my cheek in the same way I'd done to him. "Don't you think I would have fucked you in my bed if I was going to do it at all, principessa?" His words were like hot butter sliding off his tongue. He didn't blink as if proving he wasn't lying and for some reason unknown to mankind, I released my grip on the doorframe.

He kept his eyes locked with mine as he guided me toward the shower, turning me around and using the knife to cut my shirt off along with my bra. I clutched the scraps of material to my chest and Rocco flipped me around again. He'd kicked off his pants and boxers, leaving him completely naked before me. His body was divine, thick muscles and firm lines built atop his broad frame. I'd already stolen a glance at his lower half this morning and I fought the urge to do so again.

"Either you drop those clothes and unbutton your jeans yourself or I'll do it for you." He waited and my pulse drilled into my skull. Letting a Romero look at my naked flesh was a sin in itself. I was meant to uphold the sanctity of my skin, but that had been a decision made *for* me. Not for myself. And I'd ignored it before...

The dare in Rocco's eyes was making me want to be reckless. The second I let go of the clothes, it felt like stepping off the plane in Italy times a thousand, breathing in free air.

Rocco's lips twitched, but no hint of amusement crossed his features. His eyes said desire, pure and simple.

A blush ignited in my cheeks as I opened the button of my jeans and pulled them down, unable to help pulling Rocco's hand with me. His fingers skimmed my thigh, my calf then lingered on my ankle as I stepped out of them, everywhere he touched bursting with fire.

I left my panties in place, standing upright then moving straight past him into the shower. He shut the door as he entered the narrow unit behind me and I turned the water on a second before his dick grazed my ass and showed me how hard he was.

Despite the warm water, goosebumps rushed up my spine and a deep burn built in the pit of my stomach.

He pressed closer, reaching past me for the shampoo as I kept my back to him and I felt every inch of him digging into me.

I used the shower gel but when he didn't put the shampoo back, I glanced over my shoulder, finding he'd put it on the floor behind him.

"Shampoo," I demanded.

"By my feet," he answered with a smirk.

My gaze dipped down to the water streaming over his broad shoulders, the muscles that rippled and flexed everywhere I looked. We were so close and I could feel his gaze devouring me as keenly as I was him.

"Pass it to me," I ordered, holding out my hand.

"Sure," he said, too easily. He reached down with the hand which was chained to mine and I gasped as I was forced to turn and my face was dragged into his shoulder.

He stood up and suddenly I was too close, my breasts pressing against his firm chest and my nipples giving away how much his body was turning me on. He wasn't smirking anymore; his eyes penetrated my soul as I stared up at him, his hard length throbbing against my stomach.

He's my freaking kidnapper. I have to stop this!

I stepped back, heat taking my body captive as it filled every space inside me. I rubbed the shampoo into my hair, forcing his hand up to join mine as I scrubbed the eggs and flour out. His fingers pushed into my hair and a lump rose in my throat as he helped me wash it out. A tingle ran down my spine and I tried not to think about how good his hands felt on me.

When I finally had it clean, I helped him clean his too before I turned the water off, needing to get out of here and put a stop to the raging hormones invading me.

Rocco stepped out, grabbing a couple of towels and tossing me one while my eyes fell to his perfectly sculpted ass. I mean Jesus Christ, did he squat daily or was that shit natural?

I settled on staring at the wall as I wrapped a towel around me and hugged it tight to my body. Rocco secured his towel around his waist then led the way out of the bathroom and headed to the closet. He grabbed out a pair of boxers, dropping the towel and tugging them on one handed while I tried not to stare at how hard he still was.

I was caught in a storm of thoughts, wondering what it might be like to have something that size inside me while trying to remember he was my goddamn kidnapper. Being with him would be like blasphemy against my entire family. Let alone my own self-worth.

He turned to me with a large shirt in his hands. "You'll have to pull it up your legs."

He knelt down, giving me no option about accepting his help and I leaned forward to rest one hand on his shoulder while the other was yanked down to assist him. I stepped into the neck of his shirt and he drew it up over my body, dragging it over my breasts slower than was necessary. His thumbs skimmed my sensitive flesh, drawing a gasp of surprise from my lips.

I schooled my expression as he stood upright and I tucked my free arm into the sleeve, leaving the other one over the top of the shirt, avoiding his gaze. But he'd definitely heard that noise and it had been no innocent inhale; it had been pure pleasure and he knew it.

"Your panties are wet," he stated.

"They are *not*," I balked, a blush heating my cheeks at his words and the fact I *was* so hot for him. It was clearly written all over my face.

"You showered in them, bella. But good to know you're wet for me too." He winked and my soul died. Like literally bashed its own head in with a rock. Dead. Gone. Poof.

Congratulations, Sloan. You're hot for the scariest Romero in the house. And now he knows it.

Rocco

I strode into my bedroom with Sloan trotting along a step behind me as she hurried to match my pace. A day of this shit hadn't made it any funnier, despite the way my brothers seemed to feel about it. I didn't appreciate being the butt of their jokes. And I *definitely* didn't appreciate the fact that I'd spent the whole day tethered to Sloan while she wore that shirt which gave me such a perfect glimpse of her peaked nipples pressing through it. I'd pretty much been hard for her all day and I couldn't even go and jerk off over it.

My mind was full of that shower we'd shared this morning and the way her body had looked with water gliding over it. Not to mention how damn good it had felt each time her naked flesh had brushed mine.

I was pretty sure I'd be begging to get into her panties if this went on much longer and that wasn't the way this was going to play out.

I blew out a breath as I walked towards my side of the bed and moved to climb into it.

"We have to swap sides," Sloan said, tugging on the cuffs just enough to draw my attention.

"What?"

"You can't sleep on the right side of the bed tonight. The way we're cuffed means we have to swap."

I clenched my jaw, my gaze flicking to the window where the snow was falling gently again. With the demons that lay in the recesses of my mind, I wasn't likely to get any sleep if I couldn't lose myself in that view, but she had a point.

I huffed my irritation and dropped my sweatpants as I sat back on the bed.

Sloan pulled my hand towards her as she unbuttoned her fly and my fingers brushed her inner thigh as she pushed her jeans down her legs.

She sucked in a breath as I skimmed my fingers all the way down the inside of her leg to her ankle. She could have asked me to try harder not to touch her but she didn't. I was starting to get the distinct impression my little hostage had a dark side of her own.

She stepped out of her jeans and I flicked the lights off before shifting back on the bed, moving fast enough to yank her down after me so that she damn near fell in my lap.

She cursed beneath her breath as her palm lay flat on my stomach and I smirked to myself as she failed to pull away as fast as she should have.

I lay on my back and waited as she got herself comfortable beside me. Our chained hands lay in the empty space between us, our fingers brushing against each other.

We both fell quiet and I closed my eyes, willing sleep to come.

It felt like I lay there for hours, the churning emotions that warred within me feeding on the darkness and sending me too many thoughts for me to deal with if I wanted any hope of sleep.

With a huff of irritation, I rolled onto my side and tried to look over Sloan to the window and the view beyond it.

It was my ritual. I fell asleep looking out of a window and let my worries slip away into the sky.

"This isn't going to work for me, bella," I said sharply, tugging on the cuff as she mumbled something sleepily.

I didn't give her any longer to respond, catching her shoulder in my grip and rolling her towards me. I flipped her all the way around so that she was lying on my chained arm with hers falling over her stomach to meet it and her back to my chest so we were spooning and I could see beyond her to the window. We were pressed together and I could feel her heart thundering through the point of contact between us.

"What are you doing?" she breathed fearfully like she still imagined I might force myself on her. But I didn't get my kicks out of forcing women to do anything. If she was going to give me her body, she'd be doing it more than willingly, begging me for every inch I offered her.

"I can't sleep unless I can look out of the window at the sky, so this is how it's going to work," I replied simply.

The curves of her body fit perfectly into the cage created by mine, but she wriggled like she wanted to move away from me again.

"Why?" she demanded.

"Why what?"

"Why do you have to look out of the window? And I don't want some bullshit excuse, if you seriously expect me to spoon you then I'm going to need a valid reason."

I considered that for a moment. I didn't really have to tell her shit. But if I had any hope of getting some sleep tonight, then maybe it was better if I just gave her enough of the truth to get my way.

"I'm sure you've gathered by now that I'm not a good man, Sloan," I said in a low voice. "There are things I've done, things I've seen and stuff I've lived through that fills all the quiet corners of my mind. But if I can see the sky when I'm trying to shut my brain off, then I find it easier to remember that none of it matters. I'm just a tiny blip that takes up space in the time between nothing and nowhere. It doesn't really matter what I do or what I've done because in the end when all is said and done, every one of us will be forgotten by eternity."

Sloan stayed quiet for a long moment but some of the tension eased from her body and she shifted minutely closer to me.

"Who knew having so much power could be so lonely," she murmured and I frowned. I'd never thought of myself as lonely, but I guessed she was right in a sense. We all came into this world alone and left it that way too. It didn't matter if I loved my brothers or fought with all the passion of hell for vengeance in the name of my mother and Angelo. The dead forgot us anyway.

"Well we can't all live the life of the spoilt principessa," I replied. "It's not so perfect out in the real world, bella. But then maybe you're starting to realise that now."

She scoffed lightly like I was the most clueless asshole she'd ever met.

"I've lived my entire life in a cage, Rocco," she muttered. "The only difference here is that my chains are on show to the world."

We both fell silent and I shifted to get a little more comfortable, drawing her closer to me. She pushed back against me, easing the tightness in the cuff by moving nearer and I stilled as her ass ground right into my crotch.

I placed my right hand on her thigh just below the line of her shirt, *my* shirt, my thumb painting a mark along the edge of the hem.

Her breath caught in her throat as I toyed with the idea of pushing my hand an inch higher. Despite the situation we were in, I was starting to get the feeling she might actually want me to do it.

She shifted again, pushing back against my body so every hard inch of me pressed into her ass.

She continued to move and I growled in warning, drawing a soft inhale from her lips. If she wanted to test my resistance, then she was going to quickly find it lacking.

Sloan fell still but the warmth of her flesh against mine still had all the blood in my body firmly finding its way to my dick. I was heady with the scent of her, she always smelt like the sweetest form of sin, a mixture of vanilla and nutmeg that was good enough to eat. But I knew if I had a taste of her, I'd be gorging myself before I could stop.

My gaze fell on the view out of the window as the snow stopped falling and the clouds slowly withdrew to give me a look at the stars.

Sloan's breathing slowly evened out, but the ache in my flesh didn't falter. I wanted to take her body and bend it to my desire. I wanted her pinned beneath me and screaming for more while I taught her just how good it could feel to hurt for me. But that wasn't what I'd bet my brothers. I'd claimed that I could make her love me and if I convinced her to fuck me too soon, that wasn't going to happen.

I needed her aching for me, begging, pleading, down on her knees because my pleasure was all that she desired in this world.

If Sloan Calabresi was going to fall into the snare of my heart, then I was going to have to play this right. So despite the pleading ache in my balls and the desperate need of her flesh, I forced myself to close my eyes, leaving my hand just beneath the hem on her thigh.

I wouldn't take anything from her tonight and tomorrow she'd wake wishing I had and wondering why she was so drawn to a Romero.

***

We sat eating our lunch in the kitchen, my hand moving up and down with the path of Sloan's as she lifted her fork to her mouth. I had to admit that the girl knew how to cook when I didn't take the opportunity to throw the ingredients all over her and actually let her put them together. But in hindsight, I'd have probably preferred sandwiches to lasagne today as the constant yanking on the cuffs made it damn near impossible to eat.

I tried to cut my food just as Sloan reached for her drink and my knife fell to the table with a clatter.

"Enough," I snapped, pushing to my feet and glaring at my brothers. "Where are the damn keys?"

"I told you fratello, I dropped them down the toilet." Enzo shrugged innocently and I snatched my knife up again in my free hand before slamming it point first into the table right next to his fingers.

"Give me the fucking keys!" I yelled and Sloan flinched beside me, the cuffs tugging as she tried to escape my anger.

Frankie sniggered a laugh and I swept his plate of food straight onto the floor.

"Fuck this," I snapped before turning and striding away from them, dragging Sloan along behind me.

"Where are we going?" she demanded.

"To get some damn bolt cutters."

I threw open the closet beneath the stairs and searched in the back of it for the boots and coats I'd seen there. Papa hadn't cleared out all of Mamma's stuff after she'd died and the faux fur coat still held the scent of her rose perfume as I pulled it from the back of the closet.

My heart stilled as I was momentarily transported back into her arms, curled against her while she wore this coat. We were sat in the back of one of the family cars and she'd let me and Angelo snuggle inside her coat to cuddle up with her. My arms had been tight around her swollen belly where Enzo was kicking like a warrior, desperate to come meet his brothers. Angelo's fingers had brushed mine as we fought to find the spot where the new baby would kick next. I'd been happy then. Truly happy in a way I didn't even think I knew how to be anymore.

I turned to Sloan and pushed the coat into her arms. She threaded her free arm into it and tugged the other side over her shoulder which was about the best she could do in our current predicament.

A slight frown pulled at her brow as she looked at me but I turned away, not wanting her to see a part of me which was still so raw even after all these years.

I found Mamma's old snow boots next and dropped to my knees to guide Sloan's feet into them.

She had to stoop a little due to the cuff and as I looked up at her, I found a curtain of raven hair spilling all around us.

"Were these your mother's?" she breathed like she'd just taken a peek right inside my soul and could feel what was branded on my heart.

"The dead don't have much use for old coats and boots," I said roughly and she dropped the questions like I'd smacked her. Which was fine by me because I didn't need someone nosing into my business.

I grabbed a jacket out for myself, cursing as I couldn't put it on over my chained arm and hooking a button closed to hold it in place across my chest instead.

I dragged Sloan outside and around the front of the house to the garage where our cars were parked up, selecting a blue ford pickup from the line up and heading around to the driver's door.

I cursed as I reached it, glancing at Sloan who was firmly chained to my left side.

"I don't suppose you can drive a stick?" I asked her. Though as that idea occurred to me, I thought better of it anyway. If I gave her control of the car, she might try and crash it in some desperate bid for freedom.

"I can't drive at all," she replied in a small voice and I tutted. Of course Giuseppe Calabresi wouldn't have wanted his principessa driving herself around. Only chauffeur driven cars filled with body guards would do for her.

"Climb over then," I commanded and she hopped in, twisting awkwardly as I followed her so that her right arm was still in the centre of the vehicle and she was forced to lean towards me over the parking brake.

I started the engine and tugged on her arm as I placed my left hand on the wheel. She was almost yanked off of her chair and her left hand flew out to steady her, landing firmly in my crotch.

"Oh my god!" She scrambled backwards and I almost laughed.

"Do you wanna just sit in my lap?" I offered as we took off down the drive and she was left half hanging out of her seat.

"No," she growled like the idea of that didn't appeal to her at all. In fact, she sounded damn near offended by me.

We drove on down the winding road out of the mountains as the minutes slipped by and the silence stretched between us. She was watching me the whole time, though I couldn't take my eyes off of the icy road to return her penetrating gaze.

"What?" I asked eventually, shooting her a look which took in those doe eyes and pursed lips before I turned back to the road.

"I just don't understand you," she said. "One minute you're violent and terrifying and the next you're giving me your mother's clothes. And then last night…"

"What about last night?" I asked, a smile tugging at the corner of my mouth though I fought that bitch down. If she couldn't figure me out then that was fine by me. I didn't want her poking around in the depraved inner workings of my mind anyway. It would only give her nightmares and I was pretty sure the little she did know about me was enough for that anyway.

"You…we… Nothing. It doesn't matter." She turned to look away from me at last and I let myself smirk for half a second.

"Were you hoping I'd push my hand up beneath that shirt you were wearing?" I teased.

"No," she snapped, a blush pinking her cheeks.

"How far up did you want my fingers to go then, bella?" I pressed.

"I wasn't the one with a hard-on all night," she growled.

"Right. You only got wet in the shower…"

Sloan huffed and kept her mouth shut, clearly not liking the turn of this conversation though I happened to think it was funny as fuck.

We eventually pulled into Mountaindale, the little town closest to the house, though it was still over forty miles away. Sloan kept looking all around like she thought she might suddenly see a sign pointing out exactly where we were on a map or maybe she was just looking for a friendly face to beg to rescue her. Either way, she wasn't going to be getting away from me.

I headed straight for the hardware store in the centre of town and pulled the truck up right in front of the doors.

I glanced at Sloan, finding her eyes bright with hope and smirked to myself as I opened the door and helped her climb out.

I closed the door, stepping closer to her so that she was trapped between me and the truck as she looked up at me warily.

I reached out to her, pushing her long hair back behind her ear and looking down at her like she was the only woman in the world.

"What are you doing?" she breathed, thrown by my odd behaviour.

"Phil who owns this place is one of the nicest guys you'll meet up here, but he's also a nosey fucker. He'll be watching us on the CCTV right about now and wondering who my lovely lady friend is. So make sure you put on a good show for him, sweetheart."

"What?"

I answered her by catching her chin in my grip and tipping her mouth up to meet mine.

Sloan gasped in surprise and I shoved her back against the side of the truck, pushing my tongue into her mouth and stealing the kiss I'd been aching for from her full lips.

Her hands gripped my coat and she was almost pushing me back, but she didn't quite manage it, her tongue stroking mine instead.

I growled as I kissed her harder, my hand fisting in her hair and her body moulding to mine as for the briefest of moments she gave in.

I felt the second her resistance hardened as the tension in her posture grew and she bit my lip hard enough to draw blood.

The mixture of pain and pleasure only got me off more, but I broke away from her before she followed it up with a knee to the balls.

"Did it live up to your fantasies, principessa?" I teased her.

"What the hell is wrong with you?" she snarled.

"Far too much for us to discuss right now." I caught hold of her hand so that I wasn't just tugging her along by the chain that connected us and pulled her into the store.

I didn't bother heading to the racks to find what I wanted, I just strode straight to the back where Phil was sitting behind the register wearing his red check lumberjack shirt and brown wool hat like always. The CCTV feed ran to a screen beside him and he looked away from it to us as we drew close.

"Morning, Rocco," he said cheerily. "Got a new lady friend, I see?"

"Oh yeah," I agreed. "This is Sloan, she's a real handful."

"Help me," Sloan gasped, rushing forward to grab the counter and staring at him with wild eyes. "This man has kidnapped me! He's holding me prisoner up in his mansion and-"

"That's enough, sweetheart, you can drop the act while we're here," I joked, interrupting her and smiling brightly at Phil.

Phil laughed heartily. "Oh I see what you mean about her. Been doing a little role play have you?" he asked, winking at me.

"Yeah. That's actually the problem," I began but Sloan interrupted me.

"It's not a joke!" she snapped. "He's holding me hostage, keeping me chained!" She wrenched my arm up to show Phil the handcuffs which tethered us together and I smiled sheepishly.

"She got a little carried away and swallowed the keys," I said, lowering my voice like I was a bit embarrassed.

"What?" Sloan gasped.

"My wife can be the same way," Phil chuckled. "Once she puts on her French maid outfit she won't stop dusting for love nor money-"

"Call the police!" Sloan shrieked.

"I thought I was supposed to be the police?" I asked, frowning at her. "You said my name was Officer Slammer and that I'd arrested you for indecent exposure-"

"He's lying," Sloan said desperately. "He's kidnapped me and-"

"Sounds like she's got a new fantasy in mind now," Phil winked at me again. "Do you want me to cut you free or do you wanna just take some bolt cutters home so that you can play out this little kidnapper bit?"

"He threw me in the cellar and now he's forcing me to sleep in his bed," Sloan insisted.

"Oh I bet he is." Phil chuckled and Sloan looked like she might just burst into tears.

"I'll take the cutters to go. And can I grab a length of rope while I'm here?" I asked as he strolled away to find the bolt cutters. "I'll need something else to tie her up with once I cut these off after all."

"Oh yeah, I'll get the strong stuff for ya," Phil laughed as he strode away and I turned to Sloan with a smirk.

"I hate you," she hissed, tears glimmering in her eyes.

"Well lap it up, baby," I purred. "Because you ain't seen nothing yet."

Nicoli

Martello Romero's properties were all ostentatious, lavishly decorated bachelor pads in varying versions from apartments to cabins, manors to studios. I guessed that made sense for a family consisting of one man and three sons, but the lack of a feminine touch struck me in every property I'd searched. Not all of them were occupied, but I'd been just as thorough searching those that were.

I was working through the list I'd stolen from the accountant, forcing my way into property after property and tearing the places apart in my hunt.

I wouldn't stop, I barely paused for food or sleep. Nothing would keep me from my destiny. And her name was Sloan Calabresi.

When we were children we'd played together and I'd built her castles out of pillows, dens out of branches in the back yard, forts out of cardboard boxes. She'd always been my princess and I'd always been her knight. Nothing about that would change now that the monsters were no longer imaginary. I'd fight for her with the valour of a better man and the courage of the warrior she needed.

I still had the strangest of companions in my hunt. The only man to come with me on every search; Coco. It was absurd. The little white Pomeranian had walked out of buildings with bloody paws and torn through apartments filled with Romeros like he lived without fear. But as insane as it was to be taking him on these searches, I didn't have it in me to stop him from coming. He ached to get Sloan back just as fiercely as I did and we had built a strange camaraderie with that understanding.

Giuseppe had given me plenty of other men to aid in my hunt, but they came and went when they needed rest. I slept between raids for a few hours at a time or not at all. It didn't matter. I could rest when I had her back. When I'd bound her to me eternally and she was sleeping in my arms too.

Nothing mattered until that moment. And once I got my hands on her again, I'd never be letting go. She. Was. Mine.

I rode my motorcycle down a road lined with tall pines, the houses growing fewer and further between as I went. This property was one of the largest on the list. The house the family usually resided in during the summer months. I didn't expect any of the main family to be here now, but I imagined there would be plenty of armed guards on hand to protect it.

We were past the point where they knew we were coming.

By the third property we'd hit, the Romeros had been waiting for us. It was infuriating but predictable too. As soon as they'd realised that we were searching their buildings, they'd upped security in them. I just hoped it didn't mean that they'd moved Sloan somewhere outside of this list too. But it would be hard to hide a hostage from people if they were staying in a hotel, so I liked to think they'd be forced to keep her somewhere they knew. Somewhere secure.

A convoy of four cars filled with armed men followed me down the road. I got the feeling this would be one of the hardest houses to break into yet. But it was also one of the best suited to holding a captive. A large property, set away from other buildings, with modern locks and a storage basement.

Coco yapped excitedly in my saddle bag as I drew up at the side of the road just in front of the iron gates we were searching for.

The cars parked up behind me too and I dismounted, hanging my helmet from the handlebars and striding towards the gathered Calabresis who vacated the vehicles.

"They'll be waiting for us in there," I said roughly, like they might not already know that. "But it doesn't matter. There is no price too high for claiming back what has been stolen from us. Our lives are worthless if we let the Romeros rule over them."

"Too right," Blario agreed loudly.

"Il sole sorgerà domani," Christoph added fiercely. *The sun will rise again.*

"You four, lay covering fire at the main gate. The rest of us will circle the property and get in from the rear," I ordered and the men fell into their roles instantly.

I unholstered my semi-automatic pistol and strode towards the house with twelve men at my back, flipping Coco's saddle bag open as I went.

The little dog leapt out with a vicious yap before falling into step at my heels.

We circled the property and I left the men to force entry through the hedges as I carried on around to the far side of the lawn.

The huge brick house was all lit up in the dark, like a Christmas tree beckoning Santa closer. But I wouldn't be leaving any presents for my rivals, only dead bodies and bullet holes.

If Sloan was here, I'd find her. She might be in my arms this very night.

I crept towards the house under cover of night, the shadows hiding me and my men as we drew ever closer.

The silence was oppressive, the anticipation making my skin prickle with adrenaline.

I held my gun ready, my gaze locked on the back door as I approached it with intent.

Gunfire started at the front of the house and cries went up inside as the Calabresis all ran towards the commotion.

I raced forward as they were distracted, a growl of fury leaving my lips as I ran straight for the door.

One solid kick was all it took to send it crashing from its hinges and I leapt inside, firing at random in case any Romero scum were waiting close by.

Coco sped past me fearlessly, barking incessantly as he charged into battle.

Movement caught my eye to my right and I fired on a man who leapt up behind the couch. He fell back with a cry and I headed further into the huge open plan space as more gunfire came from the stairs.

I dove behind a heavy chest for cover and the man cried out as Coco made it to him, sinking his sharp little teeth into his ankle.

I took the distraction and fired a shot straight into his chest before he could hurt my loyal companion.

Coco shot upstairs to search for his mistress and I ran through the house, taking out more men and hiding behind cabinets and kitchen counters, bookshelves and even a hat stand in my bid for cover.

My rage made me fast, my fury made me fearless and in under a minute the room fell silent as our enemies were overwhelmed.

My breaths came heavily as I charged up the stairs, hunting through room after room in hopes of finding the girl who held my destiny in her grasp.

A high pitched squeal came from a room at the end of the hall and I stilled as I heard a dog yelp in pain again.

"Coco!" I bellowed, racing down the hall, not giving a shit that anyone there would hear me coming.

I fired a shot at the door as I reached it and it flew open before me as I dove inside.

I rolled as I hit the floor, taking aim at the man who held Coco by the scruff of his neck.

I fired the same moment he did and he fell to the floor, dropping the dog as pain tore through my cheek.

"Fuck!" I bellowed, clutching my face as agony flared and I was momentarily blinded by it.

I rolled to my hands and knees as Coco rushed over and started licking my arm.

I cursed, pushing myself upright and looking across the room at a mirror that hung on the wall. The bullet had grazed me, a bloody line which blazed like hellfire painted along the line of my cheekbone. But it didn't matter. It couldn't slow me down, so I didn't spare it any more of my attention.

I headed back out into the hall with Coco at my heels as we made quick work of searching all of the rooms in the building.

My heart sank as we went. I called Sloan's name as I searched, but in my heart I knew she wasn't here.

When I finally made it back downstairs to the bullet strewn living room, I found the remainder of my men waiting for me.

"There's no sign of her, Nicoli," Marco said in a low voice as if I hadn't fucking worked that out already.

"Go back to the cars," I growled. "We'll hit the next house in the morning."

They trailed out without another word and I sighed heavily as I tipped my head back to the ceiling in despair. With every property we searched, the list grew shorter. And the longer it took for me to find her, the more I started to worry about what they were doing to her in the meantime. I felt hopeless in the face of this failure.

I couldn't accept the idea that I wouldn't find her but with each passing day, hour, minute, I grew more fearful of what torture she endured.

Each photograph those monsters had sent of her had been more worrying than the last. She looked terrified, ill-treated, in despair.

Each time I saw a new image of her it just compounded this feeling of failure in my heart. I was supposed to protect her. I was supposed to have found her already. *I* was the one she should have been able to rely on.

Just as I was about to leave the house, the sound of the phone ringing caught my ear.

I hesitated, meaning to ignore it but a creeping sensation along my spine made me feel sure that that call was meant for me.

I waded through the overturned furniture and stepped over a bloody body before I found the phone.

"Hello?"

"Tut, tut, tut, Nicoli. Are you trashing another one of my family's properties?" Rocco Romero's voice taunted me from the other end of the line.

I fell still, my grip tightening on the phone until I was in danger of crushing the damn thing.

"Release my fiancé," I demanded, my voice cold and hard.

He laughed. Fucking laughed at me. My rage built to a new high, my blood boiling and visions filling my mind of a thousand different ways that I might kill this asshole and watch him bleed.

"This is a friendly warning," he said in a cruel tone. "Stop your search and the destruction of our things."

"Or what?" I growled.

"Or your beautiful bride will be punished for every move you make. You may be breaking some things of mine but I assure you, I can break her in a hundred different ways so that the pieces will never fit back together right. I won't even kill her, I'll just ruin her so thoroughly that when you're finally reunited with her, your bride will be nothing more than a walking, talking horror show. Every time I hurt her, I'll show her a picture of your face and tell her who's responsible. She'll hate and fear you more than she will me."

"You're sick," I snarled.

"I am," he agreed like that was something to be proud of. "And I suggest you don't do anything to make me prove just how sick I am."

I opened my mouth to respond, but I heard a voice on the other end of the line that made me pause. She wasn't holding the phone but she must have been in the room with him.

"What are you doing with that?" Sloan gasped.

Rocco laughed like a fucking psychopath and there was a sound suspiciously like a whip being cracked.

"Your fiancé wants me to punish you, bella," he purred and I yelled my rage to the sky, though it made no difference to what was taking place on the other end of that line.

"No," Sloan breathed. "Wait! Don't…don't!"

"Your choice, Nicoli," Rocco growled into the receiver.

My lips parted to make some response but the line went dead.

"No!" I bellowed, launching the phone across the room so that it slammed into the fireplace and shattered into a hundred pieces.

That piece of shit Romero had me by the balls and he knew it. The one thing I couldn't risk was her. She was my right, my destiny, my one true chance to become a Calabresi and live up to the fate I'd worked so hard for.

I couldn't risk her for anything. But if I stopped my search, then what? He might still be torturing her anyway. Each day she spent away from me could be filled with a thousand horrors. How was I supposed to make this impossible choice?

The answer came to me amongst the bloodlust and the rage. I had to see Giuseppe. He was her father and the head of our family. He was the only one who could make this call. Whatever he chose would determine my fate. And Sloan's.

Sloan

"Was that Nicoli?" I demanded of Rocco. He had a tight hold of my arm, his teeth bared as he practically snarled at me. He'd pulled his belt free, whipping it against the wall like a crazed man and for a moment I'd really thought he was going to hit me.

"Yeah. Your hot-headed fiancé needs to be sent a message," he growled. "He's spilling Romero blood to find you."

A breath got trapped in my lungs. His grip on me tightened as I turned away from him and mulled over those words in my mind. Nicoli was hunting for me. He was ruthless, a weapon forged by my father. If anyone could find me, he could.

Rocco growled low in his throat, shaking me to get my attention. "You better act real scared in the next five seconds, because if you don't I'll give you a good reason to. Your fiancé needs to fear for your life."

"As if I don't already," I said hollowly.

He dropped the belt and his eyes flashed murderously. Fear raced through me as his hand locked around my throat and he shoved me against the wall.

"No, principessa, I'm starting to think you've forgotten who's holding you prisoner."

I gasped as his grip tightened, bringing my hand up to claw at his skin. My eyes locked with his and that tangible energy rolled between us. I could feel the connection that had been formed between us the day he'd tried to kill me in that car pulsing in my chest.

The animal that lived in him peered from his eyes, its hunger clear. Despite myself, I shrank from him as he held me in place and gritted his teeth like he was about to break me. It didn't hurt as much as it should have and I realised too late he was just trying to get a reaction out of me.

He brought up his phone to take a photo, snapping the picture fast. He released me in an instant, but rage scorched my insides and begged for his pain in payment for what he'd done.

I snatched his shirt in my hand, refusing to let him turn his back on me. How *dare* he do that to me.

He glanced over his shoulder and I threw my fist into his face, throwing my full weight into the punch as Royce had taught me. My knuckles crunched and I groaned the same moment that he jerked back.

Satisfaction filled me as blood wet his lip and he tasted it with his tongue. A dark and twisted part of me wanted to lick it too, but I forced her down into the recesses of my mind.

"If you need an outlet for that frustration, bella, I'll gladly let you satisfy it in my bed."

My upper lip peeled back despite the warmth that spread deep into my bones in response to his words. "I thought you didn't have sex with Calabresis," I said dryly.

"That's true," he said, stepping into my personal space until the air was charged with a storm. "I don't want to have sex with a Calabresi, but I'm starting to think I'd like to fuck one."

"What's the difference?" I tsked.

His eyes glittered and I somehow felt even smaller beneath him as he pinched my chin between his calloused finger and thumb. "Nicoli didn't show you?"

I pursed my lips, glancing over at the window in a refusal to answer.

"Merda," he swore, his heated breath washing over my neck as he leaned down to speak in my ear. "It wasn't him who had you."

My jaw tightened, my lips sealed. It was a secret he had no right to, but somehow, though I'd never confirmed or denied anything about it, he'd drawn it right from my soul.

"I bet you miss what freedom tastes like," he whispered and I stilled, having expected him to say something crass. I turned my head to face him and he didn't move, meaning our mouths were less than a centimetre apart. I thought of the kiss he'd planted on me at the hardware store and a flame curled around my heart.

"Death is the truest freedom in the world," I whispered my mother's final words to me. They'd remained unspoken for years, clutched in my heart in cotton wool. But now I gave them to a Romero and I didn't know why.

"No, bella," he said, softer than I'd ever heard him say anything. "I believe you can find freedom anywhere, you just have to bleed enough for it to be granted."

He released me, walking away and for the longest moment of my life, I simply wanted to bleed.

***

My eyes were drawn to Rocco as he ate ravioli opposite me across the dining table. He was totally absorbed in his meal like I'd placed a slice of heaven itself on his plate. He ate with slow, deliberate movements, chewed, swallowed, smiled. Not a full smile, just enough to tell me how much he was enjoying his meal. A quiet satisfaction filled me at seeing him appreciate my food.

When he was done, he leaned back in his chair and tipped his head to look out of the window to his right. I continued to watch him, my food untouched, a fork clutched in my hand. He fascinated me and I'd finally figured out why. Rocco Romero was freedom embodied. His wildness had never been tamed by anyone. He owned the world because he didn't bow to its rules. Even his father didn't bend him to his will the way mine did. Rocco was only here instead of anywhere else in the world because he loved his family. He either chose to do as they asked or he didn't.

But there was something missing in him which I couldn't place my finger on. An agitation crawling under his skin, an unfilled space he was pawing at, contemplating. The way his gaze was always drawn to the sky as if he expected to find his answer there. Rocco was definitely searching for something and some strange, alien part of me wanted to find it for him.

"More wine?" Frankie asked as he returned from the kitchen. "I would offer you the finest of the Romero stock but someone smashed the whole lot." He dropped down beside me with a smirk and I couldn't fight the smile that pulled at my mouth in return. He filled my glass then did the same for Rocco and Enzo – even though Enzo had fallen asleep in his chair with his hand on his belly.

"If you keep feeding us this well, they'll start calling us the fratelli grassi." *Fat brothers.*

Rocco smirked, reaching his arms above his head and interlocking his fingers as he stretched. I couldn't imagine him looking anything other than sculpted from stone, especially when his shirt rode up and my gaze dipped to the tempting trail of hair that led beneath his waistband. *Lord have mercy on my hormones.*

The front door opened and Enzo woke up with a snore, whipping his hunting knife out of his belt. "Whasat?"

"Shit," Rocco hissed then rose to his feet.

Frankie didn't seem to know what to do with himself, settling for perching on the table and facing the door.

Footsteps thumped into the room and I turned to look at whoever had arrived. Martello stood there in a fine suit with a dark-haired woman at his side. She was beautiful, but her eyes were as sharp as razors as they fell on me. A step behind her was a skinny guy with a scar across his nose. Something in his gaze made me more afraid of him than I was of any of the other Romeros around me at that moment. Like he was missing a vital piece of humanity.

"How cosy this is," Martello said with a sneer.

"We were just eating," Enzo said lazily.

"I see that," Martello replied sharply, his eyes drilling into my head.

The woman drifted further into the room, dipping her head to kiss Frankie on each cheek. She moved around, greeting all the boys in the same way, surveying them like she was waiting to be impressed.

"It's so good to see you boys," she said lightly, gesturing for Rocco to pull out a chair for her.

He did so, but his shoulders were rigid like it caused him some discomfort to do it. She dropped into it, eyeing me across the table with hatred seeping from the pores of her flawless skin.

"Why is it sitting at the table?" she asked dismissively, not looking me in the eye.

I gazed right at her, trying to work out if I knew who she was. I had a hundred Romero names stashed in my mind, but I didn't always have faces attached to them.

"She has to eat somewhere, Aunt Clarissa," Frankie said and my heart squeezed in recognition.

Clarissa Romero was a ruthless witch who had a fondness for slitting throats. She'd killed two of my distant cousins in cold blood just months ago and the brutality of their deaths had left a chill in my bones ever since. But what was worse than that was her strange son, Guido, who must have been the guy lurking by Martello. He was a sick bastard, often used to torture information out of their enemies. If a Calabresi ended up in Guido's hands, they were in for utter hell before he let them die.

"Come sit down, Papa," Enzo said.

"I will not sit at a table with a Calabresi and it insults me that my sons would do so. Is she sleeping in one of your Mamma's beds too?" he snarled and fear daggered into my heart.

I looked to Rocco but he avoided my eye.

"Of course not," he said simply.

"She sleeps tied up in the living room," Frankie added quickly.

Martello tutted. "The cellar is the only place fit for the spawn of Guiseppe Calabresi."

"It's too cold," Rocco said firmly. "She'd be dead within a day."

"Nonsense," Martello snapped then marched from the room, leaving my heart rattling in my chest.

"I'll go calm him down," Clarissa said before rising and heading across the room. She lingered in the doorway, glancing back at the brothers. "I suggest you take that little whore where your father wants her before he returns." She disappeared and I shifted in my seat, my hands curling around the edge of the table as acid built in my throat.

Guido moved deeper into the room, dropping down into the seat next to me and sweeping a hand into his unruly hair. He moved in far too close to me, taking a breath and disgust rippled through to my core.

Rocco rested his hands on the table, glaring at Guido with intent.

"So just between us guys, what's she like?" Guido asked, speaking as if I wasn't there. "That tight little virgin pussy must have been fun to break in."

My stomach turned into an icy ball and bile pushed against my tongue.

"We haven't fucking raped her because we're not the scum of the earth," Rocco said simply, but there was a deadly undercurrent to his tone and his knuckles were turning white as he curled them into fists.

"Hey now, no one said anything about rape," Guido said with a low chuckle. "I bet she was gagging for it."

His hand immediately landed on my knee under the table and I jerked it violently, slamming it into the wood above.

"Ah!" he yelped, wrenching his fingers back. In the next second, he slapped me so hard my head wheeled sideways. Pain flared up my cheek and my hair fell over my face as I breathed heavily through the shock of it.

A crash sounded and a tremor ran through my seat. I pushed my hair back, finding Rocco pinning Guido to the floor.

"She's not yours to touch," Rocco spat in his face and Guido's eyes lit with a manic gleam.

"Share," he begged. "I'm your cousin."

"More's the pity," Rocco hissed, getting up and looking to me with an ache in his eyes.

He took my arm, guiding me to my feet while Guido scrambled upright and Frankie and Enzo looked to their cousin in rage. Both of them were on their feet and I barely had a second to process that all three Romeros had jumped to my aid.

"Cellar," Rocco announced and panic swept through me.

"No," I gasped as he hauled me out of the room. I stared up at him, desperate for him to meet my gaze, but he just clenched his jaw and glared forward as he dragged me into the hallway.

"Don't do this," I gasped as he shoved me through the cellar door and slammed it in my face. "Rocco!" I screamed, hammering my fists on the wood as the cold enveloped me.

"What a good boy," Clarissa's voice reached me beyond the wood. "Martello will be pleased."

Rocco grunted and their footsteps carried away. I pressed my forehead to the door, my heart seizing in my chest.

Whatever bond I'd thought Rocco and I had shared for half a second had been a lie. He didn't care about me. He cared about his family. He cared about controlling me in front of them. About owning me. He might have jumped to my rescue, but only because Guido had laid on a hand on his toy. I was just a doll in his playhouse, but I wasn't going to fall for the game anymore.

I sat down on the top step, curling my knees to my chest and resting my head back against the wall. I hugged my arms around myself, shutting my eyes and trying to exorcise the fear that was possessing me like a demon.

I had to be strong. Had to keep surviving until Nicoli found me. He'd tear them apart when he arrived. And when that happened, I had to be in one piece. Not broken or weakened.

I would be *me* when I walked out of this house. If anything changed at all, it would be that I was stronger.

The idea of Nicoli killing Rocco planted a dark seed into my head that grew shoots and stole my attention. Because the possibility of that happening made me ache. Like some part of me was attached to a Romero. A guy who had tried to kill me in the past and failed. I was his nightmare and he was mine. I could never let that change. I didn't want it to.

The door opened a crack and my lips parted in hope. I got to my feet, wondering if Rocco had changed his mind after all.

I pushed against the wood and the door swung wider. As I stepped tentatively into the hall, a hand slammed over my mouth and panic gripped my heart.

I was dragged back into the cellar, the door snapping shut behind us.

Guido smelt like stale cigarettes and sweat, his greasy palm pressing forcefully against my mouth and making me gag.

He held a knife to my neck as he guided me down to the bottom of the stairs, slowly releasing his hand from my mouth.

"If you scream, I'll gut you," he whispered in my ear and I shuddered in terror.

The sound of his zipper rolling down filled me with a sick kind of dread. I lurched forward but he pressed the knife to my throat more firmly and I was forced to retreat as it nicked my skin.

He ground himself against my ass and my back arched in disgust.

"Touch me and you'll regret it," I snarled, filling my voice with venom. Royce had taught me tactics to deal with rapists and my body was itching to employ them the second he let his guard down. *But what if he doesn't??*

Guido sniffed my hair as his hand slid around my waist and his fingers grazed my waistband. "Now let's find out why Rocco's so protective of his little Calabresi whore, hm?"

Rocco

"**I** don't understand why she wasn't chained down there in the first place," Papa growled on the other side of the door and I steeled myself to face him.

"She *was*," I said in a firm voice as I stepped into the living room where he'd positioned himself in a chair by the fire. Aunt Clarissa was sitting close to him on the end of the couch while Guido was nowhere to be seen. "And then we found her half dead down there because it got too cold. A dead hostage won't hold much sway over Giuseppe, will she?"

Papa's lip curled back in distaste, but the fact that he wasn't openly contradicting me told me he reluctantly agreed with my reasoning.

"And why exactly was she sitting with you in the kitchen, eating food like a house guest?" Aunt Clarissa asked, her nose upturned like she smelled something bad. Though that was the way her face always looked so it was hard to say if she was doing it intentionally now or not.

"We thought it made sense to make her work for her food," Frankie piped up. "We make her cook and clean the place for us."

"It's not like we can bring a maid up to the house while she's here, is it?" Enzo added in a bored tone as he dropped down onto the other end of the couch to our aunt and leaned back casually, looking like he was half tempted to take a nap.

"Well I wouldn't touch something cooked by a *Calabresi,*" Aunt Clarissa said with a shudder.

"Then you might just go hungry during your stay, dear aunt," I said as I took the other armchair and leaned forward with my elbows on my knees. "Because we can't cook for shit and we thought it better to make a slave of our hostage than to run around after her ourselves. Why should we have to make meals for her or clean up after her if we can put her to work instead?"

"And why exactly does she agree to do these things?" Papa asked.

"Because I punish her if she doesn't," I replied darkly.

The curt nod he gave in response was the closest thing I was going to get to praise on the way I was dealing with this, but I'd take it.

"And she really doesn't like the way you punish her, does she, Rocco?" Enzo asked with a dirty as fuck look on his face which Papa and Aunt Clarissa couldn't see.

I rolled my eyes without bothering to answer him.

I glanced around, wondering where Guido had gotten to. If he wasn't family, I would have killed that fucker a long time ago. I was all for destroying our enemies, but the things he enjoyed doing to people went way beyond the call of what was necessary.

Worse than that, he'd somehow decided that I was his rival. He went out of his way to try and compete with me and take things that were mine. I hardly even tolerated him at large functions with plenty of people to put between us. Being in a group this small with him present was about as fun as the idea of swallowing a cup of nails and shitting them out again.

In fact, if someone gave me the nails right now I'd be tempted to take that trade.

One time he pushed me far enough to make me snap. I'd beaten him half to death with a length of pipe and given him that scar on his mangled nose. Of course, Papa had dragged me off of him before I could finish him off and because Guido was the most fucked up creature I knew, his infatuation with me had only increased following his near death at my hand.

I'd changed my cell number three times before giving up and blocking him. And I didn't answer unknown numbers anymore either. A few years of that treatment had gone a long way to making him back off, but I still preferred to avoid his company when I could.

"I still think she'd be best kept in the cellar when she's not working," Aunt Clarissa said, inspecting her nails.

My hackles rose at the challenge she presented me with. I didn't like to be told how to keep my hostage and I was more than happy with our current situation which involved Sloan's ass pressed right up against my dick all night. Not that I could say that out loud, but why the fuck was she coming up here getting involved in my business anyway? As Papa's eldest son I was his second in command, though as his only sibling, Clarissa liked to think of herself as equal to me.

My gaze shifted to Papa as I wondered whether he might tell her to leave my hostage to me, but he seemed to be more interested in something on his cellphone than the turn of our conversation.

"I'm not going to let her freeze," I snapped. "She'll be worthless if she's dead."

"Just leave her down there between work. Bring her up often enough for her toes and fingers to survive and there won't be an issue," Papa said, his voice disinterested but final.

I clucked my tongue to let him know I was pissed, but didn't speak out against him. Not on this. I wasn't going to stand against my father in defence of a Calabresi. It would only make him take further action against Sloan anyway. He might even assign someone else to watch over her. Someone like Guido.

At that thought I looked around again for our unwelcome cousin and frowned as I didn't spot him.

"Where's Guido?" I asked, sitting up straighter as a prickle of warning ran down my spine.

It didn't take that long to take a piss and I had the horrible feeling he wasn't having a shit either.

"Oh you know Guidy," Aunt Clarissa chuckled. "He's always up to something."

Frankie caught my eye with a startled expression and I leapt to my feet as panic gripped me.

Enzo got up too and my brothers strode after me as I stormed from the room.

"Guido!" I yelled, my heart pounding unevenly as a feeling of pure dread slid through my veins.

He didn't answer, but he didn't have to. I made it out into the hall and I could see the cellar door ajar from here. I'd left the fucking key in the lock and it still sat there taunting me as I broke into a run.

The lights were on as I raced to the top of the stairs and muffled grunts and whimpers came from somewhere within the depths of the cellar.

I spotted him crouched over Sloan as he pinned her to the ground with a blade pressed to her throat.

A roar of pure rage left me as I leapt off of the stairs and raced towards him.

Guido looked around, the blade moving an inch away from Sloan's neck as he spotted me and a fucked up psycho smile lit his face.

I collided with him a second later, knocking him clean off of her and tumbling across the cold ground with him.

Guido scrambled away from me as I threw a punch into his side.

"C'mon Rocco," he begged. "Share her with me!" He lurched towards her again and Sloan screamed as he caught her arm.

My heart leapt with fear for her and I grabbed Guido by the scruff of his neck, heaving him backwards with all my might and launching him across the room.

He hit one of the wine racks with a cry of pain and the wood splintered around him and he fell to the floor in a heap.

Sloan's big brown eyes locked with mine and for a moment I could have sworn relief spilled through her gaze. She was looking at me like I was her saviour instead of her captor. Like I was the kind of man who might protect her from the worst things in this world and not one of the monsters who inhabited it. And for some reason, I found myself wanting to be that man for her. I wanted to ride in wearing my shining armour on a gallant steed and beat the living shit out of the motherfucker who'd dared to lay his hands on her. It might not have been poetic but it was pure, animalistic nature. I was a beast unlike any other in the depths of the woods and she was *mine*. I'd sooner tear the flesh from my own skin than let Guido have her.

I assessed her briefly, hoping I hadn't been too late to stop him from doing his worst. Her shirt was torn, her bottom lip split and her fly undone.

I saw red. Rage unlike anything I'd ever felt before filled me as I turned my back on her and violence burned like red hot magma through my veins.

I'd always hated this piece of shit. He had no code, no morals, no fucking respect for the laws we created. And now he'd gone too fucking far. He'd gone against me, flouted the rules I'd laid out in *my* house. And worse than that, he'd laid a hand on Sloan. She was my hostage. *Mine*. And he was about to find out what happened to people who tried to take my things.

I ran at him as he made it back to his feet and he raised his knife defensively just before I collided with him.

Burning pain seared across my ribs but I ignored it in favour of dolling out punishment on this piece of shit. I punched him squarely in the face, slamming my knuckles into him three times before he cut me again with that fucking knife, this time catching me across my bicep.

"Fight like a man, stronzo!" I roared at him, rearing my head back and driving my forehead down straight against the bridge of his nose.

Something cracked, blood poured and Guido staggered back, hitting the shattered wine rack behind him.

I didn't let the space between us last, closing the gap again and grabbing his wrist before he could cut me a third time.

I caught his elbow with my other hand and twisted so hard that he shrieked in pain, the knife falling from his grip with a clatter.

I shoved him away from me so that he fell back to the ground again.

I stalked after him, blood dripping from my knuckles as he shuffled backwards on his elbows.

"Alright, cugino," he gasped through the blood that poured from his shattered nose into his mouth. "She's yours. Point taken."

I snarled at him as he scrambled to his feet, my gaze narrowing on his throat as I envisioned myself squeezing the pathetic life right out of him.

There was a ringing in my ears as the bloodlust in me sharpened, my whole being locked in on the desire to rid the world of this fucking cretin once and for all.

"That's enough, Rocco!" Papa barked just as I reached my prey.

I almost ignored him. Almost took the final step to finish what I'd started, but a sharp inhale made me pause.

I stilled, glancing over my shoulder to the corner where Sloan had backed up. She was clutching her torn shirt over her chest and wielding Guido's blade before her like she thought she might fight her way past all four Romero men with it alone.

"Oh, my baby!" Aunt Clarissa gasped as she raced down the stairs, rushing past my brothers to retrieve her miserable son.

My lip peeled back as she ushered him out of the cellar and my blood finally began to cool.

"Sort out this mess and meet me back upstairs once you're decent," Papa muttered like I was boring him, but the slight upturn at the corner of his mouth told me he was secretly pleased. He'd wanted Guido put in his place for a long time, but without an excuse to punish him it was hard to do so. Now that I'd beaten him within an inch of his life for a second time, he might remember what it was like to invoke the wrath of a true Romero.

Papa turned and headed out of the cellar after my aunt and Guido and I was left with Sloan and my brothers.

Silence hung heavily as I slowly turned to look at her.

"We'll go get her some clothes," Frankie muttered. "You get that knife off of her."

"Don't forget who just saved your virtue, carina," Enzo added to Sloan as he followed Frankie out.

They closed the door behind them and suddenly we were alone.

I stalked toward her slowly. A wolf with a doe in his gaze.

"Are you going to stab me for saving your life, bella?" I asked as I closed in on her.

She held the knife like she knew what she was doing with it and the steely look in her eye said she just might use it.

I spread my arms before me as I drew closer still.

"If you're going to do it then aim for my heart," I said seriously. "Because you won't get more than one swing at me before I'm on you."

Her gaze slid from my eyes to my chest and her bottom lip quivered just a little. It looked like someone had taught her how to defend herself, but I was willing to bet she'd never sunk a blade into anyone before.

"You'll need to throw your strength into the blow," I told her. "There's a lot of flesh and bone to get through if you want me dead in one strike."

She sucked in a breath as I made it within a few paces of her.

I eyed the blade in her grip which was already stained with my blood. It was steady. She wouldn't miss if she chose to strike at me.

I widened my hands and stepped close enough for her to do it. I didn't make any move to defend myself and she held her breath as her gaze locked with mine.

"What's it to be, bella?" I asked darkly.

The moment hung between us endlessly as her eyes stared into mine and a dark energy coiled between us. It was like I was being pulled towards her and warned away in the same breath and the uncertainty of it froze me entirely.

Sloan released a heavy breath and the blade fell from her hand.

It hit the floor with a clatter and I raised an eyebrow at her as she lifted her chin.

"Tell me I'm right to think I got here before he managed to do anything to you," I breathed.

Sloan wet her lips with her tongue and the movement drew my gaze to her mouth as I stepped closer again.

"You did," she confirmed and relief spilled through me, easing the tension in my muscles. "He stabbed you," she added, reaching out to catch the hem of my shirt and push it up so that she could get a look at what he'd done.

The cut along my ribs stung but wasn't deep. Frankie would stitch it for me if it needed it, but I wasn't sure it would.

Her fingers were cold against my skin as she slid the material higher. It was wet with blood. His, mine, maybe even some of hers.

I stayed still as she inspected me, her touch lingering on my flesh like she knew she shouldn't be doing this. Like she knew she shouldn't care. But for the strangest reason, it seemed like she did.

I flinched minutely as she found the cut along my ribs and she looked up at me in surprise.

"Does it hurt?" she asked, her voice breathy like the idea of that was getting her off.

"Do you like that I'm bleeding for you?" I asked her, watching as her pupils dilated at that suggestion. "Does my pain please you?"

She inched her fingers up again, pressing down on the wound just enough to raise a grunt of discomfort from me and heat flared in her eyes.

"You're a fucked up little thing, just like me," I breathed, reaching out to her unbuttoned fly and dipping my fingers between the parted zipper.

Her breath hitched as my fingers slid across her panties for a moment and I slowly caught the zipper in my hand, drawing it back up again as the hint of a moan slid between her lips.

The door unlocked above us and I slowly buttoned her jeans for her, my fingers lingering beneath her waistband for a long moment as footsteps sounded on the stairs behind us.

I withdrew my hand and a shiver danced across her flesh. I dropped down to one knee before her and retrieved the blade as her gaze stayed fixed on me.

Frankie made it to the bottom of the stairs with a clean shirt, sweatpants and a thick sweater for her which she accepted with a word of thanks.

I turned and walked away from her as Frankie started gathering lumps of the broken wine rack into a black sack.

I didn't look back as I made it up the stairs and headed out into the main house. Enzo was lingering in the hall and he caught my eye as I approached.

"If she doesn't fall in love with you after that, then she never will," he joked and I forced a smirk onto my face.

"All part of the plan," I replied as I headed past him so that I could go and wash the blood from my flesh.

I frowned to myself as I headed up the stairs, because the strangest thing was, that that had been a lie.

Sloan

None of them had noticed, not even Rocco.

I had Guido's phone stashed in the back of my jeans. It had fallen from his pocket when Rocco had tackled him to the ground. I'd grabbed it before anyone could notice, but now I was frozen in place, still reeling from what had happened.

I could still feel Rocco's hands on me, his heated touch having wiped away the chilled touch of his cousin. Where my flesh had screamed, now it purred. Like it wanted more of Rocco's skin against it. But that was so wrong. So twisted. And I started to wonder if he'd been right. Maybe I was as fucked up as he was.

Something about Rocco unleashed the crazy in me. A secret girl who'd been living in my flesh all these years, yearning to be freed. But family customs and my father's firm hand had kept her down. Even in Italy I hadn't felt this wild. For a second I'd shared a taste of the animalistic spirit within him and I was gasping for more.

I shook my head, taking out the phone, unable to believe I'd hesitated so long in using it. The only number I knew by heart was home so I called my family's house. My father. The mere thought of hearing his voice sent a mixture of emotions rushing through me. He'd be out for blood. He'd have mobilised all of our family in looking for me. How would he react when he heard me now?

My heart drummed and my mouth dried up. I'd give him everything I had to help him find me, but something in my gut was terrified of that too. Of this house coming under attack without the Romero brothers having any warning. A whole army of Calabresis would come. They'd tear them apart with bullets. *Why does that make me feel like I wanna hurl??*

Before I could do anything batshit crazy like hang up, a click sounded on the other end. "Calabresi household."

I inhaled sharply. It wasn't my father.

"Nicoli?" I gasped, whispering even though I doubted anyone could hear me upstairs. Adrenaline washed through my veins and brought its friend panic along for the ride. *I can get out of here!*

"Sloan?" he demanded, his voice a razor slicing against my ear. "Tell me it's you."

"It's me." The line went fuzzy and I didn't hear his next words.

"Sloan?" his voice came through the static again, demanding, desperate. I frantically checked the signal, finding it low.

"Can you hear me now?" I asked hopefully, my heart ticking like a time bomb in my ears. "I need you to come find me."

"Where are y-" static engulfed his voice again and anxiety spiked through my chest.

I started garbling off everything I knew about the household, figuring he'd at least hear some of it. I told him about the snow, the mountains, the way the manor looked. I didn't know how much he caught but he said the odd word from time to time (*yes, dammit, fuckers*).

"I'm coming for you. You're mine, Sloan, no one can keep you from me," he said fiercely, passionately. My heart clenched like it was in an iron fist as I struggled for what to say. The craziest thing was, my gut reaction was to scream, *I'm not yours!*

I shoved that thought away, but another crazy one took its place. *Come find me, but please don't kill the Romeros.*

But how could I even think that? Why did I care? I should have wanted them ripped apart for bringing me here. Rocco most of all.

The cellar door opened and fear blazed through me. With fast fingers, I deleted the call history, locked the phone and tossed it away from me. It skidded under a wine rack and I tried to calm my thrashing heart as Rocco appeared a second later. If he figured out I'd had that phone, that I'd called Nicoli, he'd either move me or bring a hundred men to the house to face the Calabresis. Maybe both. And I couldn't let either of those things happen.

I frowned at the bundle of blankets in Rocco's arms, my heart softening like heated wax with every step he took closer. He knelt down, placing them at my feet with a hot water bottle on top of them. There was a thick pair of socks and one of his sweaters too.

"You have to stay here for now," he said, looking like he wasn't happy about that fact.

Does he actually give a damn that I'm down here?

I surveyed his expression, hunting for the joke. Waiting for him to grab the bundle and laugh while walking away.

"Where's my fucking phone?!" Guido's voice shook the floorboards upstairs and my blood chilled.

Rocco locked eyes with me and I gasped as he lunged forward, patting me down as he hunted for it. His hand slipped between my thighs and I smacked him across the face.

"I don't have it!" I snarled.

His eyes narrowed with disbelief and he took out his own phone, making a call and glaring at me the entire time as he sat back on his heels.

A jingling ringtone sounded from underneath the wine rack and I swallowed firmly as he moved over to it and fished it out. He tapped the screen, no doubt checking the call history before his eyes slid to me in suspicion. He ran his tongue over his teeth then stuffed the phone in his pocket.

"I've got it!" Rocco called upstairs and I wet my desert dry mouth as he moved to kneel before me once more.

I reached for the hot water bottle so I had something to occupy myself with, finding it deliciously warm.

He lifted a hand and I flinched on instinct, my guard up after my encounter with his despicable cousin. I knew what Rocco had done for me, but I was also reminded of exactly why I hated the Romeros. Guido had killed members of my family. Rocco had too. There wasn't just a line drawn in the sand between us, there was a chasm of sharp objects stained with our people's blood.

He retracted his hand and I wondered why he'd been planning on touching me at all. He released a long breath as discomfort coloured his features.

"I'm gonna sleep outside the door so no one can come down here without my permission," he said at last.

"Why?" I breathed and silence stretched between us.

Rocco grunted. "I don't care for rapists. And I certainly don't care for people laying a hand on things that belong to me."

"I'm not yours," I hissed, my spine prickling at his words, especially as I'd just heard them from Nicoli two minutes ago.

"I caught and caged you," he said with a smirk that was almost teasing. "You're mine fair and square."

"I'm not some wild horse you wrangled," I said in disgust. "You can't own people."

"Not true. To own a horse, I'd have to earn its trust. To own you, I'd have to earn your heart." His eyes blazed and heat seeped through my skin at the intensity of his gaze.

I leaned toward him, so close we were almost nose to nose. His eyes dipped to my mouth and I knew what he wanted, what he'd taken twice now and hadn't deserved.

"I'd cut it out first," I whispered, my lips twisting up at the corners in a dark smile.

"You don't have to hand it to me fresh and bloody, principessa, but thanks for the offer."

I tutted, leaning back but he caught hold of my top, dragging me close again as he fisted his hand in it.

"How long are you going to keep lying to yourself about how I make you feel?"

"I don't need to lie to myself, Rocco. I know exactly how you make me feel. You make my skin crawl and my blood curdle." My heart betrayed me, pounding so fast I feared he'd hear it drumming out my secrets in Morse code.

My mamma had always told me not to trust boys with pretty faces and carnivorous smiles. And Rocco was a beautiful apex predator. He could have any woman in the world and maybe it was starting to bother him that I didn't fall under the same spell. Maybe he was trying to prove something to himself. But if he really thought he could win the heart of a girl he'd kidnapped, he must have been even more of a cocky asshole than I'd realised. Which seemed like a stretch as his ego was already bigger than this house.

I'd never let him have me. But that wild girl inside me had her own desires. Her own wicked secrets.

She'd let him have her and she'd claim him right back in the process.

I blinked firmly, realising I hadn't done so for a long time. Rocco was smiling like he'd heard every one of my thoughts and I cleared my throat, pulling the blankets up around me and stuffing the hot water bottle beneath them.

"I don't believe you," he said in a purr. "You moan about my cock in your sleep."

"I do not," I replied, my upper lip peeling back. "And if I did it would be about ripping it off."

"I don't think so. You've tried to give me sleep blowjobs on more than one occasion. I let you suck my thumb once."

I tutted as he laughed. "You're an animal."

I waited for him to leave, but he didn't. He moved onto all fours, prowling forward like a lion and resting his hands either side of me on the wall. He gnashed his teeth together in my face, making me flinch as the snap filled my ears. His breath was hot on my skin and the smell of him surrounded me, bathing me in the scent of pine and deadly temptation.

"I can be an animal if that's what you want me to be." He snorted like a pig and a surprised laugh escaped me as I tipped my head back to create some distance between us.

He leaned away with a satisfied grin and tapped me on the nose. "Get some sleep."

"Go take your crazy pills," I shot back, battling to erase the smile from my lips.

"Crazy is just another word for interesting," he said lightly. "How boring the world would be if I knew I wasn't going to put on a tutu tomorrow and take up ballet."

"Is that your plan? Because I'm not sure they make tutus in bear sizes," I said dryly.

"That's your problem, bella. Maybe I will, maybe I won't. Plans are for normal people and I get the feeling you're anything but normal. They just made you think you are." He winked and headed up the stairs to exit the cellar.

I was left in the aftermath of his words, worrying about how much sense they made to me. The four walls of my mind had been built by my father's hands, but what had he kept out?

I tried to remember a time before I'd felt caged and my mother's face swam into my mind. I'd only been seven when she'd died, but every memory I had of her was precious. Before she'd taken her life, all I could remember was being happy. Having fun with her in the park, spending hours dancing and singing and playing make believe. She'd been my best friend. My only friend. And when she left me, the world became smaller.

Mamma hadn't let me see the bars which surrounded us, she'd sheltered me from the truth; that we were just two birds in a cage, singing at a sunset painted on a wall.

Had she been unhappy all those years and never let me see it? Had my father done all he could do to make sure she was okay? Or had he baited and trapped her, cast her in irons until she couldn't stand another moment on this earth? Even for my sake.

My soul ached with all the unanswered questions. I cherished every memory with her so deeply, but her death had tainted them. Because now I wondered whether each smile she gave me had been a beautiful lie. And whether I could have done more to soothe the pain which must have lived in her.

It was clear now that Papa had tried to force us into his idea of perfect. Quiet, subdued, compliant…

I wondered if Rocco's father had ever tried to tame him and a quiet part of me hoped he hadn't been moulded in any way. That this was his true, barbaric nature. And I envied that in a way I couldn't even begin to understand.

Rocco

I woke early with a crick in my neck and goosebumps lining my flesh from the breeze which made its way out from beneath the cellar door. Guido seemed to have learned his lesson at least. There hadn't been a peep from him during the night and it didn't seem like I'd really needed to sleep on the floor outside her door after all, but fuck it. I wasn't going to take the risk.

Sloan might be our prisoner but I wasn't going to hand her over to an animal like Guido to toy with.

I stood and stretched my aching limbs out as I retrieved the comforter I'd slept on from the floor and took it back into the living room.

I stirred the fire, adding extra logs and glanced at the clock. It was a quarter to six. No one else was up yet and they likely wouldn't be for a few hours.

I headed into the kitchen and made two steaming mugs of coffee and stacked a plate with toast before depositing that in the living room too.

I pulled the cellar key from my pocket and moved to unlock it, releasing a low breath as the door swung open.

I took my time strolling down the stairs and flipped the light on.

Sloan was sleeping in the nest of blankets I'd given her, but I could still see shivers wracking through her flesh. My breath rose before me as I closed in on her and I lifted her into my arms without bothering to wake her first.

Sloan gasped as she found herself lifted from her bed, her body tensing as she began to fight for a moment before her gaze fixed on me.

"Oh," she breathed in relief and the corner of my mouth twitched with the promise of a smile I wouldn't release.

"Oh," I agreed, holding her close to my chest as we started up the stairs.

She wrapped her arms around my neck, drawing me closer so that the sweet scent of her washed over me, tempting me with the desire to take a taste.

"Did you really sleep out here on the floor?" she breathed as we made it into the hallway.

"It was good for my back," I deadpanned as I elbowed my way into the living room and the warmth of the fire washed over us. But it held nothing to the warmth that burned through me as Sloan leaned close and pressed a kiss to my cheek.

"Thank you," she breathed, so low that I could hardly hear the words. But there they were.

I cleared my throat and sat her down in the armchair by the fire. "I wouldn't be too grateful, I still might have to slit your pretty throat when all is said and done, bella," I warned.

A frown pulled at her brow in response to that threat, but it wasn't accompanied by any signs that she feared I'd truly do it like she should. Maybe she didn't believe me. Or maybe she just didn't hold her life in high enough esteem.

I took a blanket from the back of the couch and passed it to her, followed by the mug of coffee and she stared at me like I'd had a personality transplant.

I dropped into the chair beside hers and eyed her as she drank her coffee and ate her toast, watching the way she swiped her tongue across those plump lips and imagining all the unspeakable things I'd like to do to her mouth.

"I didn't think I could hate anyone more than I hate you," she breathed as the silence stretched between us.

A dark laugh escaped me and I leaned forward in my chair, moving so close to her that she had no choice but to turn and look at me.

"I don't think that's true, bella," I said in a low voice.

"You don't think I hate you?" she asked, arching an eyebrow at me like I was insane.

"I think you hate me so hard, it eats you up. You hate me so hard you dream about me and all the awful things I might do to you. But I think that in those dreams you don't actually hate it so much when I do them…"

Her lips parted and I shifted closer to her, our breath mingling and the memory of the way I'd kissed her outside the hardware store stirring the air between us.

"You're deluded," Sloan breathed, but she hadn't moved back.

"Is that so?" I mocked, moving closer again.

I reached out slowly, pushing my fingertips into her hair and skimming them along the side of her face as she watched me.

"Is this what you want, bella? Do you want to find a soft side to me hiding somewhere beneath the mask you see?"

"You don't have a soft side, Rocco," she growled and the heat in her voice was enough to make me hard for her already. When she did bow to the desire she felt for me, I was going to be so far past ready for her that she wouldn't know what hit her.

I smiled darkly, my fingers pushing deeper into her hair until I twisted it around and my grip tightened.

"You don't want me to, do you?" I breathed in surprise. "It's not soft you're after, is it?"

She didn't respond but I could have sworn the look in her eyes was something of a plea in itself. If we were in any other situation I'd have taken her then, shown her exactly what it was she was aching to find out. But as it was, it was going to have to come from her. She was my captive, my property, *my* Sloan. But if she wanted to find out the depths of what that could mean for her, she'd have to ask for it. And when she did, I'd take hold of her so hard she'd never even think about escaping again.

I fisted my hand in her hair, yanking sharply and she moaned in a way that was so damn sexual, it was a wonder I didn't just rip her sweatpants off and fuck her on her knees right here and now in front of the fire.

"You see, baby," I purred, painting a line across those full lips with my other thumb as I kept her immobilised by my hold on her hair. "I can make you sin so bad you won't know which way is up."

Her lips parted and there was something of a dare in her eyes that set my pulse racing. She wanted to know what that felt like, wanted to feel every inch of me taking her whole body hostage. I knew it. She knew it. All she had to do was speak the dare on her lips and I'd do it.

"Fuck you," she hissed, a fire burning in her gaze.

"Oh, you will," I purred.

A thud came from upstairs before she could answer and I cursed internally as I released my grip on her, leaning back in my chair as if nothing had happened.

But as Sloan's gaze slid to the hard ridge of my cock straining against my sweatpants, we both knew there was no denying it.

She bit that full lip I'd been daydreaming about and I watched the rise and fall of her perfect tits beneath the oversized sweater she was wearing as she damn near panted for me.

"Come on, Cinderella," I growled as I got to my feet. "Time to go back to the cellar."

Sloan glanced up at the ceiling as another thud came from upstairs and by the fear that lit her gaze, I was fairly sure she was just pleased to be getting away from Guido.

She walked ahead of me to the cellar door and I paused in the hallway, grabbing Mamma's fur coat from the hook where Sloan had left it after our trip into town the other day and handing it to her.

"Thank you," Sloan breathed as she accepted it, her gaze trailing over me like she couldn't work out what to think. But that was the second time she'd thanked me this morning. She was already falling for me even if she hadn't admitted it to herself yet.

She hesitated at the top of the cellar stairs, her breath rising before her.

I stepped close behind her, my front pressing to her back as I leaned forward to flick the lights on and her ass was driven up against the urgent swell of my dick. She should have stepped away instantly but she leaned back, grinding against me in a way that had my balls aching as she turned her head to speak to me.

"Is Guido staying here much longer?" she breathed, turning those wide eyes on me and making me want to fuck the innocence right out of her.

"Hopefully not," I replied. Papa had been intentionally vague about their plans last night so I wasn't entirely sure what was going on. "While you wait for them to leave, you can daydream about all the naughty things you want to do to me once you're back sleeping in my bed again."

"You wish, Rocco," she said hollowly, pushing her ass against me one last time before walking away down the stairs as if she wasn't aching for me to fuck her just as hard as I was aching to do it.

I watched her walk away from me and growled my frustration loud enough for her to hear before closing the door with a hard snap.

I locked it and double checked it before turning and walking back to the living room. Frankie appeared yawning and shirtless a moment later and I left him to keep an eye on Sloan's door as I headed up for a cold shower. Or possibly to jerk off. Maybe even both. Because if I didn't end up nine inches deep in Sloan Calabresi soon, this frustration was gonna eat me alive.

***

"Nicoli Vitoli, didn't heed your warning," Papa said casually as he finished his lunch.

We'd brought Sloan up to cook for us and my stomach sang happily as I filled it with what may have been the best spaghetti I'd ever eaten.

She was back down in the cellar again now that she'd finished cleaning the kitchen after herself. Her own lunch had consisted of two slices of bread and butter and a banana that was on the turn - thanks to Aunt Clarissa's input. I was the asshole who had given her dog food for dinner on her first night here, but I still didn't think it was necessary to make her cook for us and not let her eat it too. Not that I'd voiced that opinion.

Guido sat at the end of the table. His broken nose re-set by his mother but the two blazing black eyes I'd given him a clear testament to which Romero had come out on top between us.

I flexed my fingers, relishing the pain of my split knuckles as I remembered pounding them into his flesh.

"The Calabresi Principessa is going to have to pay the price you promised," Papa added.

"You want me to punish her now?" I offered, my mind considering the twisted things I could subject her to in payment for her fiancé's failings. I wanted to watch her heart break as she realised his hunt for her had caused this. I wanted to watch her faith in him shatter as she found out what was done to her in payment for his crimes.

"Not yet," Papa said with a cruel smile. "I think we're going to lay a trap for the Calabresi wannabe. Nicoli Vitoli is about to find out what happens when he raids a Romero property and finds the owners at home."

I pushed to my feet with my brothers either side of me, just as keen to get to work.

"Are we leaving soon?" Enzo asked enthusiastically and I couldn't help but laugh.

"I assumed you'd be staying here, Rocco," Papa said as he stood too. "Or would you rather Guido stay to watch your captive?"

Guido practically ejaculated in his pants at that suggestion and I swear saliva even ran down his chin.

I snarled at him, baring my teeth to remind him of the beast that lay beneath my flesh and just who Sloan belonged to.

"That fucker isn't going to stay here with her," I growled.

"Well unless one of your brothers wishes to volunteer for the role, I guess it'll be you then," Papa said with a shrug.

"Or we just do ourselves out of the bother of keeping the wretch and kill her now. That will send the message loud and clear," Aunt Clarissa suggested as she plucked a piece of lint from her sleeve.

My fist clenched hard enough to cause the skin on my knuckles to split open again and I opened my mouth to bite her fucking head off, but Frankie interrupted before I could.

"Think about it, Rocco," he said, slapping a hand on my shoulder which was as much of a warning as it was a sign of solidarity. "You get to stay here alone with the Principessa and think up plenty of fun ways to torture her. And who knows, with the house to yourself for the afternoon you might even figure out a way to win that bet we made."

I flicked my gaze to him as Enzo chuckled.

"You could certainly make sure *I* win with an afternoon of freedom," Enzo added, winking at me like a dirty old man. No doubt he'd love to get back here and find out I'd fucked her and he was the winner.

Frankie clearly thought that subjecting Sloan to my winning personality one on one for a few hours was enough to put her off of me for life and make *him* the winner, but I knew better. The little principessa was tired of playing her role as the good little girl her papa had forced her to be. She was looking to break the rules and I'd been living my whole life without any. If it was freedom she wanted then I could give her a taste of living in the wild. Of course, when all was said and done she'd still belong to me, but I'd hazard a guess that being owned by Rocco Romero tasted a whole lot freer than being bought and sold like a prize pig at a fair and traded off as Nicoli's bride.

I snorted a laugh and the fight went out of me. Papa ignored our talk of bets, taking zero interest in the games the three of us played as usual. He didn't care how we got our jobs done, only that we did.

Guido seemed much more curious, but I ignored him as if he didn't exist.

"Fine," I bit out, sounding none too happy about staying behind. Though as I considered it, it probably wasn't the worst thing that could happen to me.

Sloan would need a shower and I was starting to think letting Enzo win the bet wouldn't be the most terrible tragedy in the world. With the right amount of effort, I could probably have her panting beneath me within the hour.

Though as much as that idea appealed to me, I wanted more than that. If she gave in and fucked me, it might stay with her, confuse her, make her look back on her time in captivity and think she'd gone temporarily insane. But if I got her to love me, she'd never be able to move on from it when I destroyed her.

I'd stay with her forever, haunting her dreams and her memories, scarring her so deeply that it could never be healed. If I rushed her into sex, it might ruin that plan. I wanted her begging for me mind, body and soul. And when she was desperate for even the slightest bit of my attention, I'd take her body and ruin her so thoroughly she'd dream about me forever more.

Nicoli

Sloan's whispered words had seared themselves across my heart and scarred the flesh there irrevocably. *I need you.*

And I wasn't going to let her down.

The line had been patchy at best, but I'd heard a few of her desperate words. *Snow, trees, huge house, cellar, the three Romero brothers.* It wasn't much to go on, but it had helped me to narrow down my hunt. There were only five properties left on my list which completely fit the bill. And to make things even easier for me, my men had reliably informed me that Frankie and Enzo Romero had been spotted out near one of their largest houses on the outskirts of town.

This was it. I was certain of it. I had twenty men and Coco with me. And I was going to save my bride from the Romeros and kill the lot of them in one fell swoop.

They wouldn't see me coming. We would charge in like an unstoppable force and they'd rue the day they ever stood against the Calabresis.

We'd parked the cars up on a street to the north of the huge farmhouse and we stalked through the woods as the snow poured down on us. It had been difficult to even drive up here in this blizzard, but I'd refused to wait it out. Every day they held Sloan was another day she might be tortured, abused, degraded by those monsters. I wouldn't let it stand a moment longer. I was getting her out of their clutches *tonight.*

The house was dark but a dim glow behind one of the curtains made me feel sure at least one person was home. And I was certain they'd try to hide their presence wherever they'd chosen to hold her. They would be quaking in their boots at the mere idea of us coming for them. And so they should be.

I held a pistol in my grip and had a small bag on my back where Coco sat with his head poking out as he sniffed the cold air and scouted for Romeros. I'd never thought I'd be the type to want a dog, but I had to admit the little brute had won me over. He was the only one as invested as I was in this hunt and I'd grown rather fond of his stalwart company.

My heart thumped a violent rhythm in my chest as I paused before the pristine layer of snow which coated the lawn. It was over a foot deep and completely untouched, but around the front of the house it had been cleared and two cars sat on the drive. They were here. I could feel it in my gut.

I looked either side of me where my men awaited my word from the shadows.

With a firm nod, I stepped out onto the snow.

The world was quiet and snow fell so thickly it obscured my vision, but the house stood like a silent shadow, beckoning us on.

I raised my gun and stalked forward, the freezing wind battering and biting against the exposed skin of my face.

The silence stretched as we closed in on the house, and a prickle of anticipation ran down my spine.

Coco growled a deathly warning in my ear and I froze as I spotted movement by one of the upstairs windows.

"Fall back!" I bellowed, but it was already too late.

Gunfire rang out and my men screamed as bullets flew. I took aim at the window where someone was firing down on us with a rifle, unloading my clip and shattering the glass as panic tore through me.

My men fell screaming in agony and blood splattered the snow.

I ran out of ammo just as everything around me fell deathly still and cruel laughter carried on the breeze. My men were begging, bleeding, all shot in the legs so that they couldn't walk or even think straight enough to fight on and I was the only one left standing.

The glaring red light of a laser blinded me as someone aimed a rifle right at my forehead and I glared up at the house, raising my chin and facing death like a man. I'd failed her. And if this was my punishment, then it was the least I deserved.

"Hello, Nicoli!" a man called from somewhere inside the house and the sound of a door opening drew my attention. "Why don't you come on in for a drink and a chat?"

I scowled and Coco trembled in the bag on my back. They held my life in their hands and I was little more than a puppet on a string.

"If you do anything foolish, your bride will pay the price!" a booming voice came next and I recognised Martello Romero. Head of their family and ruler of their clan of miscreants.

He'd said the only thing that would make me cooperate and I gritted my teeth as I tossed my gun aside.

I took a step towards the house, but the first voice called out again to halt me.

"Sorry, sweetheart, but I don't trust you not to have a knife hidden in your petticoat. Why don't you lose the bag and the coat?" he suggested firmly.

I bit my tongue as I drew the bag off of my back and lowered it to the ground. My gaze met with Coco's for a moment and the little white dog looked up at me like I was abandoning him. But this was the best I could offer. Once I walked inside that house, I doubted I'd be walking out again and if the dog was to have a shot at survival, he'd be better off out here in the snow than inside with the monsters.

I shrugged out of my coat next, tossing it down too.

"Lose the shirt and boots too," he added and I did so with a growl of irritation. I unbuckled my pants before they could demand that as well and dropped them, striding towards the house in my boxers.

The front door swung wide as I reached it and I strode straight in, refusing to balk. They may have had me beaten, but they'd never have me broken.

"Who ordered the stripper?" Enzo Romero called cheerily as he stepped into my path with a hunting knife held in his grip.

His brother Frankie appeared on the huge wooden staircase behind him with a rifle pointed straight at my forehead and a wide smile on his face.

"Oh fratello, you know how I like 'em flat chested and brawny," he cooed, giving me a once over as I glowered at the two of them.

"What say you give us a little show, bella?" Enzo asked suggestively. "Give us a twirl so we can check you haven't stashed anything up your ass."

Frankie laughed, raising his rifle an inch in warning so that I was given no choice but to turn around for them.

Enzo whistled at me like I was a hooker on a street corner and Frankie's boyish laughter rang out again. They were actually having fun here. No doubt the third brother would appear at any moment to complete the party.

I turned back to look at them once they were satisfied I hadn't stashed any weapons. "So what now?" I demanded.

"Well, now we're going to make sure you learn a little lesson. And then we're going to teach it to your pretty Sloan too," Frankie said with a grin.

"After you," Enzo added, pointing at a door on my right.

I stepped towards it just as something small and white raced over my foot and launched itself at Enzo.

Coco snarled as he leapt forward and Enzo cursed as the little critter sank his teeth straight into his ankle.

"Ah! What the fuck is that?" Enzo yelled, swinging his hunting knife and my heart plummeted into my gut.

"Don't hurt him!" I bellowed, diving forward before the little dog met his death at the end of that knife.

Pain blazed across my back as the knife sliced into my skin and blood spilled.

Enzo's boot connected squarely with my chin and I fell back with Coco in my arms.

Frankie moved to stand over me with a snarl of anger, his rifle aimed right at my face. "Give me another reason to pull this trigger, stronzo," he growled. The carefree laughter had fled from him, his boyish features were hard and cold. The youngest Romero might have seemed more innocent than the others, but I didn't doubt he'd pull that trigger.

"Did you bring a fucking Pomeranian with you on a job?" he asked as his gaze slid to the snarling dog in my arms.

Enzo started laughing and I pushed myself up on my elbows, holding Coco tightly so that he didn't get away again.

"He's Sloan's," I growled, not needing to explain myself to him any further.

Frankie laughed too, stepping back so that I could get up and directing me into the room again.

I did as I was told, holding the little dog close like I might be able to protect him even though I knew nothing but death awaited me in that room.

Two more men sat inside and my gaze trailed over them coldly. I wouldn't give them an inch of my fear. If I'd met my end, I'd go out the way I'd lived: with my head high and my will iron.

Martello Romero sat in a wing-backed chair in the corner of the room, his ankle resting on his opposite knee as he reclined in it like it was a goddamn throne. He watched me enter with an impassive look on his face and didn't even bother to speak a word to me.

The second man stood with his back to me, looking out of the window with his hands clasped behind him as if he was admiring the snow.

The rest of the furniture in the room had been pushed aside, but one solitary wooden chair sat in the middle of the space on top of a plastic sheet.

I walked straight to it without hesitating and sat down.

"Look at the balls on this fucker," Enzo said with a laugh as he followed me in. "How much do you think those things weigh, swinging around down there? They must be made of pure lead for him to swagger into this psycho death pit without even blinking!"

"We could find out if you'd like?" the guy by the window offered in a voice that made my skin crawl. "I saw some scales in the kitchen. We could take bets on how much they weigh before I cut them off."

It took every inch of my resolve not to shift uncomfortably in my seat at that suggestion. Torture I expected. Cutting my balls off? I'd fight to the death before I'd let them do that.

"What the fuck is wrong with you, Guido?" Frankie spat as he strode into the room with a large cardboard box in his arms, kicking the door closed behind him. "There isn't a world in which I want to have the visual image of a man's balls being cut off seared into my brain. That shit would haunt me for life."

I looked at the youngest Romero with the strangest feeling of relief flooding me and even a little gratitude. Frankie winked at me like we were old friends in on a game together and my brow pinched in confusion at the action.

"It does stick with you," Guido said enthusiastically as he turned to look at me, his gaze dipping to my crotch eagerly. I knew more than enough about the reputation of the twisted Romero cousin to believe he really had done that to some poor fucker in the past. I just had to hope the others decided to stay for the next part if they really did intend to curb his worst impulses.

"Enough!" Enzo snapped. "We aren't savages. Cutting off fingers is one thing but I draw the line at balls."

Guido huffed in frustration and returned his eyes to the snow outside.

"Put the dog in here, mio amico," Frankie said kindly, holding the box out for me.

Coco started growling and I straightened my spine, having no intention of doing any such thing.

"I promise I won't hurt him," Frankie said seriously, painting a cross over his heart. "I might kill the odd mean fucker like you, but I'm not going to hurt a puppy."

I wanted to tell him that Coco was a fully grown dog with bigger balls than the lot of them but I bit my tongue. If he believed he was just a pup maybe he really would spare him. I didn't have to take the dog down with me.

I hushed the little beast as I slowly placed him in the box and Frankie quickly closed the lid to keep him inside. He started barking right away and Frankie headed back out of the room, taking my last friend with him. My heart sank at parting with him but as Enzo moved closer to me, swinging his hunting knife in his grip, I forgot all about it.

My mouth was dry and my heart thumped with the desperate urge to run, but I remained in place.

"Our brother gave you a warning when you spoke to him," he said casually, like we were two friends out for a drink not a captive and a murderer waiting for the inevitable.

"He did," I agreed darkly. "And where exactly is the great *Rocco*?"

"Why is everyone so obsessed with him?" Enzo asked dramatically, pacing before me. "Even your little virgin bride has been screaming his name in ecstasy like he's the fucking messiah."

"Don't speak about Sloan like that," I growled in warning and Enzo's eyes lit like I'd just offered him a prize.

"You know, she really got the hang of the whole captive thing pretty quickly," he taunted. "She figured out that Rocco is so much kinder after having his dick sucked and now all he has to do is walk into the room and she's on her knees with her mouth gaping-"

I leapt out of my chair and my fist collided with his face before he could stop me.

Enzo laughed like a maniac, tossing the hunting knife aside and throwing his fists at me in return as if he'd just been aching for a fight like men.

I drove my knuckles into his side, his face, his stomach and he met every blow with a savage ferocity of his own before Frankie caught me around the throat and heaved me off of him again.

I made a move to fight Frankie off but suddenly Guido was in my face with the hunting knife pointed right at my eye.

"Sit down, Mr Vitoli," he purred.

Frankie guided me backwards and my ass hit the hard chair for the second time.

Enzo was still laughing as he got to his feet and he spat a wad of blood from his mouth before grinning at me like I'd just done him a favour.

Guido shifted forward with the knife, pressing the blade to my chest and breaking the skin so a bead of blood ran down to my navel.

"You can pick a punishment, Nicoli," Frankie offered as he leaned back against the wall, raising his gun in a casual threat. "A, B or C…"

"What's the difference?" I growled.

"Call your brother," Martello commanded and I looked his way. He didn't seem to want to take much part in this, but he was clearly going to stay for the show all the same.

Frankie grinned at me as he took his cellphone from his pocket and dialled. "B it is then." The call connected quickly and he turned the screen towards me as Rocco Romero answered the FaceTime call.

"Well look at you," he purred with an excited glint in his eye. "Are you here to watch me punish your little principessa?"

"Don't," I begged, not caring about doing so on her behalf. I'd never speak a word of protest against anything they might do to me, but I didn't care what I had to do to try and protect her. I'd carve my own flesh from my bones to pay for her safety. To have and to hold. To honour and protect. She was my responsibility. Mine.

"But I made the rules clear," Rocco replied sadly. "And I've been so looking forward to bruising that beautiful bronze skin of hers."

"Stop!" I commanded, though we both knew I held no authority.

"I'm gonna go ahead and mute you," he said with a cruel smile. "But feel free to watch the show."

The camera flipped around so that I could see a wooden door and Rocco's hand as he turned a key in a lock.

He headed down a dark staircase into a cellar and my limbs froze solid as he moved to place the camera down on a step near the bottom, facing a bare stone wall. He walked away but I couldn't tear my gaze from the screen as a shriek of fear came from the speakers.

Rocco reappeared with Sloan over his shoulder and she cried out again as she was tossed to the ground.

"What are you doing?" she gasped as Rocco stalked towards her, grinning like a fucking psychopath as he unhooked his belt buckle and slid it from the loops.

"How much do you care about her?" Enzo asked, raising an eyebrow at me as I tore my gaze from the screen to look at him. "Will you bleed for her, Nicoli?"

"Yes," I agreed. "Anything."

The brothers exchanged a dark look and Sloan shrieked as Rocco swung his belt like a whip and cracked it against the floor by her feet.

"If you don't fight back, Rocco will go a little easier on her then," Frankie promised before cutting off the call.

My heart leapt with fear as I tried to figure out what was happening to her now.

"But if you break into any more of our properties then we'll give her to Guido for an afternoon," Martello promised darkly.

Fear slid through my veins at the excitement in Guido's gaze at that suggestion.

I held my position as Enzo slammed his fist into my face. Frankie's blow knocked me from my chair a second later and I bit my tongue as I forced myself not to fight back. It went against every instinct in my body to let them do this to me, but I had to. Not for me. For her. My Sloan. I would take this punishment in her place and they would soon rue the day they ever took a stand against either of us.

They kept punching and kicking, battering my body until pain was all I was and all I could feel.

As oblivion snatched me, I could only think of her. And somehow, that made my demise all the sweeter.

Sloan

Rocco stood above me with his belt wrapped around his fist and I threw up my foot with a yell, trying to kick him squarely in the dick.

"What is it with you and my balls?" he laughed, catching my ankle before I could land the hit and flipping me over so my knees hit the floor.

I struggled wildly, expecting the lash of his belt at any moment, but he released me and I scrambled away. I leapt to my feet, turning around with my fists raised only to find him looping his belt back around his waist.

"The blizzard's getting worse, they probably won't be able to get back here tonight," he said like we were in the middle of some casual conversation about the weather.

"Why did you attack me?!" I demanded, my fists clenching tighter. I was ready to run, fight, *destroy*. But Rocco didn't seem interested in continuing his assault. I glanced at the phone on the stairs, my heart slowing as I realised it must have all been for show.

"Just driving the message home to your fancy little fiancé," he said lightly.

My breathing became shallow and I dropped my arms as he turned to leave. I hurried forward, catching his sleeve as fear washed over me. "Please don't hurt him."

He remained quiet a long moment and my grip became bruising as my heart clenched into a tight ball.

"Rocco, is he okay?" I begged the answer of him. I couldn't bear the thought of anything happening to Nicoli while he was hunting for me.

"He'll live," he said at last, pulling free of me then jogging up the stairs. The key turned in the lock and I dropped down onto the bottom stair with some relief bleeding through me. I hated the idea of Nicoli hurting for me, but they weren't going to kill him. I had to hold onto that fact and pray his suffering would be swift.

I gazed up at the door with my heart sinking like a deflated balloon. The house was empty, but Rocco still wasn't letting me out. It looked like things had gone right back to the way they had been.

A repetitive banging started up somewhere and I gazed up at the ceiling with a frown. It slowly moved all across the manor and music soon joined it, the thundering bass reaching me through the floorboards.

I chewed on my lower lip, wondering what the hell was going on as I leaned back against the wall.

The door swung open and the music spilled in so I could hear Gun In My Hand by Dorothy playing. I got to my feet as Rocco reached the middle of the stairs then leapt down the remaining few.

He landed with a smirk, his hair falling forward into his eyes and a bottle of dark rum swinging in his hand. A hammer was tucked into his belt and his chest was entirely bare, drawing all of my attention for a few agonising seconds.

"You're free – so to speak. Everyone's gone and I nailed down every window in the house."

"So by free you mean I have a bigger cage?" I asked, moving up a step, happy at least to get out of this freezing pit.

"Got a couple of brain cells in that head of yours, haven't you bella?" He grinned, leaning closer and the smell of rum and man rolled from him.

I jogged upstairs, shrugging off my coat the second the heat of the house hit me. Rocco took it from me, tossing it onto the stair banister then kicking the cellar door closed. There was a finality in the sound that sent relief skittering through my body.

He rested a hand on the small of my back, pushing me toward the bathroom in the hall. "Wash that pretty face of yours and come join me for a drink." He nudged me into the room and I frowned as he left me to it. I shut the door firmly and hurried to the window on instinct, but Rocco was true to his word. It had been nailed shut so it looked like he wasn't taking any chances with me. Except he was drinking, so that might make him careless…

I stripped off and stepped into the shower, deciding to play along with him for a while. Maybe he'd drink himself into a coma and I could find the key to the front door.

Steam filled the room as I soaked myself in heat to drain the cold from my bones, keeping my hair out of the flow.

When I was done, I stepped out of the unit and wrapped myself in a towel. I hunted the floor but realised Rocco had taken my damn clothes. I was about to shout for him and demand he give me something to wear when I spotted a dress hanging on the back of the door. It was a full length navy gown with a split up one leg. It was silk, luxurious and made for the kind of ostentatious events I'd attended my entire life.

A note was pinned to it so I tugged it off and read Rocco's scrawling handwriting.

Don't make me party alone, I'll end up in a fist fight with myself.

I released a breath of laughter, glancing at the dress again. I wasn't about to walk out there naked so I didn't really have much choice. Besides, I'd decided to go along with his madness for now. At the very least, it would buy me a little more freedom today.

He hadn't left me any underwear or shoes so I pulled the gown on without them and combed my fingers through my hair. I stopped myself suddenly, curling my hands into fists. *What does it matter what you look like, idiot?*

I rolled my eyes at myself, tugging the door open and stepping out into the hall. I followed the sound of the music upstairs and through the huge halls, wondering if it would lead me to Rocco.

I found my way to a large bedroom beyond which was a balcony overlooking the forest below. A wall of glass windows stood before it and a slanted roof kept everything but the railing out of the snowstorm which was raging beyond. A large hot tub bubbled and steamed to one side of the balcony and on the other, Rocco was dancing, dressed in a black three piece suit with a navy tie that matched my dress. The bottle of rum hung loosely between his fingers as he moved to the pounding music. He was a good dancer but he didn't seem to care what the beat told him to do, swaying to his own rhythm as he intermittently sipped on the rum and sang loudly at the sky.

To anyone else he might have looked insane. But to me, he looked like temptation. Like a man held to no boundaries or rules, who didn't give a damn what anyone thought of him.

I crept closer, feeling like I was approaching an animal in its natural habitat and not wanting to disturb him. As I opened the sliding door, he looked up, his eyes shimmering under the glittering fairy lights strung around the roof. His gaze sank down to my cleavage, my waist, the slit up my leg and I raised a brow.

"Done leering?" I asked and his mouth split into a grin.

He lunged forward, catching my hand and forcing me to twirl under his arm. "How do you think my parents' clothes suit us, bella?"

"This was your mother's?" I looked down at the dress with a lump in my throat.

He tugged me closer, skimming his fingers over the delicate detailing on my waist. "It was just sitting in the closet waiting for the moths to come. I thought I'd give it a night out."

"How thoughtful of you," I said lightly.

He held the rum out to me and the scent of spices sailed from it, invading my senses.

Keep him sweet.

I took it, swallowing a mouthful and grimacing as it burned all the way down. Heat spread out from my belly and I smirked as I shoved it back into his hand.

I pulled my fingers free from his, moving to the edge of the balcony and gazing across the view. Except what I was actually doing was looking for a way down. A drain pipe to my right looked like a decent bet. I could shimmy down it right to the ground. So long as I didn't lose my nerve over the icy sheen encasing it…

Rocco moved beside me, resting his elbows in the snow on the railing and taking in a deep breath through his nose. He released it and an icy mist spilled from his lips, captivating me for a moment as I studied his chiselled features. He knew exactly how beautiful he was, but I wondered if he knew how magnetic he was too. The longer I looked at him, the more my body begged to be nearer; I could feel the pull of him soul deep. But why I'd feel something like that for a Romero, let alone my kidnapper, was beyond me.

My gaze skidded over a thin scar on his neck just above his shirt collar. "How did you get that?" I asked, reaching out to touch it on instinct. He tilted his head, letting my fingers trace it then I pulled my hand back, unsure why I'd wanted to. Any touch I shared with him should have been violent, not gentle. And definitely not *tender*.

"Bullet," he said offhandedly like it was a regular occurrence. "One centimetre to the left and I'd be less of a problem for you, bella. Of course, I'd still haunt you from beyond the grave. Not quite as effective as doing it in the flesh though, is it?"

"Is that what you'd spend your time doing if you were dead, Rocco?" I asked coolly, turning to face the view again and watching the snowflakes tumble from the heavens.

"Undoubtedly," he said with a note of amusement in his voice. "On this plain or any other, I'll be your nightmare."

"Well maybe you'd be haunting me already if I'd remembered the safety catch on that gun four years ago."

He laughed obnoxiously and I stole a look at him from the corner of my eyes. "Even if you'd had it off and taken the shot, it's more likely the wall behind me would have needed some open-heart surgery. There's no way you would have hit me."

"You were three feet away!" I rounded on him in anger.

He swigged from the rum bottle. "Two, and you still would have missed." He grinned easily and I bit the inside of my cheek so that his smile couldn't infect me.

"Psh." I waved him off, snatching the rum from his hand and taking a long drink. "You just can't admit I would have killed you that day."

"Even if the barrel of your gun had been rested against my forehead, you still would have missed. Fate wants us right here, principessa." He knocked his knuckles on the railing, dislodging a line of snow. "Can't you feel it?"

"Fate is bullshit. If you'd squeezed harder that day, you wouldn't have anyone to hold against my father."

"I seem to recall I squeezed just the right amount."

The world was suddenly too quiet as his words washed over me, the weight of them seeming to press down on my heart.

"Liar," I practically demanded. I rounded on him again, staring him down as I tried to read the truth from his expression.

He leaned in closer then shrugged. "Or maybe I'm just embarrassed about failing."

I relaxed at that, which was stupid, but everything I knew about Rocco hinged on that day. That single moment he'd tried to kill me. It was pivotal to me hating him. And I needed to hate him; it was the only thing keeping me sane in this place.

"I might not be so easy to kill the next time you try," I muttered, angling myself away from him.

"Do you enjoy having morbid conversations?" His footsteps moved away from me and I scowled down at the trees below. The wind chilled my cheeks and a shiver took hold of me.

"What do you expect me to talk about in this place? Fairytales and kittens?"

"How about vibrators and sex swings?" he offered and it took everything I had not to laugh.

I glanced over my shoulder at him, finding him stepping into the hot tub fully clothed, shoes and all. "What the hell are you doing?"

He sank down into the bubbles, stretching his arms along the back edge with a smirk. "Come in."

"No," I said immediately.

"Looks cold out there," he commented.

I scowled as the wind bit at my exposed flesh, looking out at the darkening sky. Part of me was begging to get in the tub. The part that was drunk and reckless. I couldn't make my escape right then and I was freezing my ass off. Of course, that part of me was also undressing herself and eyeing up Rocco's mouth with a greedy expression, so I had to keep her in check.

I marched over to the hot tub, hesitating a movement before climbing in fully dressed too. I didn't speak a word and sank into the heated water with a sigh. Rocco sat opposite me, spreading his legs to rest one foot on either side of my seat. He tipped the bottle of rum into his mouth, over half of it gone already.

Mischief circled in his eyes as he placed the bottle on the edge of the tub, his gaze boring into mine.

"Do you hate me, principessa?" He cocked his head.

"Yes." *No. Sometimes. Always.*

He dropped his feet off of my seat, moving toward me through the water and shedding his jacket so it floated behind him. I pressed back against the wall of the tub as he moved through the mist like a siren in a bay, steam coiling up around him.

"I hate you too," he purred like he was saying the exact opposite. "I hate you so hard it's burned my insides and left them black and hollow." He moved right up into my personal space, resting his hand on my knee.

My throat bobbed in time with his as electric energy charged the water and raised the hairs along the back of my neck.

"I don't think you hate me, Rocco," I breathed. "I think you wish you did." There was a dare in my tone, because maybe I wanted to believe my words were true. And maybe it was how I felt about *him* deep down.

His eyes dropped to my mouth with a carnal hunger, then he shifted into the seat beside mine without a word, releasing his grip on my leg. I took a steadying breath as his shoulder rubbed against mine and I tried to catch my thoughts before they scattered away on the breeze.

"Remember when you were a child and anything seemed possible?" he whispered, his voice intoxicating, laced with excitement. I nodded slowly and he leaned in close. "That's how I feel today. Will you play with me, principessa?" His breath feathered against my neck and I found myself lured in like a moth to a flame.

"We're not children, Rocco," I said, holding onto my last piece of resolve.

"There's no one else here but us. We're miles from anywhere, snowed in to this house and the only rules that exist are the ones we make. So what do you say, Sloan?"

My heart jolted at the use of my name. The first time he'd ever acknowledged that I had one.

"What do you want to play?" I whispered, giving in to the dark part of me that wanted this. Between the alcohol and the snow beating down on the house, there was a window of time created just for us to shed our family names and pretend we weren't enemies. I could already feel how temporary it was, the seconds counting down like at Cinderella's ball. So I'd soak up the minutes and forget reality like she had, because despite being captive to this man, he felt like a real taste of freedom.

"Kiss chase," he answered darkly, taking my hand and placing it against his chest. His heart thrummed like the powerful wings of an eagle beneath my palm. "Tag, I'm it." He lifted my hand and my fingers curled instinctively as he guided them to his mouth, grazing his lips across my knuckles.

My throat tightened and my belly clenched with need as I felt that kiss right through to my core.

"I'll count to ten," he said. "Then I'm coming for my next kiss."

I opened my mouth to refuse, but nothing came out.

"One," Rocco said lazily, leaning back against the edge of the tub and surveying me like a hungry tiger.

I jumped up as I made my decision (which went along the lines of *fuck it*), water streaming from my dress as I climbed out of the tub. I ran across the balcony, slipping indoors as water poured all around me. Rocco's loud counting followed me and I sensed he wanted a real game out of this. And I intended on giving him one.

As I made it into the corridor, I pulled my dress off, knowing it was leaving a trail. I carried it into a bedroom before dumping it on the bed and wiping my wet feet off on a fur coat which had fallen from the back of a chair – *oh is that Clarissa's? What a shame.*

I hurried out of the room and ran along the hall butt naked and completely silent as I sped into Rocco's room. I ran to the drawers where he kept my clothes, hooking out sweatpants and a tank top before darting into the closet and dragging them on.

My breathing came heavily as a door banged close by and a low chuckle reached me. He'd found the dress for sure.

My heart thumped solidly against my ribcage as I worked hard to block out all thoughts of how crazy this was. But maybe I wanted to lose my mind today.

Footsteps pounded in and out of rooms around me and it sounded like Rocco was tearing the place apart to find me.

The door to his bedroom soon flew open and I bit down on my lip, holding my breath as I peered between the gap in the closet doors as he strode into the room. His wet shirt clung to his muscular frame, transparent enough to see the gun tattoos which crossed over his chest.

I drank in the wild look in his eyes as he searched under the bed then turned to check the bathroom. I knew the closet was next, it was too damn obvious.

With my heart thundering in my chest, I threw the doors open, sprinting out of the room.

His footfalls pounded after me as he released a booming laugh.

Adrenaline tumbled through me as I charged toward the bathroom down the hall with a shriek, darting inside and swinging it shut. My fingers reached for the lock but the key was gone and I gasped as the door whipped open.

Rocco filled the frame, victory in his eyes as he reached out to grab me.

I darted under his right arm, making it one more step before his hands locked around my waist. He threw me to the floor, flattening me with his immense body and pressing his forehead firmly to mine to hold me still.

His eyes were so close I could see every silver fleck etched across the hazel depths of his irises. I shamelessly lifted my chin, foolishly wanting the kiss the game promised. But I was dizzy and euphoric. I wanted to feel the heat of his flesh, taste the fire in his soul and drown in the freedom he embodied. I needed to take it all and make it my own. I envied him, resented him, hated him. And I wanted him like nothing I'd ever known.

"A kiss can be the most innocent thing in the world or the dirtiest thing you've ever experienced. It depends where you put it…" He scoured my features as if deciding where to place his mouth.

"It doesn't matter where you put it, a kiss from you makes me wanna puke," I fed him the lie.

He released a deep laugh that made my toes curl and my hips buck a little – just before I slammed them back down and mentally wrapped them in chains. He did *not* need to figure out I was into this.

"Let's prove you're a liar then," he said venomously, forcing my head to one side with his chin before brushing his lips over my ear. My entire body shook like an earthquake from the faint touch and I balled my hands into fists, refusing to react any further. His tongue ran up the shell then back down again before he sucked the lobe into his mouth. My back arched as I felt every stroke of his tongue right between my thighs, the sensation resonating throughout my entire being.

My legs widened involuntarily and a wanton moan spilled from my tongue and rang out around the empty halls. I fisted my hands in Rocco's wet shirt then ran them smoothly up the firm muscles of his back. He grew hard between my legs and my eyes became hooded as I shamelessly dry humped him like a horny teenager.

My body ached for release and I hated how good it felt to be tangled around him. I had to stop this though. I couldn't let it go any further. But before I'd summoned the god-given will to push him back, he lifted his head and grinned maliciously.

"Feels good to be right," he growled then jumped up, gazing down at me and suddenly I felt small and stupid and totally naive. "I'm hungry, what's for dinner?"

He held out a hand for me, but I smacked it away, ashamed of myself as I stood up and turned my back on him. *What's happening to me??*

I headed downstairs without a word, marching into the kitchen and pouring myself a glass of water. I kept my eyes on the snow piling up beyond the window as I drank the chilled liquid, the taste of it bitter in my mouth. The sun had almost set and the snow storm was easing off a little, but there was at least a few feet piled up on the lawn.

I heard Rocco enter the room and sit at the island. The master and his slave.

I clenched my teeth, gazing at my reflection in the window pane. I could see him watching me, his brows knitted and his arms folded.

"Dinner's not going to cook itself," he said, his tone joking but it got my back up.

My gaze fell on a small bottle by the coffee machine. Sleeping pills; Enzo often took a couple of them before bed and they knocked him out all night.

I placed the glass down, adrenaline sinking into my blood as I made a wild decision. Whatever strange illusion I was under with Rocco surely had to do with Stockholm Syndrome. This wasn't me. I didn't fall for Romeros. Especially one who had taken me against my will. Any notion I'd had about him caring for me was plain stupid. He'd only saved me from Guido because of some bullshit claim he thought he had over me. It was about his ego. I was his little victory against the Calabresis and he didn't want me spoiled by his cousin.

I moved to the cupboards and took out what I needed for a bolognese before starting to prepare it. With every chop of my knife, the more angry I became. Rocco was playing me like an idiot. And I'd moved into the invisible net he'd weaved for me like a wounded animal looking for scraps. But I wasn't going to fall for his lies any longer. And I wasn't going to sit about waiting to be rescued by Nicoli either. I was going to damn well rescue myself.

"You'll feel better if you just admit you like me instead of passive aggressively decapitating carrots," Rocco said casually, pumping another wave of rage into me.

I shook my head, refusing to answer.

"If you didn't get the message from my dick yet…I like you too." His tone dropped an octave and my throat thickened at his words. I even stopped murdering carrots because I couldn't help but react.

Lies, Sloan. He's lying to get in your panties!

I turned to him, painting on a soft smile I hoped he bought. "You do?"

He nodded, his expression almost vulnerable for a second but I smelled bullshit. "Look at you, you're…"

A trophy?

He bit down on his knuckles, releasing a groan and I tossed him a flirtatious smile before turning my back on him. My smile withered and died while I continued preparing his meal, wondering how I was going to get a moment alone to add the sleeping pills.

"My feet are frozen on this floor, I'll just go get some socks," I said after a while, taking a step toward the door. Rocco jumped up, falling straight into my trap.

"Keep cooking whatever smells so good, I'll get you some. I need to get out of these wet clothes anyway." He headed out of the room and I firmly ignored the fact he was doing something nice for me as I moved to Enzo's sleeping pills and twisted off the cap. My hands began to shake and discomfort pricked my gut as I hurriedly poured them into a bowl and placed the bottle back where I'd found it.

I used the end of a rolling pin to crush them into a fine dust then held it above the sauce.

I hesitated a few seconds, anxiety slicing into me.

He's my captor. A man who's haunted me for years. He tried to kill me!

I poured the powder into the sauce, quickly stirring it in a moment before Rocco returned to the room in a pair of jeans, his chest bare. I made up a new batch of sauce for my own meal when he became distracted by his cellphone and soon served up two plates for dinner.

I placed his down with a knife and fork then sat on the stool beside him, tucking into my meal and trying to ignore the frantic racing of my heart.

Oh my god, should I have given him such a high dose?

Rocco lifted a forkful to his mouth, blowing on it so steam coiled up around him. He shot me a grin and I forced myself to smile back even though my insides were shredding like they were in a blender.

What if he can taste it?

What the hell will he do if he realises I've spiked his food??

He swallowed a mouthful and I held my breath as I waited for his response.

He smacked his lips dramatically, releasing a moan. "Delicious."

My shoulders dropped with relief.

He ate every last bite and I forced down the knot of guilt that had formed in my stomach. He blinked heavily, getting to his feet then swept me up into his arms.

"Rocco!" I gasped.

"Leave the washing up, let's go watch some TV." He smirked at me and I nodded, my heart twisting as he carried me through to the lounge and dropped down onto the couch, pulling me against his chest.

He turned the television on but before he chose something to watch, he was already passing out. His eyes fell closed and my heart hammered as I realised this was it. I'd never be this close to Rocco again. I had to leave this house and rip myself out of the snare he'd trapped me in. And not just physically, but mentally. He'd captured a piece of me and I needed to cut out that part of me and leave it here to fester.

"Goodbye," I whispered, trying not to care as I brushed my fingers along his cheek.

He grunted in his sleep and I untangled myself from his arms, hurrying out of the room. I ran upstairs to his bedroom, pulling on thick layers of clothes and two pairs of socks. I found a small flashlight in a drawer then pulled on Rocco's warmest coat, a hat and some gloves. I pushed my feet into the snow boots he'd given me and headed out of the room with determination fuelling my movements.

Adrenaline coursed through my veins as I ran back to the balcony that held the hot tub, slipping outside and moving to the edge where the drainpipe ran down the wall. I pulled off my gloves, stuffing them into my pockets as I mentally prepared for what I had to do.

Fear snaked its way through my body as I leaned over the balcony to gaze down at the drop.

Suck it up, Sloan.

I knocked the snow off of the railing then climbed onto it, my legs surprisingly sturdy as I reached out to take hold of the drainpipe.

With a deep breath, I braced my foot against the wall and pulled myself forward to hang onto the pipe. My fingers dug into the metal as I started shimmying down it, taking it one foot at a time.

I finally reached the bottom and dropped down into the thick layer of snow, wading up to the porch and racing across it. I headed down to the drive, following the snow-covered track that led off of the property.

I put my gloves back on as I ran, glancing over my shoulder to check Rocco wasn't following me, but all was quiet. I kept up a good pace, the darkness swallowing me as I left the house behind. The snowstorm was starting to pick up again and there was no chance of any vehicles getting up this road tonight. I hoped I could reach another house before Rocco woke up, even though I was sure he wouldn't be able to find me out here in this heavy snowfall anyway.

When I was far enough from the manor, I took out the flashlight and shone it at my feet to make sure I didn't trip over anything in my path.

My heart thumped wildly in my chest as I finally escaped the Romero household, but as a wolf howl split the air apart somewhere in the mountains, I feared I was far from safety yet.

Rocco

I laughed as the sound of birdsong filled the air and I reached out to pull Sloan closer to me.

"You face is so tassly," I mumbled as I nuzzled against the tassel which was pressed to my face. "And your tits are so cushiony…" I groaned with need as I rolled on top of her, grinding my hips against her curves.

It wasn't enough. I needed more. I'd been holding back for too long and I couldn't keep doing it.

"I need to feel you," I moaned, reaching between us to unzip my fly and tug my jeans down to release the hard length of me.

I groaned as I pushed myself against her, listening for her moans in response. My hips were shifting against her, her tassels were tickling my ears. Her skin was so rough, like corduroy and her buttons were grinding against my dick in a way that really…fucking…*hurt*.

"Fuck," I growled as I blinked my eyes open and dizziness swept over me. I squinted as the couch came into focus beneath me. The couch. Not Sloan. I currently had my dick wedged between two of the goddamn cushions.

And I wasn't entirely sure it even felt good.

"Sloan!" I yelled, my voice slurred and louder than my fragile head liked. "Get back to the fucking down house man!"

Shit that doesn't even make sense to me.

I pushed myself upright with some difficulty, stumbling so hard that I fell into the coffee table.

Pain slammed through my shin and bounced around the inside of my skull, making a manic laugh fall from my lips.

"Slooooooooooan!!" I yelled, cupping my hands around my mouth as I spun in a circle.

She couldn't have escaped. I'd locked the windows up tight and the front door key was still in my pocket. There was no way out…except the balcony…

"Oh fuck biscuits."

I stumbled towards the glass doors at the far end of the living room which lay beneath the balcony.

On my fourth step, my jeans fell down around my ankles and by my sixth I was falling straight towards the ground.

I groaned as my hard-on slammed straight into the wooden floor and my forehead smacked into the window.

The fucking agony of that one cut through the blur of my thoughts and I hissed between my teeth as I pushed myself up to look outside.

"Motherfucker," I growled as I spotted footprints carved into the deep snow. The blizzard had almost covered them again but I knew what I was looking at and a new emotion found its way through the fog of my brain. *Rage.*

I dragged my pants back up, putting my goddamn dick away as I turned and staggered towards the kitchen.

I fell against walls and had to drag myself through door frames as I went while the leaden feeling in my limbs just begged for me to lay down and go to sleep.

Fuck that.

"I'm coming for you, little mouse. You'd better run fucking fast," I slurred to the walls as no one else was listening.

I reached the sink and pushed two fingers to the back of my throat until I puked. My dinner came up in a mess of spaghetti and red sauce mixed with rum and whatever the fuck was making me feel like this.

I scrambled for the tap and wrenched it on, gasping as freezing cold water poured over the back of my head and made some of my tangled thoughts stick back together. I kept it running until I was shivering then flung my head back, flicking water all over the kitchen from my curls as I glared out of the window.

My gaze fell on the dark line of the forest at the far end of our land and I cupped my hands around my mouth as I howled to the moon.

I was going to catch her. And I was going to punish her so thoroughly she wouldn't even remember her name let alone mine. Her screams would echo off of the walls of this house and still I wouldn't be through with her. No one made a fool of me. Certainly not for the second time.

I shoved away from the sink and ran to the hall, smacking my shoulder against the doorframe as I misjudged it and cursing her name beneath my breath.

I'm gonna hunt you. I'm gonna catch you. And I'm gonna make you beg for me to own you like I used to because now there won't be any mercy left in me.

I fumbled for the keys in my pocket then forced them into the door and wrenched it wide.

I gave a moment of my attention to kicking my boots onto my feet but my fingers wouldn't cooperate enough to lace them and I had no time to hunt down a shirt.

The snow was falling hard and fast, the bright white colour of it seeming to glow in the darkness of the night as it coated everything.

But it wasn't enough to cover her footprints entirely. I had a perfect path, pointing me to my prey and I was going to stalk her out into the dark like the monster she thought I was.

I headed along the side of the house without bothering to close the front door behind me and carved a path through the snow to the garage around back.

I picked up the axe we left out for wood chopping and swung it at the door again and again, smashing, splintering, destroying until I'd broken the fucking thing apart and the beast inside me purred with satisfaction.

I had the key in my pocket but I didn't want it. I wanted the swell and burn of my muscles as I fought to break my way in. I wanted the feeling of a weapon in my palms. And most of all I wanted Sloan Calabresi begging for mercy at my feet on her knees.

I tossed the axe aside and ripped the remnants of the wooden door out of my way before stalking inside.

I strode straight up to the snowmobile parked in the centre of the large garage and jammed the key into the ignition with a bark of laughter.

"How fast can you run, principessa?" I hissed.

I leapt onto the machine and it roared beneath me as I loosed the throttle and shot out of the garage.

I skidded through the snow, carving a wonky path across the yard as I tore after her, feeling so out of my goddamn head that I had no words for it.

"Oh Slooooooan!" I called excitedly as I pushed the machine to its limits and a blizzard of snow whipped across my face.

The cold bit at my exposed flesh on my bare chest, waking me up and pouring fuel onto the fire of my rage.

The snowmobile devoured the path before me, eating up her footprints like I intended to devour her.

I shot between trees, bouncing off of trunks as I failed to see them properly in my fucked up brain state. The machine groaned and crunched angrily at the treatment, but I didn't care. I just had to find her. My little runner.

A high pitched howl sounded in the trees and I lifted my head at the sound of a real wolf joining the hunt. Another howl followed and another, a shiver of energy dancing down my spine at the competition. But they wouldn't get to her first. I had her scent and I'd be the only one taking a bite.

I pulled the throttle back even harder, speeding out into a clearing and laughing aloud as I spotted her.

Her black hair billowed around her as she looked back over her shoulder, her eyes widening in panic as she still tried to run.

I cupped my hands around my mouth and howled at my prey as I stood up on the snowmobile.

The machine swerved violently without anyone to steer it and a huge crash sounded as it slammed into a tree.

I was thrown off it, cartwheeling through the air as the world blurred around me before I smashed into a huge bank of snow.

I sank a foot into it, the air driving from my lungs as my body cried out in protest to the brutal treatment and I wheezed out a pained breath.

"Holy shit," Sloan breathed and I looked up as she turned and ran again.

"Don't choo run from meee!" I snarled, my words garbled by whatever the fuck she'd given me and nothing but anger filling me now.

She didn't fucking listen, racing on like she still thought she might escape me as the howls of the wolves in the forest came so close that the hairs raised along my arms in response.

I snarled like the beast I was as I scrambled to my feet and took chase.

Sloan gasped in panic, running faster as I stumbled and tripped over my own fucking feet.

I fell against a huge trunk, using it to brace myself as I yelled her name again.

She looked back once more, those big, innocent eyes staring at me full of fear for half a second before a blur of grey fur leapt from the trees beside her.

Sloan screamed as she was knocked onto her back by the wolf and a bellow of rage left my lips.

I charged straight at it, my hands curled in tight fists as pure panic blinded me. She belonged to no beast but *me*. Her life was mine, not this creature's. And I wouldn't let it steal her from me any more than I would let her run.

I dove at the wolf, knocking it off of her before it could get its teeth into her perfect skin.

His head swung around, a mouth full of razor sharp teeth aimed right at me as I swung a punch straight at its fucking face.

My knuckles crunched as they connected with its head and the beast yelped in pain, leaping away from me as I bared my teeth at it.

It scuttled back and I shoved myself to my feet, stumbling as I missed my balance.

A second wolf sprang at me and I wasn't fast enough to avoid it before the sharp slice of all those fucking teeth tore into my arm.

I growled even louder than the fucker trying to eat me as I swung my weight around and threw my fists into its side again and again and again. The bastardo held on, shaking my arm like he thought he might take it with him and pure fucking agony tore through me.

Sloan screamed behind me and I saw red. I reached out and grabbed the fucker by the muzzle, ripping it off of me with brute force.

I swung my foot up, kicking it as hard as I could and sending it crashing away from me.

Blood pissed out of my arm but I didn't care. I roared like I was the biggest, meanest monster in this forest and the damn wolves believed it too.

They shot back into the trees and I started laughing as the panic in my limbs began to fade.

My arm hurt. So. Fucking. Much.

I looked at it then looked back at Sloan.

"You wanted me to bleed for you," I slurred. "Are you happy, now?"

Her lips parted and I didn't know whether she was going to spit on me or cry for me. I didn't know which I wanted more either.

My head spun wildly and I was pretty sure I was going to pass out again.

"Guessoo gotcha wisssh," I slurred as the world faded in and out of focus.

I fought to stay on my feet. Fought to stay conscious. But I was fighting a losing battle and that hurt me more than I wanted to admit. Because as soon as I gave in to the heaviness in my eyes and oblivion took me, I knew she was going to run.

And I didn't want to say goodbye to my principessa.

I didn't want to let her go at all…

Sloan

Panic sliced my heart to shreds as Rocco staggered toward me, grunting my name. I backed up, raising a hand to hold him off as he reached for me, desperation blazing through his eyes. He crashed to his knees before he made it, swiping for me with outstretched fingers and I retreated further. He slumped down into the snow, clawing his way toward me like an injured animal and my throat thickened as his bloody arm left a trail of red in the snow.

I can't believe he punched a wolf in the face. A fucking wolf!

The wolves howled out in the trees, drawing closer once more and fear sent a line of ice down my spine. The scent of blood hung in the air and I knew leaving Rocco here equalled his death. The thought alone drove something sharp into my heart.

I dropped down before him, all thoughts of escape rushing away from me in a wave. I couldn't leave him here to *die.*

I lifted his head in my hands and he groaned, his fingers curling around my wrist. "*Sloan,*" he growled. He was angry and hell only knew what he'd do to me when the drugs wore off.

"I'm here. Get up," I hissed as another howl echoed around us.

My heart thundered in my chest as I hooked my arms under his shoulders and heaved with all my might. I wasn't strong enough to get him the whole way up, but he pressed his feet into the snow, helping me lift him at the last second.

When he was standing, I slung his arm over my shoulders and wrapped my arm around his waist as his head lolled against his chest.

I guided him to the snowmobile, gritting my teeth with the effort it took as he laid his weight on me. He collapsed onto it as I helped him and I panted as he bent at the hip and his head nearly touched the seat. I cursed under my breath as he started falling sideways, catching hold of his arm and yanking him back upright.

The bark and baying of the wolf pack grew closer again and fear slithered through me. I grabbed hold of Rocco's belt in a hurry, unbuckling it and tugging hard to pull it free of the loops.

"This-iza bad time for-a blowjob, bella, but if you insi…" he slurred and passed out.

I shook my head at him as I tied the belt around his right wrist then pushed him back, dropping down in front of him and drawing his arm around me with the belt before tying it tightly to his other arm. When he felt secure, I turned the key in the ignition, praying on all I held dear that it would start. It stuttered several times, the engine wheezing and coughing smoke.

"*Come on*," I snarled as a shadow shot past us in the corner of my eye. Fear dashed through me as I tried the key once more, begging the machine to save us.

The engine roared and I gasped my relief as I revved the throttle and turned the vehicle onto the track Rocco had carved on his way here. I'd never driven one of these things in my life, but it seemed simple enough.

I pulled the throttle and we shot between two trees, heading through the dark woodland. Rocco rested his chin on my shoulder as I felt his weight tilting hard to the left. I threw my arm back to catch him, turning the snowmobile to one side and using its momentum to jerk him back upright.

As we climbed the hill toward the property, his hands pulled tightly around my waist and I clung onto the handlebars with all my strength as I slid backwards in my seat.

"*Stupid – massive – bear – man*," I said through my teeth.

As the house came into sight, the snowmobile started to slow and I begged it to hold out a little longer. Smoke billowed out of the engine and I cursed as I lost sight of the way ahead in the thick grey plumes.

"Come on you piece of shit," I begged. "Don't die on me."

"I'm stillalife," Rocco murmured in response and a smile tugged at my lips.

I pulled the throttle hard and the snowmobile found a final burst of speed, shooting up to the porch and skidding on a layer of ice. We tilted sideways and my stomach lurched. I threw myself the other way, taking Rocco to the ground beneath me as the snow mobile keeled over and the engine banged as it died.

We sank into the snow and Rocco groaned as I weighed him down, struggling to unclasp the belt tethering him to me. I managed to get it free, tossing it aside and springing to my feet. I caught hold of Rocco's arm, pulling backwards with all my strength to try and get him up. But it was no good.

"Wake up!" I demanded, shaking his arm as blood stained the snow around his other one. My heart doubled its pace as I dropped my hold on him, hurrying around behind him and pushing him up by his shoulders.

"Get up, Rocco. Help me," I demanded.

"Can't beleef she drugged me," he muttered angrily in his sleep.

"Well now I'm saving your ass so we're even," I snapped. "Get. Up." I lost my patience, kicking him in the side.

He jolted awake and relief filled me as he used what little strength he had left to stand. I held onto him, guiding him to the porch and he nearly face-planted as he tried to walk up the steps.

He started to topple backwards and I steadied him, clutching onto his arms and pulling. He was soaked through and starting to shiver as we finally made it to the top of the stairs. I hurried to the door, finding it open as I guided him inside.

His weight pressed down on me once more and I moved in front of him to try and keep him up. His eyes fell closed and his entire body weight leaned on me like an elephant. I gasped as my knees buckled and I collapsed beneath him, trying to wriggle free of his immense body.

"You weigh a ton," I wheezed, fighting my way out from under him.

I left him there as I locked the front door and pulled off my thick coat, panting heavily. I rolled him over and slid my hands under his arms, taking a deep inhale then dragging him backwards into the living room. I hauled him all the way to the furry rug beside the fire, dumping him down on it and falling onto my ass as I caught my breath.

The sound of the crackling flames filled my ears as my breathing finally started to slow. Rocco's chest slowly rose and fell as blood pulsed from his left arm all over the wooden floor.

I hurried out of the room with my gut knotting, heading to the bathroom and grabbing some towels. I found a bottle of vodka in the liquor cabinet in the living room then returned to Rocco's side, checking he was still asleep.

I lifted his injured arm onto my knees, stuffing a towel underneath it and soaking another one in the vodka. I gently cleaned the wound, my heart clenching as I washed away the blood. The puncture wounds from huge teeth became visible, but I didn't think any were deep enough to need stitches, thank god. I poured vodka over each of the lacerations to make sure they were completely clean then bound his arm in a hand towel, tying it tightly in place.

I started removing his clothes, pulling off his sodden socks and shoes then reaching over him to unbuckle his jeans. I swallowed the lump in my throat as I shimmied them off of him, leaving his black boxers in place. No way in hell was I taking them off.

When I was done, I knelt beside him, studying his still face. I never got to look at him too closely when he was awake. But like this, I could inspect every inch of him without him knowing I was staring. My gaze travelled down to his chest and I fought the urge to sketch the hard plains of his muscles with my fingers, the inky coils of his tattoos and the raised scars that begged for my touch.

I stood and grabbed a large blanket from the back of the couch before wrapping it around him. Then I curled up in an armchair close by, tucking my knees to my chest as I watched him, wondering how the hell he was going to react when he woke up.

Maybe I'd leave before dawn; as soon as I knew he was going to be alright. But even as I thought it, an ache grew in my chest. Nearly losing him tonight had rocked me to my core. And the way Rocco had fearlessly fought off those wolves for me made me see him in a new light. It made me wonder if it wasn't just me feeling these insane emotions. If maybe he was starting to care for me too.

After a long while, my eyes fluttered closed and my heart slowed to a calmer rhythm.

Staying here is crazy. But right now, leaving feels impossible.

***

I woke shivering and hurried out of my seat to stoke the fire, throwing another log on it to feed the dying flames. Rocco was still on the floor, the grey light of dawn beyond the snow clouds seeping through the window and making him look cold and lifeless.

I dropped down beside him as my heart rate spiked with panic, resting my hand to his neck. His skin was warm and his pulse thrummed keenly beneath my fingers. I relaxed full bodily, resting my head to his chest and listening to the solid beat of his heart beneath my ear.

"Mm…lower," he murmured and I lifted my head, snorting a laugh. *Typical asshole.*

I sat back on my heels as he shifted in his sleep, rolling towards the fire and falling still once more.

I headed out of the room and into the kitchen, whipping up some pancake mix for breakfast. I didn't really give a damn if Rocco didn't like sweet food. I sure as hell liked it and it looked like he probably wasn't going to wake up before midday anyway.

Once I'd gorged myself on several blueberry pancakes with syrup, I dumped the washing up in the sink without a care.

An idea struck me as I stood there and I quickly took several sharp knives from the cutlery drawer. I found some duct tape under the sink then taped one beneath the kitchen island where I usually sat and another beneath the dining room table. Next, I headed down to the basement, stashing two beneath the wine racks before leaving another beneath the mattress where I'd slept beside Rocco in his room. I didn't want to go back to being a prisoner, but with the snow falling thick again outside and the wolves having thoroughly put me off of walking my way out of here on foot, I wasn't left with many options.

I returned to sit in the armchair beside Rocco, finding him with his hand stuffed into his boxers. I pressed my lips together at the stupid look on his face and an idea struck me that made me grin.

Mr Beautiful Madman loves that face of his…

I located a black sharpie in a drawer in the coffee table, moving to kneel over him – extracting his hand from his boxers first.

I smiled down at the canvas of his face, leaning in to start painting whiskers on his cheeks. "Let's see how scary you look as a kitty cat, Rocco Romero…"

Rocco

I groaned as I came to, my head thick with a fog and a pounding headache.

"Are you finally waking up then?" Sloan's teasing voice came for me in the darkness and I peeled my eyes open to look up at her where she was perched in an armchair beside the fire.

"You stayed," I stated, my headache shifting in favour of the small miracle which sat before me. She was wearing one of my designer shirts which fell down to her bare thighs and made me wonder just what she might have on beneath it.

"I got snowed in," she replied lightly.

I frowned as I turned to look out the floor-length window at the snow which had piled up over a meter deep against the glass. She had a point, but not a good enough one. The sky was dim and I guessed it was late morning which meant I must have been out for hours.

"You could have left me for the wolves," I said, pushing myself up onto my elbows so that the blanket slid to pool around my waist.

"After you saved me from them? We aren't all as heartless as the Romeros," she replied easily. Too easily. Like she'd rehearsed that.

I pushed myself upright, the blanket sliding off of me so that I was left standing in my black boxers as I stalked towards her. Sloan eyed me nervously as I closed in on her and I titled my head to the side as I surveyed her.

"Truth or dare?" I purred.

"What?" she asked, blinking up at me like she was still expecting me to rip into her for running. But I didn't care about her running anymore. She was here and all I wanted to know was why.

"It's a pretty standard game. I'm sure even the pampered Calabresi Principessa has a grasp on the rules," I said, moving closer so that I could look right in to those big brown eyes. "So what's it to be?"

Her lips parted on a protest or some kind of refusal and I growled at her in warning.

"Did you just *growl* at me?" she asked, arching an eyebrow at me.

"Truth, or *dare*," I insisted.

She raised her chin, her eyes glittering. "Truth."

"Go on," I said in a low voice, wanting to hear whatever she had to confess.

She hesitated like she couldn't decide what to say and the hint of a smile tugged at her lips. "I think your name kinda sounds like… cocko," she whispered, reaching up to press a finger to my forehead.

"What?" I frowned at her and she bit her bottom lip to stop herself from smirking.

I caught her chin in my grip and tugged her lip free with my thumb as I pinned her in my gaze. "The next time you bite your lip like that in my presence, I'll bite it too," I promised her.

She inhaled sharply, looking up at me for a long moment as I dared her with my eyes to do it again. That was all it would take for me to pounce and I was pretty sure she knew it too.

Sloan batted my hand aside and stood suddenly, invading my personal space before brushing past me.

She moved to stand by the fire and I glanced out of the window at the heavy snow which still fell. If she hadn't run yet, I was sure she wasn't going to in the next fifteen minutes.

"I'm going to have a shower," I told her as I headed for the stairs at the back of the room. "If you wanna see how good it would feel for me to bite that lip of yours then why don't you come up and join me?"

I glanced back over my shoulder at her with a teasing smirk but instead of the temptation I expected to see in her eyes, I found amusement. In fact, it seemed like she was actually trying not to laugh.

I frowned as I jogged up the rest of the stairs and decided not to waste my time trying to figure out the mind of that woman.

I pushed my boxers off and untied the towel which Sloan must have used to bandage my wolf bite. I took a piss and my gaze caught on the row of puncture wounds as I tried to figure out how much they might scar. Or if it even really looked like a wolf bite at all. If my body was going to be scarred then at least it would have a good story to it. How many men had punched a wolf in the face and survived?

A few of the teeth marks looked swollen and redder than I'd like and I made a mental note to take some of the antibiotics we kept here in case of wounds that went septic.

I stepped straight into the shower and set the hot water running over my head, wondering if Sloan might take me up on my offer. I didn't think I'd ever fantasised about a girl the way I did over her. But then I'd never taken one hostage before either. Maybe I was on some kind of delusional power trip in believing that I could really make her fall for me. Or maybe I was buying into my own bullshit too much and falling for her too.

I barked a laugh at the ridiculousness of that idea and shut the water off. Sloan Calabresi was an itch I intended to scratch. Once I'd taken her body in every way I could imagine and I'd listened to her beg me for more until her voice broke, I'd soon lose interest. I always did. But until she bowed to the desire I was lighting in her, I was stuck in this torment of imagining the way her body would feel as it submitted to mine. How her lips would taste when she offered them hungrily and how my name would sound spilling from her lips as I brought her to ruin.

I dried myself off roughly, tousling the towel through my wet curls as I walked back into my room.

I crossed the soft carpet, heading for the closet and some clean clothes but I fell still as my gaze caught on the mirror.

My lips parted as I stepped closer, taking in the pen marks on my face. I had whiskers, a little button nose and kitty cat ears with tufts of hair sprouting from them drawn onto my skin. And across my forehead, she'd scrawled the word *Cocko*.

I stared at the artwork on my face for a long moment, surprise freezing me. I couldn't quite believe she'd had the balls to do this, but my heart was beating harder at the suggestion of this new game.

A dark smile curved my lips as I quickly grabbed a pair of sweatpants and pulled them on before fishing around in my bedside locker until I found a sharpie of my own.

If you want to play with the big boys, you'd better be prepared to lose, principessa…

I pushed the sharpie into my pocket and headed down the stairs to the living room at a slow pace.

Sloan was standing by the fire, her expression caught between fear and what I could have sworn was excitement as I stopped at the foot of the stairs and stared at her. I didn't let her see anything but a mask of cold rage as I glared at her.

"Did you…have a good shower?" she asked hesitantly.

I pushed my hand into my pocket and slowly drew out the sharpie, holding her eye as I held it like a blade poised to strike.

Sloan's full lips parted on a sharp inhale and I watched the way her chest rose and fell within my dress shirt. She had her own clothes. She hadn't needed to go into my closet and take something of mine to wear. It was like she wanted the feeling of me all over her. And if she was going to make the mistake of dressing like that with her bronze legs bare and a button too many undone at her throat, then she was soon going to find out how I felt about it.

I looked right into her dark eyes and flicked the cap off of the pen in my hand. "*Miaow.*"

Sloan shrieked as I lunged for her, turning and fleeing across the room as she raced for the door.

I ran behind her, laughing darkly as she wrenched the door open and spilled out into the hall.

My heart was pounding as I chased her up onto the wide staircase and I was gifted a view up the back of my shirt to her black lace panties beneath it.

I growled as I leapt forward, catching her around the waist and taking her down in the middle of the staircase.

Sloan squealed as I flipped her over, yanking her ankles so that she fell down a step on her ass and her thighs were wrapped around my waist.

She wriggled and hit me, shrieking again and almost laughing as she failed to put any real strength into fighting me off.

I clamped the sharpie between my teeth and grinned at her around it as I caught her wrists in my grip. I quickly transferred the two of them to one hand and reached between us to catch hold of the front of my shirt.

With one hard yank, I ripped it open and the buttons scattered around us, tumbling down the wooden stairs with a sound like falling rain.

Sloan cried out again and wriggled harder, grinding up against me in her bid for freedom and making desire pound through my body as I took in the sight of the matching black underwear caressing her bronze flesh.

My smile widened as I dragged the ruined shirt up and twisted it, locking her arms inside it as they were hoisted above her head. I wrapped the material around the bannister and tied it in a knot, immobilising her beneath me with her hands bound and her chest heaving with heavy breaths that didn't seem to be entirely caused by panic.

"What are you doing?" she gasped as I reared back and took the sharpie from my teeth.

"Just getting a little revenge, bella," I purred.

I pressed the pen to the hollow at the base of her throat and drew a line straight down the centre of her chest. I skimmed over the middle of her bra and carried on across her stomach, right down to her navel.

Sloan fought to free her arms from the shirt but she didn't seem to be trying as hard as she should have been.

I leaned closer to her as I drew a line over the curve of her full breast, watching her pant as I shifted my hand across her skin.

I caught her knee in my grip, pushing her legs wider as I drew a line up the inside of her thigh, taking my time as her hips bucked with what I was certain was desire. I didn't stop drawing until I made it to the edge of her panties and she gasped as the tip of the pen slid beneath the material for a moment.

"I think you've forgotten something, principessa," I growled as I trailed the pen back up the centre of her body, circling her other breast and sliding the sharpie beneath the lace which barely contained her hardened nipple.

"What?" she gasped as I slid the pen down across her flat stomach, past her navel and lower, marking her perfect flesh and claiming another moment of her attention for my own.

I reached the top of her panties and drew along the line of them, a fire lighting in my skin as her back arched and a soft moan slipped past her lips.

I held her eye as I slowly pushed the pen beneath her panties and she gasped as I drew a line lower, heading straight for the centre of her as her hips lifted into the movement in a silent plea.

The urgent swell of my dick was pressed against her hard enough for her to be sure of just how much I was enjoying this too and I growled softly as I slid the pen lower until she moaned with need once more.

I leaned down until my lips brushed her ear and slowly pulled the pen back out of her underwear. "You're supposed to be fighting me off," I breathed.

She stilled beneath me and I turned to meet her eyes as I tossed the pen aside.

Her lips parted on some kind of response, but I didn't give her the chance to voice it as I shoved myself to my feet and strode up the stairs.

"When you get yourself untied, you can have fun washing that off in the shower," I said as I walked away. "And when your hands are rubbing it away all over your body and between your thighs, you can think about me."

She cursed me as she struggled against the rope I'd made out of my shirt and I laughed as I strode back to my room to wash my face more thoroughly and remove my kitty cat mask.

It took me a little while to scrub the marker from my face and I headed back downstairs when I was done, smirking to myself as I heard the shower running in the main bathroom.

I made my way to the kitchen and poured myself a coffee before heading to the refrigerator to find something to eat. My head was still fuzzy from Sloan's drugging and as much as I was tempted to take some painkillers, I was willing to bet adding more drugs to my body wasn't the best move.

I pulled the refrigerator open and found a bowl of pancake batter sat in the heart of it.

I took it out and set a pan on the stove as I prepared to make them.

I dolloped a ladle of batter into the pan and leaned against the side as I waited for it to cook.

Sloan reappeared in her own sweatpants and cami just as the smell of burning filled the kitchen from the batter that had sloshed over the side of the pan and I cursed as I tugged it off of the heat.

I tossed it in the sink and set the water running on it with another curse as the fire alarm started blaring.

I reached up to shut the alarm off and swore again as I realised I couldn't open a window to let the smoke escape thanks to my work nailing it shut.

Sloan bit her lip on a laugh as I turned back to the room and my gaze fell to her mouth.

"What did I say about that?" I warned and she instantly released her lip from her teeth.

"Watching you try and cook is physically painful," she teased.

"Well now you can do it for me," I said as I dropped down at the breakfast bar and she rolled her eyes as she turned to do as I'd asked.

I watched her as she worked, my gaze trailing over the curve of her ass as she poured batter and built up a stack. She headed to the refrigerator and pulled out berries, syrup, cream and slowly stacked them up before me.

"I thought I told you, I don't like-"

"Not everything is about you, Rocco," she said as she started halving cherries and placing them in a bowl. "But I'm sure I could find something sweet that you *would* like if I tried."

My gaze slid over her. "Not likely," I replied, though I was willing to let her try and change my mind.

Sloan's gaze lit up at the challenge and she took a hot pancake from the top of the stack, spooning some sour cream onto it and adding some of the cherries and a squeeze of lemon juice.

She dug the fork into it, getting a heaped mixture of the combo onto it and reached out to feed it to me.

I hesitated for a moment then lunged forward and chomped down on the whole thing so suddenly that she gasped.

"Do you just do things like that to make me jump?" she accused as I pulled the food off of the fork with my teeth and sat back to chew it.

"Do you have something against me making your heart pound, bella?" I teased.

The food danced over my tastebuds and I had to admit that the combination of the sweet and sour balanced out to make something I could actually enjoy.

I ate the rest of my breakfast as Sloan watched me, picking at her own food with a thoughtful expression on her face.

"What is it?" I asked as I set my knife and fork down and she took them to the sink.

"I was just…"

"Just?" I pushed.

Sloan cleared her throat and turned to look at me, folding her arms as she leaned back against the counter.

"I was just wondering if we'd even hate each other at all if it wasn't for our names. I mean, why do the Calabresis and Romeros even harbour so much hatred for each other in the first place? Is it all about power? Does that really matter so much?" she asked in a soft voice.

My spine straightened and my gaze hardened as I looked at her. Because sometimes I did forget who she was. What she was. And that couldn't happen.

"It's more personal than a power struggle," I growled.

"So when you see me, all you see is the feud you hold with my father?" she asked. "Even though I've never once done anything to any of you?"

"And what did my mother do to any of you?" I snarled. "What did my brother do?"

"Your brothers?" she scoffed. "They've spilled plenty of Calabresi blood. I know for a fact that-"

"Not those brothers," I hissed, shoving to my feet so fast that my chair toppled over with a crash. "I'm talking about Angelo. He was four when your family broke into my house and burned it down with him and my mother inside."

"What?" she gasped, her gaze dropping to his name inked on my chest as I prowled towards her.

"Don't pretend you don't know. That's why we hunt you. That's why we came after your Uncle Sergio that day. He was there. He was responsible. And I won't stop until I've taken the lives of every member of your family who accompanied him."

"I don't know why you think they did that, but my papa wouldn't agree to something like that. He wouldn't involve a woman and child in your feud. He-"

"Are you really that naïve?" I demanded, caging her in against the worktop with my arms. "Or do you just prefer to turn a blind eye to the foundations your pretty palace is built upon?"

Her lips parted and I could tell she didn't believe me.

"I'll show you," I snarled, reaching out and snatching her off of her feet.

She shrieked as I tossed her over my shoulder, carrying her out of the kitchen and down the hall to the back of the house.

I kicked open the door to Papa's office and strode towards the huge mahogany desk before dropping her into the leather chair in front of the laptop and wheeling it so close to the desk that she was trapped in place.

If the little principessa didn't want to take my word for it then I would just have to show her exactly what her family were capable of. I'd watched the CCTV footage from that night more times than I could count, marking each and every man shown on it for death.

Sloan may not have wanted to believe the worst of her blood. But reality was going to come for her whether she liked it or not.

Sloan

The security footage began to play and I willed my heart to settle as I watched a group of people spill out of a large SUV on someone's drive. It was grainy, but I could make out my father leading the line toward what I assumed was a Romero property. I could see the porch and one of the front windows from the angle of the camera, but nothing more.

Two men moved past my papa as he spoke some order I couldn't hear and I drew in a deep breath as I recognised my bodyguard, Royce, on the right and Uncle Sergio on the left. My hands clenched into fists as they battered down the front door and the group surged inside with guns raised. A man I recognised as one of my father's guards, Eddie, carried a can of gasoline as he headed in after them. He'd died the day the Romeros had attacked us on the road. The day Rocco had almost killed me too.

Rocco reached over my shoulder and turned up the volume, the sound that fed through the speakers making my blood turn to ice. A woman was screaming and a child was crying. A second later gunshots sounded and fire flared in the front window. Some of the men ran back to the SUV with bundles of weapons and boxes in their arms as chaos broke out.

"My father had a cache there," Rocco said darkly. "But they didn't need to kill my family in the process of robbing it. Your father planned it that way. Why else bring the gasoline?" He slammed the laptop shut and I jumped in alarm as tears filled my eyes. My heart broke over what my family had done to his. I knew blood had been spilled between all of us for years, but this was personal, sadistic. How could they kill a mother and her child?

The tears spilled over and I turned to Rocco, his face cast in shadow as the light from the hall glowed behind him.

How could Royce have been a part of this either? He'd always seemed so moral, so kind. I'd known he'd worked for my father for years, but I'd never thought my papa would organise something so heartless.

"Why am I still alive?" I whispered, but Rocco didn't answer. "I should be dead in penance for this." Fear brushed along my spine as I said it, but it was the truth. My father had taken a child from Martello Romero, why hadn't he taken his in return?

"We're using you to bend your father to our will," he said frankly, his voice void of emotion.

I nodded, tears dripping from my chin as I pushed my way to my feet.

"So it's just a matter of time," I breathed, my body numb as I moved to walk past Rocco, sure he wouldn't want me anywhere near him right then. I must have been a constant reminder of this atrocity.

He caught my arm before I could leave the room and I turned to him with my heart hurting. "I'm so sorry, Rocco."

His jaw ticked as he drew me closer, reeling me in like a fish on a hook. "I see the truth in your eyes, bella. You didn't know."

I nodded and more tears ran down my cheeks, the horror of what I'd learned making it hard to breathe. My father was a monster. I'd never shared a deep relationship with him, but I'd always loved him. Cared for him. Thought the best of him.

Rocco lifted a hand, catching one of my tears on the end of his finger. He placed it in his mouth and I stilled as I watched him.

"Calabresi tears don't taste as sweet as I expected," he muttered to himself and my throat thickened. "Hurting you isn't the same as hurting him."

"Did you think it would be?" I asked, his hand trailing down from my wrist to wrap around my hand instead.

"I didn't take you because of *him*," he admitted and my lips parted in surprise.

"So why-"

He pressed his mouth to mine, gentle and deep and full of so many unspoken words I started to drown, before he pulled back just as suddenly.

"Because you've been mine since we first locked eyes. I was just taking back what belonged to me. There was never any plan to kidnap you."

He took hold of my throat, brushing his thumb over my pulse and making me shiver.

"I'm not a possession," I said bitterly. "Most of the people who were supposed to love me have tried to own me instead. And I'm tired of being owned."

"I don't want to cage you, principessa."

"Says my captor." I narrowed my eyes on him as anger flitted through me.

"You're my captor too," he said in a low tone, taking my hand and placing it against his heart. "We chained ourselves together the day we hesitated to kill each other. I've never been with a woman since without feeling like I was betraying you. That's how deep in my soul you are. We were together from that very moment."

He released me, striding out of the room and leaving me with my cheeks wet and my heart sore.

***

Rocco left me in the house for the afternoon, heading outside to do 'jobs'. At least, that was what he'd grunted at me when he headed out the patio door. I was wearing one of his shirts again, the scent of it keeping my heart steady, no matter how insane that was.

I decided to do some baking to take my mind off of things because every time I paused to think, I relived Rocco's words. That my father was a beast and my bodyguard was nothing but a mindless tool he'd used to hurt people. In a way, it hurt more to discover that Royce had been involved in that nightmare than it did my father. He was the man I'd looked up to as a kid, relied upon. He'd wipe my wounds when I grazed my knees, he'd held my hand when I crossed the road. And I'd always thought of him as a decent, deeply good person.

I didn't know what to do with the admission Rocco had given me either. That I had a hold over him as much as he did over me. The longer I thought on it, the more it drove me mad. And I certainly didn't want to acknowledge the wild girl in me who was dancing in circles, singing her heart out about it.

I took the cupcakes I'd made out of the oven, placing them on the counter and popping them out of the silicon tray onto a cooling rack. I'd made five in total, each my best work and each a different flavour. If Rocco didn't like one of them, I'd lose a bet with myself. I'd seen how he'd eaten the pancakes I'd made him, but this time I wanted him to devour one of these cakes and claim it as his favourite thing in the world. Maybe I was just trying to make up for my family's terrible deeds in some minuscule way, but I wanted to bring a smile to his face. It was some small thing I could offer.

The cakes needed to cool off before I could ice them so I headed out of the room to track down Rocco.

A dull thwacking noise reached me and I headed to the conservatory that overlooked the patio, my gaze falling on Rocco beyond the window. He was shirtless, his chest coated in sweat as he raised an axe above his head. His shoulders flexed and his biceps tightened before he swung it down hard and split a log in two.

I drifted closer to the floor-length window, pressing against the curtain so as not to draw his attention as I watched. My heart pumped harder and heat spread keenly between my thighs as I took in his powerful frame and the way his muscles stretched and yielded with each swing of the axe.

My fingers wound into the material of the curtain as I sucked on my lower lip and let myself fall into the trap of his body. Rocco Romero. My enemy, my nightmare. But not just that anymore. Now he was the man who fought wolves to keep me, a man whose heart had been bruised and battered by my family, and who didn't blame me for it, despite the blood that ran in my veins.

I frowned as I noticed pieces of paper pinned onto the logs lined up on the ground; each of them had names written on them. *Frederico, Paulo, Amelia, Whatshername with the big teeth, That guy who cut me up on the highway last week.*

My hands knotted around the curtain as he raised the axe above a log named *Gwen and her convenience store*, breaking another log in two with a deadly blow. His mouth was moving but I couldn't hear what he was saying, though it kind of looked like he was singing.

I was too curious not to find out so I opened the patio door, silently pushing it wide and glad when I didn't catch his attention. His voice reached me on the wind and I smothered a laugh at what he was singing.

"Sixty five fuckers standing on the wall, sixty five fuckers standing on the wall, and if one mean fucker should treat me like a whooooore…" He cut Frederico in half with a forceful strike and wrenched the axe free of the lump of wood the log had been sitting on. "There'll be sixty *four* fuckers standing on the wall."

A laugh burst from my throat and he turned his head, his mouth twisting up at the corner. "Do you like my song, principessa?"

"Yes, but I'm surprised I'm not in the line-up." I nodded to the line of logs, pressing my back to the wall as I fought the urge to go over there and inspect his bandaged wolf bite (AKA stare at him up close).

"Hm," he said thoughtfully, moving to a pile of logs which hadn't yet been named. He took a pad out of his back pocket with a pen, scribbling a name on it and picking up a log with a cut branch protruding from the side of it.

I folded my arms, expecting to see my name slapped onto it, but when he pinned it in place, I found Guido's name staring back at me. He placed it down on the chopping block, lifting the axe above his head and slamming it down. He severed the branch from the log and I smirked as I realised the gesture he was making.

Rocco scooped up the cut branch, tossing it to me and I caught it out of the air. "His dick's not that big but you get the idea." He winked, raising the axe again and cleaving Guido apart with a huge *crack*. The noise splintered through the air and made my pulse spike.

"I made you cakes," I said, wetting my lips and tossing the stick onto the ground.

"I told you I don't like sweet things, why do you keep making them for me?"

"I guess I like a challenge." I shrugged and Rocco dropped the axe into the snow, stalking toward me.

I pressed my palms flat to the wall behind me, my skin burning against the icy surface as he closed in on me. My breath hitched as he snapped an icicle off of the roof over the patio, biting off the sharp end and crunching it between his teeth.

"Is that why you're out here staring at me, bella? Am I your next challenge?" he asked, swallowing down the ice as his eyes trickled over me. "Do you think I'd be tempted by you standing out here in the cold in nothing more than my T-shirt?"

I pressed my thighs together, gazing up at him under my lashes. "Maybe I like the cold."

"Is that so?" He took another bite out of the icicle, crunching through it like it was some delicious treat. He moved up into my personal space, so close I couldn't breathe. "How much do you like it, Sloan?" He lowered his hand, running the length of the icicle over my breast and I inhaled as cold water soaked through his shirt and plastered it to my skin. His eyes remained locked on mine as he rolled it across my sensitive flesh and my nipple pebbled beneath its frozen touch.

A moan escaped my throat despite my best efforts at keeping it in and Rocco's pupils dilated. I kept my palms against the wall, fearing if I moved he'd stop. And right then I wanted more. Everything he could give.

The white shirt turned transparent over my breast and Rocco growled appreciatively. He dropped his arm, stepping back with a look of self-discipline.

I caught hold of his hand with the icicle still in it, guiding it back onto my body as I let the crazy part of me take over.

He swallowed thickly, watching as I dragged his hand onto my other breast and a dark look swept across his features.

"Are you afraid to keep touching me, Rocco?" I breathed in a challenge, my pulse thrumming in my ears. His hard-on was straining against his jeans and his muscles were taut all over. I knew he wanted me as much as I wanted him. And I was done pretending that wasn't true. Especially now I knew who he really was; a man seeking revenge for the murder of his loved ones. Me being here wasn't personal, not in the way I'd expected anyway.

"I'm not afraid of anything." Rocco moved the melting icicle over my nipple, his gaze searing into mine with a villainous hunger.

I tipped my head back against the wall, my thighs parting of their own accord as weeks of pent up desire unfolded in me and begged to be sated.

The heat of his fingers grazed my nipple and burned right through the cold that had burrowed into my flesh. I held my breath as he glided the icicle down between the valley of my breasts, skating over my stomach and down to my thighs. Goosebumps clung to my flesh as he brushed it up the centre of my underwear to the top of my panty line, pulling a needy groan from my lips.

I swallowed hard, breaking his gaze but he immediately caught my chin with his free hand. "Uh uh, bella, look at me and tell me what you want."

The ice melted against the soft flesh above my panties, dripping down between my thighs and sending a violent shiver along my spine.

"Rocco," I breathed.

"Say it."

"More," I begged and his hand slid into my underwear, sending chills rippling through my flesh. My back arched and I bit down on my lip as he rolled the smooth length of the ice onto the most sensitive part of my body.

"I'll give you more," he purred. "More of the hate, more of the spite, more of me. Is that what you want, Sloan Calabresi? Your captor making you feel like this?"

"*Yes*," I cried out, my eyes falling closed as he painted soft circles against the sensitive spot at the apex of my thighs. Pleasure collided with a bite of pain as the ice glided against me, making my head spin from the intense sensation.

He pressed hard up against me, drawing my senses to the taste of his flesh as I instinctively bit down on his shoulder. He swore under his breath, circling the icicle faster as icy water gathered in my panties and sent my body haywire. My hips rolled in time with his hand as I lost all self-consciousness and gave in to the pleasure he delivered me.

His hand suddenly dropped lower and I wasn't remotely prepared as he pushed the remainder of the icicle inside me. I bit down harder to stop myself from crying out as his thumb pressed right to the centre of me. It felt burning hot in comparison to the ice and he rubbed in smooth, delicious circles while pumping the ice in and out of me with his fingers.

Cold and heat crashed together. My thighs clamped around his hand a heady moan spilled from my lips and I came so hard my vision curtained with darkness and my knees nearly gave out.

Rocco steadied me, crushing me back against the wall with the firm plain of his chest as he pulled his hand from my panties. He placed the last of the icicle straight into his mouth and crushed through it with his teeth with a savage expression on his face.

"Well what do you know?" He smirked. "I found something sweet I like after all."

The triumphant look in his eyes brought heat to my cheeks and though I'd wanted this badly, I suddenly feared what I'd let him do to me. If I'd been a complete idiot to let Rocco slip past my defences and right into my panties. I just kept letting him get closer and closer. He might have really believed we had some connection, but that didn't mean he was going to let me go. I was still his captive. So why did I have to want him so much?

I slipped away from him, heading inside, the aftershocks of my orgasm still rippling through me as I hurried into the house. His heavy footfalls pounded after me, the sound of snow falling from his boots as he followed me across the conservatory, through the hall and into the living room.

"Do you always run from your problems, principessa?" Rocco called after me mockingly.

"I'm trying, but this particular one keeps following me around." I moved behind the couch to put something between us, turning back to him and placing my hands on my hips. My furious stance was somewhat weakened by the fact my nipples were still on show through my shirt and Rocco's gaze immediately slipped to them – *dammit*.

I swiped a pillow off the couch and hugged it to my chest.

"Bit late for that," he commented, giving me a slanted smile that made my treacherous vagina practically glow. *You don't get any more of a say in this, you've already had your fun!*

"Screw you," I snapped.

I was furious. At myself, at him, at my damn libido. I didn't know who was more to blame.

He raised a brow, tilting his head to one side in that cute as shit way that made my stomach knot. But not this time. "Why are you so angry? I gave you an orgasm, not a parking ticket."

"I'm angry because you're good at everything and I'm sick of it." I threw the pillow at him with a shout of rage and he caught it out of the air. I snatched up another one, tossing it at him and he started laughing. "You fight wolves with your bare hands, you look like the lovechild of a set of abs who had sex with a bear and you make girls come with icicles!"

"For the record, you're the only girl I did that to and I don't think any other one could turn me on quite like you did during that fucking perfect display."

My eyes automatically dropped to his crotch and his huge hard on stared back at me, drawing another wave of heat over my body. I was way too hot considering I'd just been screwed with an icicle.

I snarled in fury, anger pouring from me as I snatched up another pillow and launched it at him. He ducked it, grinning from ear to ear as he hounded forward, his knees pressing against the other side of the couch.

"Why are you smiling?" I demanded, hating that he was still grinning like a Cheshire Cat. Why didn't I get under his skin like he got under mine?

"Because you're so fucking hot for me it's unbelievable."

I gaped at him, snatching up another pillow and climbing over the back of the sofa to stand above him. I unleashed my fury, whacking him over the head with it while he laughed heartily, taking every blow I dealt him.

He eventually snatched the pillow from my hands, his laughter dying away as he gave me the kind of look which could have burned down an entire forest. "You wanna hurt me, principessa, then use your hands, claws and teeth. I wanna feel your hatred first hand. I wanna taste my own blood on your skin."

"You're twisted," I growled, shoving him in his stupidly huge shoulders. He didn't even react so I slapped him across the face as hard as I could instead. He licked his lip as it split and my heart lifted with a sick kind of satisfaction.

"Kiss it better," he demanded in a deep tone.

I swallowed the lump in my throat, my gaze falling to his mouth as my heart rate picked up again. God I wanted him. It wasn't fair how much it hurt not to have him. And I'd already gone this far. *So screw it.*

I lurched into his arms, pressing my mouth to his and he growled hungrily, snatching hold of my waist and holding me firmly against him. His blood met my tongue, the metallic tang of it making me moan. My anger spilled into the desire in me, merging to create an unstoppable creature that possessed me body and soul.

I clutched Rocco's shoulders as I stood above him on the couch, raking my nails across his muscles, wanting to tarnish his perfect skin. He caught my thighs, hooking my legs up around him and dropping me down to the couch with a fervent snarl.

I'd been thirsty for Rocco for so long, denying it to myself over and over and over, but it was time I quenched myself of him for good.

No matter how hard I tore at him, he didn't hurt me back. His hands were firm, forcing my hips down beneath him as I writhed against him. His tongue pushed between my lips and my heart galloped against my ribs as he claimed my mouth with firm strokes.

I locked my legs around his waist, squeezing hard enough to force a grunt from him. He caught my wrists, pressing them down into the cushion above my head then rolled his hips so the impressive length of him rutted between my thighs.

I arched into him, trying to forget he was a Romero as I fell into his eyes and found nothing but fire there. I longed to leap into it and let him burn me up. It was the only way I was going to rid myself of this primal craving.

He broke our kiss and moved his mouth to my ear, brushing his tongue across it and making me shudder beneath him. "You were mine the moment you pulled the trigger on me, Sloan."

Why is he bringing that up right now??

"And do you want to know a secret?" he purred.

I nodded, though a flicker of uncertainty ran through me.

"I couldn't kill you. Never could, never will." His heated breaths swept over my skin and made everywhere tingle.

The truth of his words washed through me and wrapped around my heart. I didn't know why I believed them, but I did.

He reached between us, unbuttoning his jeans and sliding his hand up my inner thigh.

"Say you want me," he murmured against my ear and I knew he was getting off on this, but in fairness, I was too.

"I want you Rocco, let's just leave our surnames out of it," I said breathlessly.

"Fine by me." He ripped my panties away with a sharp yank and my back arched as he drove himself inside me.

His eyes flicked back up to meet mine as a helpless moan escaped me, the size of him almost too much to bear. He smirked before he ravished my mouth with another filthy kiss and I sank into the darkness I could taste on his lips, sacrificing myself to it willingly.

The fullness of him was mind-blowing. I couldn't think straight as he started to rock his hips and another moan rolled over my tongue. Rocco laughed against my ear, his grip bruising on my thighs as he thrusted into me over and over.

I ran my thumb over the raised scar on his shoulder, biting down on my lip as goosebumps raised along his skin in response. My thighs tightened around his waist and he groaned deep in his throat.

"What's the name of the guy you fucked before me?" Rocco demanded suddenly, driving himself deep inside me in the same instant. My neck rolled and I cried out as he took possession of my body, leaving me unable to respond.

"Didn't catch that," he taunted and I squeezed my legs tighter around him in frustration. "Wanna try again?"

"Shut – *up*," I said breathlessly, digging my nails into his arms.

"Did he make you feel like this?" He kissed the corner of my mouth, my jaw, my neck, leaving my head spinning with every one he branded on my flesh. He circled his hips and buried himself inside me once more, his hand sliding into my hair and gripping tightly.

"Better than this," I teased as I caught my breath, a grin hooking up my lips as fire flared in his eyes.

He reached down, dragging my shirt over my head and tossing it away. His heated skin moulded to mine and I inhaled deeply at how good it felt. His muscles flexed against my curves and he groaned again as he lost himself to my body, drawing himself in and out of me with powerful thrusts.

He reached between us to skim his thumb over my hardened nipple and pleasure skittered through my flesh like a hurricane.

"If he's better, you shouldn't have any trouble telling me his name," Rocco growled.

I tried to taunt him again, but he started hitting a spot deep inside me that had me gasping for air. He hooked my leg up over his arm, having no mercy on me as he forced me closer and closer to oblivion. The intensity made my vision darken and the noises that left me were pure animal. Sweat and heat and friction made my body nearly come apart at the seams.

A burning torment grew deep in my core and the only word that made it past my lips was Rocco's name. I was begging, pleading and cursing him all at once with that single word.

His throaty laugh filled my ears as I fell to ruin, a vat of molten gold seeming to spill through me and coat my veins in ecstasy. I'd never experienced so much pleasure at once, every muscle in my body weakened by the force of nature that had just ripped through me.

Rocco increased his pace, holding me still and groaning deeply in my ear as he found his own release inside me with one final, mind blowing thrust.

We lay breathless, wound together so completely it was like we were one being. The weight of him was strangely comforting and being held against him somehow felt like the purest sense of freedom I'd ever known.

He grinned down at me like a wolf then kissed me like a lover, his tongue slow and burning against mine.

"Admit it, I just ruined you for all other men," he said cockily and I rolled my eyes at him, refusing to give him that satisfaction. Although, admittedly, I genuinely couldn't summon the name of my Italian ex-boyfriend right then. *Ricardo??*

"If your ego gets any more inflated, Rocco, your head will explode." I gave me him a sideways smile.

"Alright, I don't need to hear it anyway. Your face says it all. And if we're being honest…" He rubbed his nose against mine. "I think you just ruined me for all other women, Sloan."

Rocco

My flesh burned with the memory of Sloan's body against mine. She was like a puzzle I couldn't figure out. On the one hand she was so sheltered, so delicate, so innocent. But on the other she was wild, passionate and aching for a life without boundaries. She made me want to challenge her and force her out of her comfort zone at every turn, but whenever I thought I'd pushed her too far and suspected she might be about to blink, she only ever begged for more.

I didn't think I'd ever met a creature so desperate for life to ravage her as my little principessa. I felt like I'd stolen a wild creature from a cage when I'd snatched her from her wedding. There she'd been, all dressed up in white like a picture perfect virgin bride but beneath the veil a demon lurked, just aching for someone to free her from her shackles. And if she wanted someone to sin with, then I was more than happy to corrupt her.

Sweat coated my skin beneath my shirt as I stacked the logs I'd spent the afternoon splitting. Sloan had headed to the kitchen to make us dinner and finish up on her cakes.

I still wasn't sure why she was so determined to make me like sweet things, but I wasn't going to back down from the challenge she'd set herself.

I heaved the final stack of logs into the house and headed to the living room to stoke the fire. The flames raged as I fed them and the warmth of them washed over my chilled skin.

I headed back out to check on Sloan in the kitchen, the tempting scent of her cooking washing over me as I pushed the door open.

She stood with her back to me, wearing one of my shirts yet again and I watched her ass as she danced to the music she had playing over the speakers. It was some girly pop thing, but any objections I had to that stilled at the way she was moving to it, my shirt riding up just enough to give me a glimpse of her black panties every now and then.

"I'm going to have a shower," I said loudly and she flinched, spinning around in surprise, her lips parting as she took me in.

"Dinner will be ready in a minute," she said with a frown, like my schedule frustrated her.

"Did I suddenly acquire a wife when I fucked you?" I teased.

"No," she protested. "It's not that. It's just…" She shifted uncomfortably and I raised an eyebrow at her, wondering what could be ruining her mood so soon after I'd blown her goddamn mind.

"Spit it out, principessa," I urged, stalking towards her and caging her in against the work surface with my arms so that she couldn't run. Which she looked suspiciously tempted to do.

"It's just that when we…you know…" Her cheeks were colouring adorably and I was sorely tempted to prolong her agony.

"When we…" I reached out to run my hand over her breast but she batted me away.

"This is serious, Rocco," she said, chewing on her lip. "We didn't use protection."

"You're thinking I could have given you an STI?" I teased. "You don't need to worry about that, principessa, I don't make a habit of screwing girls without a condom." In fact she was the only one who I'd ever been so caught up in that it hadn't even crossed my mind. And if I was being honest, I had zero intention of putting any kind of barrier between us if we did it again. I wanted to feel her flesh against mine, I wanted my soul to be so close to hers that the barriers of our flesh couldn't keep them apart.

"That's not the only reason people use protection, Rocco," she growled. "What if I'm…*we're…*"

I barked a laugh and caught hold of her hips, pulling her against me. "Are you worried I've put a little Romero in your belly?" I teased, getting my answer as her eyes flashed with fear. "Don't worry, bella, there's no chance of that."

"You can't possibly be sure of that," she growled like I was just some mouthy douchebag who went around fucking girls without a condom all the time and didn't give a shit how many babies I left in my wake.

"I can actually," I said, stepping back with my jaw tightening. "Because I can't have children."

Sloan's lips parted as she stared up at me in shock. "What do you mean?" she demanded and I ground my teeth against the desire not to answer. It wasn't something I let myself think about much because if I was totally honest with myself, it wasn't something I was happy about. Who wanted to know that they were destined to never have a family? Cursed to live without the love of a child? But it also wasn't something I could change, so I didn't let myself dwell on it. But I guessed she deserved the truth from me after she'd given herself to me like that. Especially if I was hoping to have a shot at a repeat performance.

"I had mumps when I was a kid," I said with a shrug that attempted to dismiss my feelings over the shittiness of that particular batch of bad luck. "The doctor said it fucked up my sperm count or something. So end result; no baby in your belly."

"Rocco..." Sloan said slowly, reaching out to me like she'd looked beyond my bullshit without even trying and could see the scar of that information weighing on my soul.

"So in answer to your question, bella, you can keep fucking me without having to worry about being stuck with complicated consequences." I winked at her and pushed away from the work surface, backing up towards the door. "I'm gonna have that shower now."

"But, dinner..." she protested weakly.

"Don't worry dear, I'll be quick." I smirked at her and she pouted as I headed back out of the room and up to the shower.

I stripped off and headed beneath the hot flow, letting it rinse the sweat from my skin and peeling my bandage off so that I could wash the wolf bite too. The antibiotics had done their job and the swelling was already going down. I decided against re-bandaging it so that I could let the air get at it instead.

I finished up quickly and turned to get out of the shower but I paused as I found a message drawn in the steam that lined the mirror. *Wear me.* It was accompanied by an arrow which pointed to the door where Sloan had hung one of my most expensive suits.

It was charcoal grey with a matching waistcoat and she'd paired it with a black shirt and tie.

My lips twitched as I dried myself and dressed as she'd commanded, adjusting my tie in the mirror and styling my hair back with product to complete the look. If she wanted the Rocco I showed the world then she could have him, but she might be surprised by what she got. I didn't show any softness to the outside world. This suit was like a mask that covered up any and all of the lighter parts of me. So my principessa was going to have to see what I was like in the dark.

My polished shoes thumped on the wooden staircase in the centre of the house as I descended and strode into the kitchen with purposeful steps.

The pop music assaulted my ears as I pushed the door wide.

"Turn that music off," I snapped and Sloan flinched away from the stove as she turned to look at me.

She still wore my shirt despite asking me to dress up for her and a fire lit in my veins as she reached out and flicked the radio off.

"Is this what you wanted, bella?" I asked, taking slow steps towards her. "You want to see me how the world sees me? Didn't you like what you found beneath the veil?" I didn't really mean to ask her that, but now that it had slipped past my lips I found I actually cared about her answer. There weren't many people who saw me as anything other than the man in this suit and if she hadn't liked what she'd found, I wasn't sure what I would feel about it.

She drew in a slow breath between her lips and I kept my expression flat as I closed in on her.

"I liked it," she said breathily and my cock twitched with the memory of just how much she'd liked it.

"So you just thought you'd have a change?" I stilled in front of her as she looked up at me. "Even though you're still wearing *this.*" I fingered the hem of my shirt, my hand brushing the skin of her inner thigh for a moment before I released her.

"I didn't know where you kept the dresses," she admitted. "I thought you might find me one…"

"No," I replied. "I like you like this. With my shirt on your flesh and the scent of me all over you. I like the way it marks you out as mine. If the world saw you like this, there would be no doubt that you belonged to me."

Her eyes flashed indignantly as I laid claim to her once more and I stepped forward, pinning her back against the cupboard with my hips and pressing my hands down on the work surface either side of her.

"Or are you going to deny the fact that your body has been taken hostage by mine?" I growled.

"Every part of me is your hostage," she replied darkly and I laughed in response.

"I don't see any chains holding you here. And I don't see you trying to run anymore either," I purred.

"We're snowed in," she protested weakly. So weakly that I had to wonder if we were both questioning her motivations for staying now.

"Mmm." I pushed away from her and moved to take a seat at the kitchen island so that she could feed me.

Sloan dished up two huge bowls of mushroom ravioli and set one before me before taking a seat opposite. I concentrated on my food, not looking up again as I felt her eyes on me.

"Do you like it?" she asked and I growled at her, keeping my eyes on my food. She inhaled sharply in surprise then barrelled on all the same. "It's just that most people say thank you when someone does something for them-"

I dropped my fork with a clatter and looked up at her suddenly, relishing the way her big brown eyes flashed with uncertainty. "You're not eating with the man you think you know, bella," I growled. "You asked me to dress up like a Romero for you so that's who you've got. If you don't think you can handle it, then maybe you should be careful what you wish for."

Her lips popped open in surprise and I couldn't help but stare at them, imagining up the things I'd like to do with her mouth.

"So you just think you can put that suit on and it gives you free rein to be an asshole, like the world's most dickish superhero?" she asked, her spine straightening in the face of my behaviour.

"I'm *always* an asshole," I pointed out. "And you won't find some superhero lurking beneath my clothes no matter how hard you hunt for one."

"Yeah, it seems like when you get beneath your skin you just find the same old mobster asshole I've known my whole life. You're all just clones of each other. When you put aside your theatrics and your pretty lies, you just revert back to this." She waved a hand at me like that said it all. "You're actually reminding me of my father right now, acting like the big man in his big house with his big-"

I slammed my fist down on the surface, making the cutlery jump and causing her to flinch. "I am *nothing* like your father," I growled in a low warning. "Aside from anything else, I would *never* put a price on you. I would never let any man place a single bid and I'd certainly never sell you."

Sloan blinked at me as her cheeks coloured and I could see that my words had affected her. She turned her eyes back down to her meal and shrugged one shoulder in an attempt to deflect from what I'd said. "I'm not yours to sell anyway," she muttered.

My lips twitched and my grip tightened on my fork. "I know."

Silence fell between us, yet despite our outburst it actually felt liberating, like something had been banished from the empty space that divided us.

I turned my attention back to my meal and finished it without another word, spearing each piece of ravioli like they had personally insulted me and chewing them like a savage. It tasted fucking divine, but she didn't need to hear that.

When I'd finished, I shoved my plate across the breakfast bar at her and she caught it in surprise, looking at me like she wasn't quite sure what to make of me.

"What's wrong, principessa? Do you think you *can't* handle me like this?"

A fire lit in her eyes at the challenge in my tone and she took our plates and deposited them in the sink with her shoulders pressed back.

"I can handle you just fine, Rocco," she said with her back to me. "You just enjoy your little power trip and let's hope your head doesn't swell up too much."

"It's not my head that's swelling," I assured her as I got to my feet and stalked over to her.

She stilled as I came up behind her, wrapping my arms around her waist as I pressed my mouth to her neck.

She moaned softly as I ran my tongue up to her ear.

"You're so confusing, you know that?" she protested as I began to unbutton her shirt.

"Aren't you curious to find out what it would feel like to give in to me completely?" I growled. "To do everything I say…"

Her elbow caught my stomach and a laugh escaped me as I stepped back.

"How about you try out doing everything that *I* say," she suggested firmly.

"You think you can take control of me?" I teased, half wanting to see her try.

Sloan shrugged but the movement was filled with attitude which said she actually believed she stood a chance.

"You haven't tried your dessert," she said innocently, turning to look up at me beneath those long lashes.

I released a breath of frustration and she pouted at me until I relented.

"Sit." She pointed back at the breakfast bar and I arched an eyebrow at her as she tried to boss me about. She pressed a hand to my chest and exerted pressure until I relented and stepped back.

She kept pushing until I'd made it back to my chair and shoved me down into it.

"Close your eyes," she commanded, her eyes sparkling as she tried to take control of me. When I didn't comply, she reached out and tugged my tie loose. My heart beat a little faster as she slid it from my collar, stepping behind me so that she could blindfold me and I didn't object to this new game. She could have been about to pull a knife on me for all I knew, but somehow I trusted that she wouldn't.

She moved away from me and I waited as I heard her placing things down before me on the work surface.

"Okay," Sloan breathed, moving beside me and tugging the blindfold off again.

My eyebrows rose as I took in the row of utterly perfect cupcakes sitting before me. They looked like the kind of thing you'd see on TV, not in real life. Each of them was individually hand decorated in five different designs and she bit her lip as she waited for my assessment of them.

"Well if anything would ever be capable of changing my mind about sweetness then this would be it," I said slowly, turning to look at her. "Assuming they taste as good as they look."

"Better," she said with a confidence that made my pulse spike. When Sloan gave something her all, I doubted there was anything she couldn't achieve.

She reached out and pointed at the first cupcake in the line-up which had been delicately decorated with a swirl of pink and white frosting and had a fat cherry sitting on top of it.

"Cherry and almond twist," she said before pointing at the next which had yellow frosting with a tiny, intricately detailed green tree painted on it. "Lemon and lime. Salted caramel. Strawberry lemonade and vanilla pumpkin." That last one had a perfect little pumpkin sitting on top of it which looked like she'd made it entirely out of sugar paste.

"You're going to feel bad when you don't win me over, bella," I teased.

"You're going to eat your words," she promised as she reached out and selected the salted caramel cupcake from the line-up, a perfectly symmetrical crisscross design painted on the top of it in chocolate and caramel.

Sloan raised the cake to my lips like she was hoping to feed me and I smiled darkly as a better idea occurred to me.

"I can't really eat food that's not on a plate," I protested slowly, reaching up to grasp her wrist and lowering it as she frowned at me.

"You really need a plate for a cupcake?" she asked, arching an eyebrow at me.

"Yeah. I really do," I agreed.

She rolled her eyes and headed to collect a plate for me. As she returned with it, I snatched it from her grip and threw it across the room where it smashed against the wall.

Sloan half jumped out of her skin, staring up at me in surprise as I got to my feet and towered over her.

"Don't we have any plates?" I asked calmly, waiting for her to fetch me one.

Her full lips parted as she almost protested and I raised an eyebrow at her. Sloan quickly pulled another one from the cupboard and turned back to find I'd stalked across the room after her.

She gasped in surprise, almost dropping it herself before I plucked it from her fingers and launched it across the wide kitchen to join the other in a thousand pieces on the floor.

"What are you-"

"Plate?" I demanded and she drew another one from the cupboard with half a laugh like she wasn't quite sure if this was a new game or not and I smashed it just as quickly.

Sloan's lips had parted, her breaths coming faster as she stared up at me like I was insane.

All the best people are, sweetheart.

I kept claiming every plate from her and smashing them until there weren't any left in the cupboard and her hand fell empty at her side.

She bit her lip, unsure what to do and I lunged at her. Sloan gasped in surprise, releasing her lip into my keeping as I claimed her mouth and sank my teeth into the plump flesh just like I'd promised her I would if she did that again.

She moaned as I tugged it between my teeth and I drove the length of my body up against her as that sound made me so hard for her that I was almost bursting my fly.

I bit her just hard enough to draw blood and groaned as the iron tang of it coated my tongue. I kissed her harder, sliding my tongue into her mouth and revelling in the way her lips parted for me eagerly and her tongue met with mine.

I pulled back as suddenly as I'd assaulted her and she leaned back against the work surface panting with need, her thighs parting like she was hoping I'd take her right there.

"I thought you wanted me to eat your cupcakes?" I questioned darkly, looking down at her with an ache of desire growing in me which I could only control through pure force of will.

"But you don't have any plates," she breathed, her brow pinching as she clearly still wondered what the hell I'd been doing by breaking them all.

"Then we'll just have to improvise." I scooped her into my arms and twisted her around as I headed back to the breakfast bar.

Sloan gasped as her ass hit the marble worktop and I reached between us to unhook the buttons of my shirt which she still wore like it belonged to her.

"Rocco," she protested weakly, her eyes on me as I worked.

"Mmm?"

"Are you seriously going to eat off of *me?*"

"I'll go one better than that," I promised her. "If you've managed to bake a cake that I like, then I'll let you be the final course."

"What?" she squeaked, her thighs inching closer together like she wasn't sure if she wanted that or not.

I paused as I unhooked her final button and looked into the depths of her warm, brown eyes. "When your Italian boyfriend made you come, didn't he ever use his mouth to do it?" I asked slowly.

"Erm, he was a fan of…missionary position," she breathed, her cheeks reddening adorably.

"And that was it?" I asked, arching a brow. "He never changed it up, did it doggy style or with you on top?" She shook her head, getting even redder and my smile widened. "So he never went down on you?"

"No," she breathed. "I don't even know if I'd like that or-"

"Oh you'll like it, bella, I promise."

She was practically glowing now and I couldn't help but push it a bit further.

"So you've never given a blowjob either?"

Her eyes dropped to my crotch where I was straining against my fly so hard that it hurt and her tongue slid out to wet her lips.

I groaned at the sight of that, practically bursting at the thought of that mouth wrapped around my cock.

Sloan's gaze moved back to my eyes and the embarrassment was quickly turning to lust as she considered all of these options which apparently hadn't ever occurred to her before.

"Fuck, you really are a virgin," I growled hungrily. And that fucked up little bit of me couldn't help but love that idea. I might not technically be the first guy to get beneath her panties, but I could be her first everything else.

"No I'm not," she growled defensively.

"I'll admit you're not once you beg me to fuck your mouth," I whispered, reaching out to push my shirt off of her shoulders.

Her lips parted but she didn't seem to have a response ready for that one and I chuckled to myself for successfully flustering her again as I tossed the shirt aside.

I reached behind her and drew the cupcakes closer to us, lining them up along the edge of the worktop.

Sloan watched me like she wasn't sure if she should be panting or protesting and I was looking forward to showing her which.

"Underwear off," I commanded, lifting the lemon and lime cupcake and dipping my finger into the yellow and green frosting.

Sloan looked like she wanted to object as I stood before her in my full suit but she swallowed her complaints and unhooked her bra before sliding it off.

I bit my lip as I looked at her full breasts with a fierce hunger rising in me and waited as she slid her panties off too.

I reached out with my frosting covered finger and she gasped as I painted it straight down the centre of her left nipple.

I leaned forward and licked it back off again a moment later and she moaned eagerly as my mouth claimed her flesh.

I stood back with a smirk and took a bite from the cake in my hand. She'd gotten the perfect balance of sweet and sour into the mix and my tastebuds tingled as I chewed on it, I still wouldn't have said I'd exactly go out of my way to eat it, but I could appreciate her talent.

"Do you like it?" Sloan asked, watching me as I swallowed.

I swiped my finger through the frosting on the remainder of the cupcake, covering it with the yellow and green mess.

"Nope," I replied before pushing my finger into her mouth.

She sucked every last bit off of it, taking her sweet time as she looked into my eyes. My little principessa may have been innocent, but she sure as shit didn't want to be.

"Keep eating," she commanded. "There will be one you like."

I snorted at the challenge as I picked up the salted caramel cupcake next.

Sloan sat watching me eagerly which really wasn't very plate-like of her.

I growled hungrily and pushed her back so that she was lying on the work surface, completely bare before me and I took a bite out of the salted caramel cupcake next. The sweetness of it hit the back of my throat and I practically had to force it down. I didn't manage to hide my wince and Sloan pouted at me.

"I told you," I taunted before painting a line of the frosting straight down the centre of her body from her neck to her navel.

She gasped, bucking her hips before me and I tutted at her.

"Plates don't wriggle," I reminded her.

"I'm not really a-"

I pushed two fingers covered in frosting into her mouth this time and she moaned lustily as she sucked the frosting off.

"You like that?" I purred as she arched her back, her hands clamping around my wrist. "Plates don't grab either, bella."

"I told you I'm not a plate," she growled.

"Tut, tut, tut. I don't think you're grasping the rules of this game. Am I going to have to restrain you?"

Sloan stared at me in shock like she couldn't quite believe I'd suggested that and her pupils widened with desire.

"Yes," she breathed. "I think you'd better."

"*Fuck*, Sloan," I moved to claim my tie from the stool where I'd been sitting earlier and approached her slowly, wondering if she was about to blink or not.

Sloan raised her hands in offering and I bound them together tightly, before tying them to a hand towel hook on the end of the kitchen island so that her arms were pinned above her head.

She moaned with excitement and I slid my jacket off, dropping it on the floor and not giving one shit that that suit had cost over four thousand dollars.

I took the next cupcake between my hands and broke it in half, finding a centre of strawberry jam in it which I immediately painted up the inside of her thigh. She squirmed against her bonds as my fingers slid higher, moaning in encouragement as I drew closer to the centre of her, but I wasn't giving in just yet.

I couldn't say I'd ever remembered a time when I enjoyed eating jam before that moment but as I sucked it off of her silky smooth thigh, I found myself salivating with hunger. Although it wasn't so much the sugar that had me aching for more, it was the girl hidden beneath it.

I followed the line all the way to the very top of her thigh and paused between her legs, aching for a taste of the real treat on this table.

"Do you still think you won't like it?" I teased, my lips just brushing against her in the barest of touches which was enough to make her gasp. Her hips bucked in a silent demand and I had to shift back so that I didn't touch her there. Not yet. Not until she was begging for it.

I pinned her thighs to the table with my hands, forcing them wide as she gasped again. I turned my attention to licking the caramel frosting off the centre of her body, starting at her navel and moving up until I reached her neck.

Sloan ground herself against me as my weight pressed down on her and I tutted again as I reached for the strawberry lemonade cake and pushed three fingers into the frosting.

Sloan groaned wantonly as she sucked it from all three fingers at once, her tongue circling to track down every little bit of frosting as I pumped them in and out of her mouth.

I leaned over her, gripping the edge of the island to keep my weight from crushing her and my fingers brushed something hard which was stuck beneath the edge of the work surface.

I frowned, pushing myself upright as I moved around the side of the island and leaned down to get a look.

My eyebrows rose as I spotted the sharp knife taped beneath it and I reached out to tug it free.

"What's this?" I asked slowly and Sloan's eyes widened as she realised what I'd just found.

She squirmed against her bound hands, trying to wriggle away from me.

"I put that there before we-"

"La ragazza disubbidiente," I purred. *Naughty girl.*

I touched the knife to the base of her throat, the cold kiss of the blade drawing a gasp from her lips as I slowly trailed it down her body.

My heart beat harder as I moved it lower, watching the way her skin pebbled with goosebumps and her nipples hardened even more than before as I toyed with her. Her eyes were wide with what I could have mistaken for fear, but I was almost certain it was really exhilaration. I didn't exert any pressure with the blade, just caressed her skin with it as I watched her fall apart for me.

She moaned as I trailed it below her navel and a groan of pure fucking *need* escaped me as I tossed the knife away towards the sink. My fingers took up the path the knife had been painting and I dipped them between her thighs, sliding two inside her and groaning again at just how wet I found her.

She cried out, her spine arching as I drove my fingers in and out, delighting in the way she writhed before me.

"Poor little Principessa," I growled, pulling my fingers back out again through pure force of will. I wanted to finish my game with her before I gave in. "They never let you be free like this, did they?"

She shook her head as her eyes locked with mine and I stole a kiss which was a promise in itself as I licked frosting from her lips.

"I might keep you in a cage, little bird, but I'll never clip your wings," I swore.

Her needy panting was answer enough and I stood back again as I grabbed the vanilla pumpkin cupcake next.

She watched as I took a bite and the spicy, sweet taste flooded my mouth. I had to admit this was the best one yet; if it wasn't for the sweet aftertaste of the vanilla then I might have been able to say I genuinely liked it.

Sloan groaned as she read my answer on my face and I chuckled darkly as I used the pumpkin frosting to mark her breasts then let her suck it from three of my fingers again.

I ran my mouth over her perfect tits, sucking on her nipples and chasing my tongue with my teeth so that she cried out at each sting of pain.

"Please, Rocco," she begged as I slid my hand down her stomach, painting a trail towards the very centre of her.

"Please what?" I asked, sucking on her nipple again and relishing the noise she made in response.

"Just…do it," she gasped, her hips shifting again in a desperate plea.

"Do what?" I asked, drawing back and lifting the final cupcake from the table.

"Kiss me…*there,*" she ground out and I almost wanted to force her to tell me where *there* was exactly, but I was too hungry for her to keep playing.

"I actually have a secret to share with you," I said as I raised the last cupcake to my lips.

"What?"

"I fucking love cherries." I bit into the final cake with a groan as the taste of it washed over my tastebuds and Sloan smiled widely. I wasn't even faking, the thing was fucking divine. I could have eaten them all day every day, but there was one thing I wanted to eat more.

I took the cherry between my teeth then swiped the rest of the frosting off of the cake and pushed my hand between her thighs, covering her with it.

Sloan moaned with need as I pushed my fingers straight inside her and started moving them back and forth. I was getting frosting fucking everywhere but I planned on eating every last scrap of it so I didn't care.

Her hips were moving in time with the thrusts of my hand and for a moment I just watched her, getting off on the way she looked spread before me and begging for more.

I pulled my fingers back out of her and took the cherry from my mouth before placing it straight on top of the frosting.

Sloan was panting with need and I dropped to my knees before her, pushing her thighs wide and groaning as I pressed my mouth down right on the centre of her.

She cried out, bucking against me as she demanded more and I gave it to her willingly. I ran my tongue over her, dipping it inside her as I licked the frosting out of her and tasted the sweetness of her beneath it.

She tasted so fucking good that I groaned, working my way up until I was sucking and licking at that perfect spot and she was grinding herself against me and calling my name with a keen desperation. The sound of her begging me for more turned me on so fucking much that I had to fight against the urge stop this and just take her. But I wanted to own this moment. I wanted to be the author of this memory in her forever more.

Sloan cried out in pleasure, her heels digging into the work surface as she came, making her slide up it away from me.

I pushed myself upright so that I could see her as she writhed beneath me, biting my lip as I admired the perfection of her body.

She'd pushed herself so far along the surface that her head hung over the end of it, her ebony hair trailing down to the floor as she tried to catch her breath in the wake of what I'd done to her.

I moved around to kneel by her head where it hung back over the end of the island and kissed her mouth upside down, worshiping her full lips as they moved against mine in the unfamiliar way.

I pulled back and smiled at her wickedly as I untied her hands. "Do you want to try anything else while I've got you here?" I teased.

"Yes actually," she said, biting her damn lip again. "I want to know how it feels to take control of you like that."

"You want to tie me up?" I asked with a snort of amusement as I stood. She stayed where she was with her head hanging upside down over the edge of the breakfast bar right in line with my crotch.

"No. Not that." Sloan reached for me and tugged my belt loose before sliding my fly down.

I gripped the edge of the work surface either side of her head as she freed me from my pants and my heart leapt as she pressed her lips to the end of my cock in a kiss that sent my blood pumping pure fucking fire through my limbs.

I opened my mouth to say something, but whatever the fuck it had been was lost to me the second her lips slid around me.

A curse left me as she drew every fucking inch of me into her mouth and she moaned like it was turning her on as much as it was me. Which wasn't fucking possible because despite the fact that I'd fantasised about her doing this to me more times than I could count, the reality of her laying before me like this and the feeling of those full lips sliding down the length of me weren't something my imagination could compete with.

She drew me in and out of her mouth and I could feel myself losing control already. Because this girl was more than just some easy lay. She was a fucking diamond which had been trapped beneath layers of coal for too goddamn long. She rose to every challenge I gave her and exceeded my expectations every, single, time.

I groaned as I thrusted in and out of her mouth and she kept going and going until I couldn't hold back a moment longer. Her fingernails bit into my ass as she drew me in one last time and I exploded in her mouth with a groan of pure fucking ecstasy.

I pulled back out of her, dropping to my knees so that I could kiss her and taste my lust on her lips.

This wasn't just about sex, it was about her. And for the first time since I'd made that bet with my brothers, I felt kinda shitty about it. Because getting Sloan Calabresi to fall in love with me wasn't the kind of thing I should have been joking about. It was the kind of thing that would only happen if I turned out to be the luckiest son of a bitch in the entire world.

And I was beginning to hope I just might be.

Sloan

I shoved a bundle of dirty clothes into the washing machine with a stupid grin on my face. A week snowed in to this manor had been anything but a nightmare. It was like living in the deepest dreams of my heart.

There were a hundred words to describe what was between me and Rocco. Crazy, stupid, dangerous, senseless, *hot*. But the only one I could focus on was exhilarating. My blood was pumping, I was wide awake and the world seemed to present a future to me I never would have considered in a million years. That I didn't have to live under my father's rule. I didn't have to answer to anyone. Whether this thing with Rocco was for now or forever, it didn't matter. It had helped me make a decision that had never felt like it was mine to make before. I was going to get out of here, claim my life back and do whatever the hell I wanted with it.

I snapped the door shut on the washing machine and stood up. I'd been washing everything from the sheets to the towels. It was the first load I'd done since I'd been here and it looked like Rocco and his brothers had been working through every item in the house to avoid cleaning anything themselves. But I for one, did not wanna wear the same sweatpants for the fifth day in a row. I'd already done the whites which were currently spinning around in the dryer opposite me, now it was just the colours left.

"Wait." The door swung open and Rocco strolled into the laundry room, tugging his shirt off. My eyes immediately fell to his ripped shoulders and I sucked on my lower lip. "I've got a few more clothes for you."

He continued to strip and I enjoyed the show, leaning my hip against the machine as I waited. He got down to his boxers and I held out my hand with a sideways smile as I surveyed all of his hardened muscles.

"You first, bella." His eyes dropped to the blue shirt I was wearing. His of course.

I smiled teasingly. "Fine, but no touching me just because I'm naked, I have things to do."

"What things?" he chuckled.

"Maybe I have an escape plan to execute," I taunted and his face dropped.

"The snow's started to thaw," he said in a low tone.

A beat of tense silence passed between us.

"When the road is clear, will you let me go?" I asked, wondering if he really did care for me. Because surely that meant he'd let me go free, even if he did want to keep me. We hadn't spoken about what would happen when his family returned, but with each passing day those words had circled in the back of my mind, forcing me to confront them.

"If I let you go, will you really leave?" he asked, dropping his head so his forehead pressed to mine. The intensity of his gaze made my heart stutter and suddenly I didn't have a clear answer.

Of course I'd leave…wouldn't I?

I couldn't stay here in Rocco's arms forever. It was a dream, a stolen moment of madness. But at the same time, I didn't like to think of it ending. In fact, the thought of leaving Rocco made my heart start to fracture.

I glanced up at him then shrugged, not giving him a real answer. Even though it should have been easy. It should have been a yes without hesitation.

"I'm not staying here for your father to use me against my family," I said, choosing my words carefully.

"But if you could stay with me elsewhere..?" he suggested with a mischievous smile.

I rolled my eyes. "It's not possible."

"Anything's possible."

"Not this," I breathed. "Our families-"

"Forget our families," he growled. "I don't want to talk about any of that right now. I just want to enjoy you. So shouldn't you be taking that shirt off?"

My shoulders dropped and I bought into the beautiful promise of his words. If we didn't talk about it, we didn't have to deal with it. I knew it was childish, but we didn't have much longer together like this. A day or two maybe. And I wanted to enjoy them too, revel in them. In *him*.

I pulled the shirt over my head as lust twisted through my body and took me hostage. I dropped it to the floor, finding a carnal desire burning in his eyes. He immediately dropped his boxers and handed them to me and I turned to put them in the washer, hiding my blush at the sight of him hardening for me.

"No touching," I reminded him and he responded with a low noise in his throat.

When I'd set the machine to run, I jumped up and tried to hurry past him to the door with a grin. He kicked the door shut and stepped sideways to block my way. "I'm not touching you, but if you happen to get in the way…" He made his body as big as possible, spreading his arms and stalking forward.

I giggled, backing up until my ass hit the dryer and the vibrations of it rumbled through me. "Cheat," I taunted as he closed in on me, resting his hands either side of me on the surface.

"If you're the prize in this game, Sloan, I'll do whatever it takes to win. Cheating, bribing, intimidating. You name it, I'll do it."

I leaned back as he leaned in, his minty toothpaste breath calling me in for a taste. "How about begging?" I raised a brow and he raised one back.

He got as close as he possibly could without touching me and I pressed harder against the dryer. It went into a higher gear and the buzz of the machine ran right to my core and made me gasp.

"I don't beg," he grunted, his gaze swinging to my chest then back up to my lips.

"I thought you said you'd do whatever it takes?" I questioned innocently and he released a breath of amusement that made my skin tingle as it washed over me.

"Hm," he growled, leaning in to kiss my neck. I pressed my hand to his mouth at the last moment, laughing as I tried to slip past him. He caught my hips, lifting me and slamming my ass down on the dryer so the vibrations ricocheted through me.

"God-ah-no," I gasped, jerking forward to try and get down, but he clamped my thighs down with his hands. "*Rocco!*"

"Please," Rocco purred, but it wasn't begging, it was mocking, his smile demonic. He leaned in again and I arched my back to keep away as the damn dryer went into overdrive.

"Let me up," I demanded, half meaning it, half not. Because holy shit this was starting to feel good. Rocco pressed down harder on my thighs, rolling them outwards and baring me to him.

"Please let me have you." His tone said he already had me and that it was obvious as hell. I tried and failed to get up again and the fight went out of my limbs.

He brushed his mouth over mine, but wouldn't give me more. He nuzzled and teased and drove me crazy when I tried to grab him and pull him closer.

"Please," he said, laughing and I tipped my head back as I started to come apart.

The dryer ended its cycle and I could have punched the damn thing as the tremors abandoned my body and left me wanting. I gripped the back of Rocco's neck, giving him a serious look as I locked eyes with him.

"I need you," I panted and his amusement died in an instant.

He clutched my hips, dragging me toward him and my lips parted in hopeful anticipation as he lined himself up to take me.

The sound of the front door opening made my heart nearly leap out of my throat.

"*Fuck*," Rocco hissed, dragging me off the dryer and pushing me toward a row of bed sheets which were hanging at the back of the room.

"Rocco?" Frankie's voice sounded. Before he got me behind a sheet, the door opened and Rocco shoved me behind him, shielding my naked body with his.

I glanced around his arm with dread swelling in my gut.

Frankie looked from me to Rocco, his mouth wide open. He wore a thick snow coat and had a gun hanging loose in his fingers.

"Is he in there, Frankie? I need a word with him," Martello's voice called from beyond the room and a strangled noise squeezed its way out of my throat. My heart thundered and my body ran hot all over. *Shit shit shit!*

"He's in here and he's fucking naked!" Frankie called back and horror sped through me. *He's going to tell everyone.* "I'll make sure he gets dressed and send him your way, Papa."

"Fucking typical," Martello muttered and his footsteps pounded away.

Frankie grinned his damn head off, looking between us. "Well, well, well."

"Don't start. Get the fuck out and stall for time," Rocco snapped.

Frankie smirked. "Sure." He glanced at me. "See ya, Sloan." He slipped out the door and I ran a hand anxiously through my hair.

Rocco marched to the dryer, ripping the door open and tossing a shirt and some underwear at me. "Put that on," he snarled, his voice lacking warmth.

He tugged on his own shirt then some boxers and sweatpants as I pulled on the overly hot clothes. Then he snatched my arm, tugging me firmly toward the door and my heart pounded uncomfortably in my chest.

"What are you doing?" I whispered as he pulled me into the hall and marched along it at high speed. He guided me straight to the cellar and I dug my heels in in alarm as he opened the door. "Rocco," I hissed in alarm. Surely he wouldn't put me down there after everything that had happened between us?

He shoved me inside and a crack tore across my heart. He followed me in, pulling the door to behind him. A shadow shrouded him and fear flickered in my soul as I looked upon a man I didn't recognise. Not from the past week anyway. This was the man who'd taken me, chained me, caged me.

"Get down there and be quiet." He pointed over my shoulder but I refused to move.

"You'll let me out later though, right? When they're gone?" I asked, desperately searching for some warmth in his eyes. But there was nothing but a cold, hard wall.

"Who says they're leaving?" he spat then stepped out of the cellar and shut the door in my face.

I stared at the door with my heart sinking toward the depths of my stomach. My legs were bare and it was freezing in here. Even though I knew there were blankets at the bottom of the stairs, I couldn't stand the thought of going down there and wrapping myself up in them. I rested a hand to the wood, trying to process what had just happened.

Rocco had looked so distant, like everything we'd shared hadn't happened at all. Maybe it had just been an act in front of Frankie, but then why hadn't he reassured me when he'd left?

Why was I standing here feeling like I'd just fallen prey to the biggest con ever? That I'd been locked up in a house with a guy who'd had nothing better to do than screw me to keep himself satisfied. It wouldn't have been that hard for him to pretend.

The door suddenly opened and Frankie came into view, holding a cardboard box in his hands. "Here." He placed it in my arms, pressed his fingers to his lips then shut the door again and locked it behind him.

I frowned, placing the box down as my heart beat unsteadily. I switched the light on then pulled the box open and a bundle of white fur shot into my arms. I gasped, unable to believe it as I held Coco tighter. He went mad, licking my face, my arms, any bare piece of skin he could get to.

"Coco!" I hugged him to my chest as emotion welled, spilling over into actual tears of joy. "How are you, little beast?" I cooed, stroking him as he trembled with pure happiness. I hushed him, running my hands over his soft fur. "We'll get out of here," I promised him, placing a kiss on his head.

I couldn't believe he was here. He was my only friend in the whole world. The only one I could trust. And I had the feeling I was going to need his company more than ever before.

Rocco

After a day listening to Papa and the others run through all the things I'd missed out on when they took Nicoli Vitoli down a peg, I was pretty much itching for the lot of them to fuck off again. They'd burst my bubble and I hadn't been even close to done with living in it.

I strolled back to my bedroom with a pout on my face like a little bitch.

I knew why they'd gone on about their job so much. Papa had wanted me to feel left out. And sure, I'd have enjoyed giving Nicoli a good kicking just as much as my brothers had. But even if he'd cried honest to god tears, it wouldn't have felt half as good as even spending one hour here alone with Sloan.

That girl had been a challenge before I'd claimed her, but now she was an all-out addiction. She'd driven her way beneath my skin and found her way into my darkest desires. Her name pumped through my veins with every beat of my heart and I knew there wasn't anything I could have gotten from Nicoli or anyone else that even came close to her.

I'd never met anyone like her. No matter how far I pushed, she just pushed back, said yes, begged for more. I'd thought I was one of a kind, destined to be a lonely soul, forever seeking the next adventure alone. But she truly seemed capable of rising to any challenge I could set. Hell, she might even set me some challenges of her own.

Maybe I should have meant what I'd said to her earlier. Maybe I should have been planning our escape to a Caribbean island.

I snorted a laugh at the ridiculousness of that idea and headed up the stairs to my room.

I knocked the door open and paused as I found Enzo and Frankie waiting for me.

Enzo was sprawled on my bed with his fucking shoes on and his hands clasped behind his head while Frankie rocked the chair by the dressing table up onto its back legs and smirked at me.

"Mmm, this bed smells like freshly popped cherry," Enzo said, nuzzling into my pillow and groaning like he might just come.

I kicked the door closed behind me and raised an eyebrow at him.

"That didn't take long," Frankie added with a grin.

"Did she taste as sweet as she looks?" Enzo pushed, demanding an answer with his stare.

"What happened to making her fall in love with you, big brother?" Frankie teased. "Or were you just too desperate to stick it to her in the end?"

"Did she beg for it?" Enzo asked with a dirty smirk. "Did she get down on her knees and beg you to fuck the Calabresi name right out of her?"

"Fuck off," I muttered, crossing the room so that I could shove his fucking shoes off of my fucking blankets.

Enzo swung around at my command, sitting up with his feet on the floor and planting his arm over my shoulders.

"Tell us, Rocco," he begged. "I wanna know if the Calabresi begged for Romero dick like a whore or if you had to slip it in her while whispering false promises of love in her ears."

"What the fuck is wrong with you?" I snapped, shoving his arm off of me.

"Oh come on, since when are you shy about telling us how you fucked a girl? I'm just curious. She's got that whole innocent bella thing going on, but I've caught her eye-fucking you more than once too. So I just can't figure out if she wanted you to be a gent or if she let you bend her over the closest chair?"

I rolled my eyes and pushed a hand through my hair which was still messed up and curling after Sloan had spent the early hours of the morning clawing her hands through it. I could have styled it at some point today, but I hadn't. I liked knowing I looked a hot mess because of her passion.

"I'm not just fucking her," I said, moving to lean back against my pillows.

"Has she said it then?" Frankie asked, raising his eyebrows at me in surprise. "The three little words?"

That hadn't really been what I'd meant, but what was I supposed to say? She feels like a breath of fresh air in a life that was stagnant? I think I could fuck her every day for the rest of forever and never get sick of it?

"No, she hasn't said it," I muttered.

Enzo grinned at me excitedly. "So I win?"

"No," I snapped. "She's falling for me. She just hasn't said it. Yet."

Frankie snorted a soft laugh, rolling his eyes at me. "I dunno whether to think you're the most bullshit filled stronzo I've ever met, or to be afraid of just how fucking manipulative you can be when you want something."

I smirked at him like a wolf with the biggest bone in the den and didn't comment.

"And just what are you going to do with the principessa's heart once you have it?" Enzo asked curiously.

I scraped a hand over the stubble lining my jaw as I thought about that. Because the honest answer was that I didn't fucking know. Only that if I won her I didn't plan on just letting her go.

"I'll let you know when I've decided," I said, offering a cruel smile which would give them plenty of ideas without me voicing them.

"Well, the way I see it, as it stands, I'm the winner," Enzo said, smirking like an asshole. "And until you get more than just moans of pleasure to spill from her lips, I'm gonna start thinking up ways to spend all of your money."

"Fuck that," I replied, unable to resist the urge to rise to his bait. "I've got the principessa right where I want her. She'll be pouring her little heart out and professing her undying love for me within the week. She won't even want to escape anymore. I bet I could leave all the doors wide open and she wouldn't set a foot outside them."

"Those are big words, fratello," Frankie joked. "I look forward to watching you choke on them."

I scoffed lightly. "When have you ever known me to promise something I couldn't deliver?"

"Well if I'm honest, I didn't think you'd even manage to fuck her so I'm starting to actually believe you might do this," Frankie said, rolling his eyes.

"So now we *are* fucking her?" Guido's voice sounded a moment before my door pushed open and I straightened with a growl of anger aching to break loose in my throat.

Frankie leaned forward in his chair so that the front legs hit the carpet again and Enzo's spine straightened as he narrowed his eyes on our twisted cousin.

"*We* aren't doing anything, you sick fuck," I snapped. "And you shouldn't be spying on me if you like your face in that arrangement. Although fuck knows why you would."

"Oh come on, Rocket, if you've already broken her in then why not let the rest of us have a turn?" he pressed and I was on my feet a moment later.

"Was me smashing your face in not clear enough?" I growled, stalking towards him. "Sloan Calabresi is *mine.* And I don't share well with others. If I catch you so much as looking at her with a twinkle in your fucking psycho eyes, I'll gouge them right out of your skull."

Frankie and Enzo got to their feet too, closing in behind me and backing me up. No one had ever stood against the three of us and lived to tell the tale. And this fucking worm would be no exception if he crossed me on this. His mother might have been our aunt, but he didn't even have the Romero name. He was nothing. Less than nothing. And I'd gladly rip him limb from limb to protect what was mine.

Guido raised both hands in surrender, smiling like it had all been some big joke.

"Heaven forbid I ever stand against the great Rocco Romero," he said in a tone that was just mocking enough to make me wanna pull a few of his teeth out. "Uncle Martello sent me to find all of you. He has a job we need to discuss."

My lip curled back as he said *we* like he was one of us. But he'd never even come close to entering the ring of love and honour that I held with my brothers.

I shouldered my way past him and Enzo and Frankie did the same as we left my room and headed down the stairs. It was getting dark out and I was beginning to wonder if Papa and Guido would be staying again. I didn't want to leave Sloan down in that cellar tonight, I wanted her warm and willing in my arms. I wanted to bury myself in her and taste every inch of her skin and bathe in the noises I could draw from those perfect lips.

Papa was waiting for us in the kitchen and I was surprised to find him wearing his coat while he read through something on his phone.

"You wanted to see us, Papa?" I asked curiously, wondering if it was just to say goodbye.

"Yes," Papa replied, not looking up from his phone and making us wait for him to finish before he explained.

I moved to take a seat along the breakfast bar beside Frankie, leaning back in my chair with a yawn. I really hadn't gotten much sleep last night. Not that I was complaining about that.

Papa finally pushed his cellphone into a pocket and gave us his attention.

"I have urgent business back in Sinners Bay," he said, not bothering to elaborate. "But we've also got an issue with a shipment that went missing out on the east docks. I need you to go and deal with it, Rocco."

"Me?" I asked, failing to hide the irritation at that suggestion from my tone.

"Yes, *you*. We can't have you out of sight for so long. Besides, this kind of issue really needs your touch. We can't have anyone thinking they can get away with losing our cargo."

I clucked my tongue, folding my arms in refusal. "Enzo or Frankie can deal with that just as easily as me. I've got work to do here."

"Anyone can babysit a girl in a cellar. I need *you* to deal with this shipment. No arguments."

I bit my tongue on further protests because I knew they wouldn't get me anywhere.

"So who's staying here?" I demanded, refusing to look at Guido despite the fact that I could practically imagine him bouncing up and down like an excited school kid wanting to volunteer. But there was no fucking way I'd be leaving him here with my principessa.

"I don't mind staying here," Guido offered predictably like the slimy stronzo he was.

"I'll stay," Frankie added quickly, stifling a yawn. "I need the rest."

"Fine," Papa announced as his cellphone started ringing again. "Frankie and Guido can stay. I'll meet you two in the car in ten minutes. Get your shit together and don't keep me waiting."

My lips parted on a protest, but he glared at me with a harsh finality which I knew wouldn't permit any arguments.

Papa strode from the room as he answered his cellphone and my heart beat a little faster as I realised I was really going to have to leave Sloan here with fucking Guido in the house.

I looked around at our slimy cousin and scowled. "Get the fuck out. I need to talk to my brothers."

Guido smiled in a way that showed off his missing teeth and slipped out of the room without a word.

"I won't let him near her," Frankie swore before I had to ask. "If he tries anything, I'll just shoot him."

I eyed the pistol strapped to his belt and nodded. There were two people in this world who I could rely on wholeheartedly and if my brother made an oath like that, then I knew I could count on him to keep his word.

"I'm trusting you, fratello," I growled. "I don't even want that stronzo to *look* at her while I'm gone."

"You have my word," he agreed seriously and I nodded.

"Fine. Let's just get this job done and I can get back here before dawn." I strode from the room straight along the hallway to the cellar door, pulling the key from my pocket.

The lock clicked loudly and I headed down the wooden stairs with my feet thumping heavily with each step.

Sloan was wrapped in blankets in one corner, her eyes wide with concern and her brow furrowed with suspicion. The little dog Frankie had brought back with him growled softly as I approached and she pushed herself to her feet with her arms folded across her chest defensively.

"You knew I was an asshole when you let me into your panties, bella," I said as I drew closer to her. "Don't go giving me the doe eyes like you thought fucking me would change that."

"You're like Jekyll and Hyde, Rocco," she growled, the fire in her gaze letting me know just how much she cared. "I never know what version of you I'm going to get."

"Which might be a problem if it didn't turn you on so much," I deadpanned. "Besides, Dr Jekyll only had two personalities. I've got at least nine."

Her lips twitched with an almost smile and I grinned at her like a predator eyeing a meal.

"So now your family are back, I'm just back to being chained in the cellar?" she asked, not bothering to hide her anger.

"I don't see any chains."

"I'm locked down here again."

"Hmm… well don't worry, I'll have you back in my bed as soon as I get back."

"Get back from where?" she asked, her gaze flickering with concern.

"I have a job to run. I should be back before dawn, but Frankie will take care of you while I'm gone."

The little white dog growled from the nest of blankets at her feet like it didn't much like the sound of that idea and I eyed it for a moment before looking back to her.

"You'll be gone all night?" Sloan breathed, reaching out to me like she couldn't quite help herself.

"You'll be fine," I promised. "Just stay down here, away from…" I trailed off because it might have been better not to mention the fact that Guido was staying in the house too. It would only worry her.

"From who?" she demanded, clearly not buying into my shit for one minute.

"Guido will be upstairs," I admitted. "But Frankie won't let him near you. I swear."

She looked up at me with those big eyes and nodded slowly like my word actually meant something to her.

"Do you promise you'll be back by tomorrow?" Sloan asked and the fact that she clearly wanted that made a little piece of my soul glow with excitement.

"Unless someone shoots me," I agreed.

Her eyes widened with fear, but she had to know that that was the life I lead. It wasn't exactly a surprise that I took my life into my hands every time I headed out on a job.

I caught her face between my hands and pressed my lips to hers, silently swearing that I'd be back as soon as I could.

She resisted for a moment, her anger holding her back before her lips parted for me and she gave in like she needed the kiss as much as I did.

I was the devil sent to corrupt her and if I'd been a better man, perhaps I'd have just walked away. But I wasn't done making Sloan sin for me and I planned on keeping at it for a while yet.

I broke away from her and walked out of the room at a fast pace.

I didn't look back. I didn't want to see her standing in that cellar, looking at me like I might be a different kind of man to the demon I was.

Besides, the sooner I got the hell out of here, the sooner I'd be back.

Sloan

I didn't want to fall blindly back into Rocco's arms. I couldn't let myself trust him too easily. Not when his moods were on a constant dial, swinging from hot to cold in a heartbeat. We hadn't started this crazy thing on equal terms. I was still a girl locked in his basement, held against my will by his family. And I wasn't going to forget that any time soon.

But the last few days we'd spent together had been…indescribable. It was like he saw right into my soul and nurtured the flame that lived there, adding kindling and keeping it alive. If nothing else, I had that to thank him for. That I was somehow more of a whole person now than I'd ever been in my life.

A few hours had passed since he'd left and I couldn't stop pacing, every groan of the pipes or thump upstairs making my heart lurch uncomfortably. Knowing Guido was in the house was more than enough to make me uneasy, but without Rocco here to stop him coming into the cellar, I was a ball of nerves.

When the stress was getting too much to handle, I moved up the stairs as quietly as I could with Coco clutched in my arms, lowering myself down beside the door and resting my ear to it.

It was quiet for a long time, the sound of the TV in the living room the only thing I could hear. But eventually, someone moved this way and I froze.

"I'm going for a nap," Guido's voice sounded out in the hall then his footsteps pounded up the stairs.

More footsteps followed into the hall and I strained my ears. "Good riddance, you piece of shit," Frankie muttered under his breath.

The door opened and I leaned back, looking up at Frankie with an innocent expression.

"You listening in on us, bella?" he teased, his eyes dancing with light.

"I just want to know where Guido is at all times," I said bitterly.

"I'll protect you, dolcezza," he said with a friendly smile. Frankie always seemed to be the most easy-going Romero, and yet I sensed something lurking in him that equalled the wildness of his other brothers.

My eyes fell to the gun holstered at his hip and I raised a brow. "I'd protect myself just fine if you give me that gun."

He chuckled darkly. "And have you blow my beautiful face off? I don't think so."

"It's Guido's ugly one I'm after. That would give you a thirty second head start to run," I said, trying out a wicked smile and Frankie's brows arched.

"Something tells me you really would pull the trigger on us. Is that innocent little face of yours hiding something twisted?"

"I was just thinking the same about yours. Do you always smile at people you've kidnapped?"

He barked a laugh. "Touché." He held out his hands. "Here, I'll take the dog out for a shit."

Coco growled low in his throat, tucking back into my arms.

"He's called Coco and he'll maul you if you're not careful," I warned, not wanting to part with my dog. But I knew Coco must have needed the toilet by now.

"I can handle the little stronzo." Frankie leaned down and I let him take him, even though my gut tugged as he did so.

"Bring him back," I demanded and Frankie nodded, cursing as Coco sank his teeth into his hand.

"I will, bella." He shut the door and the lock clicked again.

I sighed, rubbing my arms as the chill of this place drove into me. I rested my head back against the wall, hugging my arms around myself as I waited for Frankie to return.

My heart rate rocketed as footsteps pounded down the stairs. I immediately jumped to my feet, taking hold of the door handle in case Guido decided to try and come in here.

A few seconds ticked by, but he didn't come.

The front door opened and banged shut again, making me frown. I didn't want Guido near my dog almost as much as I didn't want him near me.

Coco started barking somewhere in the distance and my pulse thundered in my ears. I pressed against the door, trying to listen for voices, but I couldn't hear anything beyond the faraway yapping.

You touch him and I'll kill you, you creep.

The front door opened again and footsteps thumped straight toward me. A sharp lump pressed against my throat and I clutched the door handle again, holding it as tight as I could as someone unlocked the door.

The handle turned sharply and I couldn't hold it. It wrenched open and I stumbled back as Guido's shadow fell over me.

"Frankie!" I screamed over his shoulder just before Guido's weight collided with me. He threw me back against the wall and my head impacted with the bricks, making my thoughts tumble through my mind like shattered glass.

"He's not coming," Guido growled, his hot and sickly breath washing over me. He elbowed the door shut, crowding me in against the wall and I pushed at his arms to try and keep him back. "With the dose I gave him, he'll be out for hours. Plenty of time for us to have our fun, eh?"

"Get off of me!" I shouted as I regained my senses.

I shoved and kicked, but he didn't budge as he pressed his body flat against mine. He was only a couple of inches taller than me and he didn't hold any of the muscle the Romero brothers did, but he was still strong as hell.

I felt his arousal butting into my leg and grimaced as he pushed a hand between us, cupping my breast and squeezing through the thin material of Rocco's shirt.

"Get your fucking hands off of me," I spat, trying to rear forward and head butt him.

He laughed giddily, jerking back to avoid the blow. He reached between us to unbuckle his belt and my breathing became frantic. I scratched and clawed at him then smashed my knuckles into his face.

He reared backwards with a shout of rage and I lunged toward the door, my fingers brushing the handle before he snatched hold of my hair and dragged me back a step.

"Frankie!" I screamed so loud it rubbed my throat raw.

Coco was still barking somewhere and though I knew Guido had drugged Frankie, I was too desperate not to call for him, praying he might be conscious enough to come to my aid.

Guido dragged me down the stairs, forcing me along as he held my hair and I stumbled after him, shoving and scratching him in a desperate bid to get free.

At the bottom, Guido threw me against the wall face first then slammed against me from behind, grinding his crotch into my ass. I threw my elbow back, catching him hard in the ribs and hearing something crack. He wheezed, releasing me in an instant and staggering back a step.

I turned with a gasp and fled up the stairs, powering toward the unlocked door. If I could get outside, I could lock him in. I could get to Frankie.

The thump of heavy footsteps pounded after me and fear scored through my chest as I ran as fast as I humanely could.

I was two steps from the door. One-

I reached for the handle but was jerked off of my feet at the same moment by a hand locking around my ankle. I yelped as my chin hit the step and Guido's nails tore into my flesh, dragging me backwards.

I rolled over, throwing sharp kicks at him, wriggling and writhing to try and throw him off. His teeth were bared and sweat glistened on his brow as he reeled me toward him, closer and closer.

Panic clawed at my insides as I fought as hard as I could. I kicked out with my free leg again and again, catching him in the jaw, the chest, the forehead. But I was barefooted and the demonic look in his eyes said he wasn't going to give me up for anything. His fingernails were burying deeper into my skin and his grip was unrelenting.

He caught my free foot as I tried to kick him again, throwing it aside and falling over me. He pressed his weight down between my thighs, panting heavily as he ground his hard-on into my hip.

"If you put that thing near me, I'll rip it off," I snarled.

I started to thrash and kick and bite and Guido grunted in frustration as he tried to hold me down. Every time he caught one of my hands, I got the other one free. I tore at his shirt, his face, his arms, marking him everywhere with my nails and spilling his blood.

"Enough you little whore!" he spat, grabbing my face and cracking my head back against the edge of the next step up.

My vision blurred and my body fell still for too long. Far too long. I blinked away the haze, digging deep for the strength inside me and thinking over everything Royce had taught me.

"If they get you on your back, Miss Calabresi, let them think you're beat. Then go for the balls."

My vision sharpened and I shuddered as I found Guido pulling his fly down and shuffling his pants and boxers low on his hips. I clenched my jaw, a blind fury snaring me as I took in the hungry look in his eyes.

As much as it repulsed me, I let him drop over me once more, his gap-toothed smile glaring down at me.

Let him think you're beat.

Victory shone in his eyes as he reached down to pull up the long shirt covering me.

"Stay still, cherub," he purred. "Guido's ready for you now."

Before he could do anything more, I clutched his shoulders and slammed my knee between his legs as hard as I possibly could. He screamed like a girl and I sank my teeth straight into his throat, making him wail even louder. I tasted blood and dug my teeth deeper and deeper, ripping into his flesh like an animal.

He punched the side of my head and my ear rang from the blow as he forced my teeth from his neck. He scrambled back onto his knees, cupping his balls and whimpering like a kicked dog.

I drew both of my feet back with a shriek of defiance and threw them at the centre of his chest. My heels collided with his ribs and he yelped in alarm.

His arms flailed for half a second before he tumbled over backwards and crashed down the stairs.

A sickening crack sounded as he hit the concrete at the bottom and I drew in a heavy breath, slowly pushing myself upright. I spat his blood from my mouth, wiping my lips with the back of my hand as I gazed down at him, my body beginning to shake.

I'd killed him. I must have. He was too still. His neck was at an angle that was too awkward to be natural.

I couldn't make myself move for a long moment, staring at Guido's dead body with a sick satisfaction. The back of my head throbbed and bruises were blossoming across my skin where he'd held me. I was marked, but he was too. I'd fought and won. Taken on a monster and defeated him.

I felt no remorse. I felt nothing but relief.

When I finally regained my senses enough to move, I scrambled up the steps toward the door. I did not wanna stay down here with that creep's body. Even if he was deep in hell right now and had no chance of coming back for me.

I reached for the handle, but the door was wrenched open before I could grasp it. Rocco stared in at me, his brows pinching together, fear gripping his features as he took in the wounds on my flesh. I was shaking and an eternal moment of fear held me in its arms.

Guido might have been a monster, but he was still Rocco's cousin. His family. And I'd just killed him.

Rocco

I stood at the top of the cellar stairs with my heart pounding and my lips parted as I looked down at Guido's twisted corpse at the foot of them. He was dead. No question about it. Necks did not twist at that angle naturally.

Sloan stood before me, her hair loose and wild, her eyes desperate and complete panic lining every inch of her body.

Her shirt was torn, her lip bleeding and her hands were shaking.

"What did he do to you?" I demanded, stepping forward and grasping her chin so that she was forced to look up at me. Bruises marred her perfect flesh, pain flickering in her gaze as she moved.

"I…he…" Her eyes watered and her bottom lip trembled as she tried to find the words.

"Tell me, bella," I demanded, clutching her jaw and forcing her to meet my eye.

"He was going to force himself on me," she breathed. "I didn't mean to kill him, I just-"

"You're apologising for killing that stronzo?" I asked incredulously. "You think I give a shit about *him?* I'm asking about *you,* Sloan. Did he hurt you?"

Her eyes widened and the tears she'd been fighting finally spilled over as she shook her head and threw herself into my arms.

I locked her against my chest and looked down at Guido again. If she hadn't already killed him, I'd do it a thousand times over for this.

"Don't cry for him, bella," I growled, pushing her back and looking into her eyes.

"But I just killed someone," she gasped, blinking up at me through wet lashes.

"No. You just found out who you are."

"A killer?"

"A fighter. A survivor. A fucking warrior. You already proved it once when you looked me in the eye and pulled that trigger. No man will ever break your will. No monster will ever claim you."

"No monster but you, you mean?" she asked, gazing steadily into my eyes as her tears fell still.

"Yeah. No monster but me." I leaned forward and licked the tears from her cheeks one at a time, kissing her eyelashes as the salt of her sorrow coated my tongue.

"I am yours, Rocco," she breathed. "Some part of me belongs to you now."

"Good. Because I plan on keeping that part forever. No matter where you end up, I'll own it and you'll never fully escape me.

Because my soul is bound to yours, Sloan. And you're my monster too."

Her hands fisted in my hair and she dragged me down so that her mouth could capture mine. She kissed me hard, her lips bruising, her tongue captivating, everything about her demanding I submit for once and I wasn't strong enough to resist her.

She finally pulled back and the fear which had lived in her eyes had been replaced by a fire of strength.

"What now?" she demanded.

"Now I've got a body to get rid of. Papa stayed in the city but he'll have to be told." I pulled my cellphone from my pocket and took a photo of Guido at the foot of the stairs. I sent it on to Papa with a brief message saying he'd tripped.

A moment later my phone pinged with his reply.

Papa:
Deal with it. I'll tell your aunt.

Sloan's eyes widened as she read his reply. "That's it? He's not going to figure out that I pushed him?"

"You didn't push him. The stupid fucker fell," I replied with a shrug. "Besides, who'd believe an innocent little thing like you was that bloodthirsty?"

I didn't wait for her response before tugging her out of the room. The constant yapping of her little dog came from the bathroom and I yanked the door open, freeing the little fucker so that he leapt into her arms. Sloan scooped him up and held him close as I led her to the fire in the living room and planted her before it so that she could warm up while I hunted down Enzo.

We'd arrived back to find Frankie out cold on the front porch with a fucking needle sticking out of his neck. Sloan's screams had led me to her and I swear I'd never felt dread like I had in that moment.

I found Enzo half way up the stairs, dragging Frankie up them by his arms.

"Guido's dead," I announced as I moved to help him with our younger brother. "He tried to hurt Sloan and she threw him down the stairs."

"That stronzo is lucky he's dead or I'd kill him myself for this," Enzo growled.

Frankie murmured something incoherent as we carried him up to his room and I ground my jaw.

"I'd have made his death slower if it had been up to me," I snarled.

"The stronzo's been asking for it for years," Enzo muttered in agreement.

"Papa will accept it, but Aunt Clarissa won't ever let it go," I stated.

"Yeah, well maybe she should have gotten her son under control a long time ago and he wouldn't have ended up in this fucking mess," Enzo said with half a shrug.

"Got to help…Sloan," Frankie murmured in his sleep and a smile pulled at my mouth. I could count on my brothers for anything, but Guido had stooped lower than I'd ever suspected he would. To actually drug one of us to get to Sloan was fucking calculated. But I guessed sick little psycho rapists would do what sick little psycho rapists had to to get their kicks.

"We need to get rid of the body," I muttered as we dropped Frankie onto his bed.

"You want me to do it?" Enzo offered.

"Nah. You stay here with him in case he starts choking on his own vomit and I'll go burn the asshole."

Enzo laughed darkly and dropped into the chair beside Frankie's bed.

"You should ask Sloan if she wants to help you," he joked. "If that bastardo had tried to fuck me I'd wanna watch him burn."

I snorted a laugh and headed downstairs.

That's not a bad idea.

I still wore my coat and boots so I headed straight out the back and across the yard to the huge shed at the edge of the forest. I had to dig the snow away from the doors before I could open them. To the right of the space an old Cadillac sat with gleaming red paint and an engine that hadn't run for about twenty years. It had been my grandfather's pet project and no one had ever thought to get rid of it after he passed. After the Calabresis killed him.

To the left of the space we kept a huge stack of old wooden pallets and fence panels. Basically anything that we could burn when we needed to build a pyre to get rid of a dead body. Which wasn't all that often. Although it was often enough that we also kept a can of gas ready to light the fires and industrial sized bottles of bleach to wash down the fire pit afterwards. Just in case.

I set about heaving pallets out of the stack and piling them up just far enough from the shed doors to be sure it wouldn't catch light too. When I was done, I doused the lot in gasoline and grabbed a tarp and a roll of duct tape from the pile on a shelf at the back of the shed.

I pulled my coat off and tossed it aside as I made it back into the house then headed down to the cellar to wrap up our least favourite cousin like the world's shittiest Christmas present.

I dropped the tarp beside him at the bottom of the stairs, laying it out flat before kicking him until he rolled on top of it.

I looked down at his ugly face which was still battered from my attack on him last week.

I pursed my lips and thought back on all the times we'd spent together growing up. He used to follow me everywhere like a lost little mutt. I remembered him asking his mother for a duplicate of every present I got and even for the same clothes as me so that he could look the same. It was kind of sad really. Pathetic. He'd always tried so hard to be one of us, skulking along behind me and my brothers like he thought he might take Angelo's place and we'd become a group of four again.

He used to do all kinds of weird stuff to get our attention, hanging out on the edges, showing us animals he'd caught and mutilated in various gross ways or pulling up girls' skirts like we might find the sight of panties utterly hilarious.

Once he'd started torturing people instead of animals, he'd delighted in sending us details of what he'd done to them and even photographs. I'd been eating a perfectly good burrito once and he'd ruined it by sending me a slow motion video of him shooting some guy in the head. I still couldn't look at Mexican food the same way.

And one time, he'd blown out all of the candles on my birthday cake. *Worst birthday ever.*

"Good riddance, feccia," I spat, flipping the tarp over his face, just glad that I'd never have to look at it again.

I rolled it tight, securing it in place with the duct tape to be sure that no more of his blood would spill in the house. That would be a bitch to clean out of the hard wood if it got into the grain.

Once he looked like an awkward as fuck DHL delivery, I grabbed him by his feet and started dragging him up the stairs.

With each step, his head thumped against the wood and I started singing to the tune of Pop Goes The Weasel. "Guido came to get his load off, but Sloany is not feeble, he tried to take what wasn't his, so chop! goes the Guido."

Sloan poked her head out of the living room as I made it to the hallway and I grinned wolfishly as she raised an eyebrow at me.

"Do you always make jokes about murders?" she asked, frowning at the body I was dragging across the hallway.

"I mean…only when I've been out murdering." I shrugged. "Besides, this wasn't murder. It was self defence."

"Should you really be so…cheery?" she asked.

"You want me to cry over an asshole who would have raped and murdered you?" I asked, the humour slipping from my voice as I dropped my grip on his ankles and his feet thumped to the floor.

Sloan's gaze hardened at that. "No."

"And are you going to cry over him again?"

"No," she growled.

"Good. Do you wanna come watch him burn then?" I asked with a grin, holding out my hand in offering.

Sloan offered me a tentative smile in return and when mine widened, so did hers. She took my hand and I yanked her into my arms, pressing my lips to hers hard and fast.

"Never apologise for who you are, bella," I growled. "You're a warrior. *Guerrier.*"

"I like the sound of that," she replied, her palms flat against my chest.

"It suits you," I agreed.

I stepped away from her and grabbed Guido's ankles again as I started hauling him towards the back door. Sloan kicked on Mamma's boots and pulled her coat on before following me out into the snow. I set a path straight for the stacked wood I'd prepared and heaved Guido's corpse up onto the top of it.

The whole thing rattled as his weight hit it and I walked away to get the can of gasoline before pouring it all over him.

Sloan stood staring at the pyre as still as a statue and I couldn't for the life of me figure out what was going on behind those big brown eyes.

I pulled a match box from my pocket and moved towards her, sliding the canister open. I drew a match out and twirled it between my fingers as I closed the box again.

Sloan was still staring at the pyre as if I wasn't right beside her.

I reached out slowly, offering her the match.

"You want the honour?" I asked, wondering if this would be a step too far. The point at which she balked, fell back, said no...

Sloan's gaze slid to me, her lips parting on a thought which didn't leave them.

Her gaze dipped to the match and she reached for it, taking the box in her other hand.

She looked back to the pyre but my eyes were fixed on her. Watching as she slowly placed the match against the box and drew in a long breath.

As she struck the match, the flame was reflected in her eyes, dancing in the darkness of her pupils.

She flicked it and it arced away from her, hitting the pyre and setting it alight with a whoosh of flame which blazed instantly, warming my back.

Her lips curved into a smile as she watched him burn and I couldn't tear my gaze from her. This creature of mine. This mystery I ached to unlock.

As her smile widened, mine couldn't help but follow and I cupped my hands around my mouth, howling to the moon as the bonfire blazed behind us.

Sloan laughed, her eyes finally falling on me.

"Take your shirt off, bella," I said, my gaze slipping down to her bare legs where they showed beneath her coat.

"Why?" she asked with a frown.

"Gotta burn everything with DNA evidence on it," I pointed out.

She pursed her lips then shrugged out of Mamma's coat, handing it to me. I waited until she'd pulled my shirt off too and took that as well, smirking at the sight of her in her white underwear standing out in the cold.

She reached for the coat again, but I tossed it straight onto the bonfire alongside the shirt.

"What the hell?" she demanded angrily.

"Cross contamination," I explained with a wink as I pulled my shirt off and threw it on the fire too.

"It's freezing out here, Rocco!"

"Let me warm you up then." I stalked towards her and she backed up a few steps before I caught her.

Sloan squealed as I lifted her into my arms and kept going until we made it into the shed where I dropped her on her ass on the hood of the Cadillac.

"You deserve something special, principessa," I purred, gripping her knees and slowly inching them apart as I looked down at her.

"Rocco, the door is wide open," Sloan hissed, looking over my shoulder where the bonfire raged, the heat of the flames enough to warm us even at this distance. There was no view of the house though, the doors didn't face it and my brothers wouldn't come out here looking for us.

"We're all alone out here," I promised, tightening my grip on her knees.

She licked her bloody lip and slowly stopped resisting me, allowing me to part her thighs.

"Tell me exactly how you want me to make you come," I breathed, drawing closer to her and slowly pushing her hair back over her shoulders.

Her lips opened on an answer but she didn't offer one. I smirked at the challenge she presented.

"Tell me what your Italian boyfriend used to do to you. Tell me what he did to make you scream and I'll prove I can do it better."

Sloan hesitated a long moment before answering, her eyes skipping back and forth between mine like she was hunting for something.

"I...well, he never really managed to...not like what you did to me with the...you know. Or when we..."

"Are you telling me I gave you your first orgasm with an icicle?" I asked her, my lips lifting at the idea of that.

"No!" she protested. "I've had orgasms before! Just on my own. I mean...no, I didn't mean...*oh god.*" She buried her face in her hands and my smile widened until I was worried it might just split my face in half. She was fucking adorable when she was flustered and I was getting addicted to making her blush.

"You wanna show me how you do that, bella?" I purred, leaning close to her ear.

"What?" she gasped, peeking out at me between her fingers.

I laughed darkly and reached out to peel her hand from her face. I slid it down her body until I pressed her fingers down between her thighs and she gasped as I increased the pressure of my hand on hers and started making her circle her fingers against herself.

"Show me how you like it," I dared her, pulling my hand back and watching her as she fell still.

"Rocco, I don't think I-"

"Do you want me to do it too?" I offered, sliding my fly down and watching her eyes widen as I freed myself from my pants. She inhaled sharply as I wrapped my hand around the hard length of my dick and the sound of her shock just made me want to push her more.

Sloan stared at me as I slowly started moving my hand back and forth, swallowing thickly as her chest rose and fell with each deep breath she took.

"This is for you," I said, my voice rough. "This is how much you turn me on. Don't you want me to see how I make you feel too?"

Her eyes slid from the movement of my hand back to my face and she slowly pushed her fingers into the top of her panties.

Her movements were hesitant, but she slowly moved her hand lower and my pulse pounded harder at the sight of her trying this for me. Because she wanted to please me.

"That's it, bella," I purred. "Can you feel how wet you are?"

Her hand slid lower still and she moaned softly as she felt it. "Yes," she breathed.

"Don't you want to come for me?" I asked as she fell still for a long moment like she wasn't sure if she could do this or not. "I thought you weren't afraid of anything, little warrior," I challenged.

"I'm not," she growled and I groaned as her hand started moving in soft circles.

"*Fuck,* Sloan, you're so beautiful," I growled as I moved my hand faster, stroking my shaft and running my thumb over the sensitive end as she started to really put on a show for me.

She moaned lustily, her head tipping back, her long hair swaying as she continued to move her hand in circles beneath her panties. Her other hand moved to toy with her breast and I watched as she slid her bra from her shoulder, freeing herself so that she could tug softly on her peaked nipple.

I growled with desire. I'd never felt so turned on by any other woman in all my life as I did by her. She was pure and innocent and damaged and dirty all at once and I wanted to drown in the depths of her secrets and gorge myself on a feast of her flesh.

I slowed my movements before I finished too soon, not wanting this to end, needing to watch her come apart for me first.

Her moans were getting louder, the closer she got to her climax and I could feel myself aching to follow her over the edge but I slowed my movements further, staring at her as her eyes fell closed.

"Look at me, Sloan," I commanded. "Tell me how good it feels to touch yourself for me."

Her eyes fluttered open and met mine, but that blush came back before she could utter a word.

"Does it feel good?" I asked, prompting her.

"Yes," she gasped, her movements growing faster.

"Tell me how wet you are," I purred.

"So wet," she breathed. "For you, Rocco."

I growled hungrily at that, my dick twitching in demand as I stroked it once again.

"Are you about to come for me, bella?" I asked.

"Yes," she gasped. "Yes…ahh."

I growled with a desperate desire as she pushed herself over the edge with a cry of pleasure and I moved forward to take what I needed. Because my hand was all well and good, but what I really ached for was the tightness of her body surrounding every last inch of me.

Sloan tipped backwards onto the hood of the car as her orgasm robbed her energy and I growled as I yanked her panties off of her. I pushed her legs further apart and she reached for me hungrily as I drove myself inside her.

"Oh, Rocco," she moaned, her legs coiling around me as I pounded my hips against hers, fucking her hard and fast and taking, taking, taking as she cried out in pleasure and begged for more.

This girl was like the sun and I was burning up the closer I got to her, but I couldn't get enough either. I was drowning in the depths of her and all I wanted was to crawl deeper, get further beneath her skin and wear it for my own.

I gripped her hips as I continued to pound into her and she cried out as I wrung a second orgasm from her body and her nails bit into my forearms, spilling blood. Her head fell back as she was overwhelmed and I groaned as I fucked her like I'd never get to do it again. Like I needed to brand my name on the inside of her and make sure she could never remove the scar.

I was building closer and closer to my own climax but I wasn't done with her yet and I moved my hand between us, circling on that perfect little raised bump at the apex of her thighs.

"Shit, Rocco," she moaned, half begging for more, half protesting she couldn't take it. But she could take it. I'd set her flesh alive with pleasure and tear every inch of satisfaction from her before I'd stop.

She was tightening around me, crying out, pawing at her breasts, my arms, fisting her hands in her hair as she tried to find some relief from the intensity of what I was doing to her.

"Come for me, baby," I demanded. "I can't stop until you do."

She didn't have words, only more moans left her lips but she grabbed my forearms and I felt the keen slice of pain as her nails broke the skin again and the scream that left her had me exploding too.

My weight fell over her as I pulsed inside her and I panted heavily in pure bliss as I stole a kiss from her perfect mouth.

"Holy shit," she mumbled almost incoherently.

And I laughed darkly, feeling pretty fucking pleased with myself for what I'd just done to her.

"Do you still want to leave me, bella?" I whispered, my lips brushing her ear and my stubble catching on a loose strand of her hair.

"Never," she sighed.

"Do you mean that?" I asked, my heart leaping with hope in a way that it had absolutely no right to do.

I shifted back just enough to look into those big brown eyes and she swallowed thickly. "If there was any way that it could be so, then yes," she agreed in a soft voice.

"What if I just never let you go?" I offered. "Your family can go on believing you're my captive but really you'll be my…"

"What?" she pressed, demanding an end to that sentence.

"*My* Sloan," I breathed passionately. "We could just be together. Here, in the city, you could choose whichever one of our properties you want to make our home."

"Your family would never accept that," she replied. "Even if mine stopped trying to rescue me."

"So we leave the city," I offered, the warmth of her body making me feel willing to sacrifice anything just so that I didn't have to ever let her go. "Spin a globe and pick a destination. The North Pole, the Sahara desert, I don't care. If you're there I want to be there too."

"That sounds like heaven," she admitted slowly, brushing her fingers along the side of my face.

"More like hell with me at your side," I reminded her. "But I'd make a palace surrounded by fire and brimstone right in the depths of it for you if you'd really come."

"I would," she breathed.

And even though that didn't mean anything, even though we had no plan or no way to even try and do this impossible thing, I couldn't help but feel a flood of relief at her words. Because when I'd bet my brothers that I could make her love me, I'd never once considered that I might fall for her too. And now that I had her, I knew there was no coming back from it.

If you cut me open, her name would be branded right on the blackened lump of my heart. And though there wasn't much to it, I would still happily cut it out for her and lay it at her feet. Because if there was one thing left in this world that I wanted to do with my life, then it would be to worship at this goddess's altar.

Nicoli

Mountaindale was a three hour drive out of Sinners Bay and pretty much the perfect place to come and hide out if you were a kidnapping scumbag. The town was central, but countless cabins and manors lay up in the mountains with their owners coming and going regularly. It was a small enough place for people to notice strangers, but we weren't a rare enough occurrence to draw too much attention. Plenty of folks came up here for weekend getaways and romantic breaks in the snow.

Of course, I didn't exactly look like I was on a romantic getaway with my face beaten half to shit and a scowl deep enough to bury treasure inside it.

But last night, the Romeros had made their first mistake. Rocco had shown his face out on the east docks and caused a scene big enough to draw federal attention. Not that the cops had actually shown up. They circled nearby but didn't attempt to intervene until they knew he was gone; even law enforcement knew better than to tango with the families that ruled this town.

He'd tied a guy to a shipping container and proceeded to aim fireworks at him like it was a Fourth of July parade.

Everyone was talking about it and half the city had seen the fireworks lighting up the night sky. The damn theatrics had gone on for nearly two hours until Rocco had gotten to the bottom of whatever the hell had been bugging him and in that time, I'd arrived at the docks.

I'd spotted his car – the same fucking one he'd stolen my bride in – parked up just on the edge of the marina. Everyone in Sinners Bay knew to stay the fuck away when Rocco Romero lost his shit so the whole place had been abandoned.

I'd parked up in the shadows and waited. And it hadn't been long before the chief motherfucker himself had come sauntering out of the docks with his asshole brother Enzo right beside him. The two of them had been laughing their heads off like a pair of fucking lunatics and hadn't paid nearly enough attention to their surroundings as they'd leapt into their car.

Even better than that, they must have been in a hurry to get back to this town because they'd headed straight out onto the highway and taken a direct route right here. To the middle of nowhere. If they owned a property up here, it sure as hell hadn't been on the list I'd taken from the accountant. Which meant it was a well-kept secret. And the perfect place to hide the Calabresi Principessa.

I didn't believe in luck. I made my own. And I was sure as hell that they'd just led me straight to my bride.

I'm coming Sloan. Soon I'll have you back in my arms.

I'd managed to tail them as far as this town, but then I'd lost them at a set of traffic lights. But that was fine. I couldn't exactly tail them right up to their front door without them noticing, but I sure as shit knew I'd tightened the net.

They were here somewhere. I could practically smell them on the breeze.

The snow had fallen still and all that was left was great white mounds of the stuff piled at the roadside.

The crisp morning air made the cuts on my face sting and I cursed beneath my breath. The Romeros would pay for all they'd done to me. They'd even taken Coco from me and I had no idea what had become of the fierce little pup now. But if they truly thought that that little display back at their other property would put me off, then they were seriously deluded. The only thing that would keep me from my destiny was death. And even then I'd try my best to haunt them from beyond the grave.

They were about to regret leaving me alive.

I'd spent last night in a motel on the outskirts of town, paying cash and saying little to the guy who ran it. He wasn't going to have the information I needed. But someone here would.

I weighed my options as I drove through the town, eyeing the various stores and wondering which of them would hold the key to this mystery.

I couldn't afford to make too much of a scene. I needed to figure out where the Romeros' house was without them hearing about me from some busybody or lookout they were keeping close.

The general store and diner were probably good bets, but they were busy too. I wouldn't go unnoticed asking questions in there.

As I reached the end of the high street, a hardware store caught my eye. If I was a fucked up little Romero keeping women hostage in my basement, then I'd probably need those kinds of supplies. Rope, duct tape, a little bit of psycho shopping definitely would have been in order.

I pulled up outside the store and gazed in through the glass shopfront as I waited for the few customers inside to leave.

Within fifteen minutes, the shoppers exited and the only person I could still see inside was the old guy behind the counter.

I got out of my car and walked up to the door.

A little bell rang to announce my arrival as I pushed it open and I turned back to twist the lock behind me, flipping the sign around to *closed* for good measure.

I moved through the store and walked up the aisle which led to the counter, picking up a length of chain as I went.

"Good morning," the guy said, not looking up from the monitor beside him.

"I'm hoping you can help me with something," I said slowly, closing in on him.

"What's that?" He turned to look at me and balked as he took in my battered face. A week had done a lot to heal the damage caused by Enzo and Frankie, but the bruising was yellow and angry, almost looking worse than it had at first.

"I'm looking for someone," I said.

The guy kept his eyes on me and slowly reached beneath the counter for the shotgun he no doubt kept ready for just such a scenario.

I continued my approach, wrapping the ends of the chain around my fists as I went.

"Who?" he asked, his arm tensing as he eased the gun into his grip.

"A man with the face of an angel and the soul of a demon," I said. "He took something very precious from me."

"I wouldn't know anything about that. Why don't you go on back to town and look elsewhere?"

"I think I'm in the right place," I replied, ignoring his suggestion. "The man I'm looking for is called Rocco Romero."

The guy's eyes lit with recognition and I smiled hungrily as I reached the counter.

"Never heard of him." He raised the shotgun suddenly, pointing it right at my face.

I remained still for a long moment then lunged forward, hooking the chain around the gun and yanking it aside just as he pulled the trigger.

The shot blasted out and a hole was ripped into the wooden floor to my left.

Before he could try and fire again, I ripped the gun right out of his hands and threw it down behind me.

"Now," I said darkly. "Let's try that answer again."

Sloan

I lay in bed with Rocco, my hand resting on his chest as it slowly rose and fell in time with his breaths. It was late morning and he'd not let me out of his sight since we'd burned Guido's body. He'd also claimed me all night long so I was aching in places I hadn't even known existed.

He couldn't seem to sate his appetite for me, and I had to admit I had the same problem with him. The way Rocco took my body was rough and possessing, like he'd die if he stopped. I couldn't get enough of it, giving as good as I got. I was starting to think a savage lived in me too.

I slipped out of bed, leaving Rocco to sleep and he remained passed out even when I laid a kiss on his lips. A small smirk pulled at my features. I couldn't help but feel a little proud that I was the reason this bear of a man was exhausted. He'd awoken a voracious creature in me and he couldn't tame it – though he sure as hell tried.

I pulled on one of his shirts and headed out the door, walking downstairs and through to the kitchen. Coco was sleeping on a bed of pillows in one corner and jumped up to lick my ankles in greeting. I dished him out some dog food, wondering why the hell the Romeros had some here, but really not sure I wanted to know at the same time. Then I started making a batch of pancakes and Enzo and Frankie soon appeared, drifting toward me like hungry wolves.

"I hope we can keep you forever, bella," Frankie said, taking a stack of pancakes as I handed them to him.

"Yeah, especially now you killed our creepy cousin. Maybe we should throw a party for you later," Enzo said with a disturbing grin, taking his own plate. It was weird how easily all of the Romeros had accepted Guido's death. I was starting to see that the three of them had their own moral code, and what was weirder was that something about it made total sense to me.

"Or you could set me free? That'd be good enough as thanks," I said lightly and the two of them laughed.

I sighed internally, thinking about Rocco. What were we going to do about us? I couldn't stay chained here for the rest of my life, even if he did think that was a viable option. And quite frankly, it angered me that he did. He might have wanted me under lock and key, but I certainly didn't want to be kept that way. I dreamed of a free life for both of us. I just couldn't see how it was possible. But I knew with all my heart that I wanted it to be.

It wasn't long before Rocco appeared, strolling into the room in grey sweatpants which were riding low on his hips. He looked edible and I half wanted to forget my breakfast and gorge myself on him instead.

"Pancakes?" I offered, holding out a plate.

He took it, grabbing the can of whipped cream and squirting it all over them with a smirk.

"You don't like sweet things," Frankie commented in confusion.

"I'm starting to." He grinned darkly and I blushed as I remembered him eating the cakes off of me right over the island his brothers were currently sitting at.

He sat down next to Enzo and I took the place beside him, his arm brushing mine as he ate.

We weren't exactly keeping it a secret from his brothers that we were hooking up, but if they hadn't realised before, I guess a night of my screams filling the house had done the job.

I'd been embarrassed for about five seconds last night before I'd been so lost to the pleasure Rocco had given me, that I'd forgotten what part of the world we were in, let alone that there were other people in the house.

Now, in the quiet of the morning, I was slightly more self-conscious over that fact.

Rocco's phone rang and he hooked it out of his pocket before bringing it to his ear. "Yeah?" he answered, then he fell very still. His bicep flexed and his jaw started to tick. "How long do we have?" he answered, rising from his seat and looking to his brothers. "Well give me your best guess, asshole." He paused for a long moment and my heart lurched as he spat, "Fuck!"

He hung up, shoving the phone into his pocket with an intense look.

"What is it, fratello?" Enzo rose to his feet, his hand dropping to the hunting knife at his hip.

"Rocco?" Frankie questioned.

My heart hammered as Rocco's eyes turned to me, looking like the world was falling apart. "Nicoli has found the house. He's on his way. Phil thinks he's already close, which means he will have an army right behind him."

My breathing grew frantic and I slid off of my seat, pushing a hand into my hair. Nicoli was coming for me? But that meant parting with Rocco, saying goodbye. And though I didn't want to be a prisoner anymore, I didn't want to lose him either.

"Sloan," Rocco's gruff voice cut through my thoughts as he turned me toward him, his gaze burning into me. "We have to run. Come with us."

Enzo barked a laugh. "Slap her in chains and take her."

Coco barked angrily, his hackles raising.

"Shut the fuck up!" Rocco roared, then snatched my arm and pulled me from the room into the lounge. He slammed the door and cupped my cheek, dragging me close. "If you want to go, I'll let you. Though it will kill me, bella. You may as well take my beating heart with you if you choose that option. But I don't want you to. I want – no – I *need* you to stay with me."

"Rocco…" I backed up, needing space to think, to breathe. What did I want? Was I really going to run from Rocco?

If I did, I'd never see him again. I'd be forced back into the life I led before, forced to marry Nicoli. I'd spend the rest of my days under my father's thumb. I'd never feel free again.

"I can't live in chains," I gasped, hardly able to draw in air as I felt the pressure of time closing in on us. How could I make such a weighty decision with not even a moment to think?

Rocco's brows pulled together, something shifting in his gaze. "I'll never chain you again, amore mio. Come with me and I'll make us a new life. I'll give up this one if I have to. I'll gift you more freedom than you've ever known."

I stared at him, breathless, trying to decide if I trusted the words he spoke. The truth blazed in his eyes, his promise clear. He'd keep it, I knew he would, but I didn't know how I knew that. The thought of going back to my old life was simply too suffocating to even consider. So this was it. The choice I had to make which wasn't even a choice at all when it came down to it.

I nodded, swallowing the lump in my throat. "I'll come with you."

He rushed forward with a look of relief, dragging me into his arms and pressing his mouth to mine. He fisted his hand in my hair, groaning as he clutched me to his chest like he feared I'd turn to dust at any moment.

A whole life opened up before me, full of possibility. A life at Rocco's side, our fates tangled together, the two of us defying our families by being united. It was the most insane idea I'd ever had and yet it made the most sense to me in the world.

"I am yours from my black heart to my tarnished soul," he growled powerfully. "Take it, own it, destroy it, I don't care so long as it's in your possession."

"I love you, Rocco," I said, my heart beating out of rhythm. I'd never said those words to anyone. Not like this. Not in a way where I felt them with every fibre of my body. It was like they were written into the essence of my being, permanently branded there to defy anyone else who sought to claim me.

He smiled boyishly, something I'd never once seen on his face. It was open and sweet and made him look so handsome. He opened his mouth but fell quiet as the door swung open.

Rocco's brothers spilled in like they'd been pressed against it on the other side.

"She fucking said it!" Enzo said in surprise.

"Merda santa," Frankie laughed, taking out his wallet. "I didn't think you could do it, Rocco, but shit, you really can make any woman fall in love with you."

I stepped away from Rocco, a horrible feeling of dread swirling through my chest. "What are they talking about?"

Rocco looked between his brothers and me, an expression of horror twisting his features.

"Come on. We need to go, we can talk about the bet later," Frankie urged, glancing over his shoulder nervously.

"What bet?" I breathed, taking another step back. My pulse was too loud in my ears and a voice in the back of my head was screaming at me to beware.

Rocco moved toward me with an apology in his eyes and I waited for some explanation, but it didn't come.

Enzo raised his brows. "You better explain, fratello. The principessa's heart is breaking. Isn't that what you wanted anyway? Might as well rub salt in the wound and enjoy it."

I turned to Rocco with a burning intensity in my gaze, everything they were saying clicking into place in my head. He gave me no answer, his expression taut.

"Tell me what they're talking about," I demanded, moving behind an armchair when he tried to get close again. I needed to hear it from him before I believed this, but I was also terrified of him confirming it. Because a small part of me was still hoping he'd deny it.

Rocco looked desperate as he stared at me. We were parted by only a meter of space but it suddenly felt like a whole ocean.

"I made a bet with my brothers," he rasped out, his features contorted. "I never thought-"

"What bet?" I snapped again, my fingernails biting into the back of the chair.

Enzo and Frankie shared an awkward look, glancing at their brother to see what he was going to say.

"I bet them that I could…" He swallowed thickly, his gaze hardening to stone. "That I could make you fall in love with me."

Panic bloomed. My world tilted and spun.

I clung to the armchair harder, feeling like I was going to come apart if I let go.

The pitiful look Frankie gave me drove a nail right through my chest. Because they were serious, this was actually happening. Rocco had faked it this entire time just for the sake of some callous bet.

He'd tricked me, lied to me. Made me think…

I cringed full bodily, turning my back on him, holding a hand over my face as I realised how stupid I'd been. I'd let a Romero into my heart so he could break it and torture me beneath my flesh. He'd wanted revenge on my family and this was it. What crueller way to harm my father than to make his daughter fall for him and break her heart?

I suddenly felt sick, my breakfast churning in my stomach and threatening to come back up.

This was all Rocco had wanted. He'd even convinced me to run away with him. How could I have been such a damn idiot?

"Sloan, listen to me-" Rocco started.

"Listen to *you*?" I spat hollowly. I turned back to face him, finding Enzo and Frankie sidling towards the door. "Fuck you, Rocco. Fuck all of you!"

"It was a game at first, but it's not anymore," he implored.

"Liar," I hissed, pointing an accusing finger at him. "At least own your lie. Drop the shit, Rocco. You're a good actor, but the scene is over."

I blinked back the tears which were searing my eyes, threatening to make me weak in front of him. But no more. I wasn't going to be his captive, his game. How dare he? *How fucking dare he?*

Gunshots rattled beyond the window and I gasped as I lurched around to look at the snowy slope outside. My heart hammered against my ribcage and adrenaline flooded my veins. Rocco's brothers burst back into the room and Coco charged in with them.

Frankie scooped him up and snatched his pistol into his grip at the same time.

Nicoli was here. He'd come for me. I didn't want to return to my father's side, but I sure as hell wasn't going to stay here with the Romeros. With *Rocco*. And once I was home, it wouldn't be so hard to slip away. I wouldn't be in any real chains. I'd pack a bag and run. I'd make my own life and no one would ever have a say in it again.

Rocco

I grabbed Sloan's hand and yanked her away from the window as the glass shattered. She screamed as we rolled across the floor and I pinned her down, creating a cage with my body to protect her as more gunfire rang out.

"I'm sorry, bella and I promise I'll make it up to you. But right now we need to get the hell out of here," I growled.

"Get to the cache, Rocco!" Frankie called from the far side of the room where he was taking cover beside the window with Enzo. "I'll cover you!"

"We'll meet you out back," I yelled as the shots rang out so loudly that I could hardly hear myself think.

He started returning fire with his pistol and I leapt up, dragging Sloan to her feet too and running from the room.

I held her hand tightly, refusing to let go as I dragged her out into the hall.

"Let me go, Rocco!" she demanded. "You said you'd let me go if I wanted to leave!"

"No," I snapped, she'd said that she would come with me before Enzo opened his big fucking mouth. That was good enough for me. I wasn't letting her run off while she was angry. She'd realise the truth in time, but right now we just needed to get the hell out of here. We were outnumbered, out-gunned and as much as it pissed me off, outmatched. There was no way in hell that the three of us could take on a hoard of Calabresis armed to the teeth. And I'd die before I let them take Sloan from me.

More shots were fired and the heavy crash of someone trying to break down the front door sounded again and again.

I dragged Sloan after me down the hall, throwing open the door to Papa's office before racing inside and pushing her into a corner so that she couldn't escape me.

I ripped a huge oil painting of a mountain scene from the wall to reveal a safe set into the brickwork. I jammed my thumb against the code reader as I punched in the code to unlock it. Mamma's birthday. He'd never changed it. Never stopped loving her, even after all this time. And I was beginning to get a sense of what that feeling was like.

I ripped the metal door open and started grabbing guns.

I threw a rifle over my shoulder then jammed three pistols into the back of my pants.

I grabbed the bag filled with ammo next, knocking a stack of cash out of the safe in my haste so that hundred dollar bills scattered all over the carpet. I tossed the bag over my other shoulder and snatched Sloan's hand again as I ran back for the door.

She dug her heels in and I stumbled as I spun back to face her.

"I need to go, Rocco," she growled.

"No," I snapped. "The bet was thoughtless and cruel and stupid but it doesn't have anything to do with what you just said to me. That was before I-"

A huge crash came from the front of the house and Enzo's pained cries made my heart leap up into my throat.

I wrenched the office door open, pulling the rifle from my shoulder and burst out into the hallway just as a flood of Calabresis poured inside led by Nicoli fucking Vitoli.

"Sloan!" he bellowed, his eyes wheeling about as he hunted for her and I took aim.

Just as I squeezed the trigger, a warm body collided with me and I was knocked from my feet as Sloan tackled me.

Sloan rolled across the floor to the other side of the hall as I my shot went wide and the Calabresis scattered to take cover. My rifle fell from my grip, clattering as it rolled out into the hall.

Footsteps pounded across the landing upstairs and my heart thundered with panic for my brothers as the Calabresis opened fire.

I snatched a pistol from my belt and fired back at random, scrambling across the hall towards Sloan as she cowered against the wall.

I dragged her through the door into the dining room and raced across the wide space with her in tow.

"Sloan!" Nicoli bellowed again and I felt her indecision as she tried to pull back against me.

I tightened my grip and dragged her through the door at the far end of the room and out towards the back of the house.

The back door was clear and I ripped it open before pulling her out into the snow. We didn't have time to grab coats or even shoes and she shivered as her bare feet met with the snow and goosebumps raced over her exposed flesh.

The sound of breaking glass came from upstairs a moment before two bodies leapt from the balcony which lined the back of the house.

"*Fuck!*" Enzo cursed as he rolled to his knees and dread coursed through me as the snow was stained red beneath him.

"We can't face them. There's too many," Frankie said as he got up, glancing between me and Sloan. He still had her little dog tucked into his arms and the furry thing didn't seem to have any intention of getting down. "We have to run."

"What happened to you?" I demanded of Enzo as I helped pull him to his feet.

"Flesh wound," he cursed. "Hurts like a bitch but I can run."

"Let's run then," I agreed.

I tossed him a pistol and I grabbed Sloan's hand again as my brothers led the way out across the snow towards the forest. We kept a hidden shed about a mile up into the woods with snowmobiles, cash, clothes, anything we might need for a situation like this. All we had to do was get there.

We ran across the snow, the cold biting at my skin and making me wish for a coat. Sloan must have been frozen in my shirt with her feet bare but there was nothing I could do about it. We just had to make it to the shed and we'd be fine. She'd be fine. I wasn't going to let those fucking stronzos take her from me.

Gunfire punctured the silence as we made it to the trees and Sloan screamed in panic as I yanked her on faster. We dashed between wide trunks and the light of the sun was stolen from us as the forest swallowed us whole.

Frankie and Enzo raced on ahead as I was slowed by Sloan.

She stumbled, crashing into me and righting herself by pressing her hands to my back.

"I can carry you," I offered, turning to her as she pulled her hand from mine.

My heart stilled as I found her glaring up at me with the pistol she'd snatched from my waistband aimed straight at my chest.

My lips parted as she raised her chin, flicking the safety catch off. "I won't forget it a second time," she growled.

"You want to shoot me, bella?" I asked, looking into those big brown eyes and finding nothing but determination shining from them.

"Why shouldn't I?" she demanded.

For a long moment I could only stare at her. At this perfect little creature who had slipped past every wall I'd ever put up around my heart and burrowed her way beneath my skin. In my desperation to keep her with me, I hadn't even considered the idea that she might really not want to stay by my side. Not now that she knew the truth about me.

"Well if you're going to do it then make sure you aim for the heart. Because you're taking it with you if you leave me anyway," I said.

Her upper lip peeled back and I tossed my own pistol aside, holding my arms out to my sides as I took a slow step towards her. I stopped with her pistol pressed right against my chest and for a moment I could have sworn something more than hurt and rage flickered in her gaze, but she banished it just as quickly.

"You don't have a heart, Rocco," she hissed and those words echoed right down to the darkest recesses of my blackened soul.

"I would have agreed with you not so long ago," I said. "But you found it. You made it beat and race and *ache*. It's yours. And if everything we've been through was always going to lead me here, then I still wouldn't change it. I'm yours, Sloan. So do with me what you will."

Her eyes widened, her throat bobbed. The wind blew a flurry of snowflakes through the air and her long, black hair twisted around her as she stood shivering in my shirt.

"Sloan!" Nicoli bellowed somewhere in the distance.

"Will you go back to him?" I asked. "Back to a man who would put you up on a pretty pedestal and turn his gaze from all the broken, tortured little pieces of your soul? Would you live the life of the well behaved little principessa and let it drain the wildness from you piece by piece until you were nothing but a shell? A perfect little ornament to be trotted out on his arm whenever it suited him."

"Better that than a girl in a cage being used by a monster," she hissed.

"You used me too, Sloan. You used me to find out who you were. And yeah, I'm all the things you think I am and probably a hundred more too. But I'm still yours."

Silence fell between us and all that we could hear were Nicoli's desperate cries as he followed our footsteps across the snow. If we didn't run now, he'd find us here. He'd kill me and take her back anyway.

"Well *I'm* not *yours*," Sloan growled fiercely, a tear sliding down her cheek. "Goodbye, Rocco."

She turned and ran from me and all I could do was stand and watch her go. A hollowness seemed to echo right through me, resounding down to the foundations of my soul.

"Rocco!" Frankie bellowed and as Sloan disappeared from sight between the trees, the pain that crashed through me was enough to torture each and every dark and depraved corner of my being. She'd made her choice. And it wasn't me.

I turned and ran on up the hill, chasing after my brothers and abandoning the wild girl who had been my perfect temptation and my undoing to a life that was so much less than she deserved.

Sloan

"Stop shooting!" I cried as I raced through the trees towards Nicoli.

"Sloan!?" Nicoli's voice came in return. "Hold fire!"

The gunfire stopped, but I didn't slow my pace, tearing toward Nicoli with my heart weighing like lead. I'd left Coco, but I couldn't go back. I knew Frankie wouldn't hurt him, but the idea of leaving him behind killed me.

Nicoli appeared racing up the hill and he crashed into me, wrapping me in an embrace that crushed the air from my lungs. "Fuck, I've got you. You're safe."

I clung onto him, pressing my face into his shirt, barely feeling the cold. I was numb, hollow. I'd made my choice. But I felt nothing for it.

"I'll get you home." He tilted my chin up and pressed a kiss to my mouth before I could think to stop it.

I jerked away, finding Royce standing beyond him with a desperate look on his face. I reached for him and he clutched my hand, his professionalism dropping as he dragged me into his arms.

The scent of gunfire and something completely him surrounded me and I gripped him tighter, feeling like a little kid again. I'd always been safe when I was with him, but I didn't think it was possible to feel safe right then. Not when my heart was running away from me, leaving with Rocco and tearing a gaping hole in my chest in the process. It hurt more than I could bear to admit. And knowing I might never see him again brought on a sob as I clutched onto Royce.

"It's alright, Sloan," he said gently. "We'll get you home."

Home. The word rang in my head a thousand times. I didn't have a home. My father's house was familiar, but that didn't make it the place I belonged. I knew with a painful certainty that Rocco had been the only thing that had ever felt like home to me. But he'd painted me a lie, filling me with hopes of a life together. A life I had almost let him fool me into taking.

Now, I was cast adrift. And as Nicoli drew me from Royce's arms and I began to feel the cold throbbing through my feet and slithering through my limbs, I made a quiet promise to myself: I was going to be my own knight in shining armour. The one who freed me from my cage for good.

Nicoli scooped me into his arms to get my feet out of the snow, hugging me close to his chest as he turned and headed back down the hill. "I'm never going to let anyone take you from me again," he swore.

I pursed my lips, because I disagreed with that entirely. I'd be taking myself far away from Sinners Bay as soon as I got the chance.

***

I was tucked under piles of blankets in my family home. My old bedroom didn't smell familiar anymore. It smelled like new bedsheets and broken dreams.

Papa hadn't come to see me yet. He was out on a job, still working even now when his daughter was freshly home from being kidnapped. *Typical.*

Nicoli was downstairs. He'd brought me food, water, a hot water bottle. He said I could have anything I asked for, but I hadn't asked for anything. Because what I wanted was his nemesis in my arms. But I shouldn't have wanted that for a second because now I knew Rocco was more cruel than I ever could have imagined. I tried to force my crushed heart to harden against him. I wanted it to turn to iron and never bleed for any man ever again.

How could I have been so naïve?

I thought of Coco and a growl of rage escaped me. I should have gone back for him, but the other Romeros never would have let me go. I'd had to take my chance. But now my little friend was left in their clutches.

He'd be okay, but he'd hate them. I didn't want to abandon him to that life, but what could I do for him now?

When the house was quiet, I slipped from my bed, taking a backpack from my closet and starting to fill it. I was done being caged. It was time to run. I wasn't going to wait until Papa returned to the house with all his bodyguards. There were plenty of men manning the property tonight, but I knew where each of them would be posted. I also knew there was a hole in the fence to the west of the grounds. I'd promised myself I'd slip out of it a thousand times since I'd found it as a child. Tonight, it was time to fulfil that promise to myself.

No one else mattered now, but me. I needed to start protecting myself from men like Rocco. Even Nicoli who so valiantly ran into save me, but only because he wanted me for himself.

When I'd packed a bag and changed into black clothes, I headed into the bathroom, pulling my hair up into a bun and tugging a hat down over it. Once I was off the property, I wouldn't be easily recognised. I had some cash in my purse which I'd stolen from Papa's office. It was enough to get me out of Sinners Bay and pay for a few months in a hotel. I'd figure it out after that. I didn't care if I ended up living on the streets, anything was better than here in my cage. I was going to break the bars once and for all.

I shouldered my pack, pulling up the hood of my sweater and heading to the window. I slid it open, gazing down at the two storey drop. The branch of an oak tree tickled the side of the house and I could just about reach it. I leaned forward, curling my hands around the rough bark and inhaling deeply before letting myself swing out to hang from it.

I bit down on my tongue as I shimmied toward the trunk, the strength in my arms threatening to fail me. But I had too much determination in my bones. I wasn't going to let go. My hands would fall off first.

I made it to the trunk, finding a foothold and breathing a sigh of relief as I started climbing down. I landed on the ground with a soft thump then glanced around to make sure no one could see me here.

My heart lifted as I realised I was in the clear and I set off at a fierce pace toward the west of the property.

"Freeze!" a voice bellowed and my heart lurched as I recognised Royce. "Hands on your head or I'll blow it off!"

I cursed under my breath, raising my hands and turning to face my old friend.

His stern face softened and he rushed forward in alarm, lowering his gun. "Miss Calabresi! What are you doing out here? Your father just arrived home to see you." He stopped a foot from me, reaching out like he longed to hug me, but thought better of it. I guessed now we were back at my father's property, he had fallen back into his routine as a guard. Though both of us knew he meant much more than that to me.

"I can't be here anymore, Royce. I need to go. Please, just let me go," I begged.

Royce frowned, planting his feet. "I can't do that, Miss, you know I can't. Are you…okay?" His gaze fell down me like he expected to see cuts and bruises from my time in the Romeros' company. "Perhaps you need to talk to someone?"

"I'm fine. Better than I've been in a long time, in fact," I said firmly. *Apart from my broken heart.* "I don't want this life, Royce. You know that better than anyone in this house. Just say you didn't see me."

He hesitated, his jaw grinding as he glanced over his shoulder. "I can't let you go off into the city alone. You won't survive the night."

"I'll survive just fine," I snarled firmly. "I survived the Romeros."

"Did they hurt you?" he asked, his expression pinching as if the words pained him to consider.

"No." *Yes. Just not in the way I expected.*

"Come inside," he urged. "I've always vowed to protect you, Miss Calabresi. And letting you go wouldn't be protecting you."

I moved toward Royce, knowing he meant it, knowing I couldn't outrun him. But I had to say my piece. "Do you know how it feels to be *protected* your whole life, Royce?" I asked coldly. "It feels a lot like a sheep being *protected* from wolves, all so it can be eaten later by the farmer."

Royce swallowed thickly, hanging his head. "It's the way of your family, Miss." He reached for me but I ignored his hand, moving around him and making my own way across the snowy ground. I wasn't sure how to feel about Royce now I knew he'd been involved in killing Rocco's mother and brother. It didn't add up with the man who'd watched over me all my life.

I headed toward the house with my hands clenched into fists. I didn't care if my father saw the backpack and the look on my face. He could know I hated it here, what difference did it make? Now I knew what he was, that I was born of a man who was as black-hearted as his enemies, I didn't care to please him anyway.

I strode up to the front door with Royce at my back and the guards there frowned, looking to Royce for direction. He waved them back and I walked inside, following the sound of my father's voice through the vast cream entrance hall to the lounge.

He stood by the fire with Nicoli and I may as well have been transported back in time to the day Nicoli had proposed. Or should I say, the day Papa had sold my womb to his prodigy.

Father swept his hair back from his eyes, looking to me with a sharp frown as he took in my attire. "What's going on?" he barked at Royce.

I answered before he could. "I was just trying to run away, then I was reminded that there's only one way out of this life. The same route Mamma took."

Papa's brows raised in time with Nicoli's, but whereas Papa looked furious, Nicoli looked hurt.

"Bite your tongue," Papa snarled. "How dare you speak of your mother this way."

"How dare I?" I said coldly. "I'm your daughter. How dare *you*, Papa. How dare you keep me naive, how dare you lie to me over and over, how dare you hide what you really are."

Papa strode toward me and Royce moved to my side. "Sir, she's quiet traumatised from her time with the Romeros," he said quietly.

I glared at my father, raising my chin as I waited to see how he'd react. It took me a moment to realise Nicoli was at his back, holding his arm. My brow furrowed at the sight, because I'd never seen him stand against my father in any way at all.

"Royce is right. She needs some time to process what happened," Nicoli said firmly, looking to me with a frown.

I gritted my jaw, staring back at him unblinkingly. "I know my own mind. I'm more sane now than I was before. I've processed everything just fine." I flipped my gaze to Papa. "Does Nicoli know about what you did to the Romeros?"

"What lies have they been spewing?" Papa scoffed, but there was a dangerous warning in his gaze, telling me to stop talking.

"I saw it with my own eyes. They showed me the CCTV footage from the night Evelina Romero and her son, Angelo, were murdered."

Papa smacked me across the face and I yelped as my head wheeled sideways, my skin stinging like hell. The sound of another thump made me look around. Nicoli had his arm locked around Papa's throat, wrestling him away from me.

"Know your place!" my father yelled, throwing him off and laying a hand on the butt of his gun at his hip.

Nicoli stared at my Papa with intent in his eyes, his hands balled into fists, but he didn't make another move. I was shocked he'd tried to protect me at all.

"Get her out of my sight," Papa spat at Royce and he caught my arm, pulling me toward the door.

I let him guide me upstairs back to my room and Royce immediately moved to close the window. He locked it in place, pocketing the key and my heart ached.

"Why do you do as he says?" I growled. "I saw you in that video too, Royce. I thought you were a good man, but I guess you're just my father's lap dog after all." My words were bitter and left a sour taste on my tongue.

Royce strode back across the room and nudged the door shut, lowering his voice. "I have done plenty of terrible things, Sloan," he said, dropping the employee bullshit. "I never claimed to be a good man."

"But I thought you cared about me. I thought we were friends." Had I been naive about that too? Was there no one in the world who I could rely on?

He moved forward, taking my hand and kissing the back of it. "Dear Sloan, I *am* your friend," he whispered. "But if I go against your father, he'll fire me, kill me even. And then who will be here to protect you?"

I swallowed the lump in my throat, turning my back on him and dragging my hand from his in the process.

"I was always very fond of your mother," he said softly and something about his words undid my heart, like he was pulling on a thread that opened the seam. "And before she died, she asked me to look after you. She asked that I do anything in my power to keep you safe."

"Being safe has made me more miserable than being in danger ever did," I whispered. "I'm in a world of monsters and maybe it would have been better if everyone had let me become one too." I took in a ragged breath, unsure how I was going to face the coming days, weeks, months. The path of my life was too narrow, barred in on both sides.

"I truly am sorry," Royce said heavily.

"What are you sorry for? That I'm miserable or that you helped make me this way?" I turned back to him, blinking away tears as I gazed on one of the few men I'd known and loved in my life. The face that had smiled at me when I'd done my first cartwheel, the hands that had pushed me on the swing while I cried to go higher, the feet I'd stood on when he'd taught me how to slow dance. There had been so much kindness in his actions but beneath it all, he'd held one of the chains which bound me.

He eyes crinkled at the corners and a part of me regretted those words. Because Royce had defied my father in some ways. He'd trained me to fire a gun and taught me some self-defence. He'd given me a chance and that was the most anyone in this household had ever given me. Instead of always being the King on a chessboard, he'd made me into the Queen, able to move around the board and fight her own battles. But it still hadn't been enough.

"I can give you all I have," he said sadly. "Which is the truth."

"What truth?" I asked as he pressed his back to the door to make sure it was shut.

"The truth about everything. About the coming days, about the past too. Which would you like to hear first? The future, or the past?"

I dropped down onto the edge of my bed, wondering what would be worse. "The future," I breathed. "What's going to happen now?"

"A wedding," he said gravely. "Your father is already rearranging your marriage to Nicoli Vitoli this very weekend. He'll be announcing it tomorrow."

I almost choked on that. I'd thought I had some time, but he wasn't giving me any. It was as if my life had been put on pause, not like I'd been kidnapped. Father had no empathy at all. Now I was back, he just wanted to get his affairs in order.

I nodded, letting that truth settle over my heart. "What else?"

"He's planning to kill the Romero brothers. He's laying a trap, but he hasn't yet shared the details of his plan with me. What I do know, is that their deaths will be prolonged and his victory over them will be spread all across Port Diavoli as a warning to the Romeros never to touch his family again."

Fear clutched my heart with razor sharp claws. I should have wanted the Romeros dead for what they'd done. But still, some part of me couldn't bear the thought of them lying in graves. Least of all Rocco. He'd shattered my heart, but there was still some piece of it which yearned for him. Belonged to him.

"Okay," I said, trying to figure out what to do with that information.

My stomach swirled and nausea made me wanna hurl. It felt like a lifetime since I'd eaten back at the Romero manor and I couldn't imagine there was anything left in my stomach to come up.

"And what about the past?" I asked, resting my hands on my knees.

Royce stepped forward, lowering his tone, seeming anxious. "It is your father's best kept secret. And it weighs on me every day…"

"What is it?" I breathed, my pulse thundering in my ears.

"The night your father went after Martello's wife, he knew she would be at home alone with her son, Angelo."

I nodded, a knife driving into my chest at knowing how callous my father was.

"He killed her in cold blood, then had us prepare to burn the place down. I wasn't happy with the whole thing, it was the worst job I've ever done." He shuddered, unable to meet my eye. "But if I went against your father, he'd do more than just hurt me. I have family he would go after." He ran a hand over his hair and my heart went out to him. "There was a little boy screaming in his bedroom. I was ready to try and step in, to stop things before they went too far – I'd *never* hurt a child. But then Giuseppe ordered me to pick up the boy and take him to the car."

My eyes widened in confusion. "But I thought-"

"We were vowed to secrecy," he cut over me. "I kept him hidden. I took him out the back of the house to avoid the security cameras."

"But why?" I gasped.

Royce bowed his head. "Your father was jealous of Martello having four sons when he could produce none himself."

My mouth parted and horror raced through me as I realised what he was saying.

"His name was changed and he was kept away from society for years while Giuseppe brainwashed him, coming up with a story for him while making him forget who he was."

"No," I breathed in disbelief.

Royce nodded, his expression endlessly dark. "Yes, Sloan. Nicoli Vitoli is Angelo Romero."

Rocco

I crept through the bushes to the west of Giuseppe Calabresi's mansion stronghold under the cover of darkness. Then I waited.

I had three things with me which belonged to Sloan Calabresi. Her dog. My heart. And the truth. I planned on leaving two of them for her tonight and carrying the other with me for the rest of my days, beating a sorrowful tune as it mourned the life we should have lived together.

Coco remained quiet in my bag, the little beast seeming to know it was important we weren't caught.

I found a spot deep within the bushes with a clear view of the house and waited as I watched the windows. Lights switched on and off as people moved about inside.

Two days without Sloan had only served to burn the blackened remains of my heart with a fire so fierce I knew it would never go out. But despite the fact that I wished for nothing more than to run to her now, to wait in her room and drag her back into my arms, I knew I couldn't. If she'd wanted this life with me then she would have chosen it. So now she deserved to hear the words it would take to fix this mess. And though a selfish part of me hoped with every fibre of my fucked up being that she might just love me despite all my flaws, I wasn't going to hold my breath. Fate had never shone so kindly on me as that.

My heart skipped a beat as Sloan appeared standing in the window of the room to the far right of the house. She hugged her arms tight around her body and stared out over the sweeping, snow-covered lawn as if she was hunting for something. Or someone.

Wishful thinking will only get you killed, stronzo.

I watched her for several minutes, my heart pounding with the desperate ache to go to her. But I didn't move. If she'd wanted a life with me then she would have stayed.

She finally moved away from the window and I waited until the light went out, watching as another came on in the stairwell and keeping my eyes on the dining room where Giuseppe sat waiting for her to join him.

The moment she entered the room, I moved.

I hugged the shadows around the perimeter of the building until I made it as close as I was going to get without having to cross the snowy yard, then I shot a text to my brothers.

Rocco:
Now.

Enzo:
Are you sure about this?

Rocco:

Distract them or I'm going in while they're all still here.

Frankie:

Calm the fuck down, fratello. We're doing it now. Who knew being in love would make you even more psychotic??

I frowned at that assessment. What the fuck would he know about it anyway? Frankie never saw a girl more than once. He didn't do feelings with anyone outside the family. Which I was starting to think was a clever fucking way of being.

I pushed my cellphone back into my pocket and looked at the building which housed my deepest desire and waited for the distraction they'd promised.

The flare of headlights shone through the gates at the edge of the drive in the distance and the dull tune of the DHL delivery truck's horn came just before it crashed into the gates with a tremendous boom.

The guards all started yelling at once, pouring out of their hiding places and racing across the yard to the gates, expecting an attack. It wouldn't look like that though, just an accidental crash with a driver who we'd paid off so damn well, I knew he'd never breathe a word of the truth.

The moment they'd moved away from me, I darted out of the bushes and ran for the house. A window was open on the ground floor and I leapt up, heaving myself inside and blinking as I found myself in a gaudily decorated bathroom.

I bypassed the gold shower and slipped out of the door into the corridor.

The stairs sat to my right and I jogged towards them, thanking Giuseppe Calabresi for his bad taste in carpets as my footsteps were muffled by them as I moved.

I made it upstairs and hurried to Sloan's room, pressing the door closed behind me as I slipped inside.

I gave my pounding heart a moment to calm as the scent of her enveloped me. She was sweeter than any sugar, more tempting than anything she might have whipped up for me in her kitchen.

I moved to the window and drew the curtains across before flicking on the lamp on her nightstand.

I pulled the bag from my shoulder and unzipped it, freeing Coco so that he could leap down onto her bed. He nuzzled into her pillows happily and I was more than a little tempted to join him.

My heart ached at the idea of being so close to her and not waiting to see her face, to touch her skin, kiss her lips… Not that I had any reason to believe she would want any of those things from me anymore.

I moved to her nightstand and pulled the letter from my pocket. I owed her this much. The truth.

I placed the letter down on her bed and my gaze caught on another envelope sitting beside her lamp. This one was thick, embossed with the Calabresi crest and just begging for me to look inside.

I picked it up and pulled out the contents, eyeing the elegant script with my heart melting into a vat of acid.

Giuseppe Calabresi requests the honour of your presence at the marriage of his daughter
Sloan Calabresi
To
Nicoli Vitoli
This coming Saturday, the 13th

I gripped the invite in my fist so hard that the thing crumpled up into a tight ball.

My heart wasn't just being melted in acid, it was being flayed, eaten by crows, cut into a million pieces and crushed in a vice so tight I couldn't breathe.

I dropped the destroyed invite and turned from the room, closing the door behind me with a snap so final it sounded like the world caving in.

I didn't bother to be quiet as I headed back down the stairs and into the bathroom. I didn't bother to run as I strode away across the snow covered lawn outside the Calabresi manor. I didn't care if they caught me and tortured me and killed me in the most agonising of ways, because it felt like I had nothing left anyway.

But they didn't do any of those things. And I just kept walking off into the night until the shadows swallowed me and all that was left was darkness.

Sloan

My father was barking orders at his men from the front door. The commotion at the gate turned out to be some DHL driver who'd skidded on a patch of ice. It sounded like he'd caused a lot of damage too. But Papa's pockets were deep enough to have it fixed by tomorrow. He wouldn't let the defences of his fortress stay down for long.

A distant yapping made me frown and I stopped stirring the coffee sitting in front of me on the kitchen counter as I listened. Papa started shouting again and I assumed I'd imagined it, continuing to make my coffee.

My mind had been knotted with a thousand thoughts since I'd spoken to Royce. I had no idea what to do now I knew who Nicoli really was. Royce had sworn me to secrecy, but how could I keep this from him? I'd want to know if my whole life had been taken from me. My father had murdered his mother and kidnapped him, twisted his mind and planted him in our lives. It was sick. I just needed to get some time alone with him, but how I was ever going to explain this?

The yapping sounded again and I frowned, abandoning the coffee and heading out of the kitchen, jogging upstairs towards my room.

My heart rate rocketed as I recognised Coco barking, certain I wasn't imagining it. I threw the door open and Coco leapt off of the bed. I gasped, dropping to my knees and cuddling him to my chest in delight.

"Oh my god, you're here," I gasped, then scooped him up and ran to the window, searching the dark grounds below for any sign of a Romero. Why would they bring him back to me? And how the hell did they get in here past the guards?

My gaze slid to the gathered guards at the gate as they waved the truck driver off down the road. I realised it was no accident at all. This was planned.

I swallowed the jagged lump in my throat, moving away from the window and rubbing Coco's head. My heart pounded a mile a minute as I tried to figure out why they'd bring him back to me.

Something caught my eye and I turned, spotting the wedding invite on the floor. It had been on my nightstand and from the crumpled looks of it, I guessed someone had screwed it up in their fist. My throat thickened as I realised it must have been Rocco who had come. But why would he care that I was getting married? Wasn't it obvious?

My eyes fell on a letter on the bed and my breathing hitched.

"What's going on?" Papa strode into the room and my heart lurched into my throat. I lunged for the letter, but he reached it first, scowling at the dog as he pieced together what had happened. "The fucking Romeros have been here?" he snarled, tearing open the letter and pulling out the folded sheaf of paper.

"Papa," I gasped, grabbing his arm to try and tear it from his fingers.

He held it above my head like I was a tiny child reaching for candy then shoved me away so he could read it himself. He snorted derisively, letting it fall from his hand a moment later. "He thinks he can come into my home and hurt my daughter again, does he?" He marched from the room, slamming the door behind him and shouting for the guards to search the grounds.

I bent down, picking up the letter with shaking fingers. I knew it was from Rocco, but now that the door was closed I could smell him here too. Pine and danger rolled around me and made my heart hurt.

I dropped onto the bed, curling my knees up to my chest as I let my eyes fall to the page, unable to get enough oxygen into my lungs as I read it.

To my sweetest hate,

The reason I'm writing this to you, is because I can't not write it. I hate you too much not to let you know it. I love that you are gone. Truly, I love the empty rooms, the silence, the lack of you at my side.

I hated every moment I spent in your company but have loved each one I spent hurting you, breaking you, spilling your tears. I hate that your soul is a dark mirror of mine and I love that I will never spend another moment with you again.

I have hated you so hard these past few days that it has split my heart open, making it bloody and raw. To love you would be my greatest weakness. To love you would be the worst thing any mortal could do and I would regret any moment I spent with that feeling.
I will hate you forever until my body is nothing but bones.
From your nightmare, your monster, your eternal hate,
Rocco Romero

I dragged in a shaky breath as tears fell from my eyes. I crushed the letter in my fist, anger rising in me and ripping at my heart.

Coco nuzzled into me, licking my hand again and again. I couldn't see through a blur of tears and I was furious at myself for letting them fall. Rocco was the nastiest man I knew, and I couldn't believe I'd fallen for his tricks.

"At least he spared you," I whispered to Coco, hugging him close.

I crumpled up the page and tossed it across the room into the trash can, falling back onto the bed to stare mutely at the ceiling.

I was broken, empty and a bride-to-be. And part of me just wanted the world to stop turning.

***

The next morning, Royce guided me out to the Bentley which was parked at the front of the house. I'd been given no information about where I was going and had the feeling my imprisonment was about to get a whole lot worse since I'd spoken out against my Father. I hadn't even been given a phone yet.

Royce opened the back door for me and I dropped into the car, frowning at him as he moved around to take the seat beside the driver.

I'd asked Royce a hundred times where I was going, but if he had any idea, he hadn't shown it. The driver pulled away, following directions on a satnav and I stared out of the window, figuring I was probably heading to a dress fitting for my wedding. I couldn't exactly wear the last one seeing as it was in shreds in the Romero trash somewhere. That dress had cost nearly twenty thousand dollars. Hand-made, the hem stitched with diamonds. Did I give a shit? Not one bit. Good riddance. I hoped some lucky garbage man had found the diamonds.

We headed deeper into Port Diavoli, queuing out towards the western docks before turning down a narrow street which was cast in the shadow of the Calabresi tower. My father owned it, the steel initials GC gleaming on top of it in the morning sun.

I frowned as the car slowed outside Doctor Dariello's private clinic and Royce hopped out to get my door. I stepped onto the pavement, unsure why we were here.

"I'm not sick," I stated.

Royce took my arm, guiding me up to the glass door, his brow heavily creased.

"What aren't you saying?" I hissed under my breath.

"It won't take long, Miss Calabresi," he said, which wasn't nearly enough of an answer.

We stepped into the waiting room which was white-walled with a polished receptionist sitting behind a crescent desk.

"Good morning. Doctor Dariello is all ready for you, Miss Calabresi. If you'd like to go through." She pointed to the door at the back of the room.

"I'll wait out here," Royce said, giving me a taut smile.

I swallowed thickly, moving to the door and pushing my way inside. I found myself in a clinical room with a hospital bed with raised stirrups on the end of it.

I immediately froze as the doctor got to his feet. He was a tall guy, slim with thinning hair and piercing blue eyes. "Ah long time no see, Miss Calabresi, how are you today?"

"Fine, doctor, what's this about exactly?"

"Oh, your father didn't say?" he asked awkwardly, moving to the door and flipping the lock.

My skin prickled as I stared at him. "No, he didn't."

"Well as you've been through quite the trauma recently, he just asked that I make sure everything is all…in order."

"What is that supposed to mean?" I pressed, folding my arms.

"If you'd like to move behind the screen and remove the bottom half of your clothes, we can get started. It won't take long."

I ground my jaw as he didn't answer my question, refusing to move.

"Miss Calabresi," he said in a serious tone. "I'm afraid this isn't exactly optional. Your father was very insistent and if I fail to give him any results-"

"And how is that my problem?" I demanded, a little shocked and a little proud of myself for challenging him.

Dr Dariello's face suddenly became stern. He might have been a doctor, but I knew enough about him to know he was dodgy as shit. He'd stitched up plenty of my father's men off the record and I knew he wasn't beyond taking bribes.

"Look, my dear, your father will simply come down here if I don't complete these tests. It's nothing major, I promise you," he said earnestly. "I'm just checking you're in good health."

I tapped my foot, knowing my father would force me to do this if I didn't agree. I knew what these so-called tests were about. He was checking whether his precious daughter's virginity was still intact in time for her wedding. Like me being raped would be less important than that fact.

Well if he wanted that information, then fine. It was going to infuriate him thinking the Romeros had taken my innocence anyway. And I was more than happy to give him reasons to be miserable since he'd proven how little he cared about my happiness.

I stepped behind the screen, tugging off my shoes, jeans and panties before wrapping the provided towel around my waist.

I moved to the hospital bed, getting onto it and lying back before putting my feet up in the stirrups. *Nothing quite like one of these beds to make a girl feel vulnerable.*

Dr Dariello settled himself before me on a stool and I stared up at the ceiling, trying to focus on anything else as he pulled on some gloves and got to work with whatever the hell he was doing.

When he was done, he directed me behind the screen again and I was soon dressed, waiting for his verdict on my virginity. *One guess what that'll be.*

He made some notes on his computer and I sat in a chair while I waited. He seemed anxious, jittery and even more so when he handed me a small plastic cup.

"I just need a little urine sample." He pointed to a door across the room, not meeting my eye as I walked away with it.

I headed into the toilet, managing to get a sample after several minutes of trying to relax. I returned to the room, placing it on the desk and he promptly took a packet from his drawer and pulled out a pregnancy test.

My gut lurched as I stared at it. I mean, Rocco said he couldn't have kids so I didn't have anything to worry about. And yet as he prepared the test, I started mentally trying to calculate my period in my head. I couldn't even think when I'd had my last one, but I hadn't had one while I'd been with the Romeros so that would mean I was due…four days ago.

Oh fuck.

My life changed even before the two lines appeared on the test. I could feel it. Something in me had fundamentally altered and it wasn't just my time with Rocco. This was physical.

"Well…Miss Calabresi, I'm afraid to say you're pregnant."

"Afraid to say?" I echoed, blinking several times. Rocco might have hated me and I might have hated him right back, but that didn't apply to this child. None of it did.

"Loretta can schedule you in for the termination tomorrow," he said frankly. "Just have a word with her on your way out. Apart from that, you're in good health."

I cupped my hand to my belly protectively, staring at him and his callous words about my child. Termination? No way. There wasn't a chance in hell.

I stood up, shaken and elated and confused as shit as I made my way from the room.

I'm pregnant with Rocco's child.

That reality sank in hard and fast with every step I took across the waiting room toward Royce. The doctor was going to tell my father. He'd book the termination himself.

What can I do?

How can I fix this?

I'd lie. It was all I had. And if I pulled it off, it would be okay. Everything would be okay.

"Are you alright? You look very pale," Royce asked and I nodded mutely, taking his arm as he led me out the door.

"I need to call Nicoli," I said. "Can I borrow your phone?"

"You can't tell him what I told you," Royce said in a low voice. "It will cause world war three."

"I'm not going to," I said firmly. *Not yet anyway.* Because I sure as hell *was* going to tell him when I could get a moment alone with him.

Royce handed me his phone and I nodded in thanks, slipping into the back of the car, my breathing growing frantic.

I twisted my fingers together, wondering if Nicoli would really pull through for me on this. I supposed I wouldn't be in any worse of a position if he didn't.

"Put the divider up," I told the driver and he did as I said.

Royce threw me a frown a moment before it closed between us.

The phone started ringing and I chewed on my lip anxiously as I waited for him to answer. My hand rested firmly on my stomach and part of me wished I could be making this call to Rocco.

A bitterness filled my chest as I thought of him. Of the lies. How could someone be so heartless? *And why does it hurt so much?*

"Hello?" Nicoli answered.

"It's me. Sloan," I said, my anxiety piquing.

"Oh, hey. Has your father not gotten you a cellphone yet? I can pick you one up today."

"Yeah sure, thanks," I garbled. "Look, I need to ask you something. You might be mad, and I understand if you can't do this for me, but you're a better man than my father, so I'm hoping you'll help me keep this from him."

"Keep what from him?" Nicoli asked with an edge to his tone.

I took a deep breath, figuring there was no perfect way to say this. "I'm pregnant."

Silence.

"And it's Rocco's."

More silence.

"And I need you to lie and tell my father me and you slept together before I was kidnapped."

The silence continued and I had to actually check the call hadn't cut out.

I chewed on my lip almost hard enough to draw blood. "Please Nicoli," I dropped my voice, my desperation clear. "If Papa finds out it's Rocco's, he'll make me terminate it."

"And you don't want to?" he asked, his tone giving away none of his feelings.

"No, I mean, I can't. It doesn't matter who Rocco is, I can't destroy this little life in me. I just *can't*."

"Sloan," he said, his voice a pained growl. "You said he didn't hurt you."

My eyes burned and I choked on my tongue. "He didn't," I forced out, knowing that I had to be honest here. I couldn't have Nicoli thinking Rocco had raped me, it wasn't right. "I wanted to be with him," I said heavily.

"Jesus, fucking….shit," Nicoli said, sounding like he was pacing. "Right, okay…."

"I know this is a big ask, but it's the only way to cover this up. Father will be mad, but he'll accept it if he thinks it's yours," I implored.

"Of course," he said at last. "Of course I will, Sloan. Are you heading back to the house now?"

"Yes," I said, my body sagging with relief. "Thank you, Nicoli. I'll tell you everything later. About Rocco and….everything." I had to be honest with him, I owed him that if he was going to do this for me.

"Alright. Your father is on his way home. I'm at the office, but I'll head over within the hour. If he hears from the doctor, then tell him it's mine and I'll back you up as soon as I get there."

"I can't tell you what this means to me," I said, my heart swelling for him. I'd always cared about Nicoli, though a part of me had worried he was just a clone of my father. But he wasn't at all, and I'd never given him credit for that.

"I told you I'll always be here for you," he said. "I meant that."

I nodded, saying my goodbyes and hanging up. Nicoli had pulled through for me. I'd always known he was a good man, but I didn't know how deep that ran till now. He'd move mountains for me, always had, always would. And my life would have been so much simpler if I could have loved him. Maybe in time, I still could…

It wasn't long before we arrived back at the Calabresi manor, pulling up the long drive to the cream stone building that stretched toward the pale sky.

I hurried inside, needing to be alone for a while to think about everything. Father's car wasn't here so I had some time to decide what I was going to say to him. If Doctor Dariello had called him already, he was no doubt racing here like a bat out of hell to shout at me, or maybe to plan Rocco's demise, deciding how he was going to detach each of his limbs.

I headed upstairs and Coco came running up to me, jumping up at my legs excitedly.

"Hey boy." I plucked him off the ground and hugged him tight as I entered my room.

I tickled his neck and frowned as my fingers snagged on a piece of paper which had been taped there. *What the hell?*

I pushed his fur aside to look at his collar and twisted the small note so that I could read it, while Coco waited patiently, enjoying the fuss as I held him still.

Hate is so very fucking close to love, my guerriera. I have felt both ways for you. I have burned with hate and I have burned with love, but one has waged war with the other and won.

Read my letter again and swap the words love and hate to find out which, I couldn't risk your father knowing in case he hurt you.

RR

Call me if there's ever a chance for us. 202-555-0149

My lips parted in disbelief. I ran to the trash can, tossing the whole thing upside down as I hunted for the letter, desperate to find it.

No no no, where is it? Where is it??

I found the crumpled ball with a gasp, flattening it out on the floor and rereading the words, swapping every *love* for *hate* and every *hate* for *love*.

To my sweetest love,

The reason I'm writing this to you, is because I can't not write it. I love you too much not to let you know it. I hate that you are gone. Truly, I hate the empty rooms, the silence, the lack of you at my side.

I loved every moment I spent in your company but have hated each one I spent hurting you, breaking you, spilling your tears. I love that your soul is a dark mirror of mine and I hate that I will never spend another moment with you again.

I have loved you so hard these past few days that it has split my heart open, making it bloody and raw. To hate you would be my greatest weakness. To hate you would be the worst thing any mortal could do and I would regret any moment I spent with that feeling.

I will love you forever until my body is nothing but bones.

From your nightmare, your monster, your eternal love,

Rocco Romero

Pure joy washed over my heart and flowed through my entire body.

"You asshole," I laughed through my tears. Because Rocco Romero didn't hate me at all. Not anymore. He loved me more passionately than I'd ever known anyone to love me. And even though I was angry for what he'd done to me, I couldn't deny that still felt like the best thing in the world. Like there was still a chance for us.

My hand fell to my stomach as I wiped away my tears.

I have to tell him.

I thought of Royce, sure he'd let me borrow his phone again if I asked. This thing between me and Rocco felt so close to happening. And now that there was a child involved, I could let go of the anger in my heart against him. He'd looked so broken when he'd told me he couldn't ever have a family of his own but now…now we could make a family together.

"Sloan," my father's gravelly voice dragged over me and a shudder raced down my spine. "What are you doing on your knees like some common street whore? Or is that what my daughter is now?"

I turned to find him in my doorway, standing up so I didn't feel so small beneath him and trying to steel myself to face him. The scent of whiskey sailed from his breath and the general darkness in his eyes said he was blind drunk and clearly enraged.

"I just got off the phone to Doctor Dariello," he said coldly. "And guess what he said?"

"I'm pregnant," I offered, backing up a step as he took one forward. I had to lie long enough to keep my child safe. Then Rocco would help get me away from here just as soon as I could contact him. "But Father, it's not what you think. It's Nicoli's, he'll tell y-" His fist crashed into my cheek so hard I was thrown back into the wall.

I groaned, lifting a hand to my throbbing face as he rushed toward me. Coco yapped furiously from the bed and I tried to tell him to hush, but I couldn't get the words out. If he drew my father's attention, he might kill him.

"Do you think I'm a fucking fool?" he snarled, his acrid breath washing over me as he leaned into my face. "You came back to my home without even a gracious word from your lips. You tried to run away that very night. So my guess would be that you've been spreading your legs for that dirty piece of filth since the first day he took you."

"I didn't!" I tried and his hand clamped around my wrist, locking so tightly I hissed in pain. "Let go," I demanded, pressing a hand flat to his chest to try and keep him back, but it was like pushing a brick wall. I knew plenty of monsters, but the one staring out of my father's eyes was the most terrifying I'd ever witnessed.

"Do you think I'll let some disgusting Romero rat be brought under this roof, raised as my grandchild?"

I lifted my chin, seeing red as he dared to say that like he wasn't the biggest hypocrite in the world. "I do actually. Because Nicoli isn't who you say he is, is he *Papa*? He's Angelo Romero."

Papa jerked backwards in shock, looking unsettled for the first time ever. "Who the fuck told you that?" he tried to laugh, but he failed.

"It doesn't matter who. The truth is I *know* who he is. So you were always planning on me bringing Romero *rats* into this home, weren't you?"

He fumbled for the gun at his hip and horror consumed me.

"Papa!" I gasped, ducking low as he aimed it at me. He fired into the wall then swung it towards Coco who continued to bark like crazy. "No!"

He hit a pillow on the next shot and Coco darted off the bed in alarm. Father angled the pistol towards me again and I leapt forward to try and run for the door. I could feel the barrel aiming my way and true fear took hold of me.

I made it out of my room, racing along the hallway as he came after me, panic sweeping through my veins.

Royce appeared running up the stairs, gun drawn and a look of pure terror in his eyes. "Sloan duck!"

Father's gun went off before Royce could pull the trigger. Royce slammed to the ground and blood pooled everywhere around him.

"*No*," I gasped, falling to my knees beside him and pressing down on the wound. He clutched my hand, drawing in a wheezing breath. "It's okay, I'm here, it's going to be okay."

I was shaking, hovering on the edge of an endless abyss as I stared down at the man I loved more than the father who was my flesh and blood.

Papa's shadow fell over me and I looked up at him, trembling from head to foot. "How could you?"

"Of course it was you who told her," he spoke to Royce. "You always liked my waste of space daughter too much," he slurred then he kicked me in the leg. "Get up. We're leaving."

I didn't move, leaning over Royce as he bled out, knowing there was nothing I could do for him. It was the most horrible feeling in the world. "I'm sorry," I said through my tears. "I love you."

"I protected you from the wrong evil, dear Sloan," Royce wheezed. "Forgive me."

Papa grabbed a fistful of my hair, hauling me to my feet and dragging me down the stairs away from him.

"No!" I screamed, trying to claw my way free. My hands were stained red and my heart was bursting with pain. "Royce!"

"Shut the fuck up and keep walking," Papa snapped.

"Where are you taking me?" I begged, staring over my shoulder at Royce's still form up on the landing.

My heart was in pieces and shock racked my body.

He's dying up there all alone.

Father's grip on me tightened as he pulled me along at a fierce pace. "To see your mother."

Nicoli

I pulled into the driveway at Giuseppe's manor just over half an hour after I'd spoken with Sloan.

My ears were still ringing with the echoes of that conversation. She was pregnant. And she had slept with Rocco Romero by choice. I couldn't understand it, but then I imagined there were a lot of things I'd never be able to understand about what it was like to be held captive like that for so long. Maybe it was Stockholm Syndrome. Or maybe she'd really seen something in that demon which had made her want to give herself to him.

Whatever it was, I wasn't going to cast judgement on her for it. If I'd just done my job better, she never would have been stuck with them for so long. Hell, if I'd acted faster at our wedding, they never would have taken her in the first place.

Besides, whatever the reasons for the situation, the baby growing inside of her wasn't to blame. I knew too well what it was like to be an unwanted child, raised by people who only cared for you because they were paid to. I knew the hunger of needing to belong to a family. A real family who truly loved you. It was what I'd spent so many years chasing with the Calabresis. And if Sloan was willing to marry me and give me the family I'd always longed for, then the least I could offer her child was the same. They would be mine in everything other than blood. And love didn't care much for DNA anyway.

I pulled up outside the house, frowning in surprise as I didn't spot Giuseppe's vehicle parked outside. I had expected him to beat me back here, but perhaps it was better that he hadn't. I'd been so surprised by Sloan's phone call that I'd barely said any more to her than just agreeing to help. She needed to hear it from my lips. Needed to see I meant it. I would stand by her no matter what. Her *and* this baby.

The front door was ajar as I reached it and I pulled my pistol from my hip as a trickle of adrenaline raced down my spine.

Something was wrong.

I paused, listening for some sign of what to do and the faint yap, yap, yap of a little dog caught my attention upstairs.

I frowned, adjusting my grip on my gun as I moved through the house, heading for the stairs before taking them two at a time to the landing.

My heart lurched as I spotted Royce bleeding out on the carpet and I quickly scanned the rest of the area for any sign of the Romeros. The barking still came from Sloan's room along the hall and my confusion grew as I recognised Coco.

I moved forward cautiously, gun ready and Royce suddenly groaned beside me.

"You still with me, buddy?" I breathed. "Who did this?"

"Giuseppe…" Royce rasped and his eyes fluttered open.

"I'll go look for him now," I agreed. "Keep pressure on that wound and-"

"No!" Royce coughed. "I mean Giuseppe shot me…he took Sloan…help her."

"What?" I frowned, wondering if he was delusional or something.

"There's something you need to know," Royce croaked, reaching out to grasp my ankle.

I hesitated a moment then dropped down beside him, taking his hand. I couldn't let a dying man's words go unheard.

"What is it?" I pressed.

"Years ago, when you were just a small boy, I was part of a group of men your father used to strike against the Romeros."

"Okay…" I frowned. The Calabresis struck at the Romeros every chance they got, so I had no idea where he was going with this.

"One night, we got word that Evelina Romero was alone in their home with one of their boys. The second born, only four years old but a strapping little fella…"

"Right." I looked away from him, glancing down the corridor in case someone else might be approaching, but the house was quiet aside from Coco's barks. "I'm going to call you an ambulance. Just keep talking to me while I'm on the phone-"

"No!" Royce reached out and knocked my cellphone from my hand. It skittered away down the corridor and stopped outside Sloan's room. "This is the least I deserve after everything. But I need you to hear the truth now. From someone who was there."

"Someone who was where?"

"The night Angelo Romero was kidnapped. The night a little boy was stolen from his mother's arms moments before she was murdered…"

"You're losing me again, Royce," I said because the only thing I really knew about Angelo Romero was that he'd died with his mother in a house fire when the boys were all very young.

"You're just not listening properly," Royce snapped. "What do you remember of your birth mother? Or father? Or siblings?"

I frowned at the odd question. It wasn't something I thought on much, but I did have some fuzzy memories of the family I'd had before I was put into care. "My mother used to smell of roses," I said slowly. "And she had the softest hands…and sometimes, I think I can remember playing with another little boy. But that can't have been a sibling because I read my file and I didn't have any." I shrugged.

"A little boy with dark, curly hair?" Royce asked. "A little boy called Rocco?"

I suddenly grasped what he was trying to say and my lip curled on a derisive snort which never seemed to quite make it out of my body. It was insane. What he was suggesting couldn't be true. The level of cunning, denial, brainwashing that it would have taken to carry out such a plan…

"Why?" I asked, not wanting to believe something so crazy. "Why would Giuseppe Calabresi want to steal a Romero child and then put a crown upon his head? He wants me to marry his daughter. He'd never want a Romero to-"

"Giuseppe longed for sons more than anything. He tried for years with his wife, even had affairs but he couldn't get them pregnant either. They resorted to IVF in the end to conceive and even at that, it took nine rounds before his wife fell pregnant. When the baby turned out to be a girl…he just lost his mind. And to rub salt into the wound, Martello Romero and his wife just kept having strong, healthy boys one after another. Rumour had it your mother was pregnant again when-"

"Evelina Romero was *not* my mother," I hissed. Though as I said it, I almost felt like I could hear the distant echo of a woman's screams, smell smoke tainting the air…

"I was *there,*" Royce growled. "Giuseppe plucked you from her arms and delivered you to a family who posed as foster carers. They fed you false information about your family, convinced you your name was Nicoli and not Angelo. They told you your true memories were dreams and showed you photographs of strangers with lies about them being your dead family. They worked tirelessly to convince you that you weren't who you had been. And after five years, they trotted you back out again, ready for Giuseppe to sweep in like a knight in shining armour and offer you the chance to become a part of his family. He groomed you to be the son he couldn't have and kept the true cruelty of your identity as his own twisted secret just for his amusement."

My lips were open but no words were coming out.

Royce started coughing and blood poured between his lips.

I reached out to try and brace him but he waved me off.

"Giuseppe knows Sloan lied about the baby. He knows she tried to run back to Rocco. He's going to kill her," Royce wheezed.

"No," I breathed, my whole world caving in in reaction to his words.

"You have to help her. He's taken her to the Inverno Bridge. The same place he took her mother when she tried to leave him."

"I thought she committed suicide?" I balked, my brain spinning with so much information that I just couldn't process it.

"You thought a lot of things Giuseppe wanted you to. He…always preferred a pretty lie to a dirty truth…" Royce started coughing more violently, gasping for breath as more blood fell from his mouth. I tried to help him but when he finally fell still, he didn't draw another breath.

I shook my head, refusing to believe he was dead, despite the way his eyes stared glassily up at the ceiling.

I needed to know more about so many of the things he'd said but more than that, I had to help Sloan.

I shoved myself upright and moved to retrieve my cellphone from the floor where he'd tossed it.

Coco's incessant barking came from the other side of the door beside me and I pulled it open for him before turning and hurrying back out of the house.

I needed to call someone to help me. But who? Giuseppe's men would never turn on him, not even to help his daughter. He was the head of the household. The kingpin. The don. The boss. No one stood against him and lived. And yet for some insane reason, I was planning on doing just that.

I got into my car but before I could close the door, Coco leapt up onto my lap.

I picked him up, meaning to move him onto the passenger seat and my fingers caught on a piece of paper which was hanging from his collar.

I ripped it off on instinct and looked down at the scrawled note from none other than Rocco Romero himself. He spoke of love among other things and something twisted in my gut at the sight of that word. Was this why Sloan had slept with him? Had she felt such a thing towards that monster? My enemy, my rival…my *brother*…

I wasn't sure I was ready to believe that, but Royce's story had a ring of truth to it which I just couldn't shake off.

At the bottom of the note, a phone number was written and my heart leapt as I spotted it.

If there was a chance he loved her then perhaps I really did have someone I could call on for help. But was I insane to attempt such a thing? I'd hated Rocco Romero for as long as I could remember. It was as if the need to hate him had been branded into my soul. And perhaps it had been. By the devil I'd been trying to impress…

Before I could overthink it, I dialled.

My car linked into the call as I started driving and as the phone began to ring, I sped out of the gates. I must have been losing my mind to be calling on him of all people.

But he might just have been the only shot I had.

Rocco

My cellphone finally rang as I was walking down the street to get pizzas for me and my brothers, which was mightily fucking depressing after getting used to Sloan's cooking.

Anticipation ate me alive as I snatched it from my pocket so fast I almost dropped the damn thing.

I only took in the fact that it was an unknown number before I'd hit the button to answer it with my heart beating half out of my chest.

"*Fuck,* baby you kept me waiting long enough," I groaned. "If hearts had balls mine would be so fucking blue right now. Kinda like my actual balls which are currently, really fucking-"

"This isn't Sloan," Nicoli spat and I straightened my spine as I recognised his voice.

"You'd better not have laid a finger on her," I growled, because the only way he could have my number would be if he'd found my note. And if that was the case, then he might have figured out that there was so much more to me and Sloan than just kidnapper and hostage. So much fucking more it cut me open and bled me dry. But if he'd punished her for that fact, then I'd personally cut him into a thousand pieces and scatter them to the sea.

The sharks would feast on the blood of this motherfucking, stuck up, piece of-

"I need your help, Rocco," Nicoli demanded as if he had any right to ask anything of me.

"Go fuck yourself." I'd sooner cut my own dick off than help a Calabresi wannabe like him.

"*Sloan* needs your help!" he shouted half a second before I could end the call.

"What?" I asked, my heart thundering at those words. The only words he could have uttered to make me stay on that line. "What's wrong with her?"

"Giuseppe found out about you and her. He knows about the baby, he knows about all of it. And he-"

"What baby?" I interrupted because my fucking ears must have been malfunctioning. The world seemed to narrow in around me and I stopped walking dead in the middle of the sidewalk, causing people to curse as they almost bumped into me. But I didn't give a shit because that fucker had most definitely said *baby*.

"*Your* baby," he snapped impatiently.

"My baby…in Sloan?" I was just standing there. Just fucking standing there. Because that wasn't possible. The doctors had told me. I'd had mumps. *Mumps!*

"That's what happens when you fuck a girl and don't use contraception."

My mouth was hanging open. Because no, I hadn't used contraception because I knew there was no fucking way I could get her pregnant. No chance at all. Even if we *had* been fucking like the sky would cave in if we didn't. Even if I might as well have been giving it my best fucking shot at putting a baby into her-

"The point is, Giuseppe knows and he's going to kill her!" Nicoli yelled and I heard the blare of a car horn in the background.

"Where?" I demanded, stepping straight out into the road in front of an oncoming car.

"Inverno Bridge. I'm on my way there, but Rocco, we have to hurry-"

"I'll be there." I cut the call just as the car skidded to a halt barely a foot away from me.

I strode straight up to the driver's door and yanked it open.

"Get the fuck out!" I roared and despite the fact that the guy driving it was probably twice the size of me, he leapt out like a little bitch and practically pissed himself.

I was in his seat before he'd even finished murmuring his prayers and his girlfriend was only half way out of the passenger side as I hit the accelerator.

She fell out with a scream as I tore away from them and the doors slammed shut. I weaved traffic, climbed the sidewalk and sped down side alleys in my desperation to get to Inverno Bridge.

I didn't want to exist in a world without Sloan Calabresi in it. I would get to that bridge and tear Giuseppe limb from limb for even thinking about hurting her. Her and our baby. An actual, fucking *baby*.

A crazed laugh spilled from my lips as I imagined the three of us together. There was this whole life waiting for me on the other side of this moment. All I had to do to claim it was cheat death. And I'd cheated meaner fuckers than him before and lived to tell the tale.

I'm coming for you amore mio. Don't give up.

Sloan

"Please don't do this, Papa," I begged for the hundredth time.

I was sitting in the passenger seat of his car while he drove like a maniac toward the outskirts of Sinners Bay. He had one hand on the wheel while the other pointed a pistol at me. I wanted to believe he wouldn't pull that trigger, but a more honest part of me knew he would. I'd tried to see good in him all my life when I should have been looking for the bad. If I'd let myself see it, maybe I could have escaped this fate. Maybe Royce could have too.

We sailed along the water's edge, the bay impossibly still, looking like a sheet of iron under the dusky evening sky. I wrung my hands together as I tried to come up with a way out, panic making my thoughts a blur.

Papa took the next exit, racing up the hill into the forest and the road quickly fell dark beneath the canopy.

"Where are we going?" I demanded, trying to keep my voice steady. But it wasn't just me he was pointing that gun at. I had a whole other life to protect. Maybe if I hadn't, I'd grab the wheel, take my chances. Because something told me I did not wanna reach the destination of this journey. But I couldn't risk hurting this baby. I'd never forgive myself for it.

Papa ground his jaw, not looking at me, his murky gaze set on the road.

"You're not thinking straight," I said gently, reaching out to rest a hand on his knee. He smacked it away, swerving across the road and I recoiled into my seat in alarm.

"My thoughts are crystal clear, daughter," he growled. "Your mother was the same as you. Always day dreaming about a world outside of this one. Do you think I don't see it? Do you think I can't tell my own flesh and blood is ungrateful for the life I handed her?"

"I am grateful," I said desperately, hoping I could talk him down from this rage.

"Ha," he laughed hollowly. "You're a liar like she was too. And a shitty one. The two of you have been the worst mistakes of my life."

"Don't say that," I snapped, my heart twisting sharply. "Mamma loved you."

"Loved me?" he snorted derisively. "She *despised* me. She scorned me every day. Even her body scorned me, refusing to give me a son. You're the most spiteful thing she ever did."

A jagged lump pushed at my throat. His words cut deep, slicing into my heart and carving out the piece that had always held onto the hope that Papa loved me. But he didn't. Never had. And I suddenly saw my father for what he really was: a vicious creature with nothing but hate in his heart.

"Sloan," he muttered to himself. "I always hated that fucking name."

I swallowed back the pain that was threatening to pull me apart, trying to think of a way out of this. I had to focus on my child, I had to find a way to escape for their sake. "Let me go. I'll leave the city. I'll stay out of your life."

"Pah," he spat. "And let you run into the arms of that scum Rocco Romero like a good little slut? I won't be humiliated by my own daughter."

He turned down a side road at speed, accelerating through the forest and my heart juddered as I realised where we were. I hadn't been up here for years. Not since Mamma had died. But when I was young, she'd brought me here to play at Inverno Bridge. I'd only ever come here in the summer, throwing sticks into the river and watching them twist and spin as they raced the ones Mamma had thrown. It didn't look anything like that now. There were no flowers or green grass, just snow and the dark water which ran like ink beneath the arch of the high bridge.

Papa pulled up as we reached it, the concrete structure stretching out ahead of us to the other side. There was no railing, just a low wall which was covered in snow. The trees broke around the river, the steep bank running down twenty feet to the water below.

Papa stepped out of the car, taking the keys and locking the doors the moment he left. My heart beat wildly. I opened the compartment in the dashboard, searching for a weapon. I reached under the seat, desperate to find anything to protect myself with. But there nothing.

"I'm sorry," I breathed to my child, because I couldn't see a way out. I wasn't big enough or strong enough to protect them and that was the most heart-breaking thing I'd ever experienced.

I tugged at the door handle, pressing all the buttons to get it open but it wouldn't unlock.

Papa appeared at my door a moment later, wrenching it open and reaching for me.

"No!" I screamed, throwing a kick at him. He snarled, raising his gun to point right at my head.

I stilled, the darkness of the barrel calling my name. Death lived in there and it wanted to claim me. Us.

"Get out," he commanded and terror thumped through me. He caught my wrist and yanked me out of the car as I began to shake. Then he twisted me around and threw me against it, binding my wrists behind me with rope.

"Please don't," I begged, trying to turn my head to catch his eye. "You love me."

His hardened gaze met mine as he tightened the binds so much I winced. "I've tried to love you. But you're just like *her*. And now you'll meet the same end." He shoved me along the bridge and I whimpered.

"You killed Mamma," I stated, a tear running down my cheek and freezing there in the icy wind. I was reminded of her words. The last thing she'd said to me before I'd never seen her again.

Death is the truest form of freedom.

She must have known Father was going to kill her. She must have been so afraid. She must have walked these final steps I was taking now.

"She had plenty of chances," Papa growled. "As have you." He pressed the barrel of the gun to the back of my head and pure fear ripped into me. I couldn't do anything but keep walking, praying for another few seconds of life.

The air seemed so crisp, so sweet, like it was begging me to keep drinking it in. The world around me was something out of a fairytale, the water rushing beneath the bridge, the trees reaching over the river, their branches glittering with icicles and a dusting of snow caught the moonlight. It was too beautiful a place to die.

My gaze fell on a huge rock on the wall, the snow shoved away around it. My throat closed up as I stared at it. Papa must have put it there while I was searching the car and now I wished I'd fought harder before I was faced with this fate.

I lurched backwards in fright then tried to run, darting away from him despite the gun. But this was it. Between two choices of death, I had to find life.

Papa yanked hard on the rope binding my hands and I was forced back towards him with a shriek of terror, stumbling on the icy road as he reeled me in. He bound the other end of the rope to the huge rock on the wall and I stared at my fate, refusing to accept it. Rejecting it with every atom of my being.

"Don't do this," I pleaded.

The world was too quiet, too still. Like it was holding its breath for me, waiting to see what would happen next. I always thought death would be loud, roaring, but this painful silence was worse. I could hear every thump of my heart, counting down the final beats it would take.

Father yanked me toward the wall, lifting me up and planting me on it beside the rock. I gazed down at the dizzying height below and a scream tore form my lungs as I tried to fight against the rope binding my arms. Birds burst from the trees, climbing toward the sky and I wished they could take me with them.

A car engine blared and hope bloomed as I spotted a silver Audi racing onto the road at the far end of the bridge.

The engine died and my heart juddered as Nicoli jumped out.

"Giuseppe!" he cried in rage. "Stop!"

Another engine caught my ear and I leaned back as I teetered on the edge, my father's hands suddenly leaving me. Maybe he'd calm down, maybe he'd listen to Nicoli. He'd always cared about him more than me.

I caught sight of a Volvo in my periphery, crashing into the back of Papa's Mercedes. A ragged breath of surprise fell from my lungs as Rocco climbed out of the narrow sunroof, his eyes locking on me with a fierce determination. He leapt on top of Papa's car, tearing towards me, his mouth forming my name as sheer terror filled his eyes.

Papa shoved the rock over the edge of the bridge and I had one second of utter panic before I was yanked forwards after it.

I plummeted towards the black water with a scream that echoed on into eternity.

Maybe Mamma had been right, maybe death was the only freedom life gave us. Maybe this was the key to the cage I'd been held in my entire life. But I didn't want that. I wanted a life with Rocco, our baby. Nothing sounded more free than that.

My lungs swelled with their final breath.

I crashed into the river, losing all sense of everything as I was yanked towards the bottom, the water so cold it burned.

I cursed the unfairness of the world as my heart pounded out its final tune. And I said one last apology to the child I couldn't save.

Rocco

My heart stopped beating, the world stopped turning and everything that had ever happened to me in this lifetime suddenly seemed to have all been for this one reason.

Sloan needed me.

A roar of pure rage and pain left me, shattering my soul and begging for redemption. This wasn't happening.

I won't let *it happen.*

I leapt from the hood of Giuseppe's car straight towards the water's edge, running as fast as I could before leaping off of the bridge and diving straight down after her.

I hit the surface hard and plunged beneath it, heading down, down, down, chasing after the one good thing I'd ever tried to claim in this miserable life of mine.

I won't let you die like this. It doesn't end like this!

The ice cold kiss of the water reached right down into my bones and I instantly felt the pull of the current trying to force me away from her.

I started swimming, my muscles powering me on towards the point where I'd seen her go down.

It was dark beneath the water. Too dark to even see my hand before my face, let alone the girl who held my heart in her hands.

Panic welled up inside me as I swam on and on, my arms sweeping back and forth, my heart beating a desperate, panicked rhythm as I hunted and hunted for her beneath the surface.

She couldn't be gone. I refused to believe it. There wasn't a world without her in it. Her *and* our baby. A little life that had sparked into existence amidst the darkest of circumstances. A child which was both Calabresi and Romero, bridging the impossible divide between our families. A life which had barely even begun and which I refused to let end here and now.

I kicked and kicked, desperation clawing at me as my lungs began to burn.

She wasn't going to die like this. Not here, in the dark and the cold, all alone. She was counting on me. She needed me. This wouldn't be the end of us. There would *never* be an end of us.

I kept hunting in the blackness, the cold pressing in and stealing my thoughts.

My eyes were wide and my lungs were burning with the strength of hell fire for a breath I desperately needed to take. But if I was in this much need of oxygen, then so was she.

And I wouldn't let her drown down here at the bottom of this fucking river. I wouldn't let her suffer in darkness for all of time.

If it took my life to save hers then I'd offering it willingly. What was one tarnished, blackened soul worth in payment for hers anyway? She'd never been free a day in her life. I'd stolen her from her gilded cage and wrapped her in chains of barbed wire. And though she might have come closer to freedom alongside my chaos, we both knew it hadn't been so.

She deserved a free life. Our baby deserved a free life.

And if there was a single thing that I could gift her in payment for all the wrongdoing in my rotten existence, then that would be it.

Please don't take her from this world.

Please don't take her from me.

Nicoli

"What are you doing here, Nicoli?" Giuseppe asked coldly, training his pistol on me and freezing me in place.

I knew him well enough to recognise that look in his eyes. He'd pull the trigger without a second thought. Which cut me right down to my soul. This had been the man I'd looked up to, respected, emulated. I'd worked tirelessly to please him, hoping that he might look upon me like a son the way I looked at him as a father.

But that wasn't the truth of our relationship. My whole life had just been some sick game to him. I was his little Romero pet. A beast he'd chained with years of carefully planned manipulation. But I was still a beast all the same.

"I spoke with Royce before he died," I said, my voice strong and hard as I looked into his eyes, willing him to show me some ounce of truth. To give me some indication that not all of it had been a lie. That on some level I'd been more to him than a piece on a playing board.

"I should have killed that traitor years ago. Don't tell me you bought into his lies?" Giuseppe snarled.

My gaze moved to the water far below us where he'd just thrown his own daughter to her death. Rocco hadn't surfaced. He hadn't found her and my heart thundered a panicked tune for them.

"Why would you kill her?" I demanded, my voice breaking. "She was your daughter. Your blood. She was supposed to be my wife-"

"My daughter died the day she was taken by my enemies. She spread her legs for them like a common whore and she got a death which was kinder than she deserved," he spat, no ounce of remorse in his gaze.

"But you were willing for her to spread her legs for me," I growled. "And Romero blood runs through my veins too. Doesn't it?"

"He told you then." Giuseppe sighed like I had disappointed him. "Then all my hard work with you has been for nothing. I re-built you into a Calabresi. But I suppose dirty blood will out."

His finger twitched on the trigger and I lunged forward just as he fired.

The sound of that gunshot ricocheted through the night, through my body and through my soul. It tore away everything I'd thought I was, stripped apart everything I'd built myself up to be. I was the shadow of two men and the total of none.

I wasn't Angelo Romero anymore. And Nicoli Vitoli had never really existed at all.

I collided with him as pain unlike anything I'd ever known ripped through my chest.

I was bleeding. Blood pumping from my body and agony tearing me apart. But the physical pain I endured had nothing on the war going on in my heart.

My hands locked around his throat as we hit the ground hard and the gun skittered away from us. Giuseppe cried out as I slammed his head back against the concrete, my jaw locked and fury fuelling my muscles.

He fought to buck me off of him as I tightened my grip.

Giuseppe's eyes were wild with accusation and fear as I snarled at him, my blood coating both of us but my strength never wavering.

If it took all I had left in me to rid the world of this parasite, then I would do it.

For the mother he'd murdered. The brothers I'd never known. For the girl he'd thrown to her death.

His hands clawed at my arms as he bucked and thrashed, his eyes bulging as I continued to squeeze.

This creature had stolen my life from me. And I was going to take his in payment.

I snarled with a rage so pure and raw that it cut me right down to my bones. With a surge of strength, I grabbed his chin and twisted hard. The snap that rang out was so loud that all other sounds fell silent to observe it.

Giuseppe fell still beneath me and his death was like a balm soothing my aching soul.

My world shattered into a thousand pieces and I slumped back as the pain of my bullet wound consumed me.

I crawled away from his body, moving to the edge of the bridge and peering down over the low wall which lined it into the murky water below.

Blood continued to pulse from my stomach and I pressed a hand to it as I watched the river without drawing breath. There was still no sign of them.

My heart beat faster at the thought that we'd been too late. And as the minutes dragged on, I began to lose hope.

My heart ached at the idea of coming so close only to have failed. If Sloan died then it had all been for nothing. And if Rocco died then he would leave me before I ever had the chance to tell him who I truly was. Who he was to me.

Pain flared through my stomach and my heart as I watched the water anxiously and my hope faded alongside my energy. Had we all come this far just to die here?

Was this all it came to in the end?

Rocco

My lungs burned for a breath I refused to take. My body pulsed with hunger for the oxygen waiting above me at the surface. But I wouldn't swim for it. I wouldn't leave this frozen coffin unless I brought Sloan and our baby back up with me.

If fate had decided to take her from me then I wouldn't live on without her. We would leave this river together or not at all.

Darkness reigned beneath the water, but pinpricks of light glimmered on the edges of my vision.

I was running out of time.

I blew out the breath I'd been holding and bubbles trailed away from me toward the safety of the surface.

My heart was pounding, breaking, failing.

I won't live without you, bella. Death would be a sweeter curse.

My movements were losing energy, my limbs growing endlessly heavy.

But I wouldn't give up until my body failed on me.

I kicked forward again and my fingers suddenly brushed against a hand.

My heart leapt as I kicked harder, my eyes straining to make out anything in the gloom and suddenly I saw her.

Her eyes were closed, her head bobbing in the current as she floated, weighed down by the rope which bound her to that stone.

A roar of rage left me, swallowed by the water as I clawed my way down to the rock which lay on the river bed.

My muscles flared with a desperate kind of strength as I ripped at the rope until I yanked it free of the enormous stone.

I grabbed her a heartbeat later, kicking and kicking as I headed for the surface which shone with the light of the moon endlessly high above us.

My vision faded further, my body slowing despite my need for it to speed up. But I wouldn't give in. I wouldn't fail her now. Not when she needed me most. When they both needed me most.

My head finally breached the surface and I gulped down air with desperation as I drew her head up above the water too.

She lay unmoving in my arms, her head lolling back against my shoulder and no breath passing her lips.

"No!" I roared. Not in denial but in refusal. She wasn't leaving me. She couldn't. I wouldn't allow it. I'd claimed her for my own and I refused to give her up.

I swam for the rocky shore, dragging her out of the river and slamming my hand down on her back as I tried to force the water up out of her lungs. Some came up but she wasn't coughing, wasn't helping me at all.

Pain flooded my body as I flipped her around and started chest compressions.

My lips met hers in the coldest kiss we'd ever shared as I forced air into her lungs.

Nothing.

Not a flicker of reaction.

But I wouldn't give up.

I kept pumping her chest, breathing for her time and again despite the fact that she still wasn't moving.

"Sloan," I gasped. "Don't leave me. Not like this, baby. Not like this."

I kept going. I'd die before I stopped. But as the minutes slipped by and grief fractured my soul into a million unrecognisable pieces, I began to lose hope.

It wasn't working.

She'd left me here alone.

And there was nothing in this world or the next that could ever right that wrong.

Sloan

The whole world was pain.

An agony so intense that there was nothing else. I was dying. I knew it. Nothing could hurt like this unless it was going to end in death.

I wanted to fight, but I had nothing left in me to fight with. My limbs were robbed of strength and I was drowning in an endless sea of darkness.

I thought of Rocco and the passion with which he loved me. Of Royce and the way he'd tried to do right by me. Then of my mother and her gentle smile, her warm hugs and musical laugh.

"Sloan! You passed out!" Someone was shaking me and I groaned as I came to. "You've gotta push, bella! You've gotta *push*, you're almost there, the baby is almost here!"

The lights were too bright and the pain washed back over me again in a wave.

"I can't," I groaned as Rocco clutched my hand.

He leaned across me, cupping my cheek and taking away that horrible bright light. My knight, my shade. "You can do anything, guerriera. You're my warrior, remember?"

I nodded, dragging in a breath as the midwife commanded I push once more. My nails tore into Rocco's hand as I used every ounce of strength in my body to bring this baby into the world. Our child. Our missing piece.

A scream left my lips unlike anything I'd ever heard and suddenly the pain fell away to be replaced by the most overwhelming sense of relief.

"Congratulations," the midwife said as I slumped back onto the pillow. "You have a baby girl."

Her cries filled my ears and I sobbed as she was placed on my chest. She was too beautiful for words. And so fragile. I wanted to wrap her up and keep her safe forever. But not in chains. This little girl would never be confined, controlled or owned.

Rocco leaned in to kiss her head, despite the blood, the mess, he didn't care. My heart couldn't contain the amount of love trying to live in it. It was surely going to burst.

"I can't wait to tell you all about how your mother and I met," Rocco whispered to her and an exhausted laugh fell from my lips.

"Do you have a name yet?" the midwife asked, beaming at us.

I shared a look with Rocco, a smile tugging at my mouth.

"She's named after the place where she was saved by her valiant father," I said.

It was still one of the darkest days of my life, but this little light had shone through, growing brighter and brighter until this very moment. Rocco had pulled me from the depths of the water and my father's body had taken my place amongst the reeds. It was twisted and beautiful and *us*. "River."

"River Romero," Rocco breathed, leaning in to press his mouth to mine. "I have a feeling she's going to be as much trouble as you are, mia principessa."

We'd been married the day after I'd been released from the hospital. I'd narrowly avoided hypothermia from my dunk in the river and the doctors said if Rocco had gotten me out any later, I wouldn't have made it.

The ceremony was just us, Coco and his brothers in a tiny church on the water's edge. As the sun had set, we'd sworn to belong to each other. My manic, savage, wonderful husband had made me his as soon as he could. And I would be his, free of chains, freer than a bird in the sky, for all of time.

Rocco

THREE MONTHS LATER

My phone rang and I snatched it from the nightstand before hurrying out onto the balcony to answer it so that I didn't disturb Sloan. She lost enough sleep these days without me adding to it more than necessary. I'd been surprised when Sloan had wanted to make this place our home after I'd held her captive here. But she said it was the place that had set her free and brought us together, so she loved it for those reasons.

Papa had been furious when I'd first told him about me and Sloan, but I'd told him straight that I wasn't going to change my mind in this. And as soon as River had come along, it was like he'd forgotten all about Sloan's Calabresi heritage. He'd never had a girl and the hard man he'd been for my entire life seemed to melt away when he was with her and I caught glimpses of the man he'd been while my mother was alive.

"How's my favourite girl?" Frankie's voice came on the other end of the line and I smirked as I looked out over the view of the mountains. My brothers were almost as obsessed with River as I was.

"I'm not too bad, thanks. Just been painting my nails and day dreaming about boys. You know, the usual," I replied.

"So long as River isn't getting any ideas about boys, I don't care what you get up to," he joked.

I snorted a laugh. "She's three months old. The girl is only daydreaming about milk. But when boys come onto the scene, you and Enzo can help me chase them off."

"Already on it," he agreed. "I saw a one year old giving her the eye in the park the other day and I chased him right back to his mamma."

My grin widened for a moment but as silence fell between us, I knew he wasn't calling with good news.

"You still haven't got any leads?" I guessed.

"No," Frankie sighed. "We thought we were on his trail, but it's looking like another dead end."

My heart sank at that news. Frankie and Enzo had been working tirelessly to try and hunt Nicoli down ever since Sloan had told us the truth about who he was. Papa was still afraid to believe it was true, but he hadn't done a thing to stop the hunt which was as close to his approval as we would get. We just wanted our brother home. We wanted our family to have a chance to heal. But ever since that day out on Inverno Bridge, we hadn't seen hide nor hair of him.

He'd made sure that Sloan was alright and then I'd taken him to get help for his gunshot wound from the Calabresi doctor. We'd left him there so that I could get Sloan to the hospital and we knew he'd been treated - it sounded like he'd survived the bullet just fine. But no one had heard a single word from him since. He was like a ghost. And his absence was cutting us deep.

"We'll find him," Frankie swore. "I'll let you know when I get another lead."

"Okay."

The sound of soft cries came from the bedroom and I pushed away from the edge of the balcony as I cut the call.

Sloan rolled over in our bed as she heard River stirring too but I got there first, sweeping our tiny baby up into my arms and holding her close to my bare chest. Coco eyed me from his bed across the room, cocking his head. The little bastardo had warmed to me rather quickly since I'd started feeding him some of Sloan's meatballs on the sly. And maybe I'd warmed to him too.

I wound a soft blanket around my girl and slipped back out onto the balcony as I bounced her softly and she snuggled in close, listening to my heartbeat.

I started singing beneath my breath, a song I created just for her about warrior women and an endless winter.

She nestled against me as her cries settled down and I continued to cradle her close.

"You know, babies usually cry in the night because they're looking for milk," Sloan teased from behind me and I turned to find her standing in the open doorway wearing my blue shirt.

"River cries for her papa to sing to her," I objected. "She needs a cuddle with me more than milk."

Sloan rolled her eyes and padded towards us, winding her arms around my waist so that our baby girl was cradled between us.

I leaned forward and pressed a kiss to the top of her head, inhaling the sweet scent of her as our little family were united as one.

"I think I'm the luckiest man that ever lived," I breathed.

"You say that every day," Sloan teased as she tipped her head back to offer me her lips.

"That's because it's even more true today than it was yesterday."

She laughed and I kissed her to steal her happiness. I lost myself in the fullness of her lips and the passion of her love for a long moment and I couldn't help but grin as she pulled me closer.

We moved back into our bedroom and returned River to her crib where she nestled back down with a happy murmur.

"Do you need to sleep?" I asked as I turned back to Sloan.

"No," she purred, unhooking the buttons of the shirt she wore. "I think I need you to remind me just how lucky I am too."

I smiled like a hungry wolf as I stalked towards her, turning her away from the bed and walking her back out onto the balcony instead.

If I was going to be challenged like that, then we'd be needing a closed door between us and the sleeping baby. Because if Sloan Romero wanted me to do something for her then I'd move mountains to make her wishes come true. That meant she was about to be screaming my name until she could barely remember her own.

And I was about to bathe in the joy of her love until it banished every shadow that lurked in my soul.

Printed in Great Britain
by Amazon